Praise for the first book in Les Cowan's David Hidalgo series, *Benefit of the Doubt*:

"The joy of Benefit Of The Doubt *is that the author has crafted well-rounded and highly believable characters, and meticulously researched the environments they live in. That gives the book a real sense of place. This truly is a breath of fresh air from the hard-man-style detective novels, yet the undercurrents it creates are just as threatening... Masterful!*

Living Orkney magazine

"*Well-written and thoroughly enjoyable in every twist and turn of the story. David Hidalgo is a great character and I expect to see more of him.*"

One Man in the Middle blog

"*Good storyline, which kept moving on and was a real page-turner! The author has created believable characters and this is a thriller with a bit of a difference. Really looking forward to the next instalment in the David Hidalgo series.*"

"*A gripping journey through Spain and Edinburgh that keeps you by the side of the main character, Señor David. Following his challenges through the underworld of drug barons, abductions, and personal doubts, it results in a cliffhanger ending. It's pleasing to read a realistic, yet non-graphic crime thriller that has a thought-provoking strand of spirituality running through it.*"

"*Super book. A gripping tale. The characters in this novel are very believable. The story unfolds and pulls you in. I loved all the action in Edinburgh; I'm sure I* ___ *a couple of these folk! Really interesting questions of faith are* ___ *A really gripping read. Cant* ___"

E: ___ zon.co.uk

D0865385

Books by Les Cowan

The David Hidalgo series:
Book 1: *Benefit of the Doubt*
Book 2: *All that Glitters*
Book 3: *Sins of the Fathers* (coming soon)

Non-fiction titles:
Loose Talk Collected
Orkney by Bike

ALL THAT GLITTERS

LES COWAN

A DAVID HIDALGO NOVEL

LION FICTION

Published by
Lion Hudson Limited
Wilkinson House, Jordan Hill Business Park
Banbury Road, Oxford OX2 8DR, England
www.lionhudson.com/fiction

ISBN 978 1 78264 253 4
e-ISBN 978 1 78264 254 1

First edition 2018

Acknowledgments
Scripture quotations taken from the Holy Bible, New International
Version Anglicized. Copyright © 1979, 1984, 2011 Biblica, formerly
International Bible Society. Used by permission of Hodder & Stoughton
Ltd, an Hachette UK company. All rights reserved. "NIV" is a
registered trademark of Biblica. UK trademark number 1448790.

Extracts on p. 9 and p. 283 from The Authorized (King James) Version
('the KJV'), the rights in which are vested in the Crown in the United
Kingdom, are reproduced here by permission of the Crown's patentee,
Cambridge University Press.

Cover image: © Dennis van de Water/shutterstock.com

A catalogue record for this book is available from the British Library

Printed and bound in the UK, May 2018, LH26

For Angus
Test reader, sympathetic (and knowledgeable) critic,
and encourager-in-chief

ACKNOWLEDGMENTS

Once again I want to thank all those who made this story possible both in practical ways and by way of general encouragement.

Firstly, thanks to Fiona, Angus, Dot, Mija, and Janet for reading early drafts and commenting. I'm glad you feel it has been a story worth telling.

Secondly, thanks to the many readers of David's earlier adventures in *Benefit of the Doubt*, who have pleaded for more. Can I once again apologize for the cliffhanger ending and promise that it'll never happen again. I hope you feel it has been worth the wait. In particular, thanks for your many Facebook comments, emails, and Amazon reviews. (Particular thanks to Montse in Ribadeo, who told me she had found a new hero!)

Thanks to John Ross Scott and One Man in the Middle for your favourable published reviews.

Thanks also to those who came to launch events, parted with their cash, and have said they enjoyed Book One. I hope you are willing to do the same for Book Two.

Grateful thanks to Jessica Tinker at Lion Hudson (and Tony Collins previously) for believing in David Hidalgo and doing what needed to be done to bring him to the reading public.

Thanks to Julie Frederick for your attention to detail in proof editing and for making me question things that made sense to me at the time but to no one else after that.

Thanks also to Stromness library staff for putting up with me hogging the nice window seats while writing day after day and to Soo for providing caffeine to fuel the muse.

Finally, thanks to you who are reading. I hope you enjoy this story and will let me know at lescowan@worldofdavidhidalgo.com. Find out more about this series at www.worldofdavidhidalgo.com.

Another parable put he forth unto them, saying, The kingdom of heaven is likened unto a man which sowed good seed in his field: But while men slept, his enemy came and sowed tares among the wheat, and went his way. But when the blade was sprung up, and brought forth fruit, then appeared the tares also. So the servants of the householder came and said unto him, Sir, didst not thou sow good seed in thy field? from whence then hath it tares? He said unto them, An enemy hath done this...

Matthew 13:24-28, KJV

Chapter 1

COLINTON MAINS

Juan Hernandez was just about to give the horn another blast when the tenement door he was watching opened and a slim, upright man, perhaps into his fifties, but apparently still spry and energetic, emerged. Juan leaned across and pushed the passenger door open.

"*Buenos días, hermano. ¿Qué tal?*" David Hidalgo threw a battered leather briefcase into the back seat, just missing Juan's left ear, jumped in, and took off a grey fedora.

"Ok, I suppose," he said, "in the circumstances."

Juan gave a grunt and pulled out into traffic.

"So, where to?"

David unfolded a crumpled scrap of paper.

"Colinton Mains Rise. Sixty-seven. Holy Corner then out Colinton Road. Past Tesco."

"Ok. *Venga. Vamos.*" Juan's Hacienda restaurant van gave a wheeze and a cough before getting into its stride as if unused to such an early start.

"Just us?"

"No, the others are making their own way there. Mrs MacInnes insists on taking the bus. I'm sure she thinks every free journey on her bus pass helps make up for the millions wasted on the trams."

Juan smiled as he pulled through stop-start Saturday morning traffic. If only their stalwart church treasurer had been in charge of public finances in 2008; then the crisis still raging, particularly in Spain, could surely have been avoided. Profligate bankers would have got such a telling off they would have humbly returned their dodgy millions, sacked the rogue traders, and offered to pick up litter in the park if that would have helped.

"And who are we visiting?" Juan asked.

"Sam and Mike Hunter. Do you remember Mike? He worked for Sabadell in Madrid for three years. Then there was some sort of deal with Salamanca Bank and he was transferred to Edinburgh."

"I think I do. He's English but he called himself Miguel then. Yes, I remember. He helped a lot with church finances when we were starting. Drove a black Audi convertible, didn't he? Looked more like a drug dealer than the real thing."

"Well he's completely respectable now. Married another financial wizard and they have a massive house with a huge living room. It makes sense to meet there since there's going to be a few of us today."

Juan pulled up at a pedestrian crossing to let a wave of students heading down to the library, young mums with buggies, and serious Saturday morning walkers stream across in front of them. David took the time to glance around. There was a solid row of Victorian tenements on one side and a lettings office, accessories boutique, and a hairdressers on the other. It wasn't *Gran Via* but he was getting used to Bruntsfield and liked it. Near the heart of the city but still with a village feel from all the independent shops and acres of green space on the Links. And since his flat had been transformed from something approaching a second-hand furniture dump to a liveable, and maybe even slightly stylish, personal space, he was beginning to feel at home. The only thing he still regretted was passing up a 1948 Selmer Super Balanced Action tenor sax in favour of a washing machine. Tending the body or feeding the soul – a tough choice. If the bloke in Steptoe's had known what it was worth he could have retired on the proceeds.

"And remind me what it's all about then?" Juan broke in as the lights turned green.

"You remember that Southside Fellowship joined the Edinburgh Council of Churches last year? This is a sub-group called the City

Learning Forum – mainly just to share what seems to be working for each of us. No big agenda. No minutes. No decisions. Just sharing and learning. This month it's our turn – hence a need for the three-line whip."

"A what?" Juan's English had improved hugely since he and Alicia had opened Hacienda two years ago, but really understanding a language also means knowing a million facts about the country and its customs – something he found endlessly frustrating.

"It just means everybody present. You could say 'All hands on deck' or 'All present and correct'. It's a parliamentary term."

"So everyone gets whipped three times if they don't show up, no?"

"Not quite." David smiled. "Though not a bad idea. Anyway, I thought it would be good to have a variety of viewpoints so we can each say what we think."

"Well, we are growing, so something must be right. Anyway, that's it? We just talk about what we do and how things are going? Y nada mas."

"More or less. Oh, one other thing. Mike has some financial thing he wants to talk about afterwards so I'll make my own way back. Probably nothing, but he called me last night and sounded a bit concerned."

"Suits me. You know I hate meetings."

Another wait at Holy Corner lights, then finally a right out past Starbucks, Napier University, and into leafy suburbia. David could never quite decide if Holy Corner was a joke, a blunder, or postmodern irony and therefore very clever. So-called for having four churches, one at each junction, it had probably started as a wisecrack. It wasn't as if holiness was meant to be taken seriously after all. But maybe even that was changing in a world where nothing seemed to stay the same for long. All that *Eat, Pray, Love* stuff seemed to be going down pretty well. At any rate, so many Edinburgh churches seemed to be stuffed with under thirty-fives these days there was clearly something going on. Maybe even holiness was making a comeback.

They drove a mile in silence until, finally, Juan couldn't contain himself any longer.

"You know, Señor David," he said, "some people would say you've been incredibly lucky."

"Except we don't believe in luck – as you're always telling me."

"I'm just saying *be careful*. There may be angels around you; just don't keep them so busy. That's all."

"You don't need to remind me."

"The stitches will be out soon, I suppose. You'll be back to normal in a couple of days. *Seguro*."

David looked out at the tranquil rows of homes and gardens sliding past, apparently so far removed from shootouts, drug dealers, kidnapping, and violence.

It'll take a bit longer than that, he thought, but didn't say it. *If I had the faintest idea what normal is supposed to be any more.*

Less than a fortnight had passed since Reverend David Hidalgo and Dr Gillian Lockhart had slipped away from their welcome home party at Southside Fellowship on South Clerk Street, back home more or less intact after a series of events no one could have predicted and David still could hardly believe. The search for a teenage runaway in Edinburgh had turned into an armed attack in Holyrood Park, an abduction to Spain, and a SWAT team shootout in a medieval castle. But it had also turned into a journey from utter black despair to the beginnings of hope again: you rescue me, I rescue you. They had crossed the road hand in hand and paused to look into the window of Rings and Things. The engagement diamond solitaires seemed particularly interesting. Then, without any warning, a series of shots had blown the evening apart. A body had slumped against David, the jeweller's window splattered with blood. The early evening hum was shattered with screams. David felt a searing pain on the crown of his head, put his hand up, and drew down fingers sticky with blood. Gillian was crouching on the pavement, hands clasped over her head, trembling, covered in fragments of glass. Then the screech of car tyres and a black 4x4 disappearing through the traffic. In an instant all of the satisfaction of a difficult task brought to a safe conclusion had disappeared like smoke. David had knelt, expecting the worst. The image of Gillian looking up with an expression of horror was still as vivid in his mind as the moment it happened. A young man lay groaning at his feet as the blood began to pool. David didn't have it in him to help; he just pulled out a handkerchief, clapped it on top of his own head, and slumped against the shopfront, gripping Gillian to him as if she were the one thing he had to hold on to in a world beginning to teeter and sway.

"Some people might say you're a very lucky man," DI Thompson had said, dropping his pen on the desk and pushing back his chair some hours later in an interview room.

"I wish people would stop saying that," David had replied wearily. "It just means I've very nearly been extremely unlucky." Thompson inclined his head, conceding the point.

"So, what do you make of it, then?" he had asked.

David had taken his glasses off and was rubbing his face almost as if trying to wash it all away.

"I think someone close to Raúl Álvarez was looking for revenge. Or a bit of glory. Or just for the fun of it. They came to Edinburgh, watched the church, saw us come out, and took a shot. Simple as that."

"That's obvious. What I mean is, how did they miss? You weren't exactly a moving target."

"Well, that's maybe where what you call 'luck' comes in. We were looking in the window. Gillian saw something she liked. I suppose we must have leaned forward to take a closer look just when the gun went off – so the other guy got it. How is he, by the way?"

"He'll live. Got him in the shoulder. Lots of blood but luckily – or whatever you call it – there was a medical student passing. She applied enough pressure till the ambulance arrived. Otherwise he'd have been a gonner."

"So, lines of inquiry?"

"The usual – passport control, ports of entry, known associates. Needle in a haystack really."

Now all David had to show for it was a row of stitches in his scalp, some cuts on the way to healing, and an earnest desire for a boring life.

Another half an hour and Juan's Hacienda van, complete with a Flamenco dancer on the side, pulled up outside a 1930s detached villa with a neatly clipped hedge and lions on the gate posts. *Wow*, he thought. *Qué ricos. I wonder if there'd be a market out here for home delivery. "Hacienda at Home". I'll have to see what Alicia thinks of that.*

Seconds later a silver MX5 drew to a halt from the other direction and a petite figure with jet black hair climbed slowly and painfully out. Dr Gillian Lockhart gradually straightened up, smiled in David Hidalgo's direction, and carefully closed the car door.

David smiled back. Gillian: the one he'd found against all the odds, who had come in and transformed his life. The one he'd lost and found again in Spain, and finally almost lost for good in a mixture of gunshots, blood, and glass in an Edinburgh street. Sometimes he felt like his life was turning into a remake of *Jaws*. Just when you thought it was safe to go back into the water…

"I feel such a fraud," she whispered in his ear as they wandered up the drive past the Jag and the Boxster. "I've been at Southside less than six months. Isn't this supposed to be a leaders' thing?"

He squeezed her hand reassuringly. "Yes and no. The group's about learning, so I suppose it doesn't matter who we learn from. I would say a key problem is that we're all so used to living in the bubble that we don't even register how it must seem to outsiders. So you have a really useful perspective. It'll be fine."

Just as he was about to ring, the door was opened by a young woman in skinny jeans, trainers, and a polo shirt with "Edinburgh Athletics" on it.

"Hi, saw you coming. Come on in. There's a few here already."

"Sam, can I introduce Gillian Lockhart? David gestured to his left. "Gillian – Sam Hunter. She's big in the city, you know. Expert in everything involving numbers."

"As if!" Sam made a face. "I'm all big picture now. Mike's the numbers man. Pleased to meet you, Gillian." She paused, softening her tone. "I've heard the story about Spain and what happened a few weeks ago. How are you?"

Gillian managed half a smile.

"Still sore," she said. "I got some cuts and bruises at the time but I hurt my back falling against the shop window and that's what's taking longer to clear up."

Sam put a hand on her arm.

"So glad it wasn't anything worse. Anyway, we're in the conservatory. Just go straight through."

About a dozen had already gathered. A couple from Central, some from Kings Church, St Andrew's, and a few others. A tall rangy guy with olive skin, a Scotland rugby top, and designer stubble appeared in the doorway with a tray of coffees. He quickly scanned around, then, spotting David, set down the tray and sat beside him.

"*Hombre*. Glad to see you in one piece. I hear it's been a bit full on."

"Hi Mike. You could say that. Peace and quiet – that's what's needed now."

"Wait till you see what I've got for you later. Not sure you'll get what you want."

Once the coffee things had been cleared away, Sam did a welcome then immediately passed to David, who in turn passed immediately on to an elderly but clearly robust woman to his right who had just arrived.

"Irene MacInnes is our church secretary, treasurer, stalwart – and a few other things. I think she should start. She's really the one that has kept Southside going for the last twenty years."

"Well, I'm sure that's an overstatement. We all just do what we can. What can I tell you?"

Irene MacInnes did a reasonable job of looking flattered and slightly flustered but David wasn't fooled. Ladies from Morningside don't do flustered. You'd think they'd all come from Navy SEAL boot camp, not The Mary Erskine School for girls. Mrs MacInnes briefly, concisely, and efficiently told the story of Southside right up to when David Hidalgo, an unknown quantity, subject of a recent tragedy, had been suggested as leader – largely as a stopgap, till somebody more suitable turned up. Then David told about Southside as it was when he arrived, the changes they'd made, what now seemed to be more or less working, and what they were still working on. Next up, Gillian briefly described her first impressions, then what she liked and what she still found uncomfortable – the friendly family feel and the worship songs, respectively. Finally, Juan spoke about Warehouse 66, the church David and his wife Rocío had founded in Madrid about fifteen years before, and how the cultures differed but many of the needs were the same. Then into some Q&A, explanations, and discussion.

Fascinating and useful as it all no doubt was, Gillian began to feel herself wandering. She still often had to do a mental double take at the weirdness of her situation. Last summer she'd still been getting over the divorce – in theory amicable, civilized, adult; in reality none of these things. For months after the final event she'd felt she was walking around with a banner over her head or that lottery pointy hand thing with a caption that said, "Failure, Muckup, Abandoned." The normal grown-up tools of rationalization, tell-yourself-you're-not-to-blame, etc, didn't seem to be working. She drifted into work each morning at the Scots Language Department of the university, drifted through staff meetings, gave lectures and tutorials in her sleep, and drifted home again. Slumped through rubbish TV and drifted off to sleep. It was some consolation that more than half her colleagues seemed to be in the same boat, but they didn't seem to be drifting. They dated, they went to salsa class, they managed to swing conferences in nice locations and took a "friend". They encouraged her not to take everything so seriously but somehow *pick yourself up, dust yourself off, and start all over again* didn't seem to be working.

"How are you, Gilli? You look beautiful, as usual." Her dad's weekly greeting at the nursing home in Silverknowes never changed and she didn't want it to. His body was gradually giving out but the spirit inside was only slightly dimmed – a candle flame through gauze.

"What do you think I should do, Dad?" she had asked, perplexed, one week. "I just can't make myself feel bright and positive. It's not like turning on a tap."

"I know. When your mum was drinking I tried to keep things going for you and Ros… Feeling bright and positive isn't always easy."

"You did fantastically well. You know that, don't you?"

"Well, one makes an effort. Stiff upper lip and all that."

"No, seriously. You did. You kept us safe. Now I just feel I don't have any direction any more. Like being homeless, you know?"

"I do. Life does that to you sometimes. But sooner or later you have to get back on the horse. Why not take a break? Go and see Charlie and Rosa in Andoain. They'd be pleased to have you."

"Mmm. That's worth thinking about. I haven't seen Charlie for years. And the new Mrs Charlie. She's Spanish, isn't she?"

"Basque, I think. Don't get caught calling a Basque woman Spanish. They're less than half an hour inland from San Sebastián. You can see the city and the country."

"Well, if I'm going to do that I'd better brush up on my Spanish."

So that was it. Check out the Modern Languages Department extramural programme and find a top-up conversation class. Somebody called David Hidalgo. Sounds Spanish, at any rate. Give it a go. And the rest, as they say…

"Gillian? Any thoughts on that?" The conversation had paused and the room was looking at her expectantly but not unkindly.

"Eh, sorry – I must have drifted off a bit…"

Finally, it was over. Sam rounded things up and drew some tentative conclusions. Then it was hats and coats till only Sam, Mike, David, and Gillian were left.

"Well then. What's the big deal?" David asked. "Financial irregularities in the parish?"

Mike grabbed a black ring binder and dropped it on the coffee table.

"You could say that. Actually, it isn't funny." Mike hadn't contributed much in the meeting and David had thought he seemed a bit disconnected. Now he was sharp and focused.

"We should have had another agenda item today. Three new congregations that want to join. I've been asked to do the financial health check. Apparently we don't want any dog-and-bone operations signing up – not good for the image. So they're asked to send in three years of accounts and some other stuff, which I have a look at then give them the ok. That's the theory anyway. Have a look at this."

The first page of the folder looked like a routine summary of accounts – text labels with numbers next to them in neat columns with underlined totals at the bottom. Gillian bent a bit closer, scrutinizing the figures.

"I don't know about church accounts but I used to do our local chamber orchestra's books. It all looks ok. Is something the matter?"

"Not at all. This is Maranatha Centre, Morningside. Income from offerings nine thousand or so. Outgoings just under seven. Three grand in the bank. All hunky dory."

"So what's the problem, then?" David asked. "Finance isn't my strong suit. Maybe we should have asked Mrs MacInnes to hang on a bit."

"Actually no," Sam put in firmly. "The fewer people involved, the better, at least for the time being. "Let them see the next page, Mike." The second page looked remarkably like the first.

"Same thing. This is City Life Centre. A bit more in, a bit less out, a bit more in the bank. One year up a bit, next a bit down. Nothing exciting. With me so far? Ok. Now the last one. They call themselves Power and Glory Church. Sounds a bit whacky but you never can tell these days. Three years again. They seem a bit more prosperous but there's not much in it really. All perfectly normal. Offerings. Pastor's salary. Heating and lighting. Travel and transport. A bit out to foreign missions and a bit in from sister congregations."

"Sorry, Mike. I think I really must be missing something. There's nothing here so far that's going to hit the *Evening News*."

"Indeed. Now here's the bit we don't want blabbed around or I lose my job. You know I work for Salamanca's Scottish operation? Right now I'm in what's called S&V – Scrutiny and Verification. The government have put a huge onus on the banks to track down the proceeds of crime – money laundering, ill-gotten gains, etc. So we're looking for accounts that seem disproportionate to the enterprise behind them. A corner shop that's turning over hundreds of thousands a month. A tanning studio that's taking in twenty times what it should be."

"Or a church, I suppose," Gillian put in.

"Exactly. You're on the right track. I wouldn't normally expect to see anything unusual in church accounts, but you never know. So we have an algorithm that does it all for us. Accounts are allocated what we call a model profile. If they deviate more than 10 per cent from that, we have a closer look. Now. Here we are." He turned to the final page in the folder. This time the figures were anonymous. No church name, letterhead, or logo, just three neat tables, one for each of the last three years, each one with columns for date, amount, and balance.

"But these are tiny sums," David said. "£1.24, £2.30, £4.55. What's the problem?"

"Actually, not so tiny," Mike said quietly. "That's not £4.55. It's four and a half million."

The room fell silent. A carriage clock on the sideboard gave a slight whir and a car horn sounded outside in the street.

"These columns are for transactions over the past three years. You can see the numbers are building. Not many transactions each year but they're getting bigger. Look at the bottom figure on the right. There's the final balance as of 5 p.m. yesterday." He pointed to a figure in bold: £21.3.

"How on earth does a start-up church in Edinburgh wind up with £21 million in its accounts?" Gillian whispered. The question hung unanswered for some moments till finally David spoke.

"That's one question, Mike. Others might be, which church is it and why are you telling us this?"

Mike closed the folder and was about to speak when Sam interrupted him.

"Before we go into that, there's something else. Just so as we're all clear. There are good reasons for sharing everything you've just heard. But if anything of what we're talking about gets back to senior level at Salamanca a lost job might be the least of it."

Mike took a deep breath and rubbed his temples.

"Everyone knows confidentiality is high on any bank's agenda. Customers need to know their information is as safe as their money. Despite all the recent scandals, confidentiality is still a high priority. So no names, not just yet."

"He hasn't even told *me*," Sam put in with a pointed look at her husband.

"At this stage let's keep it to a church in the Edinburgh area."

"A church that might be applying for membership," David added.

"Well, you may think that – I couldn't possibly comment," Mike replied pointedly. "Anyway, there are very strict procedures for reporting this sort of stuff. The government wants the profits from illegal activities out of criminal hands and into the public finances on the double. So the case officer – me in this instance – reports to his superior, then a report goes to the Serious Fraud Office within forty-eight hours and they have a team that take it from there. Since I'd been doing some basic background on the churches about to sign up, it kind of stuck out when I spotted this one. I passed it on, but then a week later I thought I'd take another look just to see what was happening. Call it professional curiosity. Nothing. No report.

Nothing pending. No note in the file to say what was happening. So I mentioned it to my next up and got a very funny reaction. Special measures, I was told. Nothing to do with us. Bigger fish to fry. Some sort of flannel like that."

"Which you don't buy…" David asked, more a statement than a question.

"I don't. There is no way a church that size, any church I've ever heard of, should be messing around with these sorts of sums. And for that not to be reported is itself a criminal act."

"And with that amount of money floating around there might be incentives to prevent disclosure," Sam summed up.

"And you're telling us this – why?" David asked.

"Well, you seem to be the organized crime expert around the table – more coffee anyone?"

There wasn't a rush to restart when the coffee arrived. Eventually David spoke.

"Just to get this straight, Mike. You are checking up on some basic accounts as part of the process of churches applying to be part of the Edinburgh Council of Churches. Everything they send you seems fine but as part of your job you notice something odd and the name rings a bell. A church name you might have seen recently – don't answer that – seems to be up to something peculiar. You report it to your boss, who seems to ignore it or cover it up. You're telling us that in itself is illegal. So why not just report it to the police?"

Mike took another sip and put his cup down.

"Fair question. Breach of confidentiality for starters. Whistleblowing isn't something you undertake lightly. If I go to the police I'm basically accusing my superiors of one crime and concealing another. I have to be absolutely sure of what I'm doing before I try that one on. And it'll be obvious where the leak has come from – I'm the case officer, remember? So breach of customer confidentiality and accusing senior staff of criminal conspiracy.

If I'm not 100 per cent correct, either one of these is a hanging offence. Both together and I won't be able to keep the accounts for a sewing bee. I'm not sure I want to take that risk. And if I am right I have absolutely no desire to tangle with organized crime. I just add up numbers all day. This is way out of my comfort zone."

Gillian gave him a look. "I hope you don't think what we've been through was comfortable."

"No, of course not. But you have contacts in the police, and you've got experience. Maybe you could speak to someone and give me some idea how to proceed. I don't think I can just ignore it. Not if I'm being asked my professional opinion. Doing something about it just feels like the right thing to do."

"So hanged if you do, hanged if you don't," David summed up.

"Exactly. Rock and a hard place. All of that."

"But if I say something to a police officer they're just going to come straight back to you."

"Not if you don't tell them where the information came from," Sam put in. "Then they could do their own investigation."

"But isn't that going to implicate Mike anyway?" Gillian asked.

"Well, do you have a better idea?"

"Just a minute," David said. "Maybe it's not just either or. I agree that something needs to be done, but what that is and who does it I'm not clear on at all. To be honest, Gillian and I are just a matter of weeks back from Spain. I'm not sure either of us has the energy to get into something else right now. Let's at least take a couple of days to think it over, and meet up again midweek. Maybe there's another way forward we haven't thought of yet."

"Ok," Mike agreed, closing the folder. "I've got a bit of time. But no later than that. This is a big deal. I'll keep on digging, but when sums like that are involved there's no telling what people might do."

Chapter 2

THE TRAVELLER'S TALE

They said it would cost $15,000. Who in a small town in Belarus has $15,000? Nobody, that's who. But there are ways. When you ask why it's so much they talk about forged papers, bribing guards, getting transport, arranging couriers. Risks, dangers, unexpected expenses, whatever. Anyway, it's $15,000. Take it or leave it. So when I met up with Andrei and he had a business idea, I jumped at it as a way to come up with that sort of cash. It wasn't dangerous – not really. Just moving packages from here to there. Pick something up outside the airport and deliver it to somewhere outside a railway station. You don't need to be Einstein to know what that means. Anyway, none of that was going to stop me. Who in their right mind would want to stay in a nation where you could either be a gangster or a pig farmer and not much else? Ironic really: to get away from the gangsters you have to pay them, trust them. "If I'd known then what I know now," as they say.

Once you've got $5,000 you can book a place. You hand over the cash and they say they'll let you know. As my grandmother used to say, "Nadezhda umiraet posledney" – hope is the last thing to die. You pay up and hope for the best. Of course they want the other ten so it's in everybody's interests to offer you something. What you get in the end isn't what you thought you were paying for, but isn't that always the way? I mean, you never know exactly what you're going to get when you put your hand up for anything. If I was praying for anyone except myself now I would pray they don't get what I got. But that's not going to happen, is it? Anyway, I'm getting ahead of myself.

It started when I was fourteen. The other girls in my class just wanted to get married and live like their mothers and grandmothers. The only thing they talked about was who was available: Oleg the butcher, Yuri the mechanic, even Sacha the doctor. Then making babies. In ten years' time you might be able to afford a washing machine or a freezer. But by then he's behaving like his father or grandfather and spending more on vodka than you can save to make your life just a little bit easier. I thought I'd rather kill myself quickly and be done with it. I've thought about that a lot since then. But when you're a teenager you think you'll live forever. They tell you smoking will kill you early but dying at fifty-five doesn't sound too different to dying at 500 when you're that age; that day will never come. In every practical sense you might as well be immortal. So everyone started smoking – except for me. I had a different plan. I worked out how much I might have been spending on cigarettes and put at least that amount in a shoe box under the bed every week. I didn't spend anything on make-up or magazines or parties either. Anything I did spend was an investment in the future. There was a stall at the Saturday market where they had cheap novels in English. I used to buy them and sit for hours with a dictionary, trying to understand. I don't think Jane Austen wrote for a teenage girl in 2005 in Belarus. But I loved it anyway. *1984* I understood right away because I was good at history. I was Winston but I was Julia too. Unlike them, I had a way out – or that's what I thought then.

I had known Andrei at school. We'd even gone out for a bit. He wasn't very good-looking but he was smart, ambitious. We were both outsiders and we shared our dreams. He wanted to go into business, so he studied Apple, General Electric, Hewlett Packard, and others. Bill Gates was his hero. He used to say, "Imagine, a business that started in a college dorm that now rules the world. I'll do that one day." I'd like to know if he has, but of course there's no way I can find that out now. Sometimes I watch TV and hope I might see his face on the news. Anyway, when he contacted me again I was working in an office and still saving. At that rate it was going to take twenty years. He gave me a way to make it happen quicker. So, first of all I worked for him. Then I worked *with* him. Then we moved in together and worked together. But I always told him I was going to leave. I didn't want there to be any doubt.

Once I started collecting packages from Brest on the border and taking them on to Orsha, Slutsk, Mogilev, or Minsk, my little egg really started to grow. Andrei was organized, his instructions clear. He made me learn them and not write anything down but I didn't find it hard. I was a college student going home to my family for a weekend, a granddaughter travelling to grandma's funeral, a secretary on my way to start a new job, plus a dozen other variations. I was good at it. He had a hacker friend that could usually give us a tip-off from the police computers whenever there was to be a major crackdown; then we'd lie low for a bit. Sometimes it took a bit of "fraternizing" when papers – or packages – were checked. But I was good at that too. I'm not bad-looking – at least I wasn't then. So Andrei was pleased and always paid the agreed amount and on time. "Well done, Tati," he would say. "You're a natural. I know I can trust you."

Then finally the big day came. I had paid the $5,000 a year before and now I had the ten. All the plans were made. Date, time, pickup point. I told Mum I was going to visit a friend who had just moved to Minsk. She didn't seem to care much, and Dad was usually drunk when he wasn't driving lorries full of sheep – sometimes even when he was. Only Andrei knew. They only let you take minimal stuff so I packed my little black backpack and waited by the entrance to the railway station. It was raining, the van was late, and I was wet and cold by the time they arrived. But I didn't care. This was my new beginning. Andrei came to see me off and waved from under the awning of the shops. I'd like to see him again, but the way things are now that's not going to happen. I'd like to see Mum and even Dad again. I'd like to see my home town, the school, the church, the park. Anything except these four walls.

Chapter 3

GORGIE DALRY

Diana Krall was singing "'S Wonderful" and David believed it truly was. *What they call the Jazz Age is often criticized for being superficial and trivial. All that glitter and glamour for rich parasites like Jay Gatsby, while salt-of-the-earth Steinbeck characters were starving in the dust bowl. That's true of course at one level, he thought, but on the other hand it did bring out some wonderfully witty composers and wordsmiths. And George and Ira were up there with the best. Maybe they even were the best.* David had been humming along to their sophisticated melodies and perfectly crafted lyrics for forty years and they seemed as fresh as ever. He could always find something applicable to the moment. There had been a time when, like Fred Astaire, he had the constant feeling there might be trouble ahead, but now he found himself humming "'S Wonderful". The song was all about utter astonishment that the girl in question should really, truly care. Well, she apparently did and he was duly as astonished as required.

Sunday afternoon was his favourite time of the week. Drinkmonger just down the hill kept a few Ribera del Dueros (though at eye-watering prices compared with Madrid's), which seemed to bind his former life in Spain to the present reality. Spanish sunshine bottled. Sunday morning church was great when it worked. Passing on something of value, encouraging the flock, noticing unspectacular but significant signs of growth in damaged lives – all good. But Sunday afternoon was his time for unwinding and allowing himself some satisfaction in it all. He and Gillian had fallen into an unspoken routine alternating between David's Bruntsfield flat – now finally warm and comfortable – and Gillian's posher premises in Marchmont. They had also come to

26

alternate between Spanish and Scottish. David did *merluza en salsa verde* while Gillian did Balmoral chicken. Or she did a perfect paella while he did roast pork with fantastic crackling – very hard to get in Spain. And nobody cared. Southside folk knew their minister had a girlfriend – what a hopelessly inadequate word that was – and that she wasn't from their sort of background, but they trusted him – and her – and couldn't deny the difference it had made. It was barely a shell of a man who had come to them a year ago, but now he seemed to be a human being again. Sunday evening services had been abandoned as both unnecessary and in the way of family time and Monday was his day off. So David's Sunday afternoon was like everyone else's Friday night. The weekend starts here. *'S awful nice. 'S paradise. 'S what I love to see.*

With the post-service formalities and handshaking over, they went back to whichever venue was due and put on some music – Diana Krall, Paul Desmond, or maybe a relaxing bossa nova from The Sound, Stan (the Man) Getz. Then that other magical sound, a cork popping, and an hour or two of unwinding as the Sunday lunch slowly cooked. And the talk just as nourishing as the food. They both felt they had a lifetime of catching up to do; the eight months they had been together had done nothing yet to reduce the flow. Memories, ideas, points of view, even trivia and *tonterías* – it was all good. The undemanding comfort of trivial things. Then whatever they fancied, depending on the weather: walking in the Braids, high tea at the Old Bakehouse in West Linton, or maybe Mozart at Queen's Hall. Finally back home at the end of the day.

David was feeling particularly content. He had just finished a series on "The *I ams* of John". Today had been "I am the Good Shepherd" from John 10:11. Even preaching in English he still couldn't help thinking in Spanish. *Yo soy el buen pastor. El buen pastor da su vida por las ovejas.* It was such a perfect passage for talking about relationship contrasted with religion. What could be less like a religion than sheep and a shepherd? Try getting sheep to even walk through a gate together, far less draw up statements

27

of faith, creeds and councils, doctrines and dogmas, or a sheepy sort of hierarchy. All they know is the voice of the shepherd and follow accordingly. Despite where the analogy broke down, David remained convinced this was the heart of the matter – the irreducible core – that needed to be constantly reinforced. And it was so beautifully simple: sheep, a shepherd, wolves, and walls. Neat. And this morning he felt he had maybe finally got it right. So he was a bit surprised when, a forkful of Andalusian lamb halfway to his mouth, Gillian had said, "Not sure I was 100 percent with you this morning, *caballero*."

"Mmm. Why's that?"

"Well, I entirely get the relationship/religion thing." Gillian paused, sipping her glass of Ribera. "I remember Mariano saying exactly the same when we were at Warehouse 66 in Madrid. No problems with that."

David also took another sip to help the lamb on its way.

"What then?"

"The bit about the sheep following because they know his voice and not going after strangers who would do them harm."

"And…"

"Well, just that it's entirely untrue. If you look at the history of the Christian religion, I mean. People are constantly deceived and damaged. Heretic leaders, rival Popes, tele-evangelists, all that stuff. It's just not as simple as sheep hearing the shepherd. Or have I got the wrong end of the stick?"

David munched for a moment, both for thinking time and so as not to be spraying the table with fragments of lamb and garlic.

"Yes, that's a slightly different angle from what I was taking, but I see your point."

"I suppose it's all inevitable – humans being who they are – both the deceivers and the deceived. And I'm not arguing against the relationship thing; that makes perfect sense. The problem is, how on earth are you supposed to tell one from the other?"

"The good guys and the bad?"

"Maybe not so clear as that but it's pretty murky waters, isn't it? Like which varieties are going to turn out to be following the shepherd – more or less – and which are more about fleecing the sheep. Before we met I would never have even considered church. If I had I wouldn't have had any idea where to go – St Giles or some backstreet bunch with a website and a TV channel? D'you see what I mean?"

David took another mouthful, topped up their glasses again, then got up and changed the CD.

"I suppose I was taking it from a more personal point of view, outside of the structures. But you've absolutely got a point. What I can't stand is tele-evangelists on stage repenting of their Ashley Madison account and being embraced and forgiven by their wives – all because it just got hacked and posted online. And the whole thing live on cable."

"Exactly. So, speaking basically as an outsider, how are we supposed to know who to trust? Who's not going to have a scandal next week? Who's worth putting your faith in?"

"Nobody, I suppose, including me. I suppose we would say you can only trust the shepherd."

"But the reality is that human beings are the way in. Front-of-house staff, if you like. That's how people hear and learn – from another human being. Do you just have to pay your money and hope for the best?"

"Maybe I've never had a really bad experience so I don't see the problem so clearly. But, as you say, someone who has no way of knowing could easily be led up the garden path. Maybe we just have to accept there will always be rogues and encourage due diligence, like you would with your car insurance or the bank."

"Speaking of which…"

David gathered up the plates and took them over to the sink, then peered into the fridge and found two chilled plates of *arroz con leche*.

"Yes, I know. I haven't forgotten."

"What'd you reckon then?"

"To be honest I've got that sinking feeling but I'm trying *not* to think of it. In fact, I've got an idea for this afternoon that might take our minds off it."

"Pray tell."

"That bloke that took the bullet meant for me – they've finally given me his address. I thought I ought to go around there and apologize."

Gillian's silver MX5 snaked around the maze of one ways approaching Haymarket, then swung up Dalry Road past Hay Sushi and the Passion Hut, tattoo parlours and cafés, then downhill heading west.

"I think this is it," David said, *Edinburgh A-Z* on his knee and a scribbled address in his hand. "In between the Saltyard Café and Dalry Primary. Cathcart Place."

Gorgie Dalry wasn't an area he was too familiar with, but it didn't feel that different from Villa de Vallecas in Madrid: low rent, cheap shops, old housing, and few of the more obvious signs of prosperity. The Villa had been an important place for him, where he'd begun to see things differently. Gillian swung around the right turn, then they were onto backstreet cobbles.

"This is it – Duff Street. Hmm... Looks better than it sounds."

Many of the old Victorian tenements had been knocked down and replaced by modern four-storey housing association flats. They looked smart, well cared-for, and in good condition.

"So not so Duff after all?" Gillian paused at the junction. "What number?"

They drew in at the one remaining old-style tenement, a narrow fringe of scrappy shrubs behind railings along the front and a To Let sign jammed above the common front door.

"Top floor. Naturally. Flat A. Once more, dear friends..."

"... into the breach."

Together they squeezed past bikes, buggies, undelivered

post, and what looked like the remains of chicken chop suey and trudged up three floors. More bikes shackled to the banister at the top. The door of flat A had a *World of Warcraft* poster on it and was slightly ajar.

"Seems to be this one," Gillian whispered, as if in the hope it might turn out not to be after all.

"Here we go. I did call him to say we were coming... "

David knocked. Waited. Knocked again. Waited. Then pushed the door open a few inches and shouted. Still nothing. Then a scuffley sound from within and finally a bellow like a battle cry.

"Yessss! You are mince!!!" A short guy like a baby gorilla, about as wide as tall, emerged from the darkness with a grin on a face that was too unshaven to be designer but not quite enough to be hipster. He had on torn black jeans and a black T-shirt featuring a *Star Wars* stormtrooper with his head in his hands, with the caption "These really were the Droids you were looking for".

"Sorry about that. Just plastered the Death Star. It blows up in such cool way!" Then, as if suddenly back in the twenty-first century, he wiped a paw and stuck it out. "Hi, I'm Spade. You David Hidalgo? You really should be dead y'know."

David and Gillian edged into a dark hall littered with unopened post, several still shrink-wrapped copies of the yellow pages, and fliers for double glazing and takeaways.

"Nice of you to come round. I've got the bullet in a jar if you want to see it? Sorry about the mess. Not too many visitors. Let's try the living room."

They followed as far as Spade opening the door and peeking in then changing his mind.

"Maybe not. Kitchen then."

This time they actually got inside before everyone could see the problem. A huge TV dominated one wall, with a maze of trailing cables to hand controllers dumped on a red corduroy sofa littered with dirty dinner plates, takeaway tubs, and notebooks. The one free sitting space was deeply indented, no doubt to fit the behind that was just ahead of them. Where the sink should be stood a teetering tower of dirty plates and cups seeming to defy gravity.

"So... maybe not in here either... I guess it'll have to be the office."

Backing out again, they followed their host through yet another door, this time into almost total darkness.

"Sorry about this. Just a sec." Spade hunkered down a shade too quickly for Gillian to look in another direction. "There we go. Let there be light." And there was. It was weird. Having realized this wasn't the *Ideal Home* show flat, the state of the "office" was more surprising than anything they had seen so far. It was meticulously tidy and set up like a control room. The window was completely blacked out and the walls were all painted matt black. In front of them was a full-width work surface with three widescreen monitors and matching keyboards. Above were racks of electronics with rows of winking lights. One side wall held another rack of shelves with neatly labelled ring binders showing month and year. Trays of CDs occupied the lower shelves. The remaining wall was almost entirely taken up by a whiteboard with columns of dates and numbers and random strings of characters that looked like they might be passwords.

"Sorry the rest of the place is a bit of a mess. Like I said, not too many visitors. Have a seat."

Spade pulled out a massive black leather CEO swivel armchair, spun it around, and dropped his entire weight into it. The chair gave a soft hiss. Looking around, David and Gillian found two orange plastic stacking chairs with nothing on them. They were the only furniture that wasn't jet black.

"Sorry... can I just ask," Gillian began. "Spade? We're looking for Danny McGuire."

"And you've found him. More or less. I'm only Danny to my mum now."

"Why Spade then?"

"'Cause I dig for stuff. Not obvious?"

"What for?"

"Anything that's buried that somebody wants to find – information, that is, not spuds. I thought about calling the business Spade-you-like – you know, like the baked potato chain – but I didn't think they'd get the joke in Hong Kong. That's where a lot of the work comes from nowadays. So, to answer your question, I dig for anything somebody wants to know that's on a computer somewhere that they're willing to pay for." Spade nodded towards a safe under the desk. "And there seems to be a lot of stuff some people want hidden that other people want to find. Which is a good job for me. Anyway, what can I do for you?"

David cleared his throat.

"Well. My name's David Hidalgo – you know that already. I think I owe you an apology. About that bullet."

"Aw, no worries. Shoulder's almost back to normal. Not your fault. Mind you, I did drop off the leader boards for a bit. Knackers your game play having only one working arm an' that. Anyway, it's dead right again now. They never did tell me what that was all about though."

David explained about drugs, abduction, the hunt for a missing girl, and a SWAT assault team in southern Spain. Finally the guess that someone associated with Raúl Álvarez, the big boss behind it all, had leaned out of a car window and taken a shot at a crowd of pedestrians on South Clerk Street. They'd shot the wrong man. Spade nodded in a vague sort of way through most of the story. The only bit he made David go back over and repeat until he understood it perfectly was the code that had helped reveal where Jen MacInnes, the missing girl, was being held.

"Hey, that's pretty cool," he said. "Nobody in my line would have got it, I'll bet. But there are other ways."

"What do you mean?" Gillian asked. "Other ways of what?"

"Finding out what you want to know. More than 2 billion people online now. Then there's mobile phone users, credit cards, all that stuff. If you know where to look you can find almost anyone."

"Or *anything*?" Gillian asked, casting a sideways glance at David.

"Sure, for a price. Sometimes takes a bit of time. But, more or less, long as it's connected. Anyway, fancy a coffee?"

"No, I don't think…" David started to say until Gillian interrupted him.

"That would be great, thanks. Both the same. Milk no sugar."

David shrugged as Spade disappeared.

"*Anyone or anything*," Gillian repeated once Spade had left the room. "D'you not think that might come in useful?"

It was late by the time they emerged out onto the street. With a couple of coffees and a pile of Tunnock's Caramel Wafers in front of him Spade had seemed to relax and got talkative. When he had said "not too many visitors", it might have been more accurate to say none. Ever. Food came in and 1s and 0s went out. That was it. His expedition to South Clerk Street a few weeks previously had been to deliver a set of files even he considered too sensitive to email. Kinda rotten luck going out once a month and getting shot. Other than that, Spade seemed to think life in a digital hermitage completely normal. All those he shared his cyberspace with lived in much the same way. So what? However, given that a couple of stray humans had wandered in, he seemed to be enjoying the change. He told them about the challenge of getting through locked, barred, and bolted doors – digitally speaking. Not just by applying a mathematical sledgehammer to tackle long passwords but by getting into the mind of the target, outguessing them, thinking through the tools they had available, how they might be used, and going one better. Apparently it wasn't even just computers any more. Now there was "the Internet of Things". Wireless systems in cars, home security, drones, even baby monitors. Gillian shuddered. You mean someone on the other side of the world could take over a monitor used to check a sleeping infant? More likely some guy just a few streets away wanting to know when the coast was clear for a break-in. They didn't go into the creepier possibilities.

Apparently bank accounts were easy-peasy – at which point Gillian gave David another look – government records slightly trickier, military secrets challenging, and GCHQ currently pretty secure. But we'll get there in the end. Regarding Google he was scathing.

"They want your data!" he shouted, pounding the desk. "Don't give it to them. Knowledge for the masses, my foot. We're giving them the entire shop in exchange for the menu for Pizza Express. Please, please, please, don't use Google. If you must search at least use StartPage. Google grabs your IP address plus everything you search for, every stonking keystroke. Interests, family, politics, health – the whole lot. And leaves a shed load of cookies on your drive. Today it's mostly just to shove a bunch of adverts at you. Tomorrow governments will start demanding it, then using it to run our lives. They probably do it already and nobody knows. Fact," Spade was warming to the theme, "in 2006, AOL accidentally released three months' data from 650,000 users. It's still searchable! At least StartPage deletes your data every twenty-four hours."

Once the floodgates were open, Spade seemed to be enjoying the audience and was soon telling them about his upbringing in Larbert, university at Heriot-Watt (second-year dropout), and his current "business interests". Registering with the Revenue and paying tax he considered entirely optional. This year he had decided to pay for the first year in ten. "Got to keep the lights on," he admitted. By ten o'clock he was asking David what it was like being a minister – a species he'd never come across before. David tried to describe it in a few words, but Spade seemed to want more, until David had gone into greater depth than he would probably have done with anyone from Southside. Then, at last, after eleven – by which time both David and Gillian were absolutely famished having only managed a couple of caramel wafers each to Spade's constant munching – they managed to get away.

"What did you make of that?" Gillian asked, heading back up the hill towards Haymarket.

"Well, I clearly didn't get off my marks as quickly as you. A man who can find out anything you want to know and thinks bank accounts are easy-peasy… Might come in handy."

"Oh look. Fancy something Italian?"

Gillian pulled in sharply outside Mia, open till midnight on Sundays, and looked at her watch. "We might still be in time."

Less than ten minutes later they had two plates of carbonara in front of them and a man with a massive pepper mill adding a bit more bite. The sauce was creamy and the pasta exactly al dente. Their afternoon and evening with Spade had been so full-on they were both content to eat for a while in silence. Some anonymous lounge trio were crooning "Volare" softly over the PA. At least it wasn't Dean Martin, thank goodness, they agreed. Everything they had heard and seen over the past five hours was slowly being absorbed along with comfort Italian food. David was nearly finished and about to push his chair back when the opening notes of "Moanin'" by Art Blakey and the Jazz Messengers disturbed the peace. He pulled out his mobile and peered at it in the low lighting.

"Hmm. Sam. I wonder what she's phoning about at this time? Just a minute. Hi Sam. What's going on?"

Almost immediately Gillian saw his expression change.

"What? When? I can't believe it. Yes, of course. Absolutely. Don't tell me any more. I'm on my way."

He closed the phone case, laid it in front of him, and leaned forward, elbows on the table and head in his hands.

Gillian reached out and touched his arm.

"What is it? What's happened?"

"I can't believe it," David repeated, bewildered. "It's Mike. He's dead. Hung himself in the garage. Police are at the house. Sam says they've found child pornography images on his computer."

Chapter 4

THE BUSINESSMAN'S TALE

Franchising – that's the key. 100 per cent of nothing is still nothing, but 50 per cent of something big can be plenty. You follow? It's been the key to million-dollar businesses. McDonald's, Coke (no pun intended), Hertz: all the big boys plus a million you've never heard of. But you have to decide how big you want to be. I wanted to be bigger than just shifting fifty-gram packets on the street. Therefore – franchising, which means recruitment. Of course you can't exactly advertise in a daily like *Zviazda*, though I've heard that in the West girls with something to sell can even put it in the paper. Or the guys that run them. Franchising again, I suppose. Well, we're not in the West – yet. Which brings me to Tati.

We first met in school and even then I could see she was different. Funny, quirky, really quick when it came to anything new. Good at maths, history, English (so important), geography. So it all kind of fitted when she told me when we were just fourteen that there was no way she was going to stay in a country of bandits and peasants. She was going West. She understood our history and what had happened to communism. She said it was like a ship that was well designed and built, but it sank because it was meant to be a passenger ship but the officers thought all they had was cargo. So while they were up on the bridge making all the decisions, the passengers were locked in the hold and expected to feed the boilers. When it became obvious they couldn't keep up with the capitalist ship alongside they tried letting in a little sunshine to persuade the passengers to work harder, but all they wanted to do was jump overboard. While the officers were trying to stop them they didn't see the rocks ahead. You see? Tati was a philosopher as well as everything else. Good-looking, smart, ambitious – and leaving.

But you need money to leave and she didn't have any. I swear I would have given her some if I'd had it, but back then we were both broke – little rats running around searching for crumbs while the gangsters enjoyed the banquet. Actually, they were the same ones who used to be the officers on the ship, but that's another story. *So what do you want to be*, I asked myself, *a little rat all your life or maybe get your own place at the table?* I started buying a little and selling it for a little more. Then I could afford to buy more and sell for even more. It's not rocket science, is it? *Buy and sell what?* you might ask. Well, not vegetables, but unlike most of the trade, I never used. It's my firmest rule. Most of the small-town dealers only do it to pay for their own habit. That's a hobby not a business. And feeding a habit means you're not in control. Anyway, things grew nicely till it got to the point I couldn't handle it all myself – so franchising. Bring in someone you can trust, give them a share of the business. Not working *for* you – working *with* you. Then they have no reason to steal and cheat; they'd just be cheating themselves. But who? Then I remembered Tati. We had gone out for a bit at school. I think we both realized we were different. She didn't want to get married at seventeen and spend her whole life in the same town breeding till her husband got bored, started drinking, knocked her about a bit, and spent the housekeeping on younger models. I didn't want to run a hardware store selling nails to her husband for forty years until I could afford a dacha in the country. It was just the means of achieving our dreams that was different. She was going to the West; I was going into business. Anyway, I remembered Tati and tried to find out where she was. Maybe we could help each other. Turned out she was a secretary in a town about 35 km away, still saving as much as she could and still watching English movies at the weekend. No husband. No boyfriend. Actually, no friends at all. Everyone thought she was crazy. And she did act a bit crazy. She was by far the smartest, quickest (and best-looking) girl in the office so they didn't want to sack her, but she was so bad-tempered even the boss had to ask her nicely if there was anything extra they needed done.

I got in touch. We met; I explained. She understood immediately, as I knew she would. She started working just the weekends to begin with, collecting a package from here and delivering it there. If it needed longer she'd phone in sick. Nobody dared to challenge her. It worked very well. We grew closer. We were still both outsiders, but she wanted to be right outside while I wanted to get right inside – if you see what I mean. So she moved in with me – a partner, in every sense. She was brilliant at the travel, the deliveries, and even the record-keeping. You do need to do that, you know – not for taxes, of course, but information is oxygen. I had a buddy who was an IT wizard who helped us set up the systems and kept an eye on the police computers so he could tip us off if there was going to be a crackdown. Tati loved that side of it and made up all sorts of charts and tables saying how much we'd be making in three or five years' time. But she always said to me, "Andrei – you know I won't be here then. You do understand, don't you?" And I did. Perfectly. But I won't say I wasn't sad when I saw her go. She had helped me recruit a dozen other girls and boys to take over her job and grow the business. She was a fantastic judge of character. But I knew she couldn't stay. Just as soon as she had the $15,000 they said it cost – plus a little more to set something up when she got to England – I knew she'd leave.

I saw her get into the van that night, just with a little black backpack and big dreams. I don't know how rain can be so cold and not be hail, but that night it felt like icy needles in my face. I stood by the side of the road with my hood up and my hands deep in my pockets. I took a hand out to wave and I remember she turned just before she got into the van. The wind whipped her black hair across her face as she waved back. She was smiling. She was on the way to her dream. I hope she found it. I haven't heard from her since she left – over six months now. Every day I hope

I'll get a postcard or something. I know she's tough and if anyone can make it Tati can. Still, I worry.

Chapter 5

SOUTH BRIDGE

The previous morning Colinton Mains Rise had seemed the very model of peaceful suburbia: respectable villas with neat lawns, trimmed hedges, posh cars, and busy, successful people all minding their own business. Now it looked like a scene from a disaster movie. The road outside the Hunters' home was jammed with police cars, a doctor on duty's van, and an ambulance. Fire brigade and coastguard would have made it a full set. Individuals and couples stood out on the street, pretending to walk their dogs after midnight, while, slightly less blatantly, all along the road curtains were twitching. Flashing blue lights added a lurid glow. Gillian had to park fifty yards away, the entrance to the drive sealed off by uniformed officers and yellow tape.

"Hi, my name's David Hidalgo. We're friends of Samantha Hunter."

"I'm sorry, sir. This is a potential crime scene. I'm afraid I can't let you through." The officer concerned seemed anything but sorry or afraid.

"She called me half an hour ago. She's expecting us."

"I'm still sorry, sir. I'm not at liberty to let anyone through."

"Would it help if I were her minister?"

"Are you?"

"More or less. Look, can you at least tell her David Hidalgo's here?"

"Wait here, sir. I'll pass it on."

Moments later Sam came out dressed much as the previous morning but entirely different in her demeanour. She saw David and

41

headed towards the tape, walking as if her body still remembered how but her mind had disengaged. She was stopped halfway by a burly figure in a dark suit. They exchanged a few words, then the dark suit came up to the tape.

"Reverend Hidalgo. We seem to keep bumping into each other."

"So it appears. Gillian, this is Detective Inspector Thompson. He was involved in looking for Jen MacInnes last year, then interviewed me after the shooting." Gillian nodded.

"And the inspector bit is partly thanks to you – and Raúl Álvarez. So it's not protocol but the lady is pretty shaken up and she wants to speak to you. Let's just assume you *are* her minister." He hoisted the tape. "Do what you can."

Uniformed officers and figures in non-contamination suits were coming and going in the flashing blue light. Sam seemed to be a tiny isolated figure ignored by everyone else and bypassed by the action around her. She was ashen faced and red eyed but not crying.

"Thanks for coming," she said. "Hope I didn't drag you out of bed."

"The least we could do," David replied. "How are you? I'm sorry – that's a stupid question."

"How am I? Not really sure. Running on adrenalin I suppose."

"If there's anything – absolutely anything we can do…" Gillian put in.

"Of course. I know."

"What happened?" David asked.

"I found him about two hours ago." Sam nodded towards the garage. "Like I said on the phone. But whatever it looks like, I know my husband, David. Mike did not kill himself. And all that – that stuff on his computer – it wasn't his. I swear to God."

Just then the garage door opened and a wheeled stretcher emerged. DI Thompson came up and whispered in Sam's ear. She shook her head.

"No, I've seen him. It's enough."

Thompson turned to David. "Reverend Hidalgo, can I just have a word with you?" Sam and Gillian went into the house, leaving the two men standing where they were.

"This one's landed on my desk," Thompson began. "Actually, it's not unhelpful that you're around so I'm going to bend the rules and treat you as a fellow professional. Anything you can do to support Mrs Hunter would be really helpful. We'll have a trained counsellor around in the morning but it would be good if someone could be with her tonight. We're trying to raise our game for the victims these days."

"Of course. We'll both stay. Am I allowed to ask what happened?"

Thompson shrugged and pulled out a notebook.

"By all means – in confidence. Michael Hunter was pronounced dead…" – he looked at his watch – "about an hour ago. Topped himself, on the face of it. Hanged from a beam in the garage. Mrs Hunter is emphatic that her husband did not take his own life but until we see any evidence to the contrary, that's the story right now."

"Any note, phone call, something?"

"None so far." He consulted the notebook again. "Just jumped from a chair in the garage and it's goodnight Vienna. Pathologist reckons cause of death is cerebral hypoxia – interrupted blood flow to the brain as a result of constriction of the arteries in the neck by a ligature tightened by the weight of the body. Like I said – topped himself."

"I was at a meeting here with Mike yesterday morning. There was absolutely no sign of anything that might lead to a suicide."

"Ah well, that was before the events of Saturday afternoon, wasn't it? We got a call into our Oxgangs station yesterday…" – another brief glance at the notebook – "at 16.27. Someone claiming to be a neighbour but wouldn't give a name. Male. Claimed they had observed Mr Hunter sitting on a bench in the park with his laptop taking zoom-lens photos of kids. The caller claimed they approached Mr Hunter and that a heated discussion ensued, which ended with the caller telling him…" – Thompson flipped the page – "quote, 'Filth like you don't deserve to live. I'm going to get you put away where they know what to do with your kind', end quote. Caller stated he then went straight home and phoned us."

"And you came out right away?"

"No. That sort of call would normally go into the lottery – sorry, 'the allocation process' – then out to someone – not necessarily me. Investigation in due course 'as resources permit', as they say. We're here because Mrs Hunter phoned 999 about two hours ago." He flipped another page. "She says her husband was highly agitated on Saturday evening but didn't mention anything about an argument. He went to bed about 1 a.m. but got up again in the night – exact hour unknown. When she came down in the morning he was still in pyjamas and looking like he hadn't slept, and had something on his laptop that she admits he tried to hide. Normally they go to church on Sunday mornings. This week Mr Hunter stayed home and wasn't about when Mrs Hunter came home at about 1.30. She tried his mobile but it was turned off. Apparently he'd been under a lot of pressure at work so she assumed he might have gone in to catch up on something."

"That not a bit unusual on a Sunday?"

"Apparently, but not unknown. Anyway, Mr Hunter was not to be found all afternoon and into the early evening, at which point Mrs Hunter says she began to be more concerned. She phoned a few friends but nobody had seen him so she went for a walk."

"I can imagine."

"Anyway, when she got back she noticed the garage light was on. Seems they don't use the garage much and just leave the cars in the drive. Went into the garage and found her husband – not, as you might say, a pretty sight. He looked like he'd been out for a run and still had his jogging gear on. She phoned 999 and got a uniformed patrol. They confirmed what she had said in the call and got the police surgeon out. Cross-checking picked up the earlier call. Child abuse images are a hot ticket right now so I got hauled out."

"And…"

"Just what you're hoping not to find. Mr Hunter's laptop was on his desk in the study. Mrs Hunter typed in his password and Bob's your uncle. Apparently right in the middle of a slide show from the hard drive. No doubt about the content. So all the laptops in the house and two desktops are now in the back of that van. There's a national child abuse unit that'll look at it in due course. But there you have it. In a nutshell."

David let out a long sigh, staring into the night sky far above the blue lights and yellow tape.

"I've known Mike Hunter for ten years," he said. "I just can't believe that of him."

"No doubt. The ones you can believe it of are on the sex offenders' register already. It's the ordinary blokes, pillars of the community, doctors, lawyers – ministers if you don't mind me saying so… Nobody can believe it until they're presented with the evidence. And we have pretty clear evidence as far as Mike Hunter goes. Naturally none of this is to go any further, though I'm sure Mrs Hunter understands where we're coming from."

"Well, I suppose she won't deny what's in front of her eyes. But she's sure Mike didn't kill himself."

Thompson shrugged.

"Well, right now that's what it looks like: motive, means, and opportunity. Anyway, I think we're about done here. Back in the morning but that's it for tonight. As I say, we'd appreciate it if you can keep an eye on Mrs Hunter. Not the perfect way to round off the weekend."

Sam and Gillian were sitting in the kitchen. They each had a coffee in front of them but were neither drinking nor talking. They looked up as David opened the door. Ever since getting Sam's call and running out of the restaurant, David had been struggling both with the horror and disbelief but also with what they were going to find when they arrived and what on earth to say. There was a lead weight in his gut that wouldn't go away. This wasn't the first time he'd faced something like this. The thought of Mike's lifeless body hanging from a rope brought another image to mind – twenty-five years ago when he'd left work early and found another figure hanging by the neck. Years of depression after a series of miscarriages had finally proved too much for his lively, funny, intelligent young wife and Rocío had decided enough was enough. He'd opened the door just in time to pick up the chair she'd kicked away and support her body with one arm while struggling to loosen the rope with the other. As she regained consciousness she had clung to him, which is probably the only way he had managed. The whole sequence probably took less than three minutes but it felt like hours and now came back to mind in vivid technicolour. He had pondered many times the question of what had made him leave the paperwork on his desk and head for home just at that moment. Now another question was uncoiling like a snake in his mind: why had he arrived in time and Sam had not?

Standing in the doorway, David was still hoping the right words might materialize from somewhere, but he was disappointed. Sam took in his confusion, stood up, came around the kitchen table, and gave him a hug.

"Thanks so much for coming. I didn't know who else to call." She turned and clicked the kettle on again. "We like to think we're more sophisticated than our parents but here I am doing the very same as they did in the Blitz. Get a friend round to sit with you and put the kettle on. Can't say I'm feeling much of the spirit of the Blitz, though. You read about it but never imagine it could happen to you."

Turning back with a jar of coffee in one hand and a teaspoon in the other, she looked straight at him.

"Whatever happened, David, Mike did *not* kill himself. He was a strong-minded man. Giving up or running away just wasn't part of his personality. The images on that computer weren't his. Whatever this is, it's not suicide. I can assure you of that."

Sam resisted every attempt either to get her to stay with one of them overnight or have someone stay with her. The on-call doctor had given her a sedative, she said, and she'd be fine. Well, not actually fine – but… well, you know. She'd phone in sick in the morning and arrange some compassionate leave, then maybe a few days with her sister up north waiting for release of the body. Then a small private funeral. Maybe David might say a few words. *No, honestly. I'll be fine. And yes – I'll call if I need anything. I'm sure there are other things I need to do but I just can't think right now. I'll take the phone off the hook. Can you speak to the police and let me know if they need to contact me?*

They made their way back to the car. The yellow tape had been gathered up, the emergency vehicles had left, and neighbours had gone back inside still wondering what it was all about. According to DI Thompson, if nothing new turned up, it looked as if it was going to be a pretty open-and-shut case. As with all unexplained deaths and particularly suspected suicides, there would be a report to the Procurator Fiscal, who would decide what was to happen next. Probably a postmortem would happen within the week, then the death certificate would be issued and the body released. In the final analysis, just some pathetic bloke with an abhorrent – and illegal – interest that had got out of hand and spilled over into the community and onto his computer. You've got to have some sympathy with that bloke that phoned it in. Nobody wants that in their neighbourhood. And then it turned out he was a coward as well as a paedophile and so would never actually end up where "they know what to do with your kind". Hard luck on the wife though. Bet she never knew a thing about it. You wake up in the morning and think life's jogging along ok, then by night-time it's all come crashing down and the person you live with turns out not to be who you thought they were. Didn't even have the decency to leave her a note or apologize or anything. Still, at least it's a saving to the taxpayer not having to prosecute.

Gillian pulled up outside David's Bruntsfield flat and turned the engine off.

"You ok?" she asked.

"Not as good as I was three hours ago. I'm just completely stunned. You know something similar happened to me once. I'm afraid this brings it all back."

Gillian reached for David's hand. "I'm so sorry. This can't be easy for you, after all you've been through."

"No, it's not... but it was different for me. Rocío lived; Mike didn't."

They sat in silence for some minutes.

"So what do you make of it all?" Gillian finally asked.

"Well, for a kick-off I think Sam is 100 per cent correct in saying this was no suicide, from what we know about Mike and what we talked about yesterday morning."

"Do you think the police will see it that way?"

"I'm pretty sure they won't. They have what looks like a suicide and what looks like a good reason for it."

"And all that about him being agitated – supposedly after the argument – and hiding something on his laptop."

"That's right. We interpret it one way – he was anxious about the investigation and didn't want Sam implicated by knowing who he was investigating. But, from the police point of view, it all fits together very reasonably. Secretive paedophile tries to conceal illegal images on his computer, takes a risk in the community, gets caught, terrified of the exposure, can't stand the disgrace, and decides to end it all. I imagine this is not the first time that little scenario has played itself out."

"But if it wasn't suicide, if whoever he was investigating found out and acted to protect themselves, how are we to get the police to see it that way? We don't even have a name now – just a page full of numbers that could have come from anywhere. How did they do the deed, and how on earth did that stuff get onto his laptop in the first place?"

David didn't answer, just sat silently staring out into the night. Edinburgh, like a thousand other big cities, never entirely goes to sleep, but the type of people out and about at 2 a.m. are very different

48

from those at eight o'clock the next morning. Late-night partygoers wending their tipsy way home. A few taxis, invariably taken. Night shifters heading to work. Bin lorries out on the busier routes when traffic is lightest. His thoughts returned to Mike. How was it that knowing just a few key facts – and knowing Mike personally – could lead to such an entirely different conclusion from the way the police were bound to see it? It seemed like what you believe all depends on where you're standing. He knew Mike was not a paedophile, had not been taking photos in the park, had not installed a collection of child abuse images on his computer, had not hung himself. Or did he just *think* he knew? Maybe the police interpretation was right and the finance thing was just a massive coincidence. And if it wasn't suicide, how had it been done with no signs of a struggle? And the puzzle of the images…

Suddenly David snapped out of it, unclipped his seat belt, and opened the door.

"Busy day tomorrow," he said. "DI Thompson and I need to have a chat."

David Hidalgo wasn't exactly sure what ethnicity of food detective inspectors typically favoured but thought it was a safe bet to offer some inducement for a meeting and that maybe a curry wouldn't go amiss. The lack of a good curry had been one of his few culinary complaints about Madrid, but when Lavapiés had started going all ethnic and one Indian restaurant after another had opened near his old office at Tirso de Molina, all needs were met. In Edinburgh, he'd heard good reports of Mother India on Infirmary Street near Blackwell's on South Bridge. Checking online, it turned out they did a tapas-style menu. That felt like a good omen and turned out to be sufficient incentive for DI Thompson to agree to a lunchtime meeting on Tuesday of that week. David had spent most of the previous day with Sam. Gillian had come as soon as she finished work. Sam had remained insistent throughout that things were not as they appeared and urged him to try to get the police to at least keep an open mind.

"I'm not sure what I should be calling you," David began as they found a corner table and pulled in their chairs. "DI Thompson seems a bit formal since we seem to be bumping into each other so often. And congratulations by the way."

"Thanks. It's Charlie, and you're David, aren't you?"

"I am. I hate the 'Reverend' thing so David's much better."

"Fair enough. So... thanks for the lunch, and what can I do for you?"

David paused to reorganize the table as their drinks arrived.

"It's connected with Mike Hunter, as I'm sure you've guessed."

The detective inclined his head in agreement and took a sip from his glass.

"Sam is still certain it wasn't suicide," David continued.

"Well, it wasn't an accident so that doesn't leave many alternatives."

"Ok, but before we get to that I need to fill you in a bit. As I said I had a meeting with Mike Hunter on Saturday morning, connected with the Council of Churches. Mike does – or did – the financial checking for new applications. He told us he'd found something funny connected with one of the latest batch but it only came to light though his job with Salamanca, not from the information they sent in. Large amounts of money – millions actually – in an account belonging to a smallish church. It seemed suspicious so he tried to flag it up but found he wasn't getting anywhere. He was taken off the case and told to forget about it."

Just then steaming, wonderfully aromatic portions of butter chicken, lamb karahi, fish pakora, and chilli king prawns arrived and took a bit of arranging on the tiny table. Thompson sorted his chicken and rice out, took a generous forkful, and pondered.

"So, joining the dots, he reckoned this was connected to criminal activity, not normal church life?"

"Exactly. His job was making sure the bank wasn't holding accounts from the proceeds of crime. He thought the amount itself and the fact that his superiors didn't seem to be taking any action on it were all suspicious. On Saturday morning we had a routine meeting about something else but he mentioned it and said he was going to do some further digging. We agreed to meet again tomorrow."

"Not going to happen now, of course."

"Don't you think it seems too much of a coincidence that an investigation into possible proceeds of crime should be cut short by the unexpected suicide of the investigator?"

"Very convenient for the guilty parties, I suppose."

"Exactly."

"I take it you have some documentary evidence of all this?"

"Only some figures Mike produced at the meeting."

"No name?"

"He felt he couldn't breach confidentiality further without something more to go on. Not even Sam knows the name – all we have is a choice of three."

"And what about the anonymous phone call and images on his computer?"

"Spurious. I think the call was completely bogus. The images – well, I have no idea how they got there but likewise I'm suggesting they were planted to make a suicide make sense."

"And your conclusion?"

The restaurant was quiet on a Monday lunchtime but nevertheless David lowered his voice.

"Mike Hunter was set up as an online paedophile and was murdered to cover up having found illegal activities under the front of an Edinburgh church."

Thompson tore a large hunk off a naan bread the size of a doorstep, dunked it in the butter chicken, and managed to get it to his mouth with not more than a speck ending up on his tie.

"It's a theory that accounts for some of the facts but raises more problems in relation to others. One, how did any criminal conspiracy find out they were being investigated? Two, how did they get illegal images onto a laptop that never left the Hunters' home over the weekend? Three, how was the murder itself carried out – no signs

of violence to the body and no signs of a struggle in the garage?
Suicide as a result of threatened exposure makes sense of all the
facts – the financial thing could just be a coincidence. From what
you're saying I can see there is another possible interpretation but
I'll need more than that to take it up the line for a major change
in direction."

"Like what?"

"Well, any of the above really. Right now I'm still waiting for
postmortem results and something from the computer team. I
just don't think there's enough in your theory yet to persuade the
powers that be to open a murder inquiry." With that the subject
seemed closed and DI Thompson turned his attention to the chilli
king prawns.

Back out on the street David couldn't decide which direction to turn
or where to go. Charlie Thompson hadn't been exactly obstructive
but, perhaps understandably, he needed some convincing. He already
had a perfectly good explanation that fitted the facts. Monkey
business in the church didn't disprove anything in the suicide
picture – it was just an extra piece that maybe wasn't even part of
the puzzle at all. Trying to add in that odd-shaped new piece would
mean rearranging everything else. So he wasn't ready to change the
entire scenario yet. Why would he? Something more would need to
come up – something neither of them knew yet but might be out
there that would change their whole perspective and make room
for the extra piece. It was like the many times a week David mislaid
his glasses, watch, wallet, or phone. It was somewhere here but the
question was where? He realized he was also probably still in shock
after the weekend, not to mention hardly yet recovered from being
shot at not far from where he was now standing. Looking for Jen
MacInnes in Spain already seemed like another reality that had
happened to another man.

He came out onto South Bridge just opposite the grand facade
of the University of Edinburgh's Old College Law Faculty. *I wonder*

what the law professors would make of this, he wondered, then mentally corrected himself. Their job wasn't investigation and the uncovering of evidence – just presentation to the court and the judgment of guilt or innocence – a tricky matter but different. As he saw it right now someone was guilty all right, but who was it and how to get them as far as a court?

For lack of anything better to do he crossed into Chambers Street and decided to take a wander around the National Museum. Maybe something new would strike him among the stuffed lions and tigers, the mummies and the replica machines. It had been a special place throughout his life and still had a certain magic that might be just what he needed. He remembered so many times walking around the halls and exhibits with his father – the sort of father-son moment all too rare between them and so all the more special because of it.

Hidalgo senior had been a campaigning investigative journalist in Spain until one too many investigations had led him to make discretion the better part of valour and, along with his Scottish wife, jump on a plane before Franco's henchmen reduced him to some remains in a sack in a backstreet of Carabanchel. So back to Edinburgh, where David's mum had come from. In fact, if all the family mythology was true, they had met not far from here. David's dad had been at some journalistic conference in Edinburgh, thought he'd take the chance to sample a few whiskies around the city centre pubs, ended up taking that crucial "one too many", keeled over in the street, battered his head on a lamp post, and ended up in casualty at the Royal Infirmary on Lauriston Place. Just then Mum (to be) happened to be doing an A&E practicum for her medicine degree. Somehow they seemed to connect over the blood and bandages and thankfully Dad still had sufficient mental capacity to get her phone number. So turn the wheels of fate. No visit to Edinburgh, no pub crawl, no tumble in the street, no pretty student doctor – no David Hidalgo. Later on, when they had to run from Spain, this was naturally where they ran to. Stayed with in-laws for a bit, what the Spanish mysteriously call *la familia politica*, then eventually Dad had started selling some magazine articles, writing what he used to call "tourist trash" about Spain for the emerging holiday market. Gradually they managed to get back on their feet again; then, in due course, David arrived.

But, as the years went by, he turned out to be everything his father was not: laid back, not driven; bookish and solitary in his teens; neither political nor practical but more interested in philosophy and abstractions. It didn't make for much common ground. The National Museum of Scotland seemed to be the one place they both loved where they could feel comfortable with each other. Perhaps it was being in such *uncommon* ground that made it work – everything either so gigantic or so tiny, intricate or massive, imposing or intriguing. All in a series of huge Victorian halls that by their very size made you speak in hushed tones and realize you were in the presence of something bigger than yourself, like a cathedral of science and discovery. Of course the blue whale was their favourite; it was everyone's. A huge white skeleton slung from the rafters the entire length of one of the halls. Next to that no one felt too sure of their own importance. So, wandering around, more or less in silence, every year almost from his earliest childhood, this had become the one place that managed to bridge the gulf between them, not by looking each other in the eye, but by looking away to something else that seemed to put their smaller lives into context. Next to the blue whale, maybe they weren't so different after all. David still came here when he needed to get outside of himself, to think, to regroup, to clear his mind and let a new perspective form.

The recent remodelling had improved things in a host of ways, from decent level access, right up to the new rooftop café with all-round views from the Castle Rock, past the spire of St Giles to Holyrood Park and the Southern Uplands. But the blue whale had apparently had to go. He wasn't entirely sure the trade-off was worth it but tried to keep positive and wandered in. He hadn't even got halfway round marine mammals when his mobile went off with a jarring jangle and he had to head back out again.

"Hello, David Hidalgo."

"Hi David. Sam here. Can we meet somewhere? We've got a witness."

Chapter 6

THE DRIVER'S TALE

Look, I'm just a driver. Before this job I used to drive a vegetable van and before that a bus. Actually, this isn't much different from being a bus driver. I pick up passengers and take them where they want to go. It's just that these passengers want to go a bit further than the average. So, like I say, I'm a bus driver, not a kidnapper or a blackmailer or a rapist. You'll have to speak to someone else for that. I've got a wife and family – three under ten – and I need regular work. That's almost impossible – you know, 200 guys chasing a kitchen assistant job that pays next to nothing. And round here jobs go with connections: brother, uncle, former colleague from the Party, or just friend. Without connections it's more like a million to one. So I do what I have to do and I don't apologize for it.

Anyway, I knew this bloke who used to sell fake watches in the market. I helped him out a bit, looked after the stall when he had other things on. One day he said to me, "Do you want to be poor all your life, Sergei? I can get you a job that pays more than a doctor. Then your children can eat enough and your wife can get a new coat." Of course I said yes. Then this guy, he knew another guy who knew someone else who knew someone else. You get the idea. Which means that actually, I have no idea who I'm really working for but I get paid and that's what matters. Fifty US dollars for every warm, breathing body delivered to Hamburg. That's ten times what I used to get as a bus driver, but then it's a longer run. I'm not paid to make friends and I'm not paid to think about it. I hope it works out for them but they have to take their chances like all of us. I don't know what happens after I hand them over and I don't ask. So my wife has her new coat and the kids get toys at Christmas. She doesn't ask where it comes from and I don't tell her.

But you want to know about Tati. I've taken dozens across now, and when you're driving through the night you don't look at the faces or remember the names. It's better that way. But I remember her. She was different. Everybody's nervous, but if she was, she hid it well. She looks you straight in the eye and she says what she thinks. Most of the girls have been promised a job – a nurse or a cook or a waitress or something. I don't suppose any of these jobs really exist but, like I said, that's none of my business and I don't ask. But Tati didn't want some menial job like they were promising her. She had her eyes on something more. She told me she was going to start an agency for other girls from Belarus. Once she got established she would bring them over without paying $15,000 to the mafia for a ride in a bus. She claimed to already have some funding ideas and I believed her. She said she had good English and I wasn't surprised. Nothing would surprise me about her.

Anyway, it was a filthy night when I picked her up. Outside the railway station is the usual place and she was waiting in the rain. I'd been stopped for running a red light so I was late. Cost me $10 out of my own pocket. I was late and I wasn't happy. I had two more to pick up after Tati so I was in a hurry. It's all the more surprising that I remember her so well – slim, dark shoulder-length hair, very pale skin but bright red lipstick, a sharp little nose, bright eyes. Her bag looked better quality and she had a pendant on – a circle with a flame inside it – on a chain. That's how I remember her. *Ogonyok*. Little flame. She looked like she had something inside of her you couldn't put out. At least I hope so.

She was sitting next to me and talked all the way. Most of the girls don't have much to say. They're young, scared, alone. They eat bread and sausage and look out of the window. They certainly don't talk to me. What does a girl that age have to say to a man like me? But Tati, like I say, was different. She told me about her family, how she loved reading in English or listening to English pop music. She asked me if I was married, how many kids, the usual stuff, but she seemed to really want to know. So I told her. I told her too much. Things hadn't been going so good between me and Ludmila for a few years then – even despite the extra money. I told her that as well. I told her I shouldn't drink so much. I told her sometimes in the night I have nightmares about the girls I take in my bus. All the little girls going off to the West to find their way. I don't know what happens to them and I try not to think about it, but I can't stop the dreams. She just laughed and said, "Well, you don't need to worry about me, Sergei. You'll read about me in the paper when I have a big success."

Halfway across Poland I had a crazy idea. A girl like her would be a great help to me. We could share the driving, she could look after the girls – I mean, talk to them, show them where to go when we stopped, reassure them. And I'm pretty sure she'd be able to sweet talk the border guards better than an old fool like me. They give me all the papers but sometimes there's a problem or a question and it can get tricky. If I don't get a girl to Hamburg I don't get paid and sometimes they don't all make it through. I didn't stop to think; I just said to her, "Why are you going to the West, Tati? A bright girl like you could make money here. Work with me. As we say – *artelnie garshok guschee keepeet* – with a helper a thousand things are possible." But she just laughed at me. "It's not the money," she said, "it's the life. I want to be where I can breathe, where I can be somebody."

Well, we got to Hamburg. The pickup was there and gave me a hard time for arriving late. But I got paid and the girls were handed over. Normally it doesn't bother me but this time it did. I was sorry to see Tati go. Fifteen hours in a van and she felt like my daughter.

Chapter 7

THE GRANGE

Dr Gillian Lockhart had just finished her 2–3 p.m. graveyard shift tutorial on the origins of the Scots language vowel system with particular reference to the Scottish vowel length rule, commonly known as Aitken's Law. Unfortunately, studying in the 1990s she had just missed A. J. Aitken's tenure as Professor of Scots Language at Edinburgh. He was still widely revered as the man who had more or less invented the subject and even after his death continued to tower over it. But, however loved and respected he might be in academia, he was apparently not held in such high esteem by her Tuesday afternoon tutorial group. The mixed group of late teens and so-called "mature" students had other things on their minds, though the vacant stares didn't give much away. The tutorial papers asked for the previous week had mostly passed – before immediately passing into obscurity. The "student interaction" had been torturous in the extreme and had mostly consisted of Gillian describing a point and looking to the group for examples of which very few were forthcoming. Nevertheless, finally it was over and the teenagers could head off to the Union and the middle-aged to the supermarket then home to cook the tea. She yawned, stretched, took off the glasses she now found she increasingly needed for close reading, and got up to wipe the whiteboard.

"Hi Gillian. Got a minute?" A tallish, still fairly slim figure in a Steve Jobs black polo neck and Armani jeans, a goatee beard, and a wave of steel grey hair that would have got surfers excited stood in the doorway. Gillian was never sure how to feel when Dr Stephen Baranski stopped by her room, which he seemed to be doing with increasing frequency. True, he had the reputation – probably a bit exaggerated – as the Department's lothario, but at the same time he was also a smart guy, published widely, spoke at international conferences, not painful to look at, and could be quite amusing. What's not to like? Gillian had decided some time ago that being all these things was all very well; the problem was when you knew it. She had started thinking of him more as the Department's Richard Gere, an actor she always wanted to step into the movie and slap whenever she saw him. Maybe it was just a traditional Scottish "let's not get above ourselves now" attitude. Stephen was from New England and had no such reservations.

"Sure. Come in. I'm just done."

"Exciting and dynamic as usual?"

"No. Boring and exasperating. If I'd wanted to pull teeth I could have been a dentist."

"Not them – I meant you, of course!"

Gillian resisted the temptation to roll her eyes and just smiled. Stephen smiled back though perhaps in a slightly different way.

"So. The Boss at Hampden on the nineteenth," he continued, holding up a small envelope. "You were going to think about it. Interested?"

Had it been anyone else Gillian might have wrestled them to the floor, applied a Ranger chokehold, and pried the Springsteen tickets out of their feeble, dying hands. As it was not anyone else, she carried on cleaning the board before pausing for a second to give sufficient suggestion of checking her mental calendar.

"Ah. What a shame. I forgot all about it. My dad's birthday party is on the nineteenth. I'm sure it'll be fantastic."

"No problem. He only comes every second year though. See you later."

Phew. That had been a bit awkward. She had been sure all her colleagues now understood she was "in a relationship", as Facebook euphemistically puts it these days. But, whether he knew or not (she guessed he probably did), Dr Stephen Baranski was still willing to have a go. She knew she should feel flattered but it just left her feeling muddled. She kept on wiping the board until it was cleaner than it was the day it arrived.

Dr Stephen Baranski, Revd David Hidalgo – or Someone Else for that matter. She was now over forty; the clock was ticking. Where was it all going? When all the events connected with the disappearance of Jen MacInnes had started cartwheeling out of control the previous year she had been very careful at the start just to be a helpful bystander, like the motorist willing to stop for a car crash and phone the ambulance – not take the injured home and give them hot soup. But almost immediately it had fired off in a direction she could never have predicted; both the investigation and her thoughts and feelings for that mysterious man, David Hidalgo. He was funny yet serious, wise yet foolish, careful yet reckless, tough yet weak, clear yet confused, and a few dozen other contradictory adjectives. Her feelings seemed to swing from pole to pole in sympathy. They had both uttered the fateful "I love you", but what did it all mean? She had wondered if things were on the verge of a more decisive turn the night of the shooting; then, in all the ensuing panic, the moment had passed. Besides, he was more than ten years her senior, and although that wasn't a problem in itself, they did seem to come from different generations as well as different cultural and faith backgrounds. Did they have enough in common, or maybe it was opposites attracting and all to the good?

There was one thing she felt sure of: she knew she could trust him. He was the sort of man who might take a while to work out what the right thing was, but once fixed on it she knew he would stick to it relentlessly, however difficult. His lonely, apparently one-way, drive from Toledo to Calatrava to find her, in the aftermath of looking for Jen MacInnes, had proved that. In a funny way he reminded her of Bilbo Baggins, who "knew his duty as a host and stuck to it however painful". The thought of David Hidalgo as a hobbit made her almost laugh out loud. Then she stopped herself. That was interesting – a ridiculous image but it seemed to crystallize something in her mind. David *was* ridiculous in a lot of ways: terrible dress sense, hopeless with any expression of emotions, probably believed a bunch of crazy things most twenty-first-century people would find bizarre. But he was honest and entirely trustworthy – what the lonely hearts call "sincere". She was pretty sure that Dr Stephen Baranski was none of these things. Not to mention that David had saved her life a couple of times and was great fun to be with when they weren't being shot at. Maybe it was ok after all. Maybe even what he still seemed to believe and she endlessly struggled with would just have to go on the back burner. Juan Hernandez was always fond of saying that El Señor was at work – it just hadn't all worked out yet. Maybe that was enough. Just then her mobile rang, interrupting her thoughts. It was David. Could she meet as soon after work as possible? There had been a development.

Gillian, Juan, Sam, and David met at Lovecrumbs on West Port near the Usher Hall.

"Great cakes, terrible location," Gillian commented, nodding out the window towards a trio of sleazy bars nearby as they took a corner table. "I didn't realize strip clubs still existed, and here we have three of them inside fifty yards. And no doubt prostitution and maybe even trafficking all mixed in." She gave a shudder as she set down the tray. "I suppose it never really goes away..."

"How are you, Sam?" David asked, getting the subject back where it should be as they shuffled in around a tiny table. "I tried your mobile a couple of times but just got voicemail. I thought you were going away for a bit anyway?"

"That's three questions," Sam replied, concentrating on her coffee but aiming to be at least superficially lighthearted. "How am I? Ok – and terrible. To be honest I think just numb. I know it's real but just can't believe it yet. I keep thinking of things I have to tell Mike or ask him or remind him... then I have to stop myself. I decided not to go and stay with anyone. I thought that might just make it all the harder coming back. My sister's coming down this afternoon. In fact, I've to get her at the airport around seven. What else? The mobile? I've gone a bit incommunicado too, I'm afraid. I just couldn't stand having to tell people what's happened. Or tell them how I am. I know everyone wishes me well but... I suppose I'm used to being on the giving side of things and maybe I'm not so good at taking sympathy."

Although they had met only once, Gillian had instantly liked Sam and now felt an almost overwhelming sense of sisterly affection. She wanted to turn the clock back and make it all go away, or failing that, gather her up in cotton wool until it was time to come out. Neither of these being possible, she reached across and squeezed her arm.

"It's really early yet, Sam. You've had an incredible shock. I think most people would be doped up to the eyeballs for the first fortnight."

"Well, that was one thing I didn't want. The police liaison officer they sent out suggested seeing my GP, but as well as the shock there's part of me that's just incredibly angry. I know Mike didn't kill himself and if I'm out of action I can't do anything to find out what really happened. I need to hold it together for his sake and get through it. Then I can collapse once we know the truth."

"Señora, we are praying for you," Juan put in. "Alicia, myself, David, everyone who knows you."

"I know – and I'm grateful for your prayers and for the practical help. Mrs MacInnes came round last night with a huge shepherd's pie. I didn't need to say anything to her. She just left it on the doorstep, rang the bell, then waited in the car and waved. She's a surprising lady."

"*Sal de la tierra* – salt of the earth," Juan summed up.

"So, a witness, Sam..." said David, moving them on again.

The conversation paused as a middle-aged mum and student daughter squeezed past with a loaded tray.

"It was a good thing I didn't go away. A few of the neighbours have been round. Actually, the house is full of flowers, which is nice. Anyway, Mrs Ingram from across the road – to be honest a one-woman neighbourhood watch – she knocked on the door this morning. I wasn't exactly enthusiastic about letting her in, but anyway… In the course of a long, rambling story about her youngest daughter's second husband's first wife – you get the idea – she mentioned she had been a bit worried about Mike when he came back from his run on Sunday morning: 'What a good job these young men had been around to help him.'" Sam put on the Edinburgh genteel twang. "So I asked her exactly what she'd seen. Finally, after another ten minutes it turned out that she'd noticed Mike go out for a run at about half-eleven, then around twenty minutes later a car pulled up at the door and two young men got out more or less carrying him between them. She said she wondered at the time if he'd been taken ill when he was running."

"Did she see what happened next?" David asked, coffee and cakes now forgotten. "Did they go into the house or the garage?" Sam frowned.

"That's the frustrating part. She says that at that point her sister from Toronto phoned and she didn't see any more."

David leaned back and studied the ceiling in frustration but Gillian leaned further forward.

"That's amazing. That's the first bit of evidence we've had that it wasn't a suicide at all! Anything else?"

"Well, yes and no. Could be nothing, but I was trying to think through how all of these images got onto Mike's computer. Honestly, I feel like a greyhound running round and round after the hare but never getting to the finishing line. I think of one thing, then realize it doesn't make sense, then think of something else, then back to the first one. You know? Anyway, it struck me last night that one of the sets of church accounts Mike got was delivered on a memory stick, which seemed a bit odd. I mean, what's a page of figures – 50KB or less? Why deliver it on a 4GB memory stick? Someone actually came to the door with it about ten days ago. I remember Mike went and spoke to them for a couple of minutes and then remarked on it." Sam reached into a pocket, pulled out a tiny pen drive in transparent red plastic, and held it up.

"Exhibit A," she said, laying it on the table.

"Do you know which church it was from, Señora?" Juan put in.

"Sadly, no. One of the three, that's all. But the point is, why would someone hand over a memory stick just for a file you could easily email?"

"Because there was something else on the stick that had nothing to do with church accounts," Juan stated as if it were a bald fact that everyone should know. "I did an IT evening class last year to help with the accounts at Hacienda. They were really strict about bringing in anything from home on a USB stick. They said just plugging the thing in could upload all sorts of stuff without you knowing or even touching the keyboard."

"That's what I was thinking," Sam continued. "So maybe if we found out what else was on the stick, it might give us an idea about the images on the laptop."

"Have you plugged it in to have a look?" David asked.

Sam gave him a look.

"I might not be Mark Zuckerberg but I'm not that dopey. If there is something nasty on this I don't want it on my computer as well. I suppose we'll need to explain what we're thinking to the police and get them to examine it."

"Hmm… not sure about that," David said with a grimace. "I met DI Thompson for lunch today. He's pretty reluctant to change his tune. I think the firmer the evidence we can give him for an alternative scenario the better."

Gillian gathered up her last forkful of coffee and walnut cake, drained her latte, and piled the plates on top of each other with an air of decision.

"I think I know exactly the man to ask," she said.

About eight hours earlier Alexander Benedetti – known to his friends as Sandy – had been calmly browsing through the headlines and financial section of *The Scotsman* over breakfast while his Romanian wife Sonia fussed around getting the kids ready for school. Except on days he had to go in early this was his invariable morning routine; he found it left him settled and grounded for the day. He had recently gained a very responsible position in Edinburgh's Salamanca HQ and understood perfectly well that when things went wrong in his area it was his job to fix it. Sometimes that meant going in early or long hours over the weekend trying to track things down. Today there wasn't any particular flap on, so he felt justified in taking his time. Yesterday had been a special pre-budget briefing at a nice hotel (nice lunch paid for by KPMG); today would involve a bit of catching up – nothing to get too stressed about. So he turned the page, took another sip of Valvona & Crolla's Napoletano blend, and continued browsing.

By nature he was an organized thinker, with a methodical turn of mind well suited to the task of tracking down anomalous needles in financial haystacks. In fact, he had developed a reputation as an effective fixer and it was largely that reputation that had landed him his present post. Not brutal, bullying, manipulating, or aggressive, but firm, clear, straightforward, and rigorous. The new role was called Head of Financial Security and covered internet and credit card fraud, scrutiny of accounts that might be linked to crime, insider trading, and a host of other stuff all aimed at keeping on the right side of a mountain of legislation. No one needed to remind him how much the sector had taken a hammering during the crisis and that restoring public confidence – in practice meaning the Chancellor's confidence – was one of their highest priorities now. Windfall taxes on banks, the banking levy, and excessive bonuses had meant that financial services had become a toxic brand. His job was to help restore Salamanca, at least, to being a trusted name in Whitehall and the High Street. That meant being alert to anything that might pour trouble on oily waters. Hence the morning routine of financial news while trying to screen out the hunt for gym things, homework, lunch money, and parental consent forms.

He often vaguely wondered whether this went on in every household with kids or whether his was something special. He and Sonia had only been together three years. In a sense he was still getting into the routine of things so didn't want to judge. She had been badly treated by her ex and needed space, time, and a quiet, dependable man to help both her and the kids recover. He was still single in his mid-thirties and was looking for a quiet, peaceful, dependable woman. They had met at a Central Library book group, got into a conversation about *A Short History of Tractors in Ukrainian*, and it just went from there. Despite the adjustment of having gone so quickly from living at home with his Scottish-Italian family in Prestonpans to a very nice (and frankly quite expensive) family house in the Grange with Sonia, Florian (ten), and Adriana (six), he much preferred the new life to the old and felt no need to complain. Sonia was the archetypal multitasker and managed to keep all plates spinning with no more than minor stress, which impressed him enormously. To be truthful, the entire family seemed to be doing very well, thank you. His career, if not actually stellar, was definitely gaining altitude. Sonia was finally getting the chance to study and hoped to make it to university in two or three years. The kids were happy, healthy, and bright. The past seemed to be behind them both.

Besides all that, the new church Sonia had found a year ago, in which all four of them now seemed to feel at home, also played a part. Important as career, family, and lifestyle were, he had come to see that life was about something more. Going along to church, first to keep Sonia company then fully in his own right, he had come to see that without a central core of meaning and purpose, the rest was all just window dressing. Opening a door to the spiritual had made everything else richer, not poorer, even accounting for the church's strong teaching on tithing. As his career developed this was not a trifling sum but, hey-ho, it was part of the deal so he signed the standing order and kept on smiling.

In the midst of all this sunshine there was, however, one nagging anxiety as he scanned the paper that morning – a fly in the ointment, you might say; a spanner in the works. He was doing something he knew his superiors, colleagues, and the FSA would agree he shouldn't be doing. The more he tried to justify it, the less convinced he felt. And the more he tried not to think of it, the more it kept flitting back like a pigeon returning to its loft no matter how far away you released it. "We'd never ask you to do anything against your principles," the Prophet had said to him in a friendly way one Sunday after church, "but you know it's more important to obey God rather than man – Acts 5:29. So when human rules and regulations get in the way of what God is doing… well, I'm sure you understand. The thing is we're currently gathering funds for a major advance in the kingdom of God right here in Edinburgh. I'm not at liberty to say where these funds come from or what they'll be used for; let's just say nothing is going to be the same again. Just think of the benefit you and Sonia and the children have had these past few months and imagine multiplying that by ten. Or a hundred. Remember last week's text from Malachi: "'Bring the whole tithe into the storehouse, that there may be food in my house. Test me in this," says the Lord Almighty, "and see if I will not throw open the floodgates of heaven and pour out so much blessing that there will not be room enough to store it."' Well, that's what we're planning to do, Sandy. We're bringing a substantial sum into the storehouse from God's people all over the world. With that money we believe God will pour out a blessing on Edinburgh, on Scotland, such as we've never seen before. But in the meantime we need, how can I put it, a safe storehouse. All the regulations and red tape surrounding investments could get in the way of making the most of our tithe while we're waiting for the right time. We need confidentiality and discretion. I'm sure you understand. We've been wondering about an account with Salamanca. It would be ideal if we had one of our own family keeping an eye on things. And I imagine bringing in that amount of new business might have a tangible benefit for you too. What do you think?"

Alexander had immediately thought, *Did I really hear what I just thought I heard? Am I being asked to hide an investment from proper scrutiny?* But the Prophet had a way of putting things that was difficult to resist. "Loyalty and obedience," he had said, "not to us, of course – we are merely fallible human beings – but where the kingdom of God is concerned we all have a responsibility. You know our motto: *If Jesus Christ gave everything for me then my true worship is to give everything for him.*" "Well, since you put it that way," Alexander had replied. "Wonderful," the Prophet said. "God will certainly bless you for this."

So an account was opened that started getting alarming sums into it on almost a monthly basis. This wasn't just coming from tithes and offerings; each and every member of the congregation would have to be donating their entire salary every week to add up to sums like this. Alexander duly kept ignoring the flags that kept popping up about "variance from model profile". This did not make him feel very blessed. Every week he had to keep telling himself, *It's not for me; it's not even for the church. This is for the kingdom of God. Sacrifices have to be made. We must obey God rather than man. Opening the floodgates of heaven. Where your heart is there will your treasure be also.* The problem was that rather than the treasure being where his heart was it was the other way around. His heart and mind were constantly circling back to where the treasure was. And to make things even more complicated, all staff were incentivized with respect to new business, and since the new account was credited to his name, that was how the frankly quite expensive house in the Grange had come about.

All had been well for the first six months or so based on regularly and consistently ignoring the exception reports that landed on his desk every Friday. He tried to make sure that his left hand didn't know what his right hand was doing and sometimes nearly succeeded. But then, a few weeks ago, one of his team had come to him with a query. "Have a look at this," Mike Hunter had said. "Looks a bit fishy, don't you think? What's a church doing with sums like this?" "Yes, yes, I see what you mean," Alexander had had to say. "Leave it with me, I'll have a closer look." But there was no need for closer looks since he knew the details intimately already. Mike thought it looked fishy; Alexander knew it was a pile of stinking guts and bones. But in the kingdom of God, not everything is as it seems. So instead of going to HM Revenue and Customs he had gone to the Prophet and explained that the account might be coming under a bit of scrutiny that might be hard to resist. The Prophet hadn't offered any advice. He had just spoken a bit more about the kingdom and told Alexander he had perfect confidence in him handling things for the glory of God.

Try as he might, he simply couldn't think of how. The bank's procedures were entirely clear, thorough, and unequivocal and both he and Mike Hunter were well aware of them. In fact, while he was prevaricating, Hunter had come back to him with more awkward questions. He had tried to fob him off again but it was getting less and less credible. If they didn't do something soon there was a danger of whistleblowing, and that might lead to criminal charges both for the bank and him personally. "Don't worry," the Prophet had said. "I can see that your heart is in the right place but human rules and institutions get in the way. I'm disappointed you haven't been able to deal with things but I have an idea that might help. Don't worry, Alexander. We'll take it from here. What did you say was the name of your colleague?"

Now, glancing down the minor stories in the financial section that morning, Alexander's feeling of unease suddenly got a whole lot worse. A spoonful of crunchy nut cornflakes stopped halfway to his mouth, which had suddenly gone dry. "Popular financial figure found dead" read the headline. The text went on to briefly report that a well-known and popular officer in Salamanca's Scrutiny and Verification section, Mike Hunter, had been found dead at his home the previous Sunday evening. Early indications were that Mr Hunter seemed to have taken his own life. Police were not aware of any suspicious circumstances but inquiries were ongoing. Being out of the office on a course you expect things to have moved on a bit, but not for a colleague to have topped himself. Alexander coughed, sank his head in his hands, and let out a wail of anguish.

"Sandy!" Sonia scolded him. "Please. Not in front of the children!"

Chapter 8

THE SMUGGLER'S TALE

It's incredible really – everything in the papers and on the news about organized crime and exploiting vulnerable people. I feel like a celebrity. In the old days I used to move cigarettes and drugs. It was called smuggling and nobody made much of a fuss. After all, the only losers were the tax men and nobody cares much about them. Now there's more to be made from human beings, so that's what we move and suddenly we're the scum of the earth. Well, excuse me but who are the consumers of what we move about? I'll tell you. The politicians. The businessmen. The policemen. The respectable people. And the rest of them who haven't the guts to get a real woman are sat over their computers consuming the self-same product. So, if anyone's to blame, it's them, not us. We're only fulfilling a demand. We only exist because they do. Anyway, what's the difference between smoking illegal cigarettes and sleeping with a girl who has no rights of residence in your country? They're both on the wrong side of that arbitrary line we call the law. What's legal or not all depends on who you are, where you are, when you are. I've heard that in Spain sex was legal at the age of twelve until 1999. If you did that in Britain they sent you to jail. One hundred and fifty years ago there weren't laws against it anywhere. Now it's the battle cry of all the politicians and civil rights groups that are looking for more support and donations. Even now, when Berlusconi sleeps with an underage prostitute he pays his lawyers to drag it through the courts for years and his party supporters stand by him because they're hoping for kickbacks in the future. And the man in the street laughs and says, "Good on him if he's still got the energy at that age." Now I hear they're investigating top people in Britain for "historical crimes". They're historical all right because it's been going on throughout history. But the rich get away with it, that's all. I'm not rich yet so I have to be careful. Anyway, the point is that as long as there's a demand someone's going to fulfil it and get well paid. Why not me?

But there is one thing I don't understand: why would anyone in their right mind volunteer to get on that bus? I call it the ghost train because they come and go like ghosts in the night and you never see them or hear about them again. Why do they do it? The German press is full of warnings so I suppose it must be the same in Belarus. Why would anyone trust themselves to people like us? You'd have to be mad. Or desperate. Anyway, whether I understand it or not doesn't matter. I do it and I fulfil my side of the deal and give them what they're asking for. Maybe not exactly what they expect but we get them into Britain and that's what they're paying for. Every fortnight Sergei rolls up with another van of hopefuls. They meet some guy who tells them there's a job in the West for a smart girl like you, all papers supplied. Hand over your bus fare and two weeks later you'll be in London working in a nice clean office with nice clean people. We'll arrange accommodation, health care, your first job. Then you're free to do as you please. What they forget – all these hopefuls – is that if something seems too good to be true then it probably is. Pity help them.

So they get out of Sergei's van and into mine. My job is to get them to London. Sergei isn't the brightest bulb in the building, which is just as well as he has the easy job. Starting in Minsk, a couple of other pickups elsewhere in Belarus, then into Poland, across into Germany, and finally the drop off in Hamburg. About fifteen hours in all. He gets $50 for every one delivered. Not bad money in Belarus these days and not too much risk. Then back home to his wife. I think he has a market stall during the week and sells the fake watches he buys in Hamburg. I have more risks so I get paid more. Ivan is my contact in London and I'm happy when I see him. That means no more problems. Calais is the bottleneck though. We used to take them in the boot of a car but that was before they brought in more security – extra guards, dogs, electronics. So they got a special tanker made with a double skin. Now we can take eight at a time and so far it's never been stopped. Of course it's not very comfortable in the dark, with the smell and the heat and the lack of air. But by that time they don't have much of a choice. They've come too far and paid too much to go back. So in they go dreaming of their new home, the friendly English people, the pop music, the fashion. If it's not going to be exactly what they expected when they arrive that's not my fault. My attitude is, if they want to leave so badly then they must know the risks. And it's not all one-sided. I've come a long way to get to this point. You don't see jobs like this in *Bergedorfer Zeitung*. I've been through some hard times. Had my nose broken a few times – and broken a few other noses and jaws – so I know the score. Now I'm well enough paid for the risks, and sometimes there are fringe benefits. It's not exactly permitted but they turn a blind eye so long as it's only every once in a while and nobody gets hurt.

So little Tati. She's one I took a particular interest in. Most of them won't look you in the eye. You are the driver taking them where they want to go, but they know you're not their friend. So they look at the ground or the footsteps of the girl in front. But Tati looks you straight in the eye and tells you she's going to be a big success. She was so confident it almost made me believe her. Maybe she will be, but I doubt it. She was bright, cheerful, organized. She had enough food and water for the trip and even enough to share with some of the girls who didn't have enough. They all spoke some local dialect so I didn't understand them but she cheered them all up and told them jokes. She made it feel like a Sunday School trip. In the space of a couple of hours she had already become their big sister. She comforted the ones who were crying, encouraged the ones who were sad, and reassured the ones who were worried. Of course that made my job a lot easier so I was nice to her. Then, pretty soon I was treating her like an assistant, not like a package to be taken from A to B – no different from 10,000 cigarettes or a couple of kilos of dope. I don't know how she did that. She was good-looking enough but this wasn't anything to do with skin or hair. She had something in her spirit you don't often see. Naturally I would have liked to have got to know her a bit better – if you take my meaning – but somehow I didn't dare. For the first time in years she made me feel like I could be a better man if I wanted to. I treated all the girls well on that trip. I don't know what they have in store for her but I can guess. Picking a beautiful orchid blossom and stamping it into the ground isn't a good thing to do. I have to admit that sometimes I'm not as sure about it all as I like to sound. Taking Tati was one of those times.

Chapter 9

CYBERSPACE

Spade wasn't used to this. Normally he had no visitors at all – none, *nada*, *nie*, *nyet*, *nikto*. Who'd want to visit an internet recluse who lived in a slum? But that didn't really matter. You didn't have to see people face-to-face to communicate nowadays; face-to-face was old-fashioned and inefficient. He had plenty of other ways to communicate. It wasn't a bad thing – it was just different, that's all. Despite all of that, he'd been surprised how much he'd enjoyed an evening of normal chat with affable guests who had turned up in person and were neither computer geeks nor dysfunctional neighbours. Then, not content with that, within the week they were back again. This might be worth a post on the "Sociopaths Anonymous" subreddit.

Now he held up the little red memory stick David had handed him; not because he thought looking at it would convey any more information, just to absorb the disproportionate impact such a small device seemed to have had. He was perfectly used to tiny bits of code that unlocked powerful secrets, but he'd never come across a computer virus that might have killed a man. Now he was holding it in his hand. He wouldn't have been surprised if it had started vibrating slightly. David had explained that Mike Hunter had been investigating a dodgy account that might be connected to the proceeds of crime. Shortly afterwards he'd been found hanged. It seemed at least plausible that these two things might be linked, but the only tangible connection was the tiny memory stick before them. What they needed to know was, could a USB stick have directly uploaded a collection of images onto Mike's computer without his knowledge, or maybe even allowed third-party access to deliver the files some other time?

"Of course. Totally. Either," was his immediate response. "A few years ago two big American power companies had critical systems infected from a USB stick. Probably some dipstick that wanted to play Tetris at work and brought a copy from home. Cost them megabucks to fix. Then there's a thing called Stuxnet. Supposedly developed as a cyberweapon by the US and Israel – naturally denied by both – aimed at Iran's nuclear research programme. It got in on a USB stick, then it grabbed control of a centrifuge used in fuel production and made it run so fast it blew itself to bits – which is kinda cool. You wouldn't want to be at work that day though. So – yes to both questions. It's absolutely routine."

"So the next thing is, how exactly did it work in this case?" David pressed him. "I mean, can we tell whether it introduced the files then and there or just opened the machine to outside control? And if it was from outside, who was doing the controlling?"

"We can certainly look and see what it installs and what that does – sure. As regards who, if it's a trojan we can get the IP address it links to – it has to say hello to somebody – but after that it gets a bit more complicated."

"Meaning what exactly?" Gillian asked. "Isn't there any sort of list of who uses what address?" Spade rearranged himself slightly in his massive office chair, took another bite of a caramel wafer, and tried to imagine what it must be like to not understand even the basics of internet connectivity.

"Well, we call it an address but it's not really like the address you live at. For a start, computers can share IP addresses but then, on the other hand, a single machine might get a new address every time you reset the router. So it would be like everybody in Gorgie swapping flats when the music stops – plus a few of them deciding to move in together. An IP address doesn't necessarily always link to a single consistent entity."

"Is that as far as we go then?" David asked, still trying to nail it down.

"No," Spade said slowly. "We can go a bit further. IP addresses are issued by ISPs. We can certainly find out which service provider issued the address and which country they're in. It's then that things get more complicated. ISPs are pretty sensitive about releasing who's been allocated a particular address. Normally it needs a court order – at least in the countries that have any legal system in place, and half of them don't."

"So a dead end at that point?" Gillian asked. "Country of origin."

"Well yes – officially. It doesn't mean you can't find out, just that you're not supposed to. Which is more or less what keeps me in a job. Basically you have to hack the ISP's own records. It can be done. It just takes a bit more time, that's all."

"Ok then." David picked up the stick again. "Sixty-four-thousand-dollar question. What's on it?"

Spade took the stick a little gingerly, as if distasteful of what it might have been responsible for, reached down under the desktop, and pushed it into a slot.

"Aren't you worried something might get onto your computer?" Gillian asked as the drive whirred and the stick began winking at them.

Spade uttered something between a grunt and a laugh.

"I'd like to see them try," he said. "I've more protection here than GCHQ."

From that point on, what Spade was doing, how, and why became impossible to follow. Released from having to explain the obvious to the uninitiated, he lapsed back into normal service. Windows were opened, dialogue boxes popped up, commands and parameters were typed in, lists of results appeared, were noted and then closed, and on to the next one almost before David and Gillian could register that a new application had started. The only sound besides rhythmic keyboard clatter and the stop-start whirr of the drive was an occasional grunt of apparent satisfaction and the odd slurp of coffee. At one point he unexpectedly said "magic756" without explanation, then carried on. His guests might have vanished into cyberspace for all the attention he paid them as he settled into the zone.

After about fifteen minutes of focused attention but not a single word, Gillian slipped out, braving the bomb site of a kitchen, and came back with three coffees and yet more chocolate biscuits – apparently the staple diet of computer hackers. Nothing had changed. David had given up trying to follow and was reading something on his phone. Half an hour more and Gillian had begun to pace up and down behind Spade and his bank of computers. Spade had made it all sound relatively straightforward, but now the seemingly relentless succession of windows, pop-up boxes, scrolling lists, and warning alerts were starting to look as if it wasn't proving so easy in practice. He occasionally scratched an ear, scribbled something down or grunted – nothing more. Finally, after fully an hour of silence and absorption, Gillian was unable to manage the suspense any longer.

"Problems?" she asked softly. It took a few seconds for Spade to register. He gave a short laugh.

"Naw! Baby stuff. I got the IP address and ISP forty minutes ago. Just thought I'd do a bit more roaming around, that's all. I must have got a bit distracted. Sorry. So... first question: was there something nasty on the stick? Yes. Did it download stuff by itself or actually pass control of the PC to some third party? The latter. Who did it communicate with? Here's the address." He held up a scribbled set of numbers on a Post-it note. This IP address was issued three years ago by a service provider called Unibel, which operates from Minsk in Belarus. Can you get a court order to find out who owns the IP address? No chance. You might as well ask for your granddad's horse confiscated by the Red Army back. However, luckily we don't need to ask. I've found out the address is used by a group calling itself SiS. What that stands for I have no idea but there is a registered address in Minsk. Although the IP address was issued in Belarus it seems to connect to a PC in Britain. The traffic was handled by a server in Basingstoke, then came to Edinburgh. I can't be more specific than that. As regards the event you're interested in, it's impossible to say exactly when the trojan was installed but it began communicating about two weeks ago. Then there's a huge burst of data on... eh, what's the date today? Twelfth? Big burst of data on Saturday night. I can track that back to let you see what they sent if you like... No? Right. I didn't think so. Anyway something like 200 JPGs. So that's it. Seems you're on the right track. Sorry for the interruption to normal service."

Gillian pulled out onto Gorgie Road with very different emotions from the previous Sunday evening. There was satisfaction of a sort in the fact that Sam had guessed correctly, but that didn't feel anything like as good as it should have. David had Spade's printout with all the key data – their tame hacker wasn't keen on speaking to the police himself and asked them not to say where the information had come from. "It won't be a problem, though," he'd reassured them. "Hand them this and their IT guys can follow it up easily enough themselves." Now, regardless of being right and having a page of numbers to prove it, that didn't change the reality. Mike Hunter was dead and Sam Hunter was a grieving widow. The damage had been done and all the data in the world wouldn't change that. It was like knowing the exact thickness of the ice, its chemical composition, breaking point, and all the physics that had contributed to a good friend falling through and being drowned in an icy lake. So what? You could put up a warning sign and catch whoever was responsible for the path across the lake but that wasn't the problem. What they really wanted was just as inaccessible now as it had been two hours ago. They drove back to Bruntsfield in silence.

"What now?" Gillian finally asked as she pulled in outside David's tenement entrance.

"I suppose I tell Sam. She has the right to find out first. Then a call to DI Thompson. If this doesn't change it to a murder inquiry and write off the images on his PC then I don't know what will, though we're still no further forward in knowing who we're actually talking about – I mean, which of the three congregations turns out to be not quite what it seems."

"And how do we do that? We can't go around accusing innocent churchgoers of money laundering and murder."

"And likewise we can't ignore the guilty. It's telling the difference that's the problem."

"As it always is."

"Indeed."

"Isn't it just what you were preaching about the other week – the parable of the wheat and the tares? Everything goes on growing together until the end of the age when the angels gather it all in then separate things out. We don't have that luxury."

"Well, I suppose this is less a theological problem than a criminal one."

"Except that they're posing as a church. That's the bit that gets me. There are going to be real people involved who haven't any idea of what's going on behind the scenes. I suppose they listen to the sermons week by week, send their kids to Sunday School, put their fiver in the plate, and think they're doing what they should. All the time what they're really doing is supporting a criminal enterprise that's responsible at least for disseminating images of child abuse and for murder, and maybe a bunch of other things besides. I wouldn't be surprised if this wasn't just the tip of the iceberg." Gillian sounded perplexed but also personally aggrieved.

David sat quietly, looking ahead of him, thinking about the guilty and the innocent. Beyond Bruntsfield Links and the Meadows further away lights were just beginning to come on in the smart apartments now occupying what used to be the old Royal Infirmary. That was where his mother had been working when his dad turned up drunk and bleeding one night. Getting plastered and banging your head on a lamp post wasn't entirely recommended, yet it had resulted in – well, resulted in him, among other things. And he had resulted in Warehouse 66 in Madrid in a roundabout way. And Warehouse 66 had saved innumerable lives through its drug rehab programme, even though it had then cost the one life dearer to him than any other. But through that horrendous bereavement he had come to Edinburgh and met Gillian. And because of that he had been able to help find Jen MacInnes, who would now almost certainly be dead if they hadn't got involved. In another sense than intended, maybe the parable was right enough, even in this life. You simply couldn't pull things apart and say with any certainty what was going to be irredeemably wicked or undeniably good in their consequences. Sometimes what looked the most horrendous could bring about inexplicably good results – or good intentions all go wrong. Despite being the closest of friends, there were times David had to confess he found Juan's absolute faith that "El Señor" was at work in ways we couldn't guess bordering on the idealistic. We just had to do our best, he maintained, surround everything with prayer, and somehow God would work it out. But idealistic or not, it gave him a solidity of faith David often envied. It was Joseph and his brothers again. You meant it for evil – God meant it for good. David hoped there might be something – anything – good that could come out of this. Right now it didn't seem very likely.

Alexander Benedetti had spent most of that week in a daze. He drove to work, dealt with his in tray, went to meetings, and drove home again without Mike Hunter's death ever leaving his mind. He cooked and washed up, read the kids their bedtime stories, and did a bit of hoovering while Sonia studied, all on autopilot. Sometimes she would ask him something or make a comment, but it all passed right through him like antimatter. "Are you all right?" she finally asked him. "I really think you're working too hard, Sandy. You need a break."

Of course Mike Hunter was all the talk around the water cooler.

Did you hear what happened to Mike? Incredible. Apparently his laptop had been full of child pornography and he thought he was about to be exposed, so he wrapped one end of a tow rope around a beam in the garage and the other end... well, you know. Just goes to show. You never really know someone like you think you do. One or two in the section seemed strangely silent on the subject of what he had on his computer but Alexander was silent for another reason. His problem wasn't the what, the how, or the why; it was the who. Although he'd been nowhere near the Hunter household he felt just as implicated as if he had been. And he had a deeply worrying feeling that he knew exactly who had been there. He called the Prophet as soon as he'd got his head together but was met only by what sounded like mild surprise and sympathy – or maybe that was what it was meant to sound like. He should "put it out of his mind", he was told. Look on the bright side. At least there wasn't going to be any more scrutiny of the accounts now. If he started delving into what had happened, that would probably only focus more attention on him and that was what we all wanted to avoid, wasn't it? Alexander couldn't be quite sure if that was a threat but it sounded like it might be. Funny how concealing the true nature of the account being illegal hadn't cropped up until now. In the meantime, being personally safer gave him no comfort whatsoever. A man had died. A colleague. Maybe he could even say, a friend. Mike's workstation was empty and his emails were going unanswered. His responsibilities were being shared around. But this wasn't a case of nipping off for a fortnight in the Maldives. Mike Hunter wasn't coming back and Alexander had a feeling he understood why.

Then there was the problem of the church. He thought he understood about the kingdom of God being bigger than human affairs, but did that include ignoring the banking laws and maybe even murder? And if that really was what had happened, how should he now regard the people he had trusted, confided in, and who'd personally helped him in so many ways? Were they all just being conned? And maybe the entire message was just as much of a con as the leaders. Perhaps most worrying of all, maybe it was going to be a bit more tricky getting out than it had been getting in.

So, what to do now? He could just keep his mouth shut like he'd been told, but that was proving uncomfortable already; he wasn't sure how long he could keep it up. Sonia wasn't stupid. She knew something was wrong; she just didn't know what. And she mustn't find out. Her world had had enough violence and trauma. Naturally, it wasn't something he could talk about at church, and going to the police was out of the question unless he wanted to answer some awkward questions on his own behalf. He wished he'd never heard of that stupid account or had anything to do with it. What was it going to be used for anyway? A great advance for the kingdom of God was looking less and less credible. He opened another email and tried to concentrate. Just keep swimming, just keep swimming...

Charlie Thompson took the printout David Hidalgo handed him and scanned down it.

"Sorry, folks; all Greek to me I'm afraid. What does this claim to prove?"

The day before, he had finally contacted Sam Hunter to tell her the results of the postmortem were available. Sorry for the delay – short staffed and all that. But at least she'd now be able to go ahead with what he'd euphemistically referred to as "arrangements". "Would it be ok to come out and go through it with her?" he'd asked. Of course. "Would it be ok," she asked, "if David Hidalgo joined them?"

"How are we doing, Mrs Hunter?" he'd begun, taking off his coat in the hall.

She had momentarily thought of saying, *I don't know about "we" – I've certainly had better weeks*, then decided not to try to be smart. It wasn't his fault. "Not fantastic," she'd admitted. "I've got lots of good friends though. It's a process."

"Of course," he'd replied and nodded, no doubt aiming at sympathetic but ending up sounding more like a plumber round to check a leak.

"I think we've got something here you should see," David said once they were all sat down.

"I told you my husband did not kill himself," Sam added. "That stuff on his computer was put there by someone else trying to protect a criminal account."

Thompson scrutinized the printout.

"Ok," he said, "apparently this all shows that Mr Hunter's computer was hacked, which you think relates to something he'd uncovered at work."

"Not 'apparently'," Sam said, beginning to lose patience. "He was investigating a money laundering account and his computer was interfered with. My husband was not a paedophile and he did not kill himself. We have a witness who says he was brought back from his run by two men who carried him in from a van. Mike was murdered and I want to know by whom."

"Ok, Mrs Hunter, ok," Thompson replied, holding his hands up in a gesture of calming things down. "I'm not disputing what you're saying; we're on the same side here. It's just a matter of evidence. Up to this point all we've had was an apparent suicide and a reasonable motive. I understand it's beginning to look more complicated than that. Moving to a murder inquiry isn't my decision though. I'll have to take the case to my Chief Inspector. But I entirely hear what you're saying. And if it's as clear as you say that the images came in from outside without Mr Hunter's knowledge – well that makes a suicide look a lot more doubtful. And now with the postmortem report here as well, we have another piece in the jigsaw." Thompson pulled the report out of his document case.

"What does it say?" Sam asked impatiently.

"More or less what we expected," Thompson continued, flicking to the final page. "Cause of death cerebral hypoxia – just what the pathologist said. Interrupted oxygen flow to the brain from constriction of the arteries in the neck. No surprises. Here's the blood report." He passed her the relevant page. It consisted of a long column of unfamiliar abbreviations. She scanned down them, feeling she ought to but not understanding what any of it meant. What value was supposed to be good and what was bad? How could she possibly tell if anything wasn't as it should be on account of toxins in the blood? She was just about to hand it back when the one abbreviation she did understand caught her eye. She looked at it, then looked again, but it was unchanged. That wasn't right.

"What's this?" she asked. "According to this, Mike was only showing 1.2 millimoles per litre of blood sugar."

Thompson took the page and looked at it.

"No idea," he said. "He was hungry?"

"That's not hungry. That's hypoglycemic."

"And what's that when it's at home?"

"It's what happens when you have insufficient glucose in the blood to run basic body systems. Healthy people almost never get hypoglycemic because the body is able to recognize what's going on and regulate blood sugar."

"What effect does that have?" David asked.

"First you get muddled; then you lose balance and mobility, then basic body functions. If nothing's done it eventually kills you."

"Do you mind if I ask you how you know all this?" Thompson asked.

"Easy," she said. "I'm diabetic."

"Poisoned with insulin?" David asked when Sam had come back with another round of coffees. "I thought insulin was a medicine, not a poison."

"It normally is," Sam explained. "It's a naturally occurring hormone produced by the pancreas to process carbohydrates from food. That turns sugars into a form the muscles can use. People with diabetes aren't able to produce their own insulin so they need to inject it artificially. But that's got to be balanced with the right amount of carbohydrate. Too little insulin or too much food – particularly sugar – and you get highs, which can cause long-term damage. Too much insulin or too little food means low blood sugar and that kills you immediately. They call it 'dead in the bed' syndrome. People go low in the night and don't notice until eventually the body simply doesn't have enough energy to run even basic systems like respiration, heartbeat, or brain function. It's called hypoglycaemia – 'hypo' for short. When the woman across the road said she'd seen Mike being carried in I immediately thought he must have been drugged or something. But this changes everything. I've been diabetic since I was sixteen. Lately I've been losing hypo awareness; I keep going low and don't realize it. First of all no energy, then disorientation, then, if it's not treated, you eventually lose consciousness. When I get like that Mike usually guesses before I do and gives me something. There's been a couple of times he's had to carry me into the house and give me a hormone injection. If that doesn't work then it's 999. Now it all makes sense. Mike was hypoglycaemic but not because he was diabetic. He must have been injected with a massive dose of insulin. Maybe somebody behind this was diabetic too. It means you have a perfect supply of poison just sitting in the fridge waiting to be used."

There was silence as the new information was absorbed.

"So that's what you were asking for, wasn't it?" David directed himself to DI Thompson. "How the images got onto his computer and how he was killed. We still don't know exactly who's behind it or how they knew they were being investigated but that's enough, isn't it?"

Thompson shuffled his papers and sat back.

"Ok," he said, "just to run through it all from soup to nuts. Mike Hunter notices a dodgy-looking account in the course of his work that rings a bell because of something he's doing privately. Wants to have a closer look and gets warned off. Whoever runs the account gets a tip-off and decides he needs to be removed from the picture. He's still working on the account on Sunday morning while you're at church, Mrs Hunter. Decides to go for a run – just to clear his mind, let's say. Maybe the house is being watched and that gives whoever's watching an idea. Instead of attacking Mr Hunter in his own house – they had no idea when you might come back – they decide to follow him on his run. I don't know if he had a regular route but whatever the case on that, someone got to him outside. He was restrained but not enough to leave marks and given a huge insulin injection. So by the time they brought him back here he was already unable to walk. Your car wasn't back yet so they had time and opportunity to make it look like a suicide. That must have already been decided on given the images already on his laptop and a bogus call. Now we have information – I won't ask from where – that gives us chapter and verse of how that material found its way onto his laptop. Is that where we're up to? Ok. I think that gives me enough to take upstairs."

DI Thompson drained his coffee, gathered his papers together, and stood up.

"Another question, Mrs Hunter. Do you happen to know who your husband would have reported to at Salamanca – who it was that might have told him to back off on the dodgy account?"

"Absolutely. Sandy Benedetti."

"Right. I think we may need to have a chat with Mr Benedetti. One final question, obvious really. Did Sandy Benedetti go to church, and if so do you know which one?"

Sam Hunter leaned forward, nodded, and began to tremble.

Chapter 10

THE MIDDLE MAN'S TALE

Middle men always make money," Uncle Nicolae used to say, and he was right. Our businesses are entirely different but the principles are the same. He had a carpet warehouse in Kiev, then he moved to chilled food wholesale, then finally central heating components – different lines but the same model: read the market, see what's selling, and get into the space between producers and retailers. It doesn't take as long to set up a warehouse as a factory or a shop. Factories take too long to change production lines and involve huge investment. Shops suffer from fashions and trends so they have to keep a huge range of stock. Even then rivals can offer it cheaper so all your "loyal" customers go elsewhere to save a couple of roubles. But middle men simply hold whatever any shop wants. They don't need to make it and they don't need to sell it. They simply find the cheapest source and move it on at a profit. When the mood changes you dump the excess and change lines. For Uncle Nicolae rugs became radishes, then radiators. I've never needed to change, though, because there's always a demand for what I do. I sell sex.

In the past, supply was a problem since there used to be borders and immigration police and the girls didn't come willingly. That meant drugging them, which can be dangerous, and you can't exactly pack them like coke into cavities in a van. So it needed sufficient space, and the more space that's unaccounted for the greater the risk. Then everything suddenly got easier. Schengen was meant to ease the movement of labour throughout the EU. Well, my product is a sort of a labour, I suppose. As the Eastern economies fell apart there wasn't anything to fill the gap, so lots of girls decided to try their luck in the West. They watch the movies and read the magazines and think they stand a chance. Then they get on a bus in Belarus and get off in Hamburg. Then into a van or a tanker bound for London. My job is to send them to whoever wants them from there. It's not exactly like Amazon but we do have a site on the Dark Web, and I have satisfied customers who come back and new contacts all the time.

Having said all that about Nicolae and his warehouses, though, there is one major difference between us. This is a people business and people are less predictable than plumbing. It can be a challenge to take a girl who has got off a bus thinking she's going to be a children's nanny then maybe break into modelling, and introduce her to the idea that she is now a commodity. How do we do it? First of all we welcome them. We give them a hot meal and a bed. While we're doing that we take their passports and papers for "safekeeping". Then, the next morning, Ivan and I speak to them one by one. I point out to each girl that she is now an illegal immigrant and if she does not want to be handed over the police immediately, losing all her possessions in the process, she will do exactly what she is told. They get a bit upset about that, which sometimes requires a firm response. Then I tell them that their new job is to sleep with whoever is presented to them. If not they will suffer the consequences then be put back into exactly the same situation to try again. A second refusal results in even more severe treatment. A third time and they will be found without any identification floating in the Thames. By that time they are beginning to realize that they no longer have a choice.

With Tatiana we got quite near the river solution. That was hard since she was really very pretty. At least she was before Ivan had a word. She simply did not seem able to get it into her head that this was the way things were. She kept on thinking she had a choice. She almost scratched the first guy's eyes out. The next one she kicked so hard in the groin we had to pay him to go back in with her to finish off. The third time she was sullen and just lay there. That was an improvement but it's still not what the punters pay for. So Ivan had to speak to her again. It was either that or the river, and I did believe we were making progress and shouldn't give up. So the fourth time – I think she's the only girl we've ever gone to four attempts with – she finally did what was required, if not enthusiastically, at least with some semblance of cooperation. I was relieved.

So, finally, where to send her? I knew she would need a firm hand and proper guidance so I had to be selective. I went through every single one of our outlets to see who had the proper credentials. Finally, she went to an operation in – well, I shouldn't actually say where. Just suffice it to say she'd have to wrap up warm and enjoy haggis and whisky. Is that enough? I hear she's doing very well now. Very popular apparently. Sometimes I do a few tryouts myself when I'm not too busy. I often regret being so busy when Tati passed through.

Chapter 11

GEORGE IV BRIDGE

A cold, bitter rain blew in sheets across the Firth of Forth, whipping the estuary into breaking waves from the Fife coast out into the freezing North Sea. A few work boats and freighters braved the gale but the season for pleasure sailing was over. If anything the storm seemed to gain in energy and violence as it hammered into Granton and Newhaven then swept up into the city, lashing trees, buildings, and the few pedestrians who had no choice but to be out. David Hidalgo gripped the lapels of his coat with one hand, holding onto his fedora with the other. The high buildings on either side of George IV Bridge seemed to act like a wind tunnel funnelling the driving rain like bullets. Having walked from Bruntsfield he was now completely soaked through but didn't seek shelter. He felt he probably deserved a drenching. Pastors, he reflected bitterly, are supposed to be the ones with words of comfort for the troubled, but that Thursday he had sat with Sam Hunter without a word to say. Somehow the chain of connections that led to Alexander Benedetti had breached her dam of coping and all the anger and pain came flooding out. DI Thompson had seemed finally convinced and assured them that he would be sending things "upstairs" first thing on Monday morning for consideration of a murder inquiry. For Sam, it was as if she had been grimly holding on over the past week, determined to prove that Mike hadn't killed himself. Now she'd achieved her aim, it all came overflowing out.

Between bouts of shuddering, silent tears, and howling like a wounded animal, she had haltingly explained how they had tried to befriend Sandy and his new wife Sonia. Sandy wasn't so senior that it was awkward and he'd let it be known that marrying a bit later in life wasn't entirely plain sailing. "Why don't you and Sonia come round for dinner some night?" Mike had offered. "Get a babysitter. We can have a bit of grown-up time. Adjustments like that aren't always easy." So they'd got to know one another and thought they were friends. Now this. Maybe Sandy hadn't really understood what he was doing. Or, worse, maybe he had. But the net result was that he'd been part of the chain that led to Mike's lifeless body in the garage. And it was all connected with his church. What on earth did he think he was doing? What church has that kind of money floating around? And what kind of pastor would want him to cover it up? David, in turn, wondered what kind of pastor could sit and listen to it all and find nothing whatever useful to say. Sam had wept and raged, while Gillian held her hand and made cups of tea. David could only think about Rocío hanging in his hall in Chamartin more than twenty years before.

The wind and rain battering the city had almost the feeling of a malevolent being raging at all things calm, secure, and sensible. The more David turned that gruelling evening over in his mind, the darker his thoughts became. Mike's investigations, their befriending of Sandy and Sonia, even the way Sandy had apparently been so enthusiastic about his new journey of faith – these were all the actions of good people trying to do good things. To say it had ended in tears was accurate in a way but a gross understatement. As David battled forward through the gale none of the Bible verses that floated into his mind seemed at all helpful. There was scriptural precedent, he knew, for believing that evil intentions might somehow be woven into good results but this was just the opposite – good intentions gone horribly wrong. And that left Sam Hunter hunched up and shuddering on her sofa and David Hidalgo sitting helpless and stupid beside her. So now, all things considered, the very least he felt he could do was try to get a good look at whoever might be behind it all. Those involved might be "helping police with their inquiries" soon enough so this was his only chance. The Minsk connection still made no sense but at least he now knew the name of the church.

As he continued up George IV Bridge checking the numbers of buildings, David might have said he was checking it out for Sam but he knew it was really for himself. This was personal. How dare they take a church that should exist for the good of the harassed and helpless and twist it into a killing machine. How dare they take up an offering "for the Lord's work" while they were sitting with millions of dirty money in a private account. Walking on stolidly into the stinging rain, he felt angry at his own ineffectiveness, angry at the abuse of believing people, and angry at those he'd had to let down even that morning. He'd phoned Juan early, explaining he wasn't going to be at church and could he possibly find someone else to cover? Worse still, he'd texted Gillian to cancel lunch. The strain of everything going on was telling on them both and he ought to be making it better, not worse. So what do you do when nothing you're supposed to be doing seems to help? Something else, useful or not, so long as it's something you *can* do. David gathered his lapels and collar tighter still, bent his head further forward, and trudged doggedly on, paused to check his bearings, then turned into the entrance of a huge, gloomy, pre-Victorian church building.

"The Power and the Glory" it said on the noticeboard outside. A student-looking early-twenties guy in a flannel shirt and torn jeans grinned at him in the foyer in a way supposed to be welcoming but in David's present frame of mind just came over as annoying and slightly creepy.

"Welcome to PGC," he announced like an overenthusiastic timeshare rep. "First time?" *Yes, and I hope it's the last,* David felt like saying but instead mumbled something non-committal, took the notice sheet, and made to head through the double doors. The welcome committee wasn't quite done though and pursued him.

"Sorry. Excuse me. If you're new… we'd love to keep in touch with you… if I could have your email or Facebook then we can let you know what's going on."

David hadn't intended to be rude but felt backed into a corner.

"I don't have either of these things and wouldn't give you them if I did," he stated. "And I don't want to know what's going on. Thanks." He turned without waiting to see the reaction – probably nothing short of a car bomb would shake the grin – and pushed his way through a heavy swing door.

The interior immediately struck him as bright and airy in spite of the grim facade. It seemed a pleasing marriage of old and new and he couldn't quite keep himself from approving. Yes, stained glass; yes, carved oak; yes, rows of formal seating; but also some colourful friezes, a contemporary band tuning up, and a general sense of relaxed but purposeful bustle. Grander premises but an atmosphere not much different from Southside in fact. He felt a bit wrong-footed, found a place in the back row, and sat down. Perhaps he shouldn't have been so hard on the guy at the door. He'd made sure he arrived good and early and there were only a few others dotted around, mostly "youth" chatting and giggling but a few greyer heads and one family with squirming children. The dad noticed him and smiled. He nodded back. Band members were gradually getting themselves organized as the data projector lit up onto a screen that had silently slid down from the ceiling. The sound guy was nipping back and forth from the desk, adjusting mikes, swapping cables, and one-twoing like mad. *Is that as far as sound engineers can count?* David wondered incongruously. Over by the piano it looked like a couple of Sunday School teachers were having a confab over materials. The drummer and bass player found themselves not needed for the moment and fired off a wee duet a bit like the Average White Band on a bad night, then broke up laughing. David felt his inner rage and frustration beginning to ease as he took off his wet coat, hat, and scarf and began to warm up. The atmosphere seemed entirely relaxed, friendly, normal. Not what he'd expected of a criminal venture.

"Good morning; nice to see you." He hadn't noticed a slim blonde girl with enormous, dangly earrings slipping into the row alongside him.

"Hi. Thanks."

"On holiday in Edinburgh?"

"No, I live here but I normally go somewhere else."

"Welcome to PGC. I'm Sonia, part of the welcome team. Hope you like it. If there's anything you want to ask or any way we can help, we all have these yellow badges on. Just ask."

Sonia. *Madre mía.* Maybe there was more than one – maybe a whole clan of them – but probably not. This must be *the* Sonia. Was Sandy here with her? What if he suddenly appeared? What would David say to him? *Hi Sandy. I'm a friend of Mike Hunter's – maybe you know him. Sorry – knew him.* In the meantime he thought he should say something – anything – just to extend the conversation.

"Thanks. Have you been coming here long?"

"About a year or so. I came with the kids first. We all liked it so I managed to get my husband along too. Sandy can take a bit of persuading." She gave half a laugh and David couldn't help a sympathetic smile, while also silently registering that yes, this is *the* Sonia married to *the* Sandy.

"We like it though. Max is a really riveting speaker."

"Max?" David asked and left it hanging in the hope of finding out more.

"He's our Prophet – what you'd call a pastor, I suppose. Anyway there's loads of stuff going on. I'd get Sandy to tell you more but he's not out this morning. Says he has to work – again!"

"No problem. I'm sure I'll be fine. Thanks."

"Remember, anything you need – just ask."

Sonia gave him another sunny smile and headed off in search of anyone else in need of a welcome.

How about that? David thought. *I'd bet my pension plan she has no idea what's going on.*

Final checking, confabs, and coordination over, it looked like every seat was taken. The clock finally ticked round to 11.00 and a young man with close-cropped, bleached-blond hair and quite a prominent scar on his cheek took the mike.

"Good morning, everyone. Welcome to the Power and the Glory. Is God good or what?"

Standard warm-up stuff, David thought. And a good attempt at Scottish English but not a native speaker. Germany? Balkans? Eastern Europe? Interesting. Then a few more remarks that didn't mean anything either before passing over to the band for twenty minutes or so of standing up, swaying, hand raising, ecstatic-looking singing, competently led by a guitar player just about visible through the hair and beard. So far, so normal. Then another new face and a quick run through the announcements for the week with a couple of videos to let everyone know what they were missing by not being a part of Life Groups/Kids' Club/Care and Share or whatever. Suddenly David noticed with surprise that his mouth was dry, his fists were clenched, and his lips tight as the list droned on. Who was the Prophet? What would he look like? What does a money-laundering murderer look like anyway?

Finally, a tall figure with the build of a boxer, in a black leather jacket, black T-shirt, and jeans stood up and walked forward in a slow, measured way. There was a definite sense of anticipation around the room. This was clearly the main event. Rather than take a band mike, the Prophet headed up a few steps to a lectern at the back of the platform. For a few moments he looked around without speaking, with a calm, almost serene, gaze. His expression was one of total self-assurance and tranquility but there was something about the eyes that made David sure the brain behind was whirring: who was there, who wasn't; who was sitting somewhere different; who wasn't entirely paying attention.

"Good morning, everyone," he finally said, barely above a whisper, still gazing around the room. The look was relaxed, confident. It seemed to say – we understand each other, don't we? – we're on the same side, aren't we? David wasn't quite sure where to place him between the Dalai Lama and a king cobra.

"I see we have a few new friends here this morning. Welcome." The gaze continued roaming around, unruffled and unhurried.

Somehow David felt like an ant under a magnifying glass with the sun about to come out. He said "friends", but there was something deeper that said, *I know who my friends are. Are you one of them?* But Sonia had been right about one thing. It was undoubtedly captivating.

A couple of miles away in Marchmont Gillian Lockhart had not been having the best of mornings either. She knew David loved lamb so she'd thought she'd try something new – a slow, pot-roasted shoulder with slivers of garlic thrust deep down inside the meat then cooked in a reducing sauce of onion, carrot, tomatoes, and thyme, all served with watercress, halved black olives, and mustard mash. Not Spanish, but hey, you have to broaden your mind. She'd just got the joint prepared and browned when the text came in. Brooke Fraser was singing "Something in the Water" on iTunes at the time, which always made her want to dance around the kitchen – and then she read the message. Her first thought was, *Who's going to eat all this lamb?* then her second was, *That man is soooo frustrating.* Would it have been so hard to phone or, better still, to mention it when they'd been out to a movie at the Dominion the previous night? In any case, what made David Hidalgo Sleuth-in-Chief? Once was understandable; twice definitely looked like carelessness. She understood that ministers had responsibilities and that sometimes families had to just grin and bear it. But David wasn't even being paid and she wasn't family – yet.

She took the lamb off the hob and slammed the pot down on a chopping board. The weekend had started off so well too, with a late email on Friday night from BBC Scotland no less. She was used to having her academic work published and acknowledged but somehow a radio producer had got hold of her name and wanted her to come on some mid-morning chat thing and talk about the language of teenagers in the new millennium. No doubt it would do a grave disservice to the subtlety of vocabulary drift and influence of English accents on TV but all the same it was flattering. She'd mentioned it to Gary, Head of Department, who'd given it his blessing. "Knock their socks off, Gilli," he'd said, and she thought she maybe would. Hence a small treat was in order. She left the university's David Hume Tower early and headed straight to the house of treats large and small – John Lewis at the top of Leith Walk. She'd been meaning to replace a slightly worn hall rug for some time so now went hunting in earnest. She decided on a "Royal Heritage Kazak" for £625. Like it said on the tin – not cheap but a beautiful weaving of geometric patterns in deep shades of red with creams and blues. *You can keep those abstract blotches that look like the results of careless house painters*, she thought. On a whim she bought some nice lacy underwear too. It was all gorgeous and she was looking forward to telling David her news and showing off (at least the rug) over Sunday lunch – the one that had just been cancelled. For half a second she thought she should have accepted the Springsteen invitation after all. Then she caught herself. *Come on Gillian*, she thought, *get a grip. It's just lunch*. But of course it wasn't; it begged the question of where this was all going. Well, I'm going to church anyway, she suddenly decided, David or no.

Juan Hernandez was a bit surprised to see her coming in her customary ten minutes early. When he'd had a call from David saying something had come up he kind of assumed that meant them both. But no, Gillian was here, poised, fresh, stunning as ever. *¡Que guapa!* he thought. There was no reason a happily married man (waiting to become a happily married dad) couldn't appreciate beauty – was there? And that girl was *la leche*, no doubt about it. Why David didn't get his act together and get a ring on her finger he could not understand; it was obvious. And he had no issue comparing her with Rocío, even though she'd been his own sister. They are both just beautiful examples of God's creativity. Hadn't Solomon put it perfectly (probably a man who knew a thing or two about beauty): *Todo lo hizo hermoso en su tiempo, y ha puesto eternidad en el corazón del hombre*. Everything beautiful in its time and eternity in the heart of man. For some reason he couldn't fathom and maybe never would Rocío's time had come and gone. But out of the ashes of that fire a new relationship had come and maybe a new faith as well. Sometimes David Hidalgo was soooo frustrating. *¡Hombre – simplemente hazlo!* Just get on and do it!

With Alicia's pregnancy progressing and more and more of the restaurant work falling to him, he knew he hadn't been seeing much of David recently and wasn't helping at all in this latest crisis. Maybe the strain was telling and David was spending so much time and focus on other people that he was missing the most important thing staring him right in the face. Sometimes Juan found himself falling back on his father's favourite insult – *¡El burro sabe más que tú!* – and in this case it was true. He felt like grabbing David by the lapels some Sunday, pushing him up against a wall, and saying *¡Mira! ¡Hombre!* When it comes to women, donkeys know more than you! What are you waiting for? She won't wait forever for you, you know. She's a clever, good-looking girl. There are lots of clever, good-looking guys out there. If you don't take your chance now... well, just do it, that's all! When he got like that Alicia would tell him to calm down. It'll all work out. "You say it yourself, *amante*, El Señor is in control. It'll work out in its own good time." In the restaurant he knew you couldn't make good paella in less than an hour – even after the rice had gone in. Maybe he needed to take a lesson out of his own cookbook and stop trying to turn the heat up or add a bit more salt. Anyway, this morning he'd been doubly annoyed not just that David wasn't getting his love life in order but also for failing to show up and preach – and dumping it at his door. *¡Madre mía!* You don't think I've got enough to do? Anyway, he had grabbed something from his daily reading that looked like it could be bulked up into a ten-minute talk and headed out the door.

Listening to Juan speaking about love – God's love, varieties of human love, what happens when you love somebody, what Jesus had done out of love – all made Gillian think back to slipping into the last row of this same room less than a year ago and listening, part amazed, part bemused, to one David Hidalgo speaking from the selfsame platform. Today was the first time she'd come to Southside without him and it felt strange. That first time he'd been speaking about the Good Samaritan, then seemed to get stuck. Not being used to "preaching" she wasn't entirely sure whether something had gone wrong or if this was normal, but as a background buzz of shuffling and murmuring began to grow she realized that everyone else was uncomfortable too. Then he'd gone on to compare the Samaritan's pretty good performance with something he was currently facing and not handling too well. It was weird but fascinating too. Not in her wildest dreams could she imagine any other type of talk that got so personal or confessional. It seemed this sort of thing wasn't very normal here either; hence the general confusion even once it was over. Getting involved in the hunt for Jen MacInnes, she'd gradually realized what it was all about and that was what really struck her first about said David Hidalgo. He was an odd animal in the modern world: well read, articulate, witty, not an offence to the eyes (despite totally lacking the fashion gene), but with a very unusual, almost anachronistic, compulsion to "do the right thing". Going after Jen MacInnes had almost been the death of both of them – hers unexpectedly, his by a deliberate act of putting himself in harm's way. So, not just talking the talk then. She remembered finding that startling and strangely compelling. Now it was looking not so much like an isolated incident – more just his normal way of life. By no means perfect of course (she was still annoyed about the last-minute cancellation), but even that was a consequence of the same guy. He was off again, looking down the barrel of a gun because it was simply the right thing to do. Admirable but also soooo frustrating. As Juan continued emphasizing the self-sacrifice and the fruits of love, she spotted Jen MacInnes with new boyfriend Carlos, recently arrived in Edinburgh to start a crime-free life. Maybe having a man so committed to doing the right thing wasn't the worst thing in the world. What was the alternative – the wrong thing or, more commonly, nothing at all? But while there were things more important than Sunday lunch on their agenda, that still didn't mean what happened today was ok. Words might need to be had.

By the time all Sunday morning sermons had finished the rain was off and David came out into hazy sunshine. A few more people were about and it looked like the worst was over. It certainly hadn't been the worst he'd ever heard – far from it. Like the warm-up guy, the accent wasn't native English but the ease of delivery made you quickly forget that. The jokes and cultural references all seemed to be spot on from audience reaction – David wouldn't have known what was in the charts or on TV – and the biblical explanation was sound – on the face of it. But somehow David found it deeply unsettling. It didn't feel right, like listening to Franco talking about reconciliation or Dalí on the virtues of self-restraint.

Max's theme had been that God loves leaders. The point seemed to be that God has a leadership role for everyone and that everyone could have a positive influence on those around them. So far, so good. Husbands in the family, Christian children among their friends, wives and young women in the workplace or the home, teens on their peer group, older people mentoring the young, etc. The point he was building to – David saw it coming from some way off – was that God has also appointed leaders in the kingdom of God and that God required good "followership" as much as good leadership. So you lead where God had placed you but ultimately everyone – this was emphasized several times – everyone has a duty before God to follow, and indeed *obey*, their leaders in the church. This was what was pleasing to God. And they lapped it up, smiling at the jokes, nodding at an apt catchphrase, and taking notes at every turn. It was a tour de force. David was impressed, not just in the talk but in the total effect. The congregation were entirely behind both the concept and the man. He half expected a Q&A at the end, when individuals would be given specific instructions. Very impressive, and totally contrary to everything he believed about responsibility, personal relationship, and each finding their own way forward. It left him thinking of Jonestown and Waco. Max's warm but knowing manner also extended to the handshaking at the end. Rather than position himself at the door, he worked the aisles, up and down and round and round, meeting, greeting, squeezing arms, and ruffling the hair of the kids. David tried to pick his moment and head for the double doors while Max was on his way to the front again but he was held up by a gaggle of teenagers and finally made it just as "the Prophet" approached from the other side.

"Good morning. I don't think we've met…" was the disarming greeting, but the look said, *Who are you? Are you going to be my friend?* David took the offered handshake and was on the point of muttering a good morning in response and nothing more but his hand and his gaze were held. He half considered introducing himself as Ralph but wondered if Max would say, *Come on now, we both know that's not true.*

"David," he said and nothing more.

"Well, welcome, David." Max smiled warmly. "I hope we'll see you some more."

I'd really rather we didn't, David thought, but noticing a quizzical look on Max's face, just said: "Sure. No doubt."

Even as he finally extricated himself from the possessive grip and made for the door he felt the knowing, slightly amused gaze boring into the back of his head. *Vaya, hombre*, he thought. That was weird. I'm not surprised Sandy Benedetti did what he was told.

Out on the street he turned left, then left again, straight into Lucano's Kitchen. That needed a double espresso, pronto. He collected his coffee and decided not to take the vacant window seat but buried himself as far back in the café as possible. That was weird too. He had no reason to hide and should be grown up enough not to be intimidated. Nevertheless, he really did not want the leadership of Power and Glory Church to come trooping in after him for post-prophetic refreshment. Sipping his coffee and nibbling a pastry he went over the morning in his mind. It felt like trying to make sense of an Escher print or tricking your mind around one of those 3D patterns. What exactly had been going on? There was nothing taken strictly on its own you could object to, but the overall effect just felt wrong. He sipped again and tried another nibble but didn't have any appetite. It was obvious that those attending – he didn't know whether to call them church members, disciples, or devotees – loved and valued it. They seemed to feel right at home and clearly there was a lot that was good mixed in with the dubious or frankly coercive. Apparently Sandy and Sonia had come to a real personal faith through "PGC" long before matters at the bank took their sinister turn. The wheat and the tares again – good and bad. All mixed up and no way of knowing exactly where one stopped and the other began.

Suddenly his mobile gave him a jolt. A call from an unknown number. He'd never make it out in this din. He grabbed his hat, picked up the paper cup, and struggled to the door.

"David Hidalgo. Hello."

"Good morning, Mr Hidalgo," said a youngish Scottish voice, clear but with a definite touch of tension. "Sorry to ring you up like this. We haven't met but I wonder if I could possibly see you. It's quite important. You may have heard of me – I'm Alexander Benedetti."

Chapter 12

THE PRISONER'S TALE

Arriving in London should have been the greatest day of my life. I'd worked, planned, saved, and paid for it. That couldn't have been farther from the truth. They took us out of the van into some sort of warehouse, where we were given tiny rooms each. First they took my passport off me, then I was sent to shower. When I came out all my clothes had gone. There was just this flimsy gown. I was told I was to have an interview to assess my suitability for work. The guy I spoke to was Belarusian. He said there had been unexpected expenses on the trip. Border security was suspicious and needed to be bribed. I owed them another £25,000. I said I didn't have it; that wasn't part of the deal. But I could see what was coming. He said if I didn't have the money then I'd have to work for it. They had work they could offer me. By now there was a hard, heavy feeling in my stomach. I remember my mouth was dry. He told me to stand up and take the gown off. I told him to go to hell. He laughed and said, "Don't you know? That's where you are already." Then another man came in. He must have been listening. He grabbed me from behind. They ripped it off me. I can't write down what they did. I try to forget it but I can't. Finally an older woman came for me then and took me back to my room and locked the door.

They brought me breakfast next morning, then I had another "interview". The man asked me if I had reconsidered their offer. The same thing happened but this time they beat me afterwards. I lay in bed for the rest of the day. The old woman bathed my face and body. They left me alone the day after. Then I was taken in again. They said I could do what they told me or I'd be reported to police as an illegal immigrant. But I knew that was a lie. I guessed I was worth too much to give away. I was taken to a room in the basement. The gown was ripped off me and I was left. There was a bed and a locker. After about fifteen minutes a man came in. He was Asian and didn't speak much English. He kept saying something I didn't understand and trying to grab me. I kicked and scratched him. I didn't let him touch me. He was fat and old and I was able to keep him off. He started screaming at me. Then the door opened and he was screaming at the woman. He went out and the two men came in again. I couldn't defend myself against them both. Later the woman took me back to my room.

All this time I didn't see any of the other girls but I could hear them crying at night. I didn't let myself cry. There was nothing left inside to come out. The next day another man came to my room. He grabbed me by the throat against the wall so I couldn't breathe. He said if I did that again he wouldn't let go. They'd dump my body in the river. No one knew I had arrived; nobody would know when I left. They'd find my body washed up in France. I had one more chance. The same Asian man came that night. He was naked. He was smiling this time and stroked my hair. I let him. He ran his hand down my face, then my neck, then my shoulders. Then I couldn't stand it any more so I kneed him in the groin. He went down like a burst balloon. He started groaning. They must have heard him outside. I knew what was coming next. I'd kept a nail file I'd picked up hidden in my hair. When the man came at me I went for his face. I almost got him but he dodged and caught my hand and laughed at me. He slapped me hard but that was just the start. I don't know how long it was before I lost consciousness.

I woke up back in my room. Another man I'd never seen was there. He was speaking to the first man. I could hardly open my eyes but I could see he was worried. He was speaking fast and low and it looked like he was counting something off on his fingers. He got to five then held up his whole hand right in the face of the other man. Five something. I didn't know what it was. I found out later it was five ribs they had broken, and my nose. After that they left me alone for days; I don't know how many. I was in more pain than I knew was possible. They gave me some aspirins and that was all. I couldn't even take them myself but the old woman helped me lift my head just enough. I lay flat all the time because any time I tried to roll over or sit up my muscles went into spasm and made me scream. Finally another man came in who I'd never seen before. He spoke in English. He said I didn't have any choices left. I had been a lot of trouble to them and I only had one chance left. They needed the room for someone who would work. If I wouldn't work then I couldn't live. It was that simple. So when I was fit to go down to the basement again I did what they wanted. Actually I just lay there till it was finished. It was a different man. He was young with a shaved head and a swastika tattoo. I try to forget his face but it's always there. It was like that for a week. Every night. By then I could move better. They said another girl needed the room and I had to leave. They had found me another job, far away. I was given my clothes back and told to get dressed. They put me on a bus handcuffed to the seat. We drove through the night. When I woke up I didn't know where I was. The woman who brought me breakfast was there so I asked her. She was Belarusian too. She said it was "Edynburh".

I was put into a room that was more like a bedroom this time. They said it was my room and I could put up pictures and arrange it how I wanted. There was a bed, a chest of drawers, a wardrobe. There was a poster on the wall with a picture of a garden and a Bible verse. I was given breakfast then told to sleep. I would have an interview at two o'clock. I fell asleep immediately but had nightmares. I was naked in the middle of my family. My grandmother was there. I wanted her to comfort me but she spat on me instead.

There was thin soup, then potatoes and sausages for lunch. Then I was taken to the office. There were two men, one younger with very short blond hair and a scar on his cheek. The older, tall man was like a wrestler or a weightlifter. He was smiling all the time. That was worse than the ones that only looked angry. He told me his name was Max and that he was my employer. I had a debt to pay back and until it was paid I had to work for him. While I was working I also had to pay for my room and food. If the customers were pleased with me I would get a bonus; if they weren't pleased I would be fined and that would be added to the debt. It was my choice. I didn't say anything. He said Mikhail would look after me and nodded at the younger man. Both of them were smiling now. Before I was taken back to my room he said I had to work out my own salvation with fear and trembling, whatever that meant.

So that became my life, the life I had given up everything for in Belarus. There are six girls in the house but I know there are other houses too. If someone's sick sometimes a girl comes from another house until she recovers. They're all from Eastern Europe, though not all from Belarus. We all have more or less the same story. I wish I could write to all my friends at home and tell them not to trust anyone. The routine is the same most days. We start work at about eight o'clock in the evening and work late into the night depending on how many men there are. Sometimes there's just one or two but usually more like four or five. They get fifty minutes each and we get ten minutes to clean up. Most are middle aged or older. Sometimes there's a young one. Once I had a man who only wanted to talk about how his wife was disabled and he couldn't have a normal married life. But normally they want what they pay for. It often hurts but you have to not show it or you get a bad report and they fine you. I started off hating the men. Then you get used to it. Now I try to ignore them. I pretend they're not real, that it's just like a video game or a dream. Sometimes you get the same man coming back every week who wants to "get to know you". I smile and make something up. When I'm working I try to think about other things. I wander through the woods around my uncle's farm or go shopping in Minsk. They have my body but my mind is my own.

We work late so we get up late next morning. The kitchen always has plenty of food so we have breakfast whenever we want. Lunch and dinner are made for us by a Scottish woman. She doesn't say much. There are two showers and toilets but no bath. The girls chat in the kitchen or the lounge. We watch daytime TV. Once there was something on the news about people trafficking from Eastern Europe. We watched it but no one said a word. To start with I only had my own clothes but once I'd been in the house for two weeks I was told I could go shopping. Mikhail, the younger man with the scar, took me. He made me put a metal collar on. He said if I tried to run away he had a remote control. When he pressed the button a shock went through my entire body and I hit the floor. He said that was only number 1. Then he put me in a car. He sat beside me in the back while the woman drove. It was the first time I had been outside since I came to London a month before. We parked the car and walked. I think it was the main shopping street. It was a very wide street with a castle and gardens on one side and shops on the other. It was beautiful. But the most beautiful thing was the clear, fresh air – and the sky, the people. There were people of all ages just walking about, talking, laughing, smiling. Normal people, who of course had no idea about me. How could they? They seemed polite. A middle-aged man with an overcoat and a fedora held a door open for me. He smiled and nodded. He looked like someone I could trust but I couldn't say anything. I think we spent more than £200 that day. Mikhail paid for everything. He said, "Smile, Tati, we're going upmarket. Max thinks you deserve the best." I had to try on expensive underwear to make sure it fitted. Then I had to choose earrings and bracelets. We went to a shop with underwear and sex stuff in the window but I wasn't allowed to go in. Mikhail smiled at me in a way like he knew something I didn't know and left me outside with the woman. He gave her the remote. After a few minutes he came out with a big shopping bag. "You'll like this, Tati," he said. "Bags of fun in here."

So that's how it goes. The girls are sisters; we help each other. If someone gets crazy and says she can't go on we try to calm her down and help her. We tell her it won't last forever, but of course nobody knows when, how, or if it will ever end. If she can't make herself do it any more they "deal with her" and she needs to be fed and washed for a week. Sometimes girls disappear. Nobody mentions it. There are men that like to hit a girl, abuse her, so quite often one of us needs something soothing rubbed on the blows. Mikhail said there are cameras in the rooms so they can stop it if it goes too far but usually they don't bother. We don't talk much about who we've been with or what's happened. We all know what goes on. Men think they're good in bed but every one's just as pathetic as the one before. Anyway, we eat, we sleep, we work. We try to forget. We regret that we trusted anyone and we remember the past when it wasn't like this, though that seems so long ago. We don't think much about the future. You can hear some of the girls crying in the middle of the night. They walk around like zombies during the day but they cry at night. They think it's over; there's no way out. We've had a few that couldn't go on and did the only thing they could. They take the body away in the morning and nothing is ever said. If you complain or make a fuss, you get fined to start with, then beaten. There are drugs you can take if you want but you have to "pay" for them and they write it down in a book. Sometimes I've tried asking how much I owe now, like I've a right to know, but you just get laughed at. We all know that's just some kind of excuse, something they say to start with to make it sound like there's some sort of sense behind it all. But everyone knows – them and us – there isn't any sense. I don't take drugs because I think that someday, somehow, there might be a chance to get out and I want to be ready to take it when it comes. But I don't know how that could happen. The house is locked, there's always staff on, and we're only allowed out with a minder. There's no phone or internet and the windows are frosted and have bars on. But I know there has to be some way out. I don't care if I get sent back to Belarus as long as I get out of here. But before I go I'd like to pay them back – Max, Mikhail, Ivan, and all the rest. They should know what it's like to lose your freedom, to lose control of your own body, to be someone else's property. They think they own me. Well they don't. Somehow, sometime, I'll find a way. And not just for me. For all the girls in all the houses. When I get free then they should watch out.

Chapter 13

SILVERKNOWES

Alexander Benedetti had asked that they meet at David's flat, not in a public place. "I know I'm in trouble," he'd said. "The police are going to want to speak to me. I just need to speak to you first."

"First question," David said, with Benedetti sitting across the Monday morning breakfast table. "How do you know who I am and how did you get my number?"

The banker was sitting with his elbows on the table and his head in his hands. He was unshaven and wore a crumpled white shirt and corduroy trousers.

"Well I'd heard your name from... Mike and Sam... before," he started, a slight hesitation before uttering the names, "so I knew you'd been involved in drugs and crime and stuff in Spain – I mean you'd been working against them, not with them. Sorry, I didn't phrase that very well. Look, do you mind if I get a glass of water or something? I'm not in a very good state right now." David could see he was shaking. Initially he'd been outraged that he'd even had the gall to call him, never mind want to meet. After agreeing to the meeting, he'd been planning to tear strips off him in person then do everything he could to make sure they locked him up and threw away the key. The problem was that the man sitting opposite him now was such a pathetic shell – unwashed, unshaved, a tousled mop of uncombed hair. He looked like he'd been sleeping in his car. Seeing him slumped in the chair with his head in his hands, David found it difficult to hold the line.

"Sure. Would a strong coffee be better?" he finally asked.

Benedetti seemed to settle a bit with a caffeine shot inside him.

He was in serious trouble and knew it. Whether he was going to tell the entire truth remained to be seen, but either way there didn't seem like an ounce of fight left in him.

"Let's try again, Alexander," David resumed in a slightly softer tone. "How do you know who I am? How did you get my number?"

"Sandy – I'm Sandy. Do you mind if I smoke?"

"Yes, I do. Now, Sandy," David said between his teeth, "how?"

Sandy Benedetti had his coffee mug cupped in two hands and was sitting hunched over as if he hoped to gain some warmth from the contents. He spoke in barely more than a whisper.

"Well, like I said, Mike and Sam mentioned you. Then, when Mike was asking about the account – that's what this is all about – he said he was part of a group looking at church finances that you were part of. That's why he was so interested. He'd seen their official accounts and knew that didn't match what we held. So he flagged it up. You know we look into accounts that don't match their profile, to stop money laundering and stuff. At least," he added as an afterthought, "we're supposed to."

"I know," David replied quietly, seeing they were getting somewhere at last and trying not to put him off his stride. "And I know it's Power and Glory Church we're talking about."

"How do you know that?" Sandy asked, suddenly startled. "Did Mike say it was them?"

"No, he did not," David said, making a strong effort to keep calm, like he was talking down an addict in Madrid. "He maintained confidentiality. But Sam guessed it must be the church you go to and PGC is one of the three we were looking at. It's not that hard to work out."

"Oh." Sandy collapsed again. "I didn't know."

"Well, we only found that bit out last week," David continued. "And my phone number – how did you get that?"

"You used to be a Salamanca customer. It's in our customer records."

David rolled his eyes. Did this man not take any of his

responsibilities seriously? As regards PGC he wasn't sure whether to mention that he'd been to pay them a visit but decided it might be best to keep his powder dry. "Go on," he said. "Mike was insistent that you follow them up but you tried to block it. Correct?"

Sandy seemed like a puppet with an erratic operator and not enough stuffing to keep him upright on his own, jerking up or down depending on the topic.

"Yes, that's right. I knew it was wrong. I knew all along. But I thought I was doing a good thing. I never dreamed it would come to this." He paused and shook his head. "You don't know what they're like," he said, "how they make you do what they want you to."

"I can imagine," David replied. After Sunday's performance it didn't need that much imagination. In spite of himself he was growing in sympathy for the hopeless figure in front of him.

"What did they say to you?" he asked, again trying to get the conversation back on track.

"That it was for the kingdom of God," Sandy said simply. "There was to be a massive expansion in Edinburgh. The money would be for outreach – to plant new churches, to reach new families. He told me it would be like taking all the benefit Sonia and I had from the church and passing it on to a hundred others. There's a lot that's been really good for us at PGC, you know. It's helped our marriage. It gives meaning to your life – not just making money, retiring, dying. You know?"

"Of course. That's what the gospel is. But hiding millions of pounds and lying to the regulators, Sandy. Did it never make you wonder?"

"You have no idea. I never felt right about it. But I couldn't tell Sonia. Every Sunday we were at church, he'd just be up there looking at me, smiling. He has this smile that makes you feel he knows exactly what you're thinking. If I'd had a bad week he always seemed to know. He'd just smile at me and say, 'Keep the faith, Sandy. For all the millions that don't yet know.' So I'd have to go into another week hoping nobody would notice."

"But Mike Hunter noticed…"

"Right. Mike was a friend as well as a colleague. They'd been kind to us. He was good at his job. When the system flagged up the account he ran the analysis and found they were like 3000 per cent at variance with the profile. There was no way this was just a church account. So I told him I'd deal with it. But he wouldn't back off. He came back to me the next week and asked what was going on. Somehow he seemed to guess there was more to it. I tried to tell him the Serious Crime Division was already involved and we had been told to sit on the account until they were ready to move. But he didn't believe me and kept on checking. I think he even phoned them to find out."

"So what did you do next?"

"What could I do? I phoned the Prophet. I thought he'd be able to tell me what to do."

"The Prophet," David interrupted to make him clarify. "What do you mean? Who's the Prophet?"

"Max. His name's Max but he calls himself the Prophet and that's how we're supposed to refer to him too. When you stop and think, I know it sounds a bit crazy. That's just the way it is though. Once you've been doing it for a bit you stop noticing how weird it must sound. Actually I have no idea what his second name is. He's not British; he's from Eastern Europe. He says that's what pastors are called in his country and that it fits with what the Bible says."

"His country?" David asked. "Where's he from then?"

"Belarus – Minsk, I think. He doesn't say much about what he used to do. I think he's been in Britain about ten years or so. He was involved in another church – Manchester maybe. There were financial problems there and the whole thing was shut down and disappeared. There was a case study about money laundering through a church at a conference I was at once and I've often wondered if that was them."

David couldn't contain himself.

"What?!" he burst out. "You had suspicions about money

laundering in the past and you still hid accounts controlled by the same man? Are you crazy?"

"I know, I know," Sandy moaned. "The past two weeks there's not been a moment I haven't asked myself the same question. I think I must be stupid. But he's really convincing. He's always talking about leaving the past behind. He calls it 'Forgiveness and Forgetfulness'. I suppose I thought he'd maybe got sucked into something that went wrong but that was behind him now. The church is really good in other ways. If it wasn't for them Sonia and I probably wouldn't even be together any more. You've got to believe me, Mr Hidalgo."

David got up and clicked the kettle on again. He stood looking out across Bruntsfield Links without speaking. He made two more coffees and quietly put them on the table.

"So," he said finally, "believing you were doing the right thing – despite all the evidence and your own misgivings – you went to the 'Prophet' to ask what to do when Mike Hunter wouldn't let it lie. What did he tell you?"

Sandy Benedetti took another sip of coffee and looked up to the ceiling as if in search of some better way of saying it. He spoke in a whisper.

"He didn't tell me anything to do. He just asked the name of whoever it was and told me they'd sort it out. He even thanked me for trusting him. He said God would remember everything I'd done. Listen, Mr Hidalgo, I swear to God I had no idea what was going to happen. I was scared. I thought I'd go to prison or something if it came out." He paused. "And there's something else too."

David's heart sank further. What more could there be?

"He kind of reminded me that I had got a bonus for bringing in the new account. He didn't threaten me or anything, not openly anyway. He just said that we all needed to see this through to the end. If not there'd be questions about more than PGC. I knew what he was talking about. Sonia had a terrible time with her ex; she needed peace and security. If I went to prison and we lost the house she'd never be able to handle it. So I hadn't any choice. It wasn't just for me, Mr Hidalgo; it was for Sonia, for the kids. I never meant for this to happen. I never meant for Mike Hunter to die."

Sandy Benedetti came to his own bitter end along with his story. He tried to dab the tears away. The words came out in broken, stuttering syllables. David couldn't help but hear an echo of Sam Hunter in the man who had caused, even if not directly, her husband's death. But he didn't go round the table and wrap his arm around anyone's shoulders this time. Mike Hunter was dead. Sandy Benedetti's blind faith and foolishness had made it inevitable. He didn't need to ask for the rest of the story. Sandy had given Mike's name to Max. They saw the writing on the wall. Exactly how they'd managed it didn't particularly matter right now. That would be for police and lawyers and forensic experts. Somehow they'd picked him up, jabbed a needle into his neck or his leg, and brought him back to 67, Colinton Mains Rise. Had they guessed there might be trouble so had installed the computer virus weeks before, or was that just routine, an insurance policy in case anything went wrong? Anyway, there was a ready-made explanation for why an apparently successful married man had decided to end it all; a bogus phone call and a burst of data from Belarus made it all look so reasonable. In the clear again, problem sorted. It certainly fooled Charlie Thompson. But it didn't fool Sam Hunter. If not for her tenacity and faith in the man she loved it all might have worked the way they had planned, and if not for a Latin American gunman who had accidentally shot a hacker who could trace the whole enterprise back to a corporation in Minsk, the truth might have been lost in cyberspace. Mike Hunter wasn't a man with a warped sexuality, amusing himself in his study once his wife had gone to bed. He was a diligent, moral man who unwittingly put himself in harm's way to find out the truth about dirty money. He had no way of knowing that his boss had been compromised or the lengths that vested interests would go to to protect themselves. God willing, he was too far gone by the time they got him home to be aware of anything else.

But there were still important unanswered questions. Sandy Benedetti had been protecting cash that came from crime. That much seemed certain. But what crime? What was PGC and its charismatic, compelling prophet up to? As that thought went through his head, David once again found his sympathy for the wretch across the table waning. Sandy looked up at him.

"Do you believe me?" he said, pleading like a child.

"Do I believe you?" David repeated, half to Sandy and half to himself. He thought for a moment, then felt a sudden, cold, rage inside. He looked Sandy Benedetti straight in the eye and spoke slowly and clearly.

"Sure, I believe you. I believe you have been naive, gullible, and reckless. I believe you never stopped for an instant to consider the implications of what you were doing. I believe you were more concerned about your own safety – your big bonus and house in the Grange – than the safety of another human being, another believer for that matter. I believe you had all the information you needed to see that the PGC account was corrupt and that you had a moral duty to do something about it. I believe you allowed yourself to be convinced against your own doubts and suspicions because it was in your own interests to do so. I believe you have never shown any interest or curiosity as to where that amount of corrupt gain had come from and who might be suffering in the process." Sandy was looking like a rabbit caught in the headlights, but David pressed on. "And I believe you should now do everything in your power to bring your 'Prophet' and whatever gangsters are working for him to justice. Yes, I believe you, Sandy, and I think the police will too."

At the mention of police Benedetti seemed to gain some last morsel of energy. He sat up.

"Police," he said, "do you... will you... I mean, are you going to tell them? Tell them what I've told you?"

"No need, Sandy," David replied. "You've done it yourself."

He reached into an inside pocket and pulled out a black plastic box about the size of a packet of cigarettes and laid it on the table.

"You get all that, Charlie?" he asked. "Maybe you should come up now. You must be freezing out there."

David's head was still buzzing with Sandy Benedetti when Gillian picked him up that evening. Charlie Thompson had made it abundantly clear just how much trouble the banker was in and that there would be charges pending. Just exactly what with would depend on the Procurator Fiscal. Without a doubt a breach of the banking regulations. As regards the murder – well, that would remain to be seen. Sandy sat without a word of protest. In a way he almost looked relieved the roller coaster ride was finally over and the brakes were on.

"Can I go home and talk to my wife?" was his only question. "I left her a note yesterday to say I was at an urgent work event and I haven't been in touch since. Actually, I was in the Balmoral last night. I just couldn't face going home."

"You're not going to do a vanishing act, are you?" Thompson asked pointedly. "I might be able to swing it for you to come in voluntarily if I can trust you."

"Absolutely," Sandy confirmed in a totally flat tone. "This has all gone on long enough. To be honest, I don't really care what happens now. I just want it to be over. But I need to talk to Sonia. She needs to hear it from me – that I did not know about the murder and I had no part in it."

Thompson paused, considering his options. "I'm going to take a risk. Go home and speak to your wife. Have a night at home; then, two o'clock tomorrow afternoon at Gayfield Square. Turn up late or not at all and we'll throw the book at you. Is that clear enough?"

Sandy nodded.

"Crystal," he said. "I'll be there."

Later on, rattling over the Dean Bridge then out Queensferry Road, David updated Gillian on the conversation and the fact that Benedetti had indeed turned up and given a statement – to everyone's relief. Gillian gave a long sigh as they sat at the Orchard Brae lights.

"I wonder how she'll take it," she said, "Sonia. I suppose she must be completely in the dark."

"Did I tell you I'd met her?" David asked.

"Sonia? How?"

"At Power and Glory. She was on the welcome team. It was quite surreal, to be honest. But I'd swear she knows nothing about it all."

"How was she?"

"Really nice actually. Welcoming – well, that's the job I suppose – but genuinely. It's plain to me that whatever else they might be up to, for her and Sandy PGC had its good points – as far as being a church is concerned, I mean. She said how much it had helped them. Like we keep on saying – good in the bad and bad in the good."

"I'm glad it's the angels that are supposed to pull it all apart, not me."

They drove on in silence as Gillian nipped in and out of the teatime traffic then onto the curiously named Quality Street and on down towards Cramond, en route to her dad's birthday do.

"Speaking of angels, Gillian," David finally said.

"Were we? Oh yes, the angels in the parable."

"So, speaking of angels, I wonder if you could pull in somewhere down here just before we get any further."

"Intriguing," Gillian said as she slowed up and found a parking spot. "We better not be long. Dad's eightieth is a big deal. We can't be late. And what's this to do with angels by the way?"

"You'll see... or at least one angel in particular. And your dad has waited eighty years for this. Ten minutes won't make a difference."

Gillian turned the engine off and twisted round as far as the sports car seat would allow.

"So, fire away," she said. "What's on your mind?"

"Something I need to say," David replied after a pause, as if he'd been trying to compose his opener but was still having a bit of difficulty getting started. *Oh dear*, she thought, *here we go. This could be good or bad. Do I really want to hear it?* They still hadn't spoken about Sunday's lunch fiasco and despite thinking it through a bit and calming down, Gillian didn't yet feel it was out of Action and into Filing. *If he doesn't bring it up I will*, she thought.

"Mmm…" she replied non-committally.

"Well, two things actually. First, I should have called you on Sunday. I thought I needed to go and see these guys but we should have talked about it the night before; I just hadn't got to the point of making up my mind. I'm sorry I messed up your day."

That's a good start at least, she thought.

"Forgiven. But you're right; it did mess up the day. I was pretty mad… and number two?"

David sat in silence again. A couple of mums walked past with buggies, babies, and shopping, laughing and chatting, heading home to get the tea on. He watched them pause on the corner. One of them pulled out a mobile and held it so they could both see. A couple of seconds watching then they both cracked up. *Probably internet cats*, he thought. *Why does half the world want to spend all their time filming cats?* Then he shook himself and snapped back to the present. *Get a grip*, he thought, *this isn't helping*, and tried again.

"Number two isn't just about yesterday, or what's going on just now – well, only partly. Remember when we were with Sam last week? I felt totally useless. I'm much better at practical things. When we worked with the addicts in Madrid I used to do the treatment plans. When they needed to talk about how they'd screwed up or were missing their wives, well, Rocío did that – or Juan, or Alicia. Anybody. I just knew I wasn't any good at it. But you were there last week and you did exactly what was needed." David held his hand up to block the denial he guessed was coming. "You did. Exactly. When Sam was talking about finding Mike in the garage I couldn't get the images out of my head – Rocío, when she tried to end it all, and then seeing her in the morgue. I don't think about it every day any more, but sometimes it just seems to pop out like it was yesterday, you know? It's like a photo album in your head with someone turning the pages and pushing your face in it. You try to close the book and move on but you can't. It's always there on the shelf and sometimes comes down at the most awkward moments.

"But then I looked at you. Sam was crying and I wasn't that far from it myself. I was able to remind myself the world had changed. The images are still there but they don't have the power they used to. Juan says I was a broken man when I got back to Edinburgh but that you put the pieces back together again – it's true. If I hadn't been for you, Sam and I would have been sitting there, both of us blubbing. Anyway, I'm just saying I'm glad you're with me – and that, thank God, Raúl didn't, well, he didn't manage to do what he tried to. And I haven't chased you off yet."

Gillian had taken David's hand as he spoke. Now she kissed it.

"*Igualmente*," she said. "Is that the right expression?"

"Well, it means 'me too' so I hope so."

"I was just managing to hold it together myself. Are you seeing her again this week?"

"Yes, I think so. But I'm not quite done yet. Sorry, you know I'm no good at this. What I want to say is I don't ever want to be thinking about the time we've spent together like it's only pictures in the past. I want it to be the present. Always in the present."

Gillian turned further round, as far as the cramped cabin would allow.

"Are you saying what I think you're saying, David Hidalgo?"

He reached into an inside pocket and pulled out a little black box – not too dissimilar from what he'd laid on the table in front of Sandy Benedetti – but with altogether a different feeling.

"I am. What do you think?"

There are places that deserve to have ugly, harsh names and entirely live up to them and others that you somehow feel well disposed to just by the sound of the word. Gillian had always thought that Silverknowes was one of the latter. Sandwiched in between upmarket Cramond and the grittier Granton, it was neither posh nor plain, which was fine. That was partly why she'd felt ok about Dad coming here when he needed more care than she or Ros could give just by popping in a couple of times a day. Initially she'd had a horror of the idea of "going into care", but the social worker had seemed human enough and the staff were really nice. The reality was that more was needed and they all had to all face up to that. The clincher was when they said of course Dad could bring his drums; they had a piano in the lounge and maybe he could entertain them if they got someone to tinkle the ivories. It was certainly going to be a lot better than finding him with a broken hip on the bathroom floor and decisions to be made in the midst of a crisis. Archie himself was remarkably sanguine about it all after a visit. In fact, he seemed to have got a bit of a thing with Juanita, the Brazilian care worker in his unit, and made his own decision without anyone having to badger him. "She says her brother can get me all the João Gilberto records I want," he reported, "even the ones not issued in Europe." So that was that. The building was new and located on Marine Drive, so there was a waterfront view as well. By and large he seemed to have been happy in the year since he'd given up the house in Corstorphine.

David and Gillian pulled up in the car park and headed in, loaded up with party food. David did the heavy lifting and Gillian kept her hands out of sight – too much excitement in one day and all that. But she was floating, her two favourite men around her.

"So this is the young man?" Archie inquired in mock Morningside when Gillian introduced David. "I've heard so much about you!"

"All good, I hope," David replied conventionally, not quite sure how to play it. "Happy birthday. They tell me you like this sort of stuff." From behind his back he produced a nicely boxed bottle of eighteen-year-old Highland Park.

"Thank you kindly, sir," Archie intoned, planking the box at his feet. "And they tell me you play tenor, which makes you not all bad. Wrap yourself around this and tell me you've brought it with you." He held out a large glass of red wine.

123

"Sadly not," David admitted. "Just birthday cake. Gillian says you used to play professionally, Mr Lockhart."

"House band at Ronnie Scott's. And Archie, for goodness' sake. Backing Stan Getz was a nightmare. He was having an affair with Astrud – Gilberto's wife. You know – the original girl from Ipanema. Well, she was an absolute peach but Getz was drunk more than sober. It could get a bit rough getting them on stage but the dressing room was horrendous. She'd be crying and begging him to sober up, trying to get me to hide his booze. He'd show up late, fall asleep when he should have been going on – all that stuff. But when you got them in front of a mike, well, that was something different. She sang like an angel and he played like a demon. They brought the house down. That was the beauty of being in the resident band. You got to play with all the greats: Paul Desmond, Ben Webster, Mulligan of course. I even backed Mulligan and Desmond together. That was a dream. Let me tell you how that happened…"

It did Gillian good to see her dad in such good form. She had heard his jazz stories so many times she struggled to look interested, but this was a new audience and he was playing it for all he was worth. And David was genuinely interested. They were both in their element. She slipped away to help the staff get the food and drinks sorted. Eventually all was ready, the lights clicked off, and the cake emerged. Gillian led the singing; the old man took a mighty puff and extinguished all eighty in a single blow. Then it was paper plates and piles of party food. David went off and struck up snatches of conversation with other residents and staff.

"Sorry Ros couldn't be here," Gillian whispered in her dad's ear. "I think they had the holiday booked for ages."

"And I suppose my eightieth birthday was a complete surprise? I know – October holidays and all these kids." He took a sip from his glass and tugged his waistcoat down.

"Anyway, on a more important subject, how are you doing, Gilli? What are you thinking?"

"About what?"

"You know about what. You and him, the boyfriend. How's it going?" Archie grabbed a passing sausage roll and popped it in whole while Gillian took a sip of her red grape juice. He always did have an alarming knack of cutting right to the chase, which didn't seem to have been softened by the years. David stood at the other end of the room, apparently all ears to the problems of maintaining Spitfire engines in the North African desert.

"Well, there's a bit of news there, Dad. I was going to tell you later once we were on our own."

"Sounds promising. Would that be good news then?"

Gillian nodded and smiled.

"David proposed on the way down here. I didn't see it coming or I would've told you sooner."

"Well, well. And how are you feeling about that, honey? I imagine you must have said yes or we wouldn't be talking about it."

She nodded.

"I said yes, and I'm feeling good – really good. We've been together almost a year. I've been wondering myself where it was all going, even where I wanted it to go. But now it's happened I feel at peace about it. It's been kind of a growing thing, I suppose – more than fireworks."

"Like Mama Cass then?" Archie asked cryptically.

"Sorry, you've lost me there."

He sang a couple of lines from "It's Getting Better" in a gravelly voice till they both ended up in fits of laughter. David raised one eyebrow at the other end of the room and hoped the joke wasn't on him. Gillian just smiled serenely back.

"And he's a vicar or minister or something, isn't he? I suppose he can't be a priest. Not now anyway."

That made her laugh again.

"He's a part-time pastor of a little church in Newington, remember?" she reminded him. "And he teaches Spanish for a living. But he was leader of a huge church in Madrid. He's part Spanish actually. I've been there. It's absolutely awesome. They do a tremendous job with drug addicts and alcoholics – all of which David started and led. Then two years ago his wife was murdered by a drug gang – some sort of retribution for loss of earnings with all the addicts that had given up. He found it really hard, packed it all in, and came back to Edinburgh. His mum was Scots and he was brought up here. That's it in a nutshell." She thought perhaps now might not be the time to say that since meeting David Hidalgo she'd been attacked, abducted, shot at twice, reduced to a nervous wreck, and was currently helping solve a murder made to look like a suicide and unravelling a money-laundering conspiracy – but regardless of that, she felt 100 per cent in love and none of that seemed to matter.

Archie twisted round in his chair with some difficulty and kissed her on the cheek.

"Congratulations," he said. "I take it he loves you?"

"Apparently so," Gillian smiled back. "He's a really sweet man. It's not always obvious though. It takes a bit of time to get to know him. But I think you'll like him when you do."

"I like him already," Archie confirmed, taking another sip. "He brought me a bottle of Highland Park. And what about the religious bit? I hope you haven't signed over your life savings and taken the pledge."

"Well, I do make a small contribution from time to time," Gillian admitted with another laugh. She seemed to be doing a lot of laughing tonight and all without a sniff of alcohol. She guessed she must be a happy girl.

"You know what I mean," Archie persisted. "I tried to bring you girls up to think for yourselves. Not to get pulled into the hocus pocus. I hope you haven't let me down."

"Not at all, Dad," Gillian said reassuringly. "I go to church, read my Bible, pray a bit, ask questions. I haven't signed up for anything but I'm learning. And if anything it's actually making more sense the further on I get."

"When I was young you had to leave your brains out with the hats and coats," Archie snorted, "and I still think faith just means seeing how many impossible things you can believe before breakfast."

"I'm not going to argue with you on your birthday," Gillian replied with mock seriousness. "I'll just say I used to think that too – or something like it. But I'm beginning to see it's a bit more complicated. I haven't sold my soul and church is great. Loads of really kind folk I've come to value. So there you are."

"Well Gilli, I just want to see you happy, not hurt. You know that."

"Course I do."

"And he's a kind man?" Archie glanced across at the animated expression on another old man's face as he told David about the day he met Monty in person, and the way David grabbed a plate of smoked salmon on brown bread and passed it round the group of old ladies in the corner while still listening with rapt attention.

"He is."

"You love him?"

"I do," she nodded.

"So do what you need to do, honey. And if I get a pair of these fancy robotic legs we keep hearing about I'll walk you down the aisle." Then he did a quick double take. "There will be a wedding, I suppose? A man of the cloth and all that."

Gillian smiled again.

"There will be a wedding. Give us a chance; I've only just said yes, but probably sooner rather than later. You'll be the first to know."

"Ok. Don't leave it too long. I want to toast the beautiful bride and the Highland Park won't last forever."

Gillian smiled again, her face getting sore from the strain.

"Love you, Dad," she said in his ear.

"You too, honey. You too."

"And happy birthday again."

As the bridge rolls, pastries, cheese puffs, and lemon meringue – not to mention the whisky – took their toll, Archie began to nod a bit. Juanita came over and whispered that maybe they should give him time for a nap then maybe he'd get a second wind in an hour or so. Would that be ok? "Of course," Gillian said, and thanked her for how well they were looking after him. She collected David, who was still engrossed in the tales of the Desert Rats.

Marine Parade was getting distinctly chilly by that time of year and that time of night. They wrapped up warm and clung to each other in the face of the biting wind. They walked a hundred yards or so in silence, Gillian gripping his arm.

"Did I do the right thing?" David suddenly asked without explanation.

"Asking me to marry you?"

"No, I don't need to check on that. I mean shopping Sandy to the police. He thought he was talking to me in confidence and I had the whole thing relayed to DI Thompson. When I phoned him to say Benedetti had asked for a meeting he wanted to be present first of all and I said no. Then he wanted to wire me for sound and I agreed. Was that ok?"

"In the light of what Alexander Benedetti has been up to I think that's a minor matter. You said he seemed relieved when Charlie came up."

"Yes... I think so. He said he just wanted it all to be over. He was mainly worried about the effect it would have on Sonia. I think he expects to go to prison and has sort of come to terms with it."

"How do you think she'll take it?"

"Not well, I imagine. The whole thing just makes my blood boil; nothing but victims in every direction – Mike, Sam, Sonia, even Sandy himself, I suppose. Guilty party and a victim at the same time. He broke the law but he was also conned. And we still have no idea where all that money comes from – drugs no doubt, plus who knows what else, which means another bunch of victims. I still can't get over the fact that the whole thing is hidden behind a church. No wonder we get such a bad reputation."

Gillian tightened her grip on David's arm and pulled in closer.

"Hang on a bit," she said. "There isn't any *we* in this. You and I, Southside, Juan and Alicia, Warehouse 66, Mariano and Maria, all these guys – all of us – we're not PGC. I don't feel the least apologetic to be part of a church that does good just because there are others that don't. The people that lump it all together have probably never been to a decent modern church in their lives. All they know is marriages, births, deaths, and the odd scandal they see on the news. It's not the same. The police just need to shut it down, get the bad guys, and send them to prison so they can stop spreading whatever poison they have. Sandy and Sonia can recover in time. They were looking for the right thing, just in the wrong place. That can be fixed. Stop worrying; you did the right thing. Absolutely."

They walked on a bit further. The Forth bridges could just be seen in the distance behind Cramond Island.

"I absolutely love you," David said. "It makes things so much different to have someone to talk it over with. Juan's a great guy but, well, it's not the same, you know?"

"I do. And I'm relieved it's not the same. I'd be worried if it was."

By the time they got back to the party Archie had recovered and was propped up behind his drums. An old dame in her nineties was perched at a piano playing "She'll Be Coming Round the Mountains When She Comes". A few of the brighter souls were trying to remember as many of the proper words as they could. David and Gillian came in hand in hand. Archie spotted them, nodded at the choir, and rolled his eyes. They waited until the final chorus had died away, then went over to where he was grimly wiping his forehead and helping himself to another refreshment.

"Hi Daddy," Gillian said. "That sounded good."

He gave her a look and continued a slow shuffle with brushes.

"You might say that, my dear. I couldn't possibly comment. Anyway, you look like the cat that got the cream. Find a lucky bag in the street?"

"Maybe," she replied. "I never showed you this, did I?"

"Showed me what?"

"Something sparkly," she said and flashed her left hand.

Archie didn't miss a beat.

"About time too," he said. "And you, Mr Whatever-your-name-is. Treat her right or I'll send round the horn section to sort you out. Some of these trumpet players are mean dudes!"

Chapter 14

HACIENDA

It was a pleasant but somehow disorientating sensation having so many well-wishers, maybe like the sort of instant celebrity *Big Brother* winners and viral Youtube stars are prone to. Everyone claimed to have seen it coming long before they did, which apparently gave them a sense of ownership and possibly even a hint of smugness.

"Finally, brother," Juan said with feeling when he heard the news. "*Me vuelves loco, amigo.* And Alicia too. But I'm glad you've seen sense at last. Now what?"

"Don't think we've got that far yet. Maybe next spring."

"But we need a *fiesta* right now, no?"

"I guess so."

"Hacienda, Sunday night, eight o'clock. Leave it to me."

Gillian went into work the following morning feeling like her head was on another planet. She should have been working on essay questions for the new first year intake but couldn't seem to get down to business. She didn't want to make a big deal of it among her colleagues but somehow it couldn't be helped. Becky the secretary noticed first and from there the news spread like wildfire. Even Stephen Baranski had the grace to offer his congratulations. Head of Department Gary was very complimentary. "What a relief," he said. "I thought you were going to take up with that bloke from Harvard two years ago. Then we'd have lost you to the States. Congratulations. And I have a conference on 'Regional Languages on the Celtic Fringe' for you in Galicia at kind of short notice. Hope you can get your head out of the clouds long enough for that."

What few were aware of was what it had cost them both to get to that point, and the questions that were still in the pending tray. David had counselled so many young folk about the need to choose a firm believer as a life companion that he couldn't help now feeling a bit sheepish. "When the passion fades, as it eventually will," he used to say, "you need to be built on the same rock – have the same goals and connections." Now the old certainties didn't seem quite so secure. He had once thought he and Rocío were built on the same rock, that if they just kept their eyes on what they'd been called to then they didn't need to worry about the risks and dangers. But it hadn't worked out that way. On the other hand, he had found happiness again and was willing to give God the benefit of the doubt. There was a big difference, he'd finally realized, between "making sense of things" and "coming to terms" with them. He still couldn't say what sense everything made, but he had somehow managed to sign a non-aggression pact with reality and maybe that was enough. Unexpected love had come his way. She wasn't going to be handing out tracts on the street any time soon but maybe neither was he. She was on a journey; a fact they were both aware of and treated with respect. Who could say where that would end? David was often struck by how often her questions, comments, and probing hit the nail on the head. *Why do you do this? Why not that? Have you ever thought about trying something else? Can you see how this must feel to outsiders? That makes no sense.* David at least had the presence of mind to realize that love and affection isn't a matter of theology. As the Spanish so nicely put it, he had found *la otra mitad de la naranja* – the other half of the orange. That was enough. Juan, who might have been expected to take a harder line, certainly had no problem with it. "You love each other," he said. "You complete each other. You belong together. Who do you think you've got to thank for that?" When the moment finally came it was wasn't hard to decide at all. He had popped into Macintyres on Frederick Street and took less than ten minutes to choose a diamond solitaire in a gold band. He'd never done anything more right in his life.

For Gillian, the idea of a relationship where religion was a factor seemed weird. Without it ever being in her top ten issues, she'd always seen Scottish "churchianity" as pretty irrelevant, end of story. Believe what you like, she'd once have articulated, but don't force it on me, don't judge my morals or those of my friends, and don't expect me to take a message seriously in twenty-first-century Scotland that comes from a Middle Eastern oral tradition built on ethnic cleansing and stoning adulterers. Except that David wasn't a sociological concept or a religious point of view. He was a bloke with his own beliefs, as well as his own doubts and uncertainties. At times it seemed more of the latter than the former. He was a guy who would once have believed a shed load of stuff she just couldn't get her head around, but then all at once he was hanging on by his fingertips – "his jacket on a shoogly nail", as her dad might have put it. So, guess what? David Hidalgo was on a journey too, and that meant it was never about barricades and slogans. They were simply groping tentatively forward hand in hand. More important than dogmas and doctrines, he was a man of integrity trying to get it right, not just looking out for number one. In fact, she sometimes thought he should put himself a bit higher up the pecking order. So, when the little black box appeared and a diamond solitaire twinkled from inside, she didn't hesitate. He was a clever, good, even godly, man who loved her and would never deceive her. A kiss in the car outside the butcher's in the rush hour wasn't perhaps the most romantic moment in her life. Or maybe it was.

"Come away in!" Irene MacInnes called as David pushed open the door of Hacienda that Sunday evening. Juan and Alicia might have been the nominal owners but that night even they had to do what they were told. The entire restaurant had been turned over to a buffet with eight tables together in the centre and chairs pushed back around the wall. Another couple of tables at the other end held reds, whites, cavas, and soft drinks for the kids. As well as the mountains of salads, tapas dishes, and Hacienda specialities on the buffet table, more seemed to be emerging all the time. Extra labour had been drafted in for the event so Alicia wasn't allowed to do much "in her condition" and was constantly being told to sit down and put her feet up. Alicia's nephew Tomas, who had originally come over from Madrid to improve his English, was now more or less permanent, as was Julie, the girl in David's Spanish class last year who had given David and Gillian their first excuse to speak. She and Tomas seemed to be an item now, and as well as letting everyone know her pivotal role in the drama she showed particular interest in the ring and insisted that Tomas have a good look and admire it as well. Jen MacInnes, now almost seventeen and in need of work experience anyway, had a professional-looking apron on, her sleeves rolled up, hair tucked back, and a brisk and businesslike attitude that her granny particularly approved of. Her mum, Alison, was also on the team but actually found it hard to concentrate. She still had to pinch herself every morning when Jen brought her in a cup of tea and a digestive and did not need constant nagging about tidying her bedroom, doing her homework, clearing up the tea dishes, not leaving stuff all round the house, and being in at a reasonable time. She sometimes thought the girl who'd been abducted by Raúl Álvarez had never come back but had been replaced by someone entirely different. They still had their moments, but once the change was made things never really looked back. Alison's mum encouraged her to give thanks to God but Alison was content to thank David Hidalgo – which she did mentally almost every day.

As well as running the tightest of ships on the catering front, Irene MacInnes had also proved herself remarkably adept as social organizer. Discreet inquiries had been made and conversations had so that most of the Scots Language Department and half of Southside Players chamber orchestra also showed up – in the latter case, to make sure they weren't going to lose their top flautist to a waiter from the Costa del Sol as the rumours had it. Along with a big turnout from Southside, it all made for an interesting mix. Normally Gillian was more at home with a pile of books researching some new point or preparing classes, but this time she just went with the flow and basked in the general approval.

"Isn't she stunning?" Gary commented to a couple of departmental colleagues.

"You don't need to tell me," Stephen Baranski answered ruefully. "I tried to ask her out last week. I feel such a dope!"

"Well, I think that's forgivable," another colleague remarked. "If you didn't know the lie of the land then Gillian is undoubtedly highly ask-outable."

"Ye awright, Davie?" Eric Stoddart slapped his pastor's back while gripping a plate of tortilla with the other. "Cameron! Tyrone! Leave they chicken legs alain. Yiz ur only alloo'd the wan each. Got it? An' Senga. Fur ony sake sit doon ur ye'll hae they olives skeitin' roun' like marbles. An' get yir maw a drink. Great feed, Davie. An' seen as wir oan aboot waddins an' tha', ur ye mindin' about oor weddin' date? Lorraine wid like to get it in afore Christmas if we can. Noo ah'm aff the drugs and the swally we're wantin' a proper Christmas for wance. Right married in aw. Awright?"

What Alison felt looking at Jen, David felt about Eric. The toerag in a shell suit he'd first met over the counter of a hot soup van in Drylaw almost a year ago bore so little relation to the smartly dressed family man in front of him who never missed a week at church, was now working for a roofing company, and was planning to spend his earnings on children's toys for Christmas instead of smack and bevvy.

"Absolutely, Eric. It will be my pleasure."

Across the room Lorraine was sitting next to Alicia, both of them happily and obviously pregnant.

Sometimes David thought things were finally all coming together; not everything inevitably went wrong. Maybe this was the beginning of normality. Just then his phone rang.

"Hello. David Hidalgo. Yes. Hi Charlie. What can I do for

you?... I'm at Hacienda. Spanish restaurant in South Clerk Street... Bit of a celebration actually... Well, if you have to, I suppose. Yes, I have actually. I was using it this morning; I think it's in the church building... Ok, if it's absolutely necessary. Right. Half an hour or so?"

"Trouble at mill?" Gillian asked, seeing David's expression. "I take it Charlie's DI Thompson."

"He is indeed. And he wants to speak to me in half an hour. Wouldn't say any more. But he wants me to have my laptop available for some reason. I can nip along to Southside and pick it up. I left it after doing the PowerPoint this morning. But I've no idea what he can want with that."

It was little more than twenty minutes before Charlie Thompson appeared with a detective constable in tow. In the interim Irene MacInnes had proposed a toast, led the singing of "For they are jolly good fellows" and three cheers, and still managed to keep an eye on the emergence and placement of each additional dish. The sounds of happy eating and contented conversation made a buzz of general well-being around the room. Kids in party frocks mixed with old folk. Eric, who had never read a book in his life but was a walking dictionary of modern urban Scots, was happily chatting with Gillian's Scots Language colleagues, who wanted him to come in and be recorded for the Modern Urban Scots audio project. They couldn't pay but there'd be a lunch in the staff club, a credit in the final version, and maybe an opportunity to talk to undergraduates. Eric earnestly agreed while Lorraine was cracking up in the corner.

"You? At the uni?" she asked, incredulous. "Daein' the roof ah could believe but getting yir name in a book an' hob nobbin' with the heid bummers? That'll gie the kids somethin' to talk abou' in circle time!" Secretly she was intensely proud and from that moment on never missed a chance to tell anyone willing to listen that her husband was giving a lecture at the university.

DI Thompson did not have a carefree look on his face as he came in.

"David Hidalgo – DC Kevin Carmichael. Is there somewhere we can speak? And have you got your laptop?"

"Yes to both. Juan has a side office off the kitchen; we can use that. The laptop's in there. Any reason why Gillian can't join us?"

The two officers exchanged glances.

"No, I suppose not." Thompson agreed. "We're all grown-ups here."

Wondering what exactly that was supposed to mean, David found Gillian showing off the ring to a group from the Thursday afternoon Ladies' Craft Club, who were looking like they'd never seen an engagement ring before, clucking and sighing over it. He whispered in her ear then ushered them all into a tiny office with two chairs and a desk littered with invoices, orders, and statements.

"This yours then?" Charlie Thompson asked, nodding at the MacBook on the desk.

"Sure. What's this all about?" David asked. "This was actually meant to be an engagement party."

"Yeah, sorry about that. And congratulations by the way. Developments in relation to our mutual friends."

DI Thompson parked his ample backside on a corner of the desk and took out a notebook.

"We interviewed Alexander Benedetti last week – as you know. A report has gone to the Procurator Fiscal. Looks like he's not going to be charged with the murder, but there's a bunch of breaches of the banking regulations, conspiracy to defraud, false accounting, etc. I doubt if he'll be spending Christmas at home. Anyway, the next thing was to freeze the account. We have a bunch of guys that specialize in financial and accounting offences. However, bit of a cock-up in the handover so it was Friday before they actually got onto it. Then, guess what?"

"It wasn't there?" David hazarded a guess.

"Oh, it was there all right," Thompson smiled. "But something like 20 million short. Transferred overnight on Thursday. Goodness only knows where. They left £666 in the account. I suppose that's meant to be some sort of joke."

David groaned, looked at Gillian, and rolled his eyes.

"So they live to ride again? I think I can guess what's coming next."

"I bet you can't," Thompson said grimly. "Of course the church is locked up and none of the principals are to be found. But, and this is the nasty bit, they've been busy in the interim. When did you last use your laptop?"

"This morning. At church. I usually do some sort of PowerPoint when I'm speaking."

"All ok?"

"Yes, of course. What's my laptop got to do with PGC church and Max whatever his name is?"

"Turn it on and we'll see."

Unable to contain a sigh at both the interruption to their event and the seemingly bizarre request, David opened up the case. He quickly typed his password at the sign-in screen, expecting the normal wallpaper of windmills in La Mancha and a selection of icons around the edge. Gillian involuntarily gasped as the screen lit up. David narrowed his gaze, unable to believe what he was seeing. Instead of Quixote giants in the evening light, the screen showed what looked like a child's bedroom. There were pop posters on the walls and My Little Pony toys around the bed. In the middle of the bed was a girl. She looked about twelve or thirteen but could have been older. She was holding something like an artist's sketchpad but looked totally naked behind it except for a tiny thong and high heels. There was a message on the pad in thick crimson marker. She was looking straight at the camera and smiling. The message read: "David Hidalgo is a Dead Man."

"Welcome to the club," DI Thompson said tersely. "Every single member of my team has the same image. You're famous."

After that it was hard to get back into the party spirit. They sat in stunned silence. DC Carmichael spoke, directing himself particularly to Gillian.

"I'm sorry you had to see that. Naturally there's no question about where it came from."

"I should think not," Gillian said.

"We're working on the assumption that this came from the same source as the material on Mike Hunter's computer – that's to say PGC church or whoever's behind it. A farewell greeting, you might say. I suppose your involvement in clarifying Mike Hunter's death and pointing us at PGC… well I think we can say that hasn't been taken very kindly."

"You can say that again," David muttered, sitting down. "Can I close this thing now?"

"Of course. Sorry." DI Thompson pulled the lid shut himself. "I'm afraid we're going to have to take your laptop away. I hope that's not too inconvenient. Anything on it you need urgently?"

David gave another heavy sigh.

"Just all the notes I need for this week's Spanish classes."

"Sorry about that," Carmichael said, not looking particularly bothered. "We'll get it back to you as soon as we can. The aim is to try and find where that stuff came from, then try to link that with the money laundering."

"Have we not ascertained that already?" Gillian asked. "We know that Mike's computer was infected from some server in Belarus."

Thompson took over.

"I'm afraid our guys in Cybercrime haven't been able to replicate what your source found so that's still to be confirmed. However, as soon as possible we want to convene a case conference and pull all the threads together. Normally that's an in-house affair, but given that you both have been so involved the DCI wants you both included if you don't mind."

David nodded wearily and looked at Gillian.

"When?" she asked.

"As soon as possible. Probably Friday morning. Maybe ten-ish?"

Gillian pulled out her iPhone and did a few quick taps.

"Can't do ten," she said. "Eleven thirty?"

"Ok," Thompson agreed. "Let's aim for that. It'll depend on everybody else being able to make it. We're bringing in pathology, the finance boys, and Cybercrime. And Alexander Benedetti is pleading guilty to all the banking charges and says he wants to give as much assistance as he can. So we're going to include him as a key witness, which will probably not do him any harm when it comes to sentencing. Now, finally, your mysterious master hacker: do you think he'd be willing to speak to us?"

"I very much doubt it," David admitted. "Let's say he operates a bit under the radar."

"Well, we know who he is from the reports after the shooting. Maybe we'll just have to be persuasive."

At this it looked as if the meeting was over until Gillian pushed the door shut again.

"Just a minute," she said. "Is there not something we're forgetting? A threat has been made against my fiancé's life. Right now what that image had to say bothers me more than where it came from."

"Of course; I should have mentioned that. We do take it seriously. We think it would be a good idea if you could drop out of circulation for a bit, David. We've got somewhere safe you can stay for a few days – at least until Friday. DC Carmichael will make the practical arrangements. So that's it from us. Sorry to be party poopers."

The celebration was still in full swing as David, Gillian, and the two detectives emerged but it was immediately obvious that something had changed. Gillian tried to keep up a smile but didn't fool anyone and David was looking grim and pale. He whispered briefly in Juan's ear, then tapped a teaspoon against a half-empty cava glass and thanked the company for showing up and all their good wishes.

There was still a mountain of food to be eaten but something had come up and he and Gillian would have to head off a bit before time. However, he would like to point out that neither of them had been arrested, that Juan was not in trouble for his VAT, and that none of their cars had been clamped. What exactly had turned up he didn't say, so the ripple of laughter was a bit half-hearted.

Fifteen minutes later they pulled up on Bruntsfield Place, behind Carmichael's unmarked car, fifty yards from David's flat. A bright yellow cherry picker with traffic cones around it was taking up three spaces opposite the front door, while a couple of guys in hi-vis jackets fiddled with a flickering street light. It didn't take long to pile a couple of days' worth of shirts and smalls and a washbag into an overnight case. With his computer and probably himself impounded, there didn't seem any point in taking his Spanish class handouts but he stuffed them in anyway, just in case. Probably a phone call to the Adult Education office in the morning would be helpful to let them know what was going on. "Couple of days?" he asked DC Carmichael. "Probably better till further notice'," Carmichael replied without batting an eyelid.

Then, just as David leaned forward to give the zip on his bag a final tug, a crack like nearby fireworks rang out and the bedroom window exploded. Razor sharp shards showered the room, mixed with fragments of plaster and wood. The crash of breaking glass mingled with a scream and a shout. David instinctively grabbed Gillian's arm and dropped to the floor. Carmichael shot over to the window and pushed open the curtain edge. The cherry-picker platform was still up as the vehicle tail lights receded up the road.

"I am so fed up with this," David Hidalgo groaned, lying on the floor with his arms around his new fiancée. Gillian's eyes were closed tight as if trying to shut it out once and for all.

Chapter 15

THE BURGLAR'S TALE

Something's going on; everybody's noticed. I've been here six months but even the girls that have been here longer say they've never seen the place like this. Hard to say what it is but the minders seem nervous and there are whispered conversations all the time. Everybody seems extra keen to make sure everything stays locked; nobody's let out, even for a shopping trip. There's this old guy that books me every week – he says I should just call him Pat. Sometimes he's not quite "up to it", you might say, so we just talk. He says there's been a big thing in all the papers about a church that turned out to be a front for a bunch of criminals. When the police tried to pick them up all the birds had flown. Police are appealing for information from the public. They're saying it's all connected with drugs and money laundering and sex – which means us, I suppose. Some of the girls that look younger have said they make them get dressed up like fifteen-year-olds and get pictures taken, or they get filmed with some punter. One Sunday I thought I'd try it on a bit and asked one of the minders if he was planning on going to church today; his response was a slap across the face. I take that as confirmation. So this whole thing hides behind a church – what an idea. Who would think a church could be involved in what we have to do day after day? But then, nobody signs a receipt when you drop money in the plate; it only gets recorded when you count it. So if you've got a couple of thousand extra from some other source you don't want to mention, what's to stop you dropping that in too? No questions, no paper trail. Perfect. And that explains odd things people say around here. If you do something wrong Max might say something like "for all have sinned and fallen short of the glory of God". Once I was complaining about a customer and refusing to see him again and Max just said smiled and said, "I urge you, sister, in view of God's mercy, to offer your body as a living sacrifice, holy and pleasing." If that's from the Bible then this place is even sicker than I thought.

How they hide the amount we're making I have no idea. Pat once said he pays £200 an hour for me. That's quite an expensive chat some weeks. Actually, there are times I feel kind of sorry for him. His wife died two years ago and he says he's never got over it. They hadn't had sex for years before that anyway so it's a wonder he remembers how. He just seems really lonely. Anyway, the weeks he is up to it he just rolls over afterwards and you can ask him anything. So £200 times the number of punters each of us has in a week. Four or five a night, times six nights, times six girls. I make that about £30,000 a week. Multiply that by the number of houses and fifty weeks a year. You can do the math. That's going to be some account that'll need special treatment before it gets to be clean money. Even in Belarus they've started tightening things up so it's bound to be tougher here. Anyway, like I said, something's going on. I hope they get them all but I'd like half an hour with a lead pipe with each of them before they make it as far as court. Then they wouldn't need lawyers. They could take what's left out in a cardboard box.

One of the guys, Dimitri, has been particularly nervous. He's incredibly overweight and just goes around the place sweating and puffing and losing things. Last night the phone in the office rang and he was in such a hurry to answer it he left the door open and his keys in the lock. It just took a couple of seconds for them to end up in my pocket. When he finished the call he started looking for his keys, couldn't find them, and went totally ballistic. He was shouting and swearing in Russian, grabbing anyone in sight and smacking them around like crazy. One of the other minders had to pull him off Irena or he would have killed her. Of course by this time his keys were at the bottom of a bottle of shampoo in my locker. When he couldn't find them, first he was shouting and swearing, then he just sank down on the floor and started crying. "He's going to kill me," he kept saying. "He's going to kill me dead." I had Pat that night so I asked him if he could do me a favour. Pat thinks I'm his friend. I told him I needed a couple of keys cut so that all the girls could at least have their own locked drawer to keep personal stuff in. "Do they not even get that?" he said. "That's a crime. It's not like you're slaves or anything, are you?" He agreed so I told him I would have something really special lined up for him next week. I could hardly eat anything till his time came round again. He did a big wink when I came into the lounge where the punters wait. I could have killed him then and there. But he gave me the keys. I put the originals back where Dimitri would find them. He was just so relieved he didn't seem to wonder where they had been for their holidays.

I waited till the next night to use the new set. I took Elvira with me for company. She's twenty-seven and been here a year. She's worried what's going to happen next since she gets fewer and fewer bookings. That's one of the crazy things this place does to your head. You hate having to do what the punters want but you're afraid of what's going to happen when nobody wants you any more. There's not exactly what you'd call a pension plan here. We met outside my room at 3 a.m. I thought my heart was beating so hard they'd hear it upstairs. At that time of night there's only one security guy on the door upstairs and they keep one girl awake just for any latecomers – so to speak. We got to the office and tried the keys. We were on to the last one before it turned. I thought none of them was going to work. We didn't dare turn the light on. There's just a desk, a computer, and a filing cabinet in the office. They obviously think the place is so secure there isn't any need for more. They probably think we're idiots that can only do one thing. Elvira started looking through the filing cabinet while I tried the computer. These guys are such morons. I just touched a key and got the home screen with an Excel spreadsheet – no password or anything. I used Excel all the time for the accounts when I was working with Andrei so this was a breeze. It wasn't even a very complicated set-up. Just one tab per house. Columns for girls and lines for nights. Each cell had the name of a punter – or whatever name they gave. That was disappointing too. I looked at my column. Big Boy, Bazooka, Gusher. Not very imaginative and certainly not very accurate – I should know. Actually each girl had three columns. Name, rate, and "Special". So last week Bazooka paid a 20 per cent surcharge for – well, I won't say for what. It's too humiliating. When this is all over I'm going to make sure I track down every single last punter and give them a "Special" they won't ever forget. Free. Then at the end of each week there are totals for each girl. It looked like if it was less than £6,000 it showed up in red. Elvira had a few greens early in the year but after that it was all red. There was a yellow comment flag against her most recent total. It just read "Retirement?" I didn't show her it.

That spreadsheet confirmed what we thought. There are seven houses listed. It looks like we are the main house where all the records are kept. The guys that run this operation are so crap-for-brains. Andrei and I could have shown them how to run a proper illegal business in our sleep. Each house even had a name: Salamander, Craigmillar, Muirhouse, Wester Hailes, Granton, and Victoria Quay. I've picked up enough about Edinburgh to know what that means. One to five are the poorest areas of town where there's going to be the least chance of standing out and the best chance that police won't care. Victoria Quay is where all the government offices are, along with the top guys with money to burn and influence. I wonder if they think they're a better class of customer? I've had a few. I can tell you they're not – just a nice Burberry coat over the same brutal, heartless wretches. Anyway, this was interesting but wasn't giving us anything we needed. Then Elvira tapped my shoulder. "Look at this," she whispered and handed me a document. I held it up in the light of the computer screen. I couldn't believe it – names, titles, phone numbers, email addresses, even IP addresses. It was on two pages. The first page was called the White List. Unless I've got it completely wrong, it looked like all the great and the good who'd had the pleasure of our services. Titles were things like JP, MP, MSP, MEP, QC, CID, then names of girls and houses – I suppose these were their preferences – and next, a percentage. It wasn't clear if that was a discount or what they paid: eighty, fifty, twenty, or zero. It doesn't take a genius to know what that might be worth in the wrong hands. The second page was called the Black List. This time it was only names and IP addresses. No titles but some had designations – journalist, police, academic, banker. I only had time to notice the couple of names at the top. "Mike H: Banker" had a red line through it. The next one was "David H: Pastor". By this time I was shaking so badly that every creak or noise outside made me jump. My mouth was dry, my shoulders stiff. I looked at Elvira and nodded towards the door. She closed the filing cabinet. On an impulse I shoved the document down my jeans. I know that was crazy but it just seemed too valuable to leave behind. We tried to leave everything else exactly as it was, then pulled the door carefully shut and headed back to our rooms. We paused at Elvira's door. She gave me a brave smile and we had a hug. I think we felt like the little shepherd boy when the first stone landed in Goliath's forehead.

I was nearly back to my door when a heavy hand landed on my shoulder.

"What have you been up to, little lady?" said a voice. I almost collapsed right there. It was Boris, who does security on weeknights.

"Are we not even allowed to go the toilet any more?" I asked.

"Fully dressed?" he shot back.

"There was a Special on tonight," I bluffed. "That's what he wanted. Normal clothes and a nice slow strip."

"That was hours ago. You should be getting your beauty sleep."

"Well, we took a little coke. I couldn't sleep. Is that against the rules?"

"Get back in your room; I'll have to log it – unless we have another little Special right now. I quite fancy a nice slow strip. Just you and me."

"Oh come on, Boris," I said. "You know that's against the rules."

"For me they're more like guidelines," he said and pushed me against the door. "There you are, Princess. Do you want it logged or not?"

The thought of that hulking brute at almost four o'clock in the morning turned my stomach. And I needed to hide the lists somewhere until I could figure out what use could be made of them.

"Just a minute, Boris. Wait here till I get ready. I think I can give you something you'll like." You could see him beginning to water at the mouth, big, greedy eyes looking me up and down. "Just a few things to get sorted," I said, went into my room, and closed the door. First of all, what to do with the document? Sometimes there are searches if something goes missing. They rip your room to shreds. There's nowhere that's safe. I'd noticed a peeling length of wallpaper that week. I wondered if it might just peel back a little bit more then maybe seal up. Surely they wouldn't take the wallpaper off the walls. The bottom edge felt loose. Gently ease it away. Then the two sheets slipped inside. No chance to seal it down yet but maybe no need. I didn't plan to be entertaining Boris this evening. Now over to the washbasin. This was going to be desperate but I needed something convincing. The shampoo bottle that I hid the keys in was lying with the lid off. I grabbed it and didn't let myself stop to think, just gulped down two huge mouthfuls and opened the door smiling at the slavering Boris. I just had time to put my arms up around his neck when the liquid hit my stomach and came up quicker than it went down. Boris got it full in the face. I think his mouth was actually open at the time. Green slime dripped down his cheeks and chin, and his shirt was covered. I fell onto my knees and kept on retching for real while Boris took a step back and started wiping his face with his hands, making the most disgusting groaning noise.

"I'm so sorry, Boris," I managed to gasp. "I think it must have been the coke on an empty stomach. I'm really sorry."

"You filthy animal," he managed to splutter. Apparently he didn't enjoy tonight's Special after all. The vomit and the retching was 100 per cent real and so was the smile on my face as I watched him reeling from one wall to the other, still spitting and groaning in search of a washroom. With a bit of luck he would stink till the relief came in at nine o'clock and then he'd have some explaining to do.

The next time I saw Dimitri he was very pale. His eyes were bloodshot and he had a huge bruise on his left cheek. He spent his entire shift going through every paper in the lounge, then we could hear shouting and swearing in Russian from the office. Then they started the search. By that time I'd managed to seal the wallpaper with a thin film of Nestle's milk – when it dries it's better than glue – and Boris didn't report me. They never said what they were looking for and they found some things the girls had hidden but they didn't find the document. I haven't seen Dimitri since then and I hope my suspicion of what's happened to him is right. Elvira and I speak in whispers at breakfast or in the afternoon when a lot of the girls are asleep. We reckon we've got a stick of dynamite. The question is how to set it off. The top name on the Black List keeps going round in my head. Who is "David H: Pastor" and how can I warn him? If Mike H. already has a line through his name maybe David H. will be next. The way things are going this place is getting more and more jumpy. Maybe there isn't much time.

A few days later it was Elvira's birthday – you know, the one day in the year you're supposed to be special and everybody pays attention to you. She just cried all day. Nobody has any money here and we can't go shopping even if we did, but the girls tried to make her something. Lara is a bit of an artist and had wanted to do her portrait but couldn't find her sketchpad. Then, suddenly it appeared again exactly where she'd left it. She did a brilliant head and shoulders that made Elvira look lovely. Marta made her a beautiful paper mobile for her room and the rest of us did what we could. We made her birthday cards. That's when I got an idea.

Chapter 16

HQ

"Can't say it looks any safer than any of the others," Gillian commented, looking at the nondescript three-bedroom detached house in front of them.

"Ah well, appearances can be deceptive," DC Carmichael replied. "There's more technology in here than at Apple HQ – motion detection, body heat sensors, dampening fields for sound, secure communications, bulletproof glass, the lot, not to mention the more traditional security – two burly blokes outside 24/7."

"Sounds convincing," David said wearily. "I was tempted to think this whole thing was verging on overkill but, well, I think it maybe is required, at least in the meantime."

After the shot came through David's window they had lain on the floor, too shocked to move for a minute or more, listening to Carmichael's urgent radio call: "All patrols to look out for a yellow cherry-picker vehicle heading east from Bruntsfield at speed with at least two men on board." As they began to pick themselves up it became clear that the sticky zip David had been bending over to undo may have made all the difference. The bullet hole showed up clearly on the door lintel. Fragments of glass were showered all over the bed and the floor, but this time at least there wasn't any blood mixed with it. They carefully brushed themselves down.

"No maybes," Gillian said pointedly as they walked up the garden path. "Something is definitely required."

Carmichael let them into the safe house and immediately pointed to a control box on the wall.

"Fifteen seconds to key in your password or all hell breaks loose.

Right now it's 'SeVastoPol-969?!' – don't ask me why. And you need the punctuation and the capitals. You can change it to your own choice but then you need to let the team know. I think it's easier just to leave it unless you have a real problem with that."

David shook his head and they went on through the living room into the kitchen.

"Fridge, freezer, and cupboards fully stocked. Anything more you buy, keep the receipts. And upstairs there's a double bed made up. We'd recommend no mobile phones, no outings, and definitely no visitors. Any questions?"

There were none, so after a few minutes more wandering around DC Carmichael left them with a cheery reminder.

"Tuesday, 2 p.m., Gayfield Square – don't forget. Have fun, you two."

Gillian waited till she heard the front door go then collapsed onto the bed.

"There goes a man with a dirty mind," she commented. "If I was wanting to 'have fun' I wouldn't be doing it here." David sat on the bed next to her, then somehow as if by mutual consent they both lay back.

"I was thinking of a tour of the Paradors for the honeymoon," he remarked in an absent sort of way.

"I was thinking of the Caribbean," Gillian replied with a smile, "but once this is over I'd probably be happy with two weeks in Wigan."

David rolled half over and kissed her hair.

"You look wonderful in the moonlight, darling," he said, which made her laugh.

"Do you think Mrs MacInnes would be scandalized if I stayed with the minister in his safe house?"

"If you did, I don't suppose all that police technology would be enough to keep her from finding out. I don't think anyone's much bothered, to be honest. They love you and I think they trust me not to corrupt you."

"You know you could have stayed at my place," Gillian said, pushing herself up on one elbow.

"Of course; I know. But I've had enough of you being in the firing line by association with me. This is better; I'll survive. I noticed a DVD player down there. I can watch the first series of *Sherlock* again."

"Now that would be appropriate! But seriously – you are not Sherlock and I am not John Watson, or vice versa. We just need to get through this and get back to normal. A minister with a small congregation and a minor academic. Deal?"

"Absolutely. None of this was by choice, I assure you. But I do still wonder where all that money's coming from. Maybe we'll find out at the case conference on Friday. The normal sources of big turnover cash are drugs and sex. I think the police have been keeping on top of the drug trade recently, so that could mean prostitution. And that would probably link into people trafficking as well, which means victims from South East Asia or Eastern Europe living in slavery conditions for the pleasure of guys you might live next door to."

Gillian leaned over and stroked his hair back.

"You think too much," she said. "I know you don't go looking for trouble; it just seems to find you. And I know that it's in your nature to try to sort out something you find that isn't right. I'm not complaining – I'm proud of my upright, do-the-right-thing husband-to-be – but let's not forget each other in the middle of solving the rest of the world's problems."

David smiled back at her.

"Yet again," he said, "the good and the bad, all mixed up. I do like the sound of that husband-to-be; even Mrs MacInnes won't be able to complain, though she'll probably get you a nice, sensible, knee-length nightie for the wedding night. I have to stop myself imagining what you're going to look like."

"Don't. But if you can't think of anything, there are some fun shops on Hanover Street I could investigate."

David pulled her to him and kissed her, lightly at first, then in earnest – then as if his life depended on it.

The week David spent at the safe house might have been the longest in his life. It was like he was in a holding pattern, not going anywhere, but with Gillian banned on account of "no visitors" there was no one to hold. He missed his Spanish classes, for the company as well as the cash. They did manage a few Skype calls but decided that was an unsatisfactory way of communicating and gave it up. He even considered inviting Carmichael's "burly blokes outside" to share whatever he'd been cooking but thought that would just come over as weird and didn't. After all three series of *Sherlock*, he went back in time and watched both seasons of *Life on Mars*, then back to his younger self and the entire *I, Claudius*. In his nightmares the "prophet" of PCG, who turned out to be Maxim Blatov by name, became the smiling demon Caligula while he was the bumbling fool, "Clau, Clau, Claudius". In both the history and the drama the fool came out on top, but not in his imagination. He didn't sleep well in a strange bed, had no view, no contact with neighbours, none of the ingredients he was used to, no red wine, and he hated cooking in an unfamiliar kitchen where they didn't have all the utensils he needed. Every time he needed a sieve he had to open six cupboards to find it. Nevertheless, Friday did eventually come and Carmichael came to cart him off to the case conference. Gillian was already waiting, and despite the temptation they managed to greet each other more or less professionally.

"Detective Chief Inspector Stevenson is going to be chairing this," DI Thompson informed them as they walked down the corridor. "He'll handle the rest of the introductions. This has been a funny one – started off a suicide and some kiddy pics well within a DI's remit, and it's been moving up the food chain ever since. Now it's at DCI. Where it's going to end up goodness knows."

It was a long time since David had been in such a high-powered meeting. Sometimes in Madrid he had to advocate from recovering drug addicts at police or court meetings but not so far in Scotland. Now there was a DCI at the head of the table, the Procurator Fiscal next to him, the pathologist next to him, and a bunch of detectives he'd never seen before, as well as Thompson and Carmichael. A couple of civilian IT staff and a financial crime analyst made up the numbers. Most surprising was to see Sandy Benedetti dressed in an immaculate business suit and tie, sitting with a pile of papers in front of him. They glanced briefly at each other and nodded as David sat down. Thompson had told him on the way that Sam Hunter had been offered the chance to come in and say a few words but not surprisingly had declined. The police liaison officer who had been keeping in contact with her came on her behalf and would report back. David and Gillian seemed to complete the attendance list.

Stevenson started without further ado. He was a big man, and everything in his manner said that he was used to being in charge. It looked like the main function of any team Stevenson led was to jump when he said jump. A variety of reports had been circulated – though not to David or Gillian – and after introductions there was a quick run around the table to see if anyone wanted to elaborate. Most diplomatically declined or added just a word or two for clarification. Finally, Stevenson closed the folder in front of him, pushed his chair back a bit, and took a sip of water.

"So, what are we looking at here?" he asked, though it wasn't a question he expected anyone else to answer. "Death in suspicious circumstances – an unlawful killing, I think we're agreed." He glanced at the fiscal, who nodded cooperatively. "And another attempted on Sunday night. A bunch of obscene images doing the rounds, including to our own officers." Here he looked pointedly at the IT team, who had the grace to look down and shuffle some papers. "Mr Benedetti, I believe you have been suspended by your employer pending the outcome of proceedings. But in the meantime you are offering assistance to the investigation. Is that correct?" Sandy nodded dutifully but without much enthusiasm. "We'll hear more from Mr Benedetti in due course. And Reverend Hidalgo and

Dr Lockhart – we need to express our appreciation to you both for what you've been through. If it hadn't been for you we wouldn't even be at this point, which brings me" – David noticed the operative "me" rather than "us", as Stevenson paused for a second to consult a sheet in front of him – "to Mr Daniel McGuire, aka 'Spade'. Now, Mr 'Spade' has declined to attend today and there's nothing we can do to oblige him, but he has spoken to our IT team and I think you can speak for him. Yes? Good. We'll come to that later.

"To summarize: we have a body constituted as a church – Power and Glory – which has, until recently, held an account at Salamanca Bank. Mike Hunter noticed it was at variance with what it should have been to the tune of about £20 million. He tried to investigate but PGC were alerted to the fact; we all know with what results." Sandy studied the papers in front of him as if they were his rich Italian aunt's last will and testament.

"At the present time the account in question is virtually empty, the church is closed, properties previously occupied by the lead pastor, one Maxim Blatov, and his assistant Mikhail Lubchenco, are now vacant. DS Quinn, I believe you've been doing previous searches?"

"Yes, sir," a ginger-haired man next to David spoke up nervously. "We ran the names and descriptions and anything comparable. Not much came up until Mr Benedetti mentioned a conference he'd attended where a similar case was described. We've been in touch with Greater Manchester and managed to track it down – different names, but we're sure it's the same two men, same MO – sorry, *modus operandi* – a church as a front. First of all it seemed they were content with some small-time drug dealing, which was laundered through the church weekly offerings. Then they began a prostitution ring. Finally they got careless and began posting flyers. In fact, a retired chief inspector got one on his car windscreen, took exception to it, and got in touch with former colleagues. Manchester were doing a zero tolerance campaign at the time and took a hard line. Blatov and Lubchenco were picked up, along with some strong-arm guys, and ended up with two years and eighteen months, respectively. Six girls from Eastern Europe were found in a locked tenement half starved to death. They were eventually offered asylum on account of what they'd been through. Blatov and Lubchenco were deported when their sentences had expired, both back to Belarus."

"So that's it in a nutshell," Stevenson summed up in a satisfied tone. "That's what Blatov and Lubchenco have been linked to in the past. However, just to put it into context: DI McIntosh, you've been doing some research in this field. Can you run us through why you think people trafficking is the big ticket now rather than drugs?"

A young-looking man in noticeably more casual dress than the rest of the CID cohort stood up and made his way to the end of the room.

"Thank you, sir. As some of you may know I'm doing a criminology thesis on this right now." An inward groan from the older hands was almost audible; however, this was more in Gillian's line and she perked up. Stevenson's expression suggested he didn't expect to be riveted by the presentation but was being obliged to tolerate it. McIntosh plugged his laptop into a data projector and pressed on.

"I won't take up time with the whole background, but just briefly…" Something was muttered to David's right and he thought he could guess what it was. McIntosh looked up for an instant, took a deep breath, and pressed on, popping up a variety of bullet points, graphs, and tables as he spoke.

"So, first of all, on the negative side, we think the drug trade in Edinburgh is more or less at saturation point right now. By that I don't mean that everybody is using and there's no further demand, but that given the economic recession, focused and effective policing, a number of gangs taken out of circulation – Reverend Hidalgo will know a bit about that – restriction of supply from international seizures, and health service harm-reduction programmes, we feel that things are more or less in balance and that it would be very hard for a new high-volume player to come into the market. Besides, £20 million-worth of new supply would certainly have been noticed at uniformed level as well as by ourselves. So we don't think that PGC are primarily drug-related. The only other candidates that could possibly generate that kind of money would either be sex work or the arms trade. The arms trade is international, not local, and while vast sums are made these tend to be by traders supplying Afghanistan, Syria, and some African conflicts – so not likely to be happening in Edinburgh. This leaves the sex trade, which has been the main focus of my research.

"The next question is, what's going on in both supply and demand that might make the PGC operation feasible? Firstly, I'm suggesting that there is a general increase in demand throughout the Western world. Obviously, sex has been in demand and indeed on sale basically forever but we are currently seeing a massive increase in its commercialization, principally through the internet. Porn sites are ubiquitous, in many cases free, and becoming more and more extreme. What was once cutting-edge porn is now the norm and child porn images have emerged as the new extreme. Now there's a national specialist agency tasked with trying to make sure these don't become tomorrow's new norm."

"Any references for that?" Gillian interrupted, apparently the only one in the room actually interested in what DI McIntosh was saying.

"Certainly. Dr Gail Dines is a leading authority. I can give you more later. Anyway, the general thesis is that more men are using porn than ever before, and that generates a knock-on to greater demand for live, paid-for sex as well. It's probably all part of general consumerism but that's another story. Police Scotland is responding to this, and as we all know there have been a series of high-profile prosecutions of sauna operators in the city over the past few years. We're also taking a much harder line on the so-called 'toleration zones' for street workers, such as Salamander Street. So, to cut to the chase…"

"Thank you, DI McIntosh," Stevenson intoned, with ill-disguised sarcasm.

"Yes, sir. To cut to the chase, the equation is that demand is increasing; we are putting more and more pressure on traditional sources of supply, so there is an opportunity to fill that with coerced sex workers trafficked particularly from Eastern Europe. The Schengen agreement has made travel within the EU much easier, so once traffickers can get the girls into the Schengen area then they are more or less free to move them wherever they want. Simultaneously, the economies of many former Warsaw Pact countries have more or less collapsed, creating an increased demand for a new life in the West and a corresponding increase in the black economy."

"So, we have criminals from Eastern Europe trafficking girls also from Eastern Europe into sex-mad Western Europe kept in locked houses because we've shut down all the saunas. That it?" Stevenson interrupted.

"Yes, sir. I… eh … think that sums it up."

"Good. Now we can move on. As it happens we've had rumours of new sex premises from a number of sources, including internet chat. It all seems to add up. If the sums going through that account are all or mainly from prostitution then we must be looking at more than twenty girls. Mr Benedetti has told us about the more conventional activities of the church and I believe you've also visited, Reverend Hidalgo. Seems to be a very persuasive cover.

"So, that's what we know. Now, what we want to find out. DI Thompson, I think you've got something to guide us through that?"

"Yes, sir." Thompson stood up and made his way to the opposite end of the room from McIntosh's presentation, where a flip chart stand that David hadn't previously noticed was set up. Thompson turned the blank page over to a numbered list.

"I've listed these more in time order than order of importance," he began. "Number one: how exactly did Blatov and Lubchenco get child pornography images onto Mike Hunter's computer? We have a general picture of that from Spade but we'd like more detail, such as the nature of the enterprise in Minsk that seems to own the IP address the trojan communicated with. We'll have to liaise with the Belarusian authorities on that. Number two: exactly how was the murder carried out? Working hypothesis is that Mr Hunter was intercepted somewhere on his run, injected with a massive dose of insulin, brought back home, and hanged when he no longer had the capacity to resist. Hence no bruising to the body or signs of a struggle, no wounds, no poisons in the blood, and no murder weapon – other than a syringe and there's plenty of them lying around in the street. Mrs Hunter actually came up with that scenario." At this the locum pathologist had the grace to shuffle a bit and look embarrassed.

"Number three: where did the money vanish to? I think the IT section have obtained permission to formally contract with Spade to look into that. He seems to be our best bet. Recovery of the cash is clearly part of the objective. Linked to that, number four, the whereabouts of Blatov and Lubchenco. Ports and airports are under observation. We have no indication that they've left the country but then no indication that they haven't. Then, finally, how was that cash generated, and if it's another prostitution racket with people trafficking thrown in, then where are these girls and are they at risk?" Thompson paused for a second for questions. There being none, he sat down and studied his notes.

"So is that a fair summary, then?" Stevenson asked the room in general, hands clasped over a more than ample girth. "Before we go on to lines of inquiry and our strategy on this one we're agreed on what we know, what we don't know, and what we're aiming for: the culprits, the cash, and whatever commodity they've been selling, in that order, ok?" Stevenson paused for confirmation but couldn't resist a smile at the nice alliteration. He'd have to remember that one for the final report. Just as he opened his mouth to continue someone else spoke.

"Actually, I'm not sure I can entirely go along with that." David Hidalgo was a bit surprised by the sound of his own voice in a meeting where he'd been determined to keep quiet and let the cops get on with it.

"Go on, Reverend Hidalgo…" Chief Inspector Stevenson said slowly, the soul of professional politeness but an edge of irritation in his voice. "What's your problem?"

David cleared his throat, took his glasses off, and gave them a wipe.

"Well, I'm entirely an amateur in this and you might say only involved by accident; maybe it's just a question of words." David was sitting upright, leaning slightly forward, and speaking directly to Stevenson. It was clear this was no mere matter of terminology. There was an edge to his tone that struck a new note in the meeting.

"If you're right in saying that these guys have previously used a church to cover prostitution and people trafficking and there's a good chance they're doing the same thing here, then firstly I have a problem with the word 'commodity'." Stevenson raised one eyebrow. The rest of the meeting had suddenly woken up and was paying attention. The cops in the room were not used to seeing the boss challenged in a public setting. They watched Hidalgo to see what was coming next.

"I appreciate you're trying to cover whatever they're selling – drugs, pornography, or sexual services – but in any of these cases I think we need to keep a focus that this is about people: the addicts, the children, the girls. I just think it's unfortunate to call any of these 'commodities'. I've worked with all of these sorts of victims. When you see what it does to them – one year, five years, even ten years after – then you stop thinking about it just as a matter of buying and selling.

"And secondly…" *This is great*, Stevenson's subordinates around the room were thinking. *There's more to come*. This Hidalgo bloke was definitely not what they had expected from a minister. He spoke clearly, concisely, and pointedly and didn't seem the least phased by the big man opposite.

"Secondly, I'm not happy with that order of priority. To my mind the cash is the lowest priority and the victims are the highest. Of course the culprits need to be apprehended, but if we get the culprits and the cash but can't help the victims, then as far as I'm concerned we have completely failed. The victims are the priority. To my mind, finding out who has been exploited and damaged and helping them matters much more than the money and even more than the perpetrators."

There was silence around the table. All eyes were on Stevenson as he fiddled with his pen. The rest of CID was enjoying the experience enormously. The DCI opened his mouth but a fraction of a second too late.

"Actually, there's one more point, if I may." Now it was Gillian's turn. This was just too good. Half of the team were already imagining the conversation in the canteen at lunchtime.

"Go ahead, Dr Lockhart." Stevenson was now almost speaking through clenched teeth.

"Thank you." Gillian smiled as sweetly as if she were presenting the weather. "It seems to me that there's one other interest that hasn't been mentioned at all. We almost had a second murder two days ago, a fact no one seems to be remembering." One or two of the CID boys actually looked a bit mystified. A second murder? Who was that? Gillian pressed on.

"This investigation wouldn't be happening at all if it wasn't for Sam Hunter's insistence and what David and I have managed to find out. Now it looks like whatever else Blatov and Lubchenco are up to, David is persona non grata right now and just missed being a body, not a witness. I fully understand all the priorities you've been mentioning, but I have to say I'm somewhat surprised that security of a key player hasn't even been mentioned. As I understand it the safe house was only supposed to be until today. I'd like to know what you're planning next." David shifted a bit uneasily in his chair, cleaned his glasses again, but said nothing.

"DI Thompson?" Stevenson deflected the question to his

subordinate as if any omission was nothing whatever to do with him. Thompson in turn shuffled a bit.

"Well, no particular plan, sir," he fumbled. "I imagined we'd just continue with the safe house until we felt the risk had passed."

"Well, we appreciate that," Gillian went on sweetly, "however, with respect, we've known that PGC is a front for something illegal and probably responsible for a murder for over a week, yet they still managed to clear out the account, post further images, and take a clean shot at David right in the middle of an active investigation. And I suppose everything in the case is going to be on computer. Well, there does seem to be at least a question over the security of the police network. Wouldn't you agree?" She turned to the IT team leader who cleared his throat and was about to say something but didn't get the chance.

"So, if whoever is behind PGC can post a threat against Reverend Hidalgo right onto the screens of the team supposed to be tracking them down, I'm not sure we can regard anything else on these computers as secure right now. And that applies to the safe house as well. Only the officers concerned knew that David was going home to pack instead of being at the party when the shot was taken. We're not accusing anyone, of course," Gillian kept the sweetest of smiles, "but there does seem to be some sort of information problem. David and I have discussed the situation. We're not willing to wait for the next shot or the next computer attack. We'll be making our own security arrangements from now on. I thought it was only fair to let you know."

"I see, Dr Lockhart," Stevenson said slowly. He was not a happy man and didn't hide it. "And are we permitted to know where you're likely to be?"

"We think it would be best just to keep that on a need-to-know basis. We'll still be getting email and we'll have mobiles so we can be contacted. Now, if that's all we can contribute, if you don't mind, we've got some packing to do."

"Remind me never to get on your bad side," David said as they drove through the afternoon traffic towards Bruntsfield. "That was a scary performance. You are one awesome lady."

"I just found that guy so annoying," Gillian replied as she put her foot down and shot past a dithering tourist. "We were clearly there just to rubber stamp whatever he'd already decided. I thought I should just clarify the agenda a bit."

"Which you did with a vengeance."

"Well, they didn't seem to have any interest in what had just happened to you. I was just a tigress protecting her cubs, that's all."

"And considerably more attractive than my last cub mistress, if you don't mind me saying so."

"Don't mind a bit. I'm not willing to let them have another shot at you just when you've agreed to take me on a Caribbean cruise for two weeks."

"Did I agree to that? Oh yes, sorry. Must have slipped my mind. Will two weeks be enough?"

"I was actually planning to spend the rest of my life with you. But two weeks can do for starters."

David quickly threw a selection of bits and pieces into a case. The bedroom window had been boarded up but there were still fragments of glass lying around. Clearly ballistics didn't see property reinstatement as part of their job. He lugged it downstairs and shoehorned it into the tiny Mazda boot. Next stop was the Scots Language Department office in David Hume Tower on the corner of George Square. While none of the modern buildings came close to matching the character of the old tenement blocks, George Square library at least made a reasonable attempt, while DHT looked like it came out of the drawer labelled "cheap, ugly, and lacking in imagination". *That's what you get for being an empiricist philosopher*, David reflected, *functional, practical, and horrible*. Besides, David Hume was the man who had concocted the weakest of arguments against the possibility of miracles so he shouldn't expect one for his eponymous seat of learning. However, that notwithstanding, Becky in the office always brightened things up and sometimes managed a few miracles of her own. The entire staff were utterly intrigued with Gillian's new status – engaged to that minister, the rescuer of lost girls, drug gang buster, and now apparently involved in yet another cloak and dagger enterprise – but none more than Becky. In spare moments around the office she toyed with the idea of actually getting a dragon tattoo and waiting to see what might happen next. Maybe some dashing sleuth would sweep her off her feet as well, though David Hidalgo could hardly be considered exactly dashing, and he was a bit on the old side. Still, appearances can be deceptive. Just look at Daniel Craig – not necessarily an icon, but once he gets that shirt off walking through that surf… She felt a shudder running down her spine as she typed in the photocopier password.

Gillian Lockhart appeared at the hatch.

"Hi Becky," she said brightly. "I think you have some tickets for me?"

"Hi Gillian. I do indeed. Please come in."

"Hi Becky. How are you?" David put in, lurking in the background. "I hope asking for the extra seat wasn't a problem."

"No bother. You'll get the bill." She pulled a folder out of a desk drawer and opened it up.

"Here you are. Two seats, Edinburgh to Heathrow to Barajas Madrid, couple of hours' layover, then to Santiago de Compostela. There's a car booked for you. It's about two hours to Ribadeo. Have a nice time!"

"We will. Anything we can bring you back?"

"Yes, Antonio Banderas if possible. If not, some more of that nice *turrón* you gave me for Christmas. Yummy."

"No problem," Gillian smiled. "Consider it…"

Just then the phone rang. Becky held up a hand as if to say, just hang on till I get this.

"Hello, Scots Language Department. Can I help you? Certainly, I'll just see if she's available." Becky looked at Gillian and pointed to the phone with a question on her face. Gillian shook her head. They needed all their time to get to the airport. No point in getting caught up in something now.

"I'm sorry," Becky carried on. "I'm afraid Dr Lockhart isn't available just now, and she's going to be away for some time. Can I take a message? No, I'm sorry; I'm actually not at liberty to say where she's going or when she'll be back, but I'm sure she'll call you as soon as possible. No, I'm sorry; I'm not at liberty to give that information. No, I'm afraid that isn't possible. But if you... oh – they hung up! That was weird."

"What?" Gillian asked.

"Some bloke wanting to speak to you who wasn't at all happy that I wouldn't tell him where you're going."

"Accent?" David said, a touch more strongly than he'd meant to. "What sort of accent did he have?"

"Hmm. Not sure," Becky murmured. "Not your average. Foreign, I think. I'm not too good at that. I can get the number they called from if you like. No, it's been blocked. Funny."

"What do you think?" Gillian asked with a shudder as they headed down in the lift. "PGC?"

"Maybe. Was it Max himself on the phone? Or maybe just a colleague from some overseas university genuinely wanting to talk to you and cross that they couldn't."

"The more I think about it the happier I am we're going away for a bit. A week's conference in the sun sounds ideal. Sorry the departmental budget isn't up to booking a Parador though."

"So what have we got?"

Gillian handed him the folder as they emerged into the light of an autumn afternoon on George Square. Leaves were beginning to fall, giving the place an air of back-to-business after the summer. Lectures must have just come out to judge by the throng of students and staff. It looked like a meeting of the undergraduate branch of the UN: African, Asian, European, Middle Eastern, and every style of dress and fashion.

"I love this multicultural buzz," David commented, shuffling through the papers. "It reminds me of the more ethnic bits of Madrid. When I was growing up here Edinburgh was much more uniform."

"You should hear some of the accents in my tutorial groups," Gillian remarked. "It's just as well they don't get marked on Scots pronunciation."

"Here it is." David found the sheet and brought it to the front of the bundle. "Seems like we're not getting a hotel at all. It's the *Aparthotel O Retorno* – lounge, kitchen, bathroom, and shower, two bedrooms.

"*Retorno* – is that just return?"

"'Homecoming.' Seems like a good sign. How long are we planning on staying?"

"The conference is a week but I've given Gary the basic overview. As far as I'm concerned, we stay until it's safe to come back."

Chapter 17

THE CONSPIRATOR'S TALE

I've heard the main reason there's a problem with drugs in prison is bent prison officers smuggling them in more than relatives. Even prisoners of war used to get the guards to bring in stuff they could use to forge passports and identity papers. But I've never yet heard of a punter doing favours for a girl before – until now. The guys we have to deal with are young or old, offhand or brutal, well off or average, local or foreign. What they have in common, though, is that they basically treat you like a piece of meat. They come here with an appetite for something tasty; I get served up. They indulge themselves until they've had enough. Then they pay up and go home till the next time. Apparently we're both members of the same species but there's no human interaction – no conversation about wives and families, no chat about work or holidays or last night's TV or football scores or what books you've read. They don't want to think that you're a human being at all who might be interested in any of these things. You are a sex "facility" to be used and forgotten about till the urge comes on again and the bank account can stand it. That's the pattern, but every now and again an exception turns up. Pat is an exception.

He's probably in his late sixties. Punters don't tell you anything about their normal lives for obvious reasons, but Pat tells me everything. He says he used to run a hardware shop but then he sold it for a good profit and retired. His wife wasn't well for the last ten years of her life and he had to look after her more and more, but in spite of that he loved her and misses her. So when he comes to me, he's not trying to prove his virility or just get a kick; I think he's trying to remember what it was like with his wife when they were young. He's shown me pictures of her. She was lovely – beautiful bobbed hair in a London 1960s style and wearing the latest fashion. I know it sounds ridiculous but she reminds me a bit of Audrey Hepburn – that same petite frame and elfin face. Maybe I remind him a bit of her; I don't know. He's gentle when we're together. Maybe it's his age but he's very slow and deliberate, and he talks to me. He tells me about their life together. His shop must have done well because they travelled a lot – all the European capitals. He showed me a photo of them sitting at a table in the Champs-Élysées, another in Rome, and another in Madrid. He has copies of postcards they sent home from forty years ago. I know he'd like to ask more about me but we both know that's pointless; he doesn't want to face the fact of who I am and what I'm doing here. He just wants me to be his wife when she was twenty-three. And I don't try to confront him with the reality. We both know that if I push him he'll just clam up or go somewhere else to try to recreate his lost love. So, is he a hypocrite? Of course. Should he be charged and convicted for what he's doing? Absolutely. Is he part of the demand that leads to girls like me being tricked and conned out of our savings, our freedom, our hopes and dreams? Without a doubt. But in Pat's case it's not an entirely one-way street. Life cheated him too. He was in love. His love grew old and sick and then died. He misses her and wants to get back any reminder he can. Is that entirely wrong? For how he goes about it, yes, but not the longing itself. Even in the midst of this disgusting exploitation there's something that once was good in Pat. I think of it like a mirror that's been smashed with a hammer. What you see is distorted, shattered, fragmented, but it may still have been beautiful once.

That's why I don't take a length of cable and make a noose at one end and a knot at the other and jump off a chair like Elvira did last night. I heard the sound and barged into her room. I didn't get there in time. She had stopped breathing and her face was purple. I couldn't do anything to bring her back. I shouted for help and one of the other girls went for a minder. He just cut her down and carried the body upstairs. I have no idea where she is now – in hospital or in the river. I don't expect to see her again. It's because I still believe in the real image, not just the broken one, that I haven't given up. For my own sake, for Elvira, for all the other girls, I have to find a way out of here. That's where Pat comes in.

Last week Elvira had a birthday party – twenty-eight years old. I suppose there's never going to be another one now. The girls made birthday cards for her. I started thinking about Andrei still in Belarus. It'll be his birthday soon. I was thinking I'd like to send him a card just to let him know I'm alive. The last time he saw me was when I was getting on that bus. Maybe he wonders why I don't contact him. Maybe he worries that something has gone wrong but he doesn't know what or how he could help. If only I could send him a little card signed "from Tati", at least he would know I'm not dead. Then he might try to follow the trail and see where it leads. I know he liked me. Maybe he was even in love with me but he knew I was going to leave him so he didn't make a fuss. If he knew I was in trouble I think he would do whatever he could to find me.

So that's what I've decided to do – send him a birthday card. I made it out of a sheet of paper from Lara's sketchpad. I drew a picture of a forest with a castle in it on the front. If you looked carefully there's a girl behind the window of the highest tower but the window has bars on it. Inside I wrote him a message. His English was never that good so it's in Belarusian. If Max or Mikhail find it they'll probably kill me anyway so I didn't see any point in saying anything other than the truth. I told him everything that had happened as briefly as I could. And I told him about the White List and the Black List, and "Mike H." with a red line and "David H: Pastor", who was next on the list. If David H. is on the Black List, he may be my only friend in this country, even though he doesn't even know I exist. He must be some sort of threat to Max and Mikhail or he wouldn't be on the list. What has he done? What does he know? Is there a way he could help? So I told Andrei that sometimes we get let out to go shopping if we need something new for a Special night. There's one coming up in a fortnight. It's going to be a really big deal. Silvia heard Boris talking about it to another of the minders. He said it's for a bunch of VIPs and that fifteen girls are going to be needed. He was saying what he'd give to get a piece of the action. I'm going to tear up as much of my stuff as I can; I'll try and make it look like some punter did it, which happens pretty often. I'll say I can't do a Special until I get new stuff. He has to take me shopping. When we do go out we always go to the same place – Sally-something on the main street. And it's always on a Thursday afternoon. Mikhail once got drunk at a Special and told me I'm "quality" and that they get 25 per cent more for me than the other girls. "That's why you get to wear nice stuff," he said. So, I'm going to make it work for me. I'll tell Andrei to try to find someone who's a pastor in Edinburgh called David and second name starting with H. There was also a computer IP address on the list so I put that in too, though what good that might do him I have no idea. Then I'll tell him to get David to be at that shop at the time I say. I'll try to get out then. I don't know how I'll recognize him but maybe I'll have good luck. I'm certainly due some. Then the hardest part. I'll ask Pat to post it for me, to my brother to wish him a happy birthday. If he gives it to Max or Mikhail I'll probably end up as dead as Elvira. If it doesn't arrive or is late or Andrei is on holiday or has moved or doesn't open his post regularly or can't find David H. or if I can't get out that day or we go to a different shop or David doesn't show up – a million ways it can all go wrong; only one way for it to work. If there's a God in heaven I need it to work. I need a break. If Pat posts it I'll show him how grateful I can be.

Chapter 18

RIBADEO

There was something about landing on Spanish soil that made David Hidalgo feel grounded metaphorically as well as physically. There hadn't been time to get out of the airport in Madrid, so as the Iberian Airbus A320 landed in Santiago de Compostela and they collected their bags and finally got out into the sunshine, David felt a weight lift off him and breathed a sigh of relief. On the one hand he was sorry that they were going to be away for Mike's funeral, but on the other hand they needed to find somewhere safe and this just seemed too good an opportunity to miss. Gillian was having to be there and he could tag along till things calmed down. Juan, Alicia, Mrs MacInnes, and all of Sam's own congregation would be there for her. No, this felt like the right thing in the circumstances.

Still, it wasn't as if nothing bad had ever happened to him in Spain. The whole Álvarez affair had been played out around Toledo, one of his favourite cities, and his deeper personal tragedy happened in Madrid. It was just that everything somehow seemed more manageable in what still felt like his own front yard rather than elsewhere. Edinburgh was a fantastic city and he could operate perfectly well in Scottish culture, but he knew that, in a pinch, under the skin, he was more Spanish than Scots, and landing in Spain felt like coming home. Galicia in particular was a special kind of homecoming since his grandparents had lived on the Lugo coast – what the locals called *A Mariña*. So even when his father was still persona non grata in Franco's Spain, he was sent to spend the long, hot summers with his grandparents on the beaches of Viveiro, Foz, Barreiros, and Ribadeo. A trip to Lugo, A Coruña, or Santiago was a treat, but Ribadeo was where they had lived, so naturally he thought it the most attractive town on the coast. Now Gillian had a week's conference on the status of regional languages around the Celtic fringe, hosted right in Ribadeo. Perfect.

Despite all of Juan's protestations about luck, he felt they were definitely due a lucky break, and if Edinburgh wasn't safe, he couldn't imagine a better place to be. No doubt the fine constabulary of Edinburgh would track down the gangsters behind Power and Glory soon enough, uncover the location of the brothels bringing in the money (if that's what it was), find out if these were simply local girls with drug habits to fund or illegally trafficked foreign nationals, give them the help they needed, and wrap the whole thing up. Next he knew it he would be reading about it in *The Scotsman* and the *Evening News* or watching Max and Mikhail being hustled into court under blankets on *Reporting Scotland* and that would be that. So the fact that they needed somewhere to lie low for a bit and that Gillian had been delegated to attend a week's event here seemed a no-brainer. While she was presenting results of her research on how Scots influenced and was influenced by standard English in vocabulary, grammar, pronunciation, and idioms, he could swan around the waterfront and the park, sit out on the *terrazas* of El Cantón, wander through the shopping streets on Villafranca and San Roque, and generally just chill out. After the strain of the past few weeks he felt he needed it. Chilling out, swanning around, and hanging out were normally not very high on the Hidalgo agenda but this time he would make himself slow down and watch the world go by. The first priority was therefore to get the hire car, get out of the city and onto the *autovía*, find their accommodation, and start relaxing in earnest. But Gillian had other ideas.

"We're surely not going to leave Santiago without looking at the cathedral?" she asked, aghast. "The Camino is the most famous pilgrim route in Europe – and the oldest – and the cathedral is where they all heading for. We can't miss it." So it turned out the first thing they were looking for once they collected the hire car was a car park.

As soon as Gillian set foot on the cathedral plaza, she realized how unprepared she was for what lay in front of her. The builders and sculptors seemed to have set themselves the challenge of not leaving any stone undecorated. Instead of a simple set of steps leading up to the entrance portico there was an elaborate twin flight of steps, each doubling back on itself, all inside a framework of ornate metalwork and railings on its way to the top and the incredible entrance arch. Then inside, the supposed relics of St James set in yet more ornate architecture and stonework, all beneath a soaring vaulted ceiling and a panoply of angels and demons. Not content with one architectural gem, the other side of the square had felt the need to set up in competition and claimed the oldest continuously functioning hotel in the world in the Hostal dos Reis Católicos. In fact, in every direction the whole city centre seemed to be like a sprawling outdoor museum or a history of Catholic piety and veneration in stone. And the throng of pilgrims lent a new meaning to the term "Catholic Mass". The sheer number was impressive, but the most surprising thing was how unlike typical visitors to Spain they looked. Instead of standard beach and bar wear of T-shirts and shorts, the pilgrims looked as if they were just out of boot camp and were about to feature in an episode of *Ray Mears' Extreme Survival*. Each one seemed to have their backpack, sturdy walking boots, wooden walking sticks or hi-tec aluminium poles, North Face jackets, and Aussie head gear. Gillian found the cathedral impressive but the pilgrims even more so.

"There must be more than 500 of them in the square and the cathedral," she mused, "times 800 kilometres each. That's a lot of walking. I hadn't realized that piety was so popular."

"Not everyone does it for religious reasons, though," David remarked. "In fact, it's probably the minority. It's just a different sort of holiday for some – a rite of passage, self-discovery, open yourself to the infinite, meet interesting people, connect with history, and a heap more. But you're right, it's an interesting phenomenon. Even though I wouldn't say it's particularly religious for most, you'd

172

have to admit there's a spiritual component. They're looking for something, even though most of them might not be that interested in organized religion."

"I think it's more than interesting," Gillian said, pulling out her iPhone and taking shot after shot, mainly of the people with the stone as a backdrop rather than the other way around. "This is the exact antithesis of those who think that science has the answers to everything, and anything you can't prove and measure is meaningless."

"Wasn't there was some Nobel physicist who said that science answers all the boring questions very well but doesn't even attempt to answer the interesting ones? That's to say, it does the whats and how manys but doesn't even look at the whys. So maybe a lot of these folk are a bit like Sandy Benedetti, trying to make sense of it all, just not entirely sure where to look, so they give this a shot. I'm sure there are revelations on the way – that they go home enriched and fulfilled."

"As well as those who go back to the office still searching."

"I can cope with that. The only thing that frustrates me is not searching – not even thinking these are important questions, just taking things at face value and not looking any deeper."

"Ros."

"Sorry?"

"My sister, Ros. You've just described her to a tee."

They spent another hour or so wandering around, did the short version of the tour, tried to ignore a certain amount of inevitable tackiness (*Your Cathedral need you become a friend €25*), then were on their way to find a bar when David noticed the time and thought they'd better get a move on.

"Still a couple of hours' driving to go," he said. "I'd like your first view of Ribadeo to be in the daylight."

They tracked down the car again and finally made it out of town. Having only seen Madrid and the south, Gillian was surprised how green and growing everything was: green fields, woodland, dairy cattle, hills and valleys, instead of baked-dry plains and the remains of bleached-white scrubby grass around the feet of ancient gnarled olive trees.

"It's actually quite a lot like Scotland," David commented. "The rainfall in Galicia isn't too different from the Highlands; it's just that it tends to fall on fewer days. At this time of year you get a torrential downpour, then ten days of sun, instead of overcast and drizzle nine days out of ten."

"And warmer," Gillian added.

"Yes – which does make a big difference. My granny used to consider it profligate if she had to turn on the heating before Christmas."

There were a couple of ways David could have gone but he favoured the short route and headed straight for Baamonde, then Vilalba, before hitting the coast at Foz and following their nose along the A8. Gillian was glad she wasn't driving so she could gaze out of the window at rolling hills and plummeting valleys as the road took them up into the clouds over spectacular bridges and viaducts.

"Switzerland," she said as they passed the cathedral town of Mondoñedo far below. "It's exactly like Switzerland without the snow."

"You should visit País Vasco," David replied. "That's even more so. I think they own the copyright on mountain scenery and the Swiss have to pay an annual licence fee."

Half an hour later they were at the sea.

"The Bay of Biscay," David said, pointing. "Or the *Mar Cantábrico*. Take your pick."

"All depending on whether you're looking south or north I suppose," Gillian added.

"Exactly. Like Frances Drake. He's a hero to Brits but to the Spanish he's *La pirata Drake*. It all depends on your perspective."

"Or like DI Thompson?"

"How's that?"

"Well, I suppose from his perspective he was being cautious and not multiplying hypotheses. From our point of view he simply refused to see what was staring him in the face."

"You mean the suicide that wasn't one?"

"Exactly. I was beginning to think he was being deliberately obtuse."

"Which reminds me – I never asked what you were meaning in that dramatic exit speech at the case conference. Were you just suggesting that the police computers had been hacked – which we know – or that someone was deliberately leaking information?"

"Leaking information and obstructing the investigation."

"Really. Is that what you think?"

"I've no idea. I think I was only meaning the computers. But Charlie Thompson did take a lot of convincing to consider Mike's death in another way. The guys that shot through your window could just have been waiting on the off chance; they could have seen something on a computer report or they could have been tipped off."

"Depending on your perspective."

"Indeed. You know you should publish something on 'The Power of Perspective'. It could enter the language like 'The Tipping Point' or 'The Wisdom of Crowds'.

They drove on a few more kilometres in quietness, then David indicated, pulled off the motorway, and drove through a series of roundabouts and links that seemed to loop around the town coming in from the inland side.

"Look," Gillian pointed. "Parador Hotel. Pity the university doesn't see how important it is for staff to get the best accommodation and service."

"Well, it must be the best because this is where Franco came for his summer holidays. Stayed in the Parador and went fishing when he wasn't signing death warrants."

"Nice. Maybe I'm glad we're going somewhere else."

The car they had hired had GPS but David had turned it off as soon as they were out of Santiago. Now he held up the address on a document Becky had given them in one hand and navigated deftly with the other. Before long he pulled up in front of a tall, narrow-looking section of a four-storey block.

"Aparthotel O Retorno," he announced. "¡Bienvenida Señorita!"

Spade drummed his fingers on the desk and looked balefully at the document in front of him – a contract to provide investigative and analytical services for Police Scotland. Talk about sleeping with the enemy. Police Scotland, and England, and USA, and everywhere else were exactly who he spent his normal working life avoiding. It wasn't that his business was supporting criminals doing criminal-type things and trying to hide it from proper law enforcement; it was just that how he found out what his clients wanted to know often did involve looking under rocks the government said were out of bounds. So, if Bad Guys A keep a bunch of secrets under Rock X, they may be, strictly speaking, within their rights to say, "That rock belongs to me and anything underneath it is private." On the other hand, if what they kept under it was going to crawl out in due course and damage or destroy fairly decent start-up IT Company B, then maybe it was morally reasonable to give start-up blokes some help into poking around and turning over some rocks now, rather than later once the damage has been done – legally wrong but morally right. Not that different, in fact, from Bernstein and Woodward chatting on the phone with W. Mark Felt, then known as Deep Throat, in a search to uncover what Nixon's aides were up to that night in the Watergate Hotel. The leaking of insider information was just as illegal then, and the powers that used to be at the White House would have cut off Felt's balls without hesitation had they been sure of his identity; the fact that he took a risk and that the *Washington Post* was willing to publish it brought down Nixon and proved a turning point in investigative journalism. Spade knew he wasn't as photogenic as either young reporter, but he liked to think he was in much the same business. In any case, an increasing proportion of his work seemed to be for corporations frightened of being hacked and losing valuable data who were willing to pay a friendly hacker big bucks to find all possible weaknesses and points of entry and stop them up. So that wasn't only morally right; it was actually legally ok too. But it was still a different matter from a deal with the guys who would probably prefer that he didn't exist at all.

He was worried: to sign or not to sign – that was the question. The zombies the police employed as so-called IT investigators hadn't even been able to understand the printout he'd given David Hidalgo, never mind catch the ball and run with it, so they had come back to him. In fact, they had even wanted him to attend a friggin' case conference like some sort of technical office boy. He had told them they could stick that invitation where the sun don't shine. But now he had a dilemma. He had had to relinquish as evidence the little red USB stick David Hidalgo and Gillian Lockhart had brought him, but its contents still troubled him. There was a lot that was troubling about this whole affair. Spade was used to fiddling around in anonymous servers kept in racks in warehouses in Cupertino or Shanghai. He was not used to people getting murdered a couple of miles away and nasty blokes keeping houses full of young women prisoner for fun and profit. The police were asking for his help in putting a stop to it and getting the bad guys – not a bad aim in itself, but once you started talking to the enforcers there was no telling where it might stop. Would they cotton on to some of the other things he did for a living and want to do a little enforcing in relation to that as well? The contract would probably be quite remunerative but frankly his needs were few and the safe under the desk was stuffed with fifties so what would he be gaining? Nevertheless, the idea of locking up those responsible and helping the girls get out and either go back home or try to stay and live a normal life in Edinburgh did appeal. David had contacted him after the case conference to let him know what was going on and that seemed to be the agenda. PGC were the bad guys and some pair called Blatov and Lubchenco certainly deserved to have their balls cut off. What to do, what to do? The aim was good but he wanted nothing to do with the authorities who needed his help to fire the gun.

He flicked to iTunes to find something to calm his thoughts and provide some inspiration. He'd heard that some people would open their favourite book – be it the Bible or Shakespeare – and take whatever advice it gave as mystic guidance. iTunes served that purpose for Spade. What would he get today? Elvis Costello – interesting. And of Elvis's output shuffle had chosen Spade's favourite – his debut on Stiff Records, *My Aim is True*. Oddly appropriate. "Welcome to the Working Week" simply reminded him to get on with things and not delay. Not really much of a help. *Thanks Elvis. I already know that.* He knew he wasn't a "Miracle Man" but he did own up to some "Sneaky Feelings". If he didn't do anything he'd no doubt end up feeling "Less Than Zero". There was simply no point in "Waiting for the End of the World" or just standing by and "Watching the Detectives". He clicked back to his favourite track again, "Alison", which contained the line, "My Aim is True." Spade had never been interested in religion other than as a backdrop to Black Sabbath records. But since David Hidalgo's visit he had started reading, just out of curiosity. Now a saying of Jesus came to mind that seemed to sum things up very well: "Nothing is hidden that will not become evident, nor secret that will not come to light." He made up his mind. It didn't really matter who else was aiming. Spade Enterprises was going to join in the duck shoot. Blatov and Lubchenco would wish they had never been born. But first he would have to call in a few favours from a pal in Minsk.

Andrei didn't get many birthday cards. He had more or less lost touch with his family these days. There was one older brother who had gone into politics and was always off being Very Important. Another had taken over the family farm once his dad had finally drunk himself to death. He only seemed to be interested in dairy yields and turnips. His mum had never recovered from years of abuse from his useless, drunken father and simply sat in the kitchen rocking back and forth, drinking tea from an ancient samovar and reading Pushkin. So who was there to send him a birthday card? In particular, who would have sent him a birthday card from Britain? He could only think of one person and found his fingers were shaking as he ripped open the envelope. It was a home-made affair with a childlike drawing of a forest and a castle on the front on rough sketchpad paper. As he opened the simply folded sheet and began to read he found he needed to sit down. Tati, Tati, my beautiful, lovely, joyful, sweet, funny Tati. What have they done to you? What have they put you through? How could anyone take such a rose and stamp it into the ground? He felt the tears pricking his eyes but he wasn't sure if they were of compassion or rage. How dare they even touch such a holy thing, never mind what they had forced her into. Andrei's business had been going very well, thanks to the firm foundations laid when Tati had been with him. Despite the potentially higher profits, he had steadfastly stayed away from the more powerful and addictive substances. His lines were strictly for fun. And he had even been branching out into legal and legitimate business – how weird was that? He secretly knew she would approve. It gave legitimate employment to half a dozen locals, all with their own dreams. From the moment he read what was in the card every ounce of spare energy, all his research capacity, and all the money his business was making would be devoted only to one goal: finding Tati and paying back in full for what they had taken from her. But first he had to find "David H: Pastor". He had a hacker buddy in Minsk who might help.

Max Blatov sat at his desk and smiled.

"You're getting things out of proportion, Mikhail," he said. "It's a setback, nothing more."

"How can you say that, Max?" the younger man demanded. "Getting rid of Mike Hunter was supposed to be the end, not the beginning. Now Benedetti's talking to the police, we've had to move funds, the case conference named us both and linked it all back to Manchester, the church has had to close, and you call it a setback! And all because of that interfering little priest Hidalgo."

"Calm down, *syabar*," Max said calmly, still smiling. "Look on the bright side. We still have access to all the computers, not to mention live contacts. There are too many high-profile customers who would go down with us. It's not going to happen, believe me."

"How can you be so sure?" Mikhail insisted, stubbing out an only half-finished cigarette and lighting another. "The number of CID guys on the books is irrelevant while Hidalgo is still out there. That dumb-ass Dimitri missed a sitting target so he's still in circulation. He's a loose cannon. He shouldn't be left rolling around on the deck. We need to make sure. And what happens if information gets into the wrong hands? We still don't know what happened to the lists."

"Mikhail, Mikhail, you worry over many things," Max said soothingly. "Only one thing is needful. Everything will be taken care of. Ultimately, if we have to move we will leave no trace behind."

Mikhail snorted with disgust.

"You can't be serious, Max," he said. "That's going too far. One dead body was necessary. That's too many. I think there's even a problem among the girls. Tati knows something. I'm sure of it."

"Well, Mikhail. 'Choose you this day whom you will serve.' And once you've chosen, we may all need to make sacrifices – even the lovely Tati."

The younger man fingered the scar down his cheek nervously.

"I'll have to think about it," was all he said as he got up and opened the door.

"You do that," Max said. "And while you're thinking send Dimitri in. Ah, Dimitri. Come in. I've a little job for you."

Chapter 19

SHORELINES

Dr James Dalrymple sometimes felt he was living in limbo – not quite working and not quite retired. Although he wasn't in theatre any more and he'd given up teaching, his research still wasn't complete, and he felt the need to arrive at some definite conclusions to pass on to the next generation of anaesthetists before finally calling it a day. So far it was clear that not all pounds of body mass are equal. A fifty-five-kilogram slim, fit woman was a different proposition from a fifty-five-kilogram grossly overweight ten-year-old. Different doses and safety margins applied. His research aimed to arrive at the optimal sliding scales to guide practitioners in what was only going to become an increasingly common problem. But when that was done – what then? No doubt the normal life of the fit, retired professional: a mixture of useful voluntary work, pursuing his private hobbies, and a good dose of winter sun. He'd already been brushing up his first aid to do some talks to local Scouts. Sarah was still fit and active and due to retire in the summer; there was no reason why they couldn't have a long, fulfilling retirement for many years doing things they liked. But now it was late October, the weather was closing in, and he was restless. No more sailing now, at least not in a twenty-six-foot Westerly with a dodgy engine. The squalls that came rushing up over the Pentlands or down from Fife were just too unpredictable. In the meantime, his only option was taking Maxi, their rather elderly golden retriever, for a morning walk down by the Firth of Forth, then getting on with inputting his data and crunching the numbers. Eventually a result would pop out; he was sure.

It wasn't particularly cold this morning and very still, but a chilly bank of fog lay flat over the Forth so you could barely see fifty yards in any direction. Not to worry, though; he knew their morning route well and so did Maxi. It was amazing how much fun a slightly over-the-hill dog could have with a simple stick thrown and retrieved. Still, this was what they were bred for, wasn't it – retrieving things? James picked up the slimy branch and tossed it again, towards the waterline, and Maxi dutifully bounded off into the fog to return any minute, slimy stick in mouth, for another round – apparently pointless for both of them but it gave some kind of pattern to their morning stroll other than just the walk.

"Maxi!" he shouted into the mist when she seemed to be a bit overdue. "Maxi! Where are you? Confounded dog!" Nothing. No doubt she had found something even more slimy and disgusting and was worrying away at it.

"Maxi!!"

Nothing for it; he'd have to go after her. He made a mental note to reduce her morning chocolate treats for non-compliance. As Dr Dalrymple advanced into the mist the honey-coloured shape of Maxi gradually appeared up to her chest in sea water, sniffing around some bulky object half-floating, half-beached, just on the waterline.

"What have you got there, old girl?" Dalrymple muttered, picking his way over the slippery rocks and trying not to fall his length in the mud. He was never sure, looking back, at what point he realized what he was seeing. One minute he was trying to get his dog to disconnect from some bag of rubbish washed up on the beach; the next he was up to his knees in icy water dragging a body above the waterline. Also, just as imperceptibly, he clicked into A&E mode – like riding a bike, they say. He got his hands under her armpits – for it was a she – and half-lifted, half-dragged, the body above the waterline to where he could find a level spot. He took off his waterproof Barbour, laid it down, and pulled the body onto it. Then he ripped away the rubbish bag half-enclosing her body. It was then he first noticed the black cable ties around the wrists and ankles. He found himself using language his wife would not have approved of. Female, between twenty-five and thirty maybe, blonde, Caucasian. Her skin was freezing cold to the touch. Breathing? Hard to say. Brief and shallow, if at all. Feel for a pulse. Nothing at the wrist, so go to the neck. Maybe something. Also hard to say, so five immediate rescue breaths, mouth to mouth. Then CPR. Thirty compressions, then two more breaths. He remembered the routine was supposed to be "till help arrives" but he had left his damn phone behind, very few people were about at this time in the morning, and in the fog, and who was going to see him anyway? So, thirty more, then two, then another thirty, then two. At the third cycle she suddenly gave a cough and spewed up a mouthful of water. Then a gasp, followed by being sick in earnest. Dalrymple got her over into the recovery position and took off his thick woolly sweater to wrap around her. Now she started moaning and convulsing – not good, but better than no response.

Being a moderately fit 63-year-old walking the dog is one thing; carrying a 120-pound dead weight half a mile to the car was quite another. With just barely enough strength, he managed to get her up in a fireman's lift and set off. Three or four times he slipped and narrowly missed twisting an ankle. He also began to notice how wet his feet were and how cold he was feeling with his coat and jumper wrapped around the body over his shoulders. Maxi, seeming to realize something was amiss, trotted along beside him, tongue hanging out, constantly looking up to check.

"Don't look at me, old girl," Dalrymple managed to wheeze once they were off the rocks, over the grassy bank, and onto the road. "I've no idea either."

He laid her as gently as he could on the back seat of his Range Rover – thank goodness he hadn't brought the Midget – started the engine, and put the heater on full blast. Normally it took a good twenty minutes to get from the shore back up to the house. This morning he did it in sixteen.

"Sarah – phone for an ambulance! And get a kettle on!"

Something either in his tone or what he was saying suddenly provoked a reaction. The girl started struggling wildly, even as he was carrying her into the living room.

"No!" she shouted. "No ambulance. No police. No police."

"Ok!" Dalrymple responded, trying to keep things calm. "No ambulance. No police. Sarah! Cancel that. But hot, sweet tea as soon as you can! And some dry clothes."

Given the trembling and shaking, Dalrymple judged it more important to get the girl's wet clothes off, even if it did cause her more distress, than leave her shivering. He went for scissors and cut the cable ties as he explained to Sarah what had happened down on the shore. Half-drowned and certainly hypothermic was certain. Looks like a blow to the head as well, so maybe concussion. Her blonde hair was gathered in dark red lumps of clotted blood, but apparently no broken bones. Pupils dilated and pulse weak but breathing more regular now. A livid red scar was around her neck. Sarah Dalrymple had done enough Friday nights herself in A&E not to be phased. Together, they got the wet things off, a warm, dry, jogging suit on, two Solpadiene into her – there wasn't anything stronger in the house and it has caffeine as well as paracetamol – and some hot sweet tea. Sarah put an extra heater in the spare bedroom, turned the electric blanket on, and went to fill a bottle.

Once in bed, her body temperature began to come up as she slept. The only sign of further distress was when the dog got into the bedroom and Sarah tried to call her out. This set the girl off screaming again, so James grabbed the dog while Sarah sat with her till she calmed down. Then he phoned and cancelled all appointments for the day. The obvious – indeed only sensible – course was to call an ambulance and get her to hospital and a drip in but something made him hesitate. At the very word "ambulance" she had been near hysterical despite the little strength she had, so he decided that keeping her calm and rested was the better course. Surely thirty-five years in theatre and thirty years in A&E between them should give them enough experience to know if things were getting critical. Sarah cut the matted hair away and cleaned the wound. It seemed basically superficial, a blunt instrument blow rather than a deep cut needing stitches. They took her temperature every half hour. At 28.5°C Dalrymple and his wife exchanged worried glances; however, half an hour later it was 30, which was going in the right direction. By lunchtime she was 35.5 and no longer officially hypothermic. Every hour they managed to get another hot drink into her before she sank back into a troubled sleep. Sarah sat with her, while Dalrymple rang their son Paul, who was halfway through his Masters in sports medicine, which he knew would certainly include hypothermia treatment for skiers. He was somewhat gratified when Paul arrived and confirmed everything that had already been done.

"She should really be in hospital, Dad, don't you think?" he ventured.

"Of course, absolutely," Dalrymple agreed, without hesitation. "But the only words we've had out of her was a big 'no, no' when I asked your mother to phone for an ambulance. She roused herself enough to shout, 'No ambulance, no police, no police.' So now she's out of the danger zone, until we can find out what this is all about, I'm going to respect my patient's wishes."

"There was one other thing," Sarah said, coming through to the kitchen to refill the hot water bottle. She seemed to react to the dog going in."

"But, now I think of it," Dalrymple remarked thoughtfully, "she didn't actually see the dog, did she?"

"Wasn't it more when you called 'Maxi'?"

"Yes, I suppose you're right. So it was the name, not the dog as such. Oh, and one other thing. She was muttering something just before I came through: 'David H. Pastor'. What do you think that might mean?"

"What indeed," Dalrymple echoed and went back through to check her temperature again.

The girl slept fitfully throughout the night. Paul stayed and they took shifts.

"Just like a night passage in *Hiawatha*," he commented as his dad came in to take his watch. "But not so rolly and chances of a better breakfast."

"You cheeky whalp!" Dalrymple smiled. "Remind me to be rude about your boat when you get one."

At about eleven o'clock the following morning the girl finally opened her eyes and looked about her. Sarah was by the bedside at the time and squeezed her hand before going for her husband.

"Good morning," he said gently as he came in. "You are a very lucky girl. How do you feel?"

"Tired," she said. "Better. You find me where?"

"In the river. And it wasn't me. You've got the dog to thank." He just stopped short of calling her Maxi. Then she put him in an awkward spot.

"Name your dog?" she asked.

Dalrymple and his wife exchanged a glance but he thought he would take a risk and see what would happen.

"Maxi," he said.

Strangely, there was no reaction at all. The girl smiled and reached a hand out. Maxi came and licked it.

"Hello, Maxi," she said, smiling. "Thanking you so much."

"Would you like something to eat?" Sarah asked.

"Pliz. Yes."

"Some soup?"

"Yes. Soup."

"Maxi found you and I brought you up here," Dalrymple explained slowly as Sarah helped the patient sit up, then put a tray with soup, buttered bread, and coffee on her lap. "You're in my house. I'm a doctor; my name is James. This is my wife, Sarah; she's a nurse. And this is our son, Paul; he's a doctor too. We haven't told anyone you're here. We have not spoken to the police. You're safe here and you can stay until you're better. Do you understand?"

"Yes. Thanking you so much," the girl repeated.

"We found you in the river. Can you remember how you got there?"

The girl looked down and hungrily took another mouthful of bread.

"Yes, I remember," she whispered, looking up. "They try to kill me. I am Elvira. They try to kill me."

The entrance hall to *O Retorno* was chic in a Belle Époque style, Gillian thought; in fact, almost more Parisian than Spanish. There were white and blue large ceramic tiles up to shoulder height, then pink painted plaster above and small framed impressionist reproductions dotted about. Being in the middle of the block, there was no natural light, but a number of antique table lamps and mirrors helped. The reception counter was in dark wood as were the stairs. There was no sign of space for a lift. A pretty girl with long dark hair, an olive complexion, and almond eyes smiled at them from behind the desk.

"Hola. Buenas tardes, Señor y Señora. ¿Podría ayudarles?"

"Sí. Tenemos una reserva," David replied. *"En el nombre de Lockhart."*

"Ah. Sí. Lo veo. Bienvenidos a O Retorno."

Formalities over, David went for their cases, then laboriously lugged them up two floors. *Keeping things authentic is all very well,* he thought, banging his knees for the third time, *but a lift would be nice.* The apartment itself was lovely inside, with mustard yellow walls and more dark wood in the dining table and chairs. The little alcove kitchen was compact but had everything they might need. And there were indeed two bedrooms as advertised; Mrs MacInnes needn't have worried. Gillian immediately went to the window. The town seemed to be built partly on the flat above a steep fall towards the Ria and partly cascading down towards the water. She could just make out the masts of pleasure craft in the marina and beyond that the impressive span of the bridge that carried the *autovía* across the mouth of the estuary and into Asturias, the neighbouring province.

The girl who had checked them in gave them a quick tour of the facilities in a sort of lilting Spanish Gillian had never heard before, with some words and expressions she had difficulty catching.

"Gallego," David said once she had gone. "I think what you're here to study, Dr Lockhart."

"Yes, I guessed that. I suppose it must be like listening to the Doric for a standard Scots speaker."

"Except that they make a big thing here that it's not an accent or a dialect. It's a language, related to Spanish and Portuguese but separate and unique. Just to give you the heads up."

"Well, we say the same about Scots as well nowadays, you know," Gillian replied, wandering around and opening cupboards. "And I imagine most of the delegates will say the same wherever they're from."

"So, remind me," David continued, taking bags through to their respective rooms. "What exactly constitutes the Celtic Fringe these days?"

"Let me see if I can remember them all," Gillian began. "Scotland, Ireland, Isle of Man, Wales, Cornwall, Galicia, Brittany – I think that's it. Actually, there are those that would argue that Galicia shouldn't really be included; however, they themselves are in no doubt and are trying hard to raise the profile, hence the fact that the University of Santiago is paying for all of this."

"So we can expect a good dose of bagpipes in the cultural evening?"

"I wouldn't be surprised."

The light was clear but soft and the temperature balmy as they came out after Gillian had showered and changed. The *paseo* hour had arrived and groups of old men, young couples with children, and bunches of teenagers had begun to appear almost like flowers that only open at certain times of day, wandering around, meeting and chatting or finding a table in any of the bars around the park. Unlike many Spanish towns there didn't seem to be any main square in Ribadeo, just the park with clean, tidy gravel paths through it and little formal corners bordered by miniature hedging and one fair-sized fountain in the middle.

"Correct me if I'm wrong," Gillian remarked as they wandered hand in hand going nowhere in particular, "but there seems to be an even higher density of bars and restaurants here than I'm used to in Spain."

"You're right enough," David confirmed. "Ribadeo is a holiday town but mainly for indigenous Spaniards, so although I think it's a really beautiful spot with the Ria and the port and so on, it's almost completely unknown outside Spain – except for the pilgrims. One of the Camino routes goes through here so there are international visitors, but they tend not to stop more than one night."

"Having their sights set on Santiago," Gillian completed the thought.

"Indeed."

Before long they found a *terraza* that wasn't too crowded, close to a very impressive grand residence complete with a gilded turret, though now in very poor repair and boarded up.

"That seems a bit grand for a small coastal town," Gillian remarked, gesturing with her *caña* glass towards the tower.

"The *Torre dos Moreno*," David explained. "Galicia has typically been one of the poorest regions of Spain so lots of Gallegos would go off seeking their fortunes in the new world."

"Another connection with the Scots then."

"I suppose so. But while the Scots went to Canada and New Zealand, the Gallegos typically ended up in Cuba or somewhere else in the Caribbean or South America. Some of those that did make a fortune came back and, as is the way of these things, wanted to show off a bit. So Ribadeo has a lot of what are called *Casas de Indianos* dotted through the town, built by those who came back from the Indies. That's the biggest, but probably also the most dilapidated, right now. There always seems to be some plan to renovate it but it never seems to get any further forward. I believe they've even started a *Fiesta de los Indianos*, where everybody dresses up like returning Cuban plantation owners from 1915, then they sit about smoking Havana cigars and drinking Cuba Libres."

Gillian took another sip of her *caña*, let out a long sigh, and gazed around.

"This is just so nice," she said. "I love this outdoor life – having a drink, watching the world going by. I think I've been living on my nerves the last two weeks with everything that's been happening. I just feel it all slipping away here. And it's good to get you out of it as well. I don't suppose many newly engaged couples have their engagement party gatecrashed by the police investigating organized crime."

David didn't immediately reply, just took a sip of his beer and nibbled a little chunk of marinated pork that had come as a *tapa* with the drinks.

"You're right; I feel exactly the same," he eventually agreed. "But something you said earlier on the drive has been playing on my mind. What if PGC actually does have connections inside the police force? What if it is a people-trafficking, prostitution thing and there are those in positions of power who may have partaken and have an interest in the principal players not being brought to book? Let's just imagine a worst-case scenario – that Charlie Thompson or even somebody even more senior likes a bit on the side and now sees himself in danger of exposure if PGC goes up in smoke. The more I think about what you said in the case conference, the more sense it seems to make. He was extremely reluctant to consider another explanation for Mike's death and there was the delay in getting the financial crime team on the case, so that by the time they were involved the money had been moved. And what if someone deliberately tipped them off that I was going to be at my flat at a certain time and that might be their last chance before the safe house, then here? I'm not saying Charlie Thompson – I don't know who – but if your theory is correct then it would have to be him or somebody senior to him."

"Well, I wouldn't call it a theory," Gillian answered slowly. "For some reason I was just a bit uneasy about saying where we were going. Not sure why; it wasn't really a thought-out thing. And in order to justify that I just strung a bunch of facts together that could be interpreted in various ways. It wasn't as fully formed in my mind as you might think – or compared with what you've just said. But I can see where you're coming from."

"Where's it all going?"

"Well, if you're right, then we're in bigger trouble than I'd thought."

"Throughout the flight and even when we landed in Santiago, I was thinking, thank goodness that's all over. It's surely just a matter of sweeping it all up now, then things can go back to normal and we can get on with our lives. But if what we're saying adds up, then who knows? It could mean we're in the firing line from more than just the obvious bad guys."

Gillian caught the waiter's eye and ordered two more *cañas*. The evening light was beginning to fade. A makeshift five-a-side football space had been put together not far away using plywood sheets to keep the ball roughly in play and a dozen or so eight- to ten-year-olds were going at it full tilt. A group of girls the same age were chasing each other around on skateboards and roller blades.

"Do you know Jeff Wayne's *War of the Worlds*?" David asked out of the blue.

"A bit," Gillian replied. "I'm not really a prog rocker but I could stand an hour in the company of Justin Hayward. Why?"

"There's a line in the narration where Richard Burton talks about how safe and tranquil everything seemed just when humanity was on the edge of extinction. That's the feeling I'm getting, like I want to think it's all over, that everything'll work out fine. But there's this nagging doubt at the back of my mind that says it won't. That we've got a lot to go through yet before this is done."

"So what do we do now?"

"I don't know. For me, I think the first thing is to just be very clear about who our friends are, who the enemy is, and who we're not sure of. Then we work with our friends and keep clear of those we're not absolutely sure we can trust."

Perhaps it was the cold beer or a slight breeze that had sprung up, but Gillian felt a shiver sweep over her.

"Who do you trust?" she asked.

"Number one – you, of course," David replied. "Sam, Juan, actually Spade, I think; in the police I'm just not sure."

"Did you notice the guy that did the presentation on trafficking, McIntosh? He gave me his card just as we were leaving. You know, he was the only one that spoke in that meeting that I really felt comfortable with."

"Agreed," David said. "So maybe McIntosh in the police. Anyway, drink up. I think we're safe here at least. I have plans for Sunday lunch but we'll need to book."

DI Thompson pushed open the gents toilet door just down from his office, looking forward to a moment of blissful relief. He'd been stuck in another stupid, pointless training session for the past two hours with too much coffee going in and no opportunity for anything out. Once he stood up it hit him full force.

"Ohhh," he said, letting out an involuntary gasp of pleasure.

"All right, Charlie?" said a voice next to him.

"Oh, didn't see you there, sir," Thompson answered.

"Forget the sir; we're in the cludgie."

"Fair enough."

There was a moment of silence as both men enjoyed the feeling of not having to hold it in any longer.

"What an utter waste of time. I do not need a teenager telling me to bend my legs when I'm lifting a box of files," the "sir" remarked.

"I'm glad it's not just me then."

"Far from it, let me assure you. Anyway, on a more important topic, how's it going?'

"How's what going?" Thompson answered guardedly.

"Don't be a smart ass. The PGC investigation."

"Oh, as well as can be expected. A few setbacks but I think we'll get it wrapped up soon enough."

"And what exactly would you term a setback then?"

"The cash disappearing, the church closing, the principals doing a runner. That sort of thing."

"Oh, I see. Well, here's what I'd call a setback. That we have no idea where David Hidalgo is, that his tame hacker who seems to knock spots off our guys wants nothing to do with us, and that Sandy Benedetti insists on telling us his life story instead of maintaining a respectful silence as his lawyers have in vain been suggesting. And another setback: I hear that some fairly important papers have gone missing. Two documents, to be precise. Have you heard of the White List and the Black List? No? Well let me enlighten you. These moronic plonkers – for want of a better description – thought it was a good idea to commit to paper a list of important and valued customers along with their preferred choice of company and preferential terms. Instead of keeping such information safer than Fort Knox in an encrypted file with a password longer than the Police Federation's constitution, they decided that for ease of use they would keep it on a sheet of A4 in a filing cabinet. Along with this interesting and highly readable list they had a second page called the Black List. This apparently held the names of those less in favour. 'Mike H' at the top, I've been told, with a red line through his name. You'll never guess who came next. So these are setbacks. And when you say wrapped up, what might you mean by that?"

"Well, I suppose finding the cash and the principals."

"D'you know, Charlie, I'm not entirely sure we're on the same planet. The cash, I grant you, but has it not occurred to you what happens when these guys get to court and are looking for reduced sentences? Who else do you suppose might go down with the sinking ship? And if our young lady friends disappear entirely that might not be a bad thing either. Do you get my drift, Charlie, or have you not been paying attention?"

"Of course I know what you mean; I'm not stupid. But as far as I'm aware it's all pseudonyms and deniable. A couple of hoodlums could name anyone they liked. Without proof it's an allegation, that's all."

"That's a remarkably optimistic viewpoint, if I might say so. One broken link in the chain, Charlie. That's all it takes – one broken link. Or one wee linnet that feels like singing. Then 'Tam, ah Tam, ye'll get yir farin' in hell they'll roast ye like a herrin', or words to that effect. I think you'll find that there are a few Tams in this town that aren't planning a holiday in hell. And some of them have been in touch with me, in forceful terms. Your job is to keep names out of the public eye. How our mutual friends clear up after themselves is their own business – tragic and unfortunate, but less tragic and unfortunate than some other outcomes we can imagine. That clear? Ok. Well get to it, laddie."

Chapter 20

MINSK

Andrei hated driving any distance on the poorly maintained Belarusian roads. It was Sunday so the roads might be quieter but he would probably still spend two hours doing twenty-five kilometres per hour behind a tractor hauling turnips. Nevertheless, he considered it wise to meet Rudi in person. They had been doing business for almost eight years and Rudi had always proved reliable, efficient, and on time. Not cheap, but then what he was providing was unique and worth every rouble, in particular the access to police computers with details of forthcoming operations. So, when it was cloudy, Andrei, Tati, and their various young apprentices would lie low and catch up on the admin. When the clouds had passed, normal service could resume. That kept them out of trouble and out of jail and kept Rudi as what Andrei liked to call a "preferred supplier". Actually, he was one of very few suppliers with that level of access in the entire country. Hacking was not a career with courses at the National Technical University, a published body of good practice, and weekly updates in popular magazines. It was something more akin to being a stock market investor or a poker player. You brought your own talents to the game, and though you might learn from others you kept the secret of your success to yourself. That seemed to be particularly true of Rudi, who communicated in single words, did not seem connected to any hacker community like Anonymous or Chaos, and did not encourage contact between his various clients. When Andrei had first approached him and asked if there was anyone he could speak to who would vouch for the quality of his work, Rudi had replied simply, "No." "No what?" Andrei had asked. "No there isn't anyone or no there isn't anyone I can speak to?" "The latter. Take it or leave it." He had decided to take a risk and took it and had been very happy with the service, but still not one whit more knowledgeable about the enigmatic Rudi. Was that his real name (unlikely), was he actually German (maybe), was he even male (probably but not even that was certain)? Now, given the urgency of what he was looking for he felt a meeting was preferable to a series of one-word emails, hence bumping along behind a tractor on the road to Minsk.

Rudi had only agreed to meet in a public place. They decided on Zerno near Nyezalyezhnastsi Prospect. Rudi had said to take the corner table next to the window. Andrei arrived on time but realized as he went in that he had no idea what Rudi even looked like. He needn't have worried. The guy sitting at the corner table next to the window looked like an alumnus of Kraftwerk. He wore a dark suit, white shirt, black pencil tie, and had dark hair slicked down to one side. Either Rudi was indeed very German or doing a good impression. This fitted well with his efficiency and economy of expression but wasn't what Andrei had expected as typical hacker style. Andrei nodded across the room, collected an Americano at the counter, and sat down. He tried some small talk but found it ignored so went straight to the main event.

"Rudi, I have something I want you to do for me – not a favour, a paid job. A friend of mine is in trouble and needs some help. That means I need to find out exactly where she is, what the circumstances are, and also I need to get in touch with a man she thinks she can trust."

Rudi took a sip of his coffee.

"Tati is in Edinburgh," he said without emotion. "She is working for PGC, run by Max and Mikhail. Unless things change she probably has about a week to live, along with all the rest of the girls. I don't communicate with her but I know the circumstances."

Andrei was stunned. He managed to lay his coffee down without spilling it but took some time to find his tongue.

"How…" he began. "How do you know it was Tati I was going to ask you about?"

Rudi shrugged.

"It's not difficult," he said. "You told me you wanted help to find a girl in the West. You worked with Tati. She left six months ago to travel to the West. Besides, PGC are my clients."

"Who are PGC?"

"The front for an enterprise run by Maxim Blatov and Mikhail Lubchenco. The front is a church but PGC is a sex business. Blatov and Lubchenco are Belarusian citizens but operate in Edinburgh. I provide informatic services for PGC."

"I've just heard from Tati. She says she is one of a group of girls controlled by a man called Max. Basically they are slaves working as prostitutes."

"That is probably quite an accurate description."

"And you work for these guys?"

"They pay me, same as you. They run an illegal organization, same as you. Some people benefit and some suffer because of what they sell, same as you. It's business."

Andrei took a deep breath. What Rudi was saying was true from one point of view, but there was no way he could see himself in the same category as what Tati had told him about. People were free to buy and use his drugs if they wanted. Nobody was a prisoner or coerced. He paid strict attention to quality control and avoided high-risk substances. He even provided safe use guidelines, and nobody was about to be murdered. But he could see how a narrow definition might make things look. He decided not to apply to Rudi's sense of decency; he would just keep things on a strictly business footing.

"Ok," he said, "I hear what you're saying. Well, regardless of the rights and wrongs, it looks like Tati is in trouble, and the other girls with her. I want to get her out. Can you help me?"

Rudi sipped his black Russian tea and lit a Camel cigarette.

"This presents something of a conflict of interest for me," he said. "I have worked for PGC longer than I've worked for you. Normally I wouldn't be able to do anything for you; however, in this case I owe a favour to a friend who has approached me over the same issue. I am therefore willing to assist."

Andrei was stuck for words again.

"Someone else has contacted you about Tati?"

"No. About the behaviour of PGC."

"Who?"

"A hacker called Spade."

"Spade?"

"In English it is an agricultural implement for making holes and uncovering things, I believe. Spade is from Edinburgh. He was approached by a local individual trying to resolve a suspicious death by hanging. The whole affair depended on child pornography images found on the dead man's laptop, which were seen by police as explaining an apparent suicide. Spade was asked about a memory stick the deceased had been given shortly before and found that it had installed a backdoor trojan. The trojan was designed by me; Spade recognized my trademarks. It gave my clients, PGC, control over the individual in question's computer, which led to the installation of a set of image files. This was intended as a cover for their intention to murder the man by hanging. Spade was subsequently asked by Scottish police to help them resolve the matter by finding out where the trojan had come from. He declined and opted to contact me instead by way of a friendly warning. We have worked on one or two projects in the past so I am familiar with his skills. I appreciate it when a colleague advises me of potential legal complications. And I did not give permission for PGC to use the downloaded files in this manner. The fact that they are selling sex in Edinburgh is really none of my business. But for the reasons mentioned, in this case I am willing to intervene."

Rudi took a long drag on his cigarette and gazed out of the window. Andrei was used to operating on the wrong side of the law but this guy was something else. The certain death of one individual and the possible death of others did not seem to move him at all. He spoke about conflicts of interest when asked to intervene to save lives. Andrei guessed that people with the skills to work as successful hackers probably were a bit out to the left field, but Rudi was coming from a different galaxy. It sounded like he was agreeing to help and that was something. Maybe the rest was none of Andrei's affair.

"So I'm not in Edinburgh and I doubt I could do much good by being there. But Tati has sent me the name of someone she thought could help. She doesn't know the full name though – just David H. and the fact that he is a pastor. Or it could be that his full name is David H. Pastor. What she wrote me didn't seem entirely clear."

"The first is correct," Rudi stated, like a teacher marking a not particularly bright student's work. "The name is David Hidalgo. He is pastor of a church in Edinburgh. He is the one who gave Spade the memory stick. The man who died was a friend of his. I have also had some interaction with his computer. My information is that police have been dragging their heels on following up the complaint and the death and have even allowed the bulk of the capital held by PGC to be moved outwith their jurisdiction. PGC will have to close down in the city but the police have an interest in not pursuing the investigation – too rigorously, shall we say."

"Why?"

"Because senior police officers are frequent users of PGC's services of course. As are members of parliament and the legal professions, etc. It's normal in any large capital city."

"So what has Spade asked you to do?"

"Deprive PGC of service. Bring some of their connections to, shall we say, a wider public. Trace the missing cash. As an acknowledgment of Spade's role in this I am willing to provide this information. Now you want your girl out. That's it, isn't it?"

"Yes. No. I want Tati out but I want all the girls out. I don't care about the police and who's been jiving on the wrong dance floor. As regards the money, again, I don't care, but PGC shouldn't keep it. In fact, it might be quite appropriate if it were redistributed to more deserving parties."

"Yes," Rudi mused. "I suspected that might be part of the deal so I've set wheels in motion. £20 million of PGC's account has already been moved to a safe holding account from which I can distribute it elsewhere in due course."

"And what about David Hidalgo? Can we contact him?"

"Certainly," Rudi said, pulling out his mobile. "Would you like to speak to him now?"

Andrei blinked. He moved his mouth but nothing came out.

"I haven't contacted him already because this is your show, but I've got his number. You can call if you want."

Andrei shook his head, overwhelmed at the speed things were moving and paralysed by his lack of English to explain a complicated life and death situation to a man he had never met. All he knew was that Tati seemed to see him as their potential rescuer. If Tati had been here she would have known what to say. But if she'd been here he wouldn't be having this conversation.

"Ok then," Rudi shrugged. "Here's the number and his email. Take your pick whenever you want to." He handed Andrei a card he'd already prepared. "And this is Spade's email – or one of them – if you need to contact him."

Andrei drove home in a daze. He'd wanted things to move quickly but was stunned by how much information Rudi had and the steps he'd taken already. *Do hackers rule the world now?* he wondered. *Is there nothing they don't know and can't do?* His grandmother would have gone to a priest if she'd wanted advice or counsel. Maybe the hackers were the priests of the new world order, just like their more religious counterparts – secretive, full of hidden knowledge, skilled in the black arts, and also effectively running the show. As soon as he got in he fired up his laptop and went straight to Google Translate.

Two thousand kilometres to the west, Spade chuckled as he opened Rudi's email confirming what had been discussed in Zerno.

The money was in quarantine, PGC had lost access to the police computers, and Andrei had been given David Hidalgo's email and phone number. Wheels were in motion or, you could say, the net was drawing in – the Internet. *Thank you, Elvis Costello*, he thought. *Your aim was true and so was mine.* He chuckled again, tore the wrapper off another caramel wafer, and sent Rudi a cheery Scottish thank you. On a bit of a roll he wondered about including a Youtube link to The Specials performing "Message to You Rudi" just for fun but reminded himself that Rudi in Minsk didn't really understand the concept so it would be a waste. Nevertheless, things were going well and it was fun for him. He hoped these hoodlums were beginning to squirm. He decided to wash some dishes and take out the rubbish to celebrate.

Also far from Minsk, Elvira was sitting up in bed, devouring another bowl of soup. This was followed by mince and tatties with doughballs, peas and carrots, then a plate of trifle with extra cream. She had previously formed a poor opinion of Scottish food based on what was provided by the lazy, dirty, bad-tempered women employed by Max. But this was delicious. It was rounded off with a cup of tea and a couple of fingers of Sarah's home-made pure butter shortbread. James and Sarah Dalrymple sat around the bed nibbling their own light lunch, Paul having left once the danger was over. They watched in amazement how much the skinny girl in the bed managed to stow away in minutes. Normally James and Sarah would have been in church at this time or just home getting the roast out of the oven, talking over what Gordon, their minister, had said that morning or what the Sunday School kids had been up to. This morning James had phoned Gordon early and explained they had an unexpected visitor and that he wouldn't manage his door duty. He had arranged a swap but was calling out of courtesy. He'd see him at the normal leadership on Wednesday – probably. Now they sat around marvelling at the transformation from two mornings ago. It was the third day since Maxi had bounded off into the mist and found something interesting in the waves lapping on the shore. The first night's sleep had brought her back from the half-dead to at least half-living. The second night had restored her to what seemed more like normality. She ate like a horse, chatted nineteen to the dozen in that particular variety of English Sarah recognized from so many Polish nurses in casualty, and couldn't stop petting Maxi, who had taken up permanent residence on the bed. James didn't have the heart to throw the retriever out. Elvira petted and stroked the dog as if she alone had saved her life. In short, her spirits seemed good and her physical recovery was advancing rapidly. Dalrymple felt the time might be right for a conversation he wasn't looking forward to. It was hard to see how it could fail to be a matter for the police, whatever Elvira might think.

"Elvira," he began after the trays were cleared away. "You seem to be improving well. And you can stay here until you are fully recovered… but we need to ask how you ended up in the water. Who did this to you? You said before that they want to kill you. To help you we have to know who wants to kill you and why. If we can't find out what has happened I don't know how we can help you be safe wherever you go from here. Do you understand what I'm saying?"

"I understand, yis," Elvira nodded, burying her hands in Maxi's deep golden fur. "Is not easy explain." Sarah poured her yet another cup of tea, which Elvira took with two massive spoonfuls of sugar. The room was warm. She was well fed. The people around the bed had saved her life. It was a long and complicated story but that was not what made it difficult. For the first time in years, she felt she had people around her who cared about her and whom she could trust. None of them was a threat. No one was going to drag her from her bed, strip her clothes off, and push her into a room with a man she had never met to do whatever he demanded. Maybe, she hardly dared to hope, that chapter was finally over and Max, Mikhail, Boris, Dimitri, Ivan, Sergei, and all the others could be consigned to the past and she could begin to live again. It was almost too much to take in. She had known the moment would come when she would have to delve back into that life and explain, but she had been putting off thinking about it. Now she owed it to the family in whose lovely home she had no right to be. But how to begin?

"I am from Belarus," she said simply. "I used to work in a shop. We sold everything from vegetables to boots, batteries to toothpaste, dresses to detergent. My father's shop. I was bored and I wanted come to the West. I met a man who told me he could arrange. He promised job in the West, but cost much money. I stole money from my father and gave him. But there was no job. They take me to a house of other girls. I am beaten. Everybody beaten. Then they put in a room and bring in a man. They say you have to do sex with the man or we beat you again. I didn't do but you know soon you must or they kill you. So I did, many times. Every day, many men. They hurt you and they force you do things is horrible. If you are not good with them they say to Max who write it in a book. They promise if you do enough good then you can go but they never let you go. And every time they write a bad in the book they tell you it take longer to go. Most of the girls more younger than me. They get good in the book. But if not many men want you, then you get worry. Some girls who not do good they make disappear. I wonder when they make me disappear too. So I worry more and then I not good with the men and I get more bad in the book. Tati try to help me. She help everybodys. We get into the office at night and find some papers, but nothing seem to happen. Tati wrote to friend in Belarus but we don know if it come right to him. One day I not able to do any more. Was my birthday. I decided I not able to live here more. And I not able go back Belarus after I take money from my father. So I decide kill myself. Tati find me and call someone. They take me down but Max say I cannot work good any more so they will finish what I start. So Dimitri take me to the river. He put plastics on the wrists and ankles. Max say him to get a boat and go far out. To put a heavy thing on my legs and put me in. But he is fat and lazy. He could not get a boat and did not know how use it. So he took me in the night to a place the boats come in. He hit me on the head and put me in a bag and push me over the wall in the water. That is it. You find me, Maxi find me. Now you know all."

The clock in the spare room ticked. Maxi yawned and licked her chops. Elvira kept stroking her fur, not looking up. Illness and injury are no respects of persons; the Dalrymples thought they'd seen a bit of the rough side of life, but this was something else. James cleared his throat while Sarah reached out a hand. In the few minutes it had taken her to tell her story James had felt his retirement plans slipping away. Modern sex slavery was going on in his city. How dare they! How dare they come here, importing people like meat and selling them on the street. And the anger he felt towards the users was no less – presumably Scottish men who had grown up with what he still considered to be largely decent human values in Scottish society, paying their money without an ounce of pity for the girls they were using. Doing whatever twisted, perverted things they wanted for a bundle of tenners on the table without a single thought for the homes, families, dreams, ambitions, or basic human dignity of the girls they were using. Did these men not have mothers, sisters, wives, daughters? Did they have no one they cared for that they might think of in the aftermath when the animal lust was spent and they wandered home alone? Was there no inner accusing thought or did they just gag the voice of conscience, think about other things, and resume their daily routine until the next time? It was both incomprehensible and appalling that this should be how a developed, mature democracy behaved. So much for the great Scottish Enlightenment.

He studied the ceiling and let out a long breath. If this was going on in Edinburgh, in the twenty-first century, with all our talk about human rights and freedoms and all the moaning about what in comparison were minor inconveniences, he simply did not see how he could pass by on the other side. The girl had come to him;

it was no accident. Gordon had been speaking just the previous week about "good works, which God prepared in advance for us to do" from Ephesians 2:10. If this didn't qualify then he had no idea what might. She had come to him; but there must be other Elviras out there. She had mentioned someone called Tati and said there were other girls. But how many? A dozen? A hundred? More? He wasn't a politician but he had connections. Once they had got to the bottom of Elvira's story some of these connections would be getting a pointed phone call. A hundred questions and potential realities spun around in Dr James Dalrymple's head, but he could already see that city breaks around the capitals of Europe, getting back to the piano, or taking up watercolours no longer held much appeal. It would be like standing by during Kristallnacht and watching while the homes of his Jewish neighbours were firebombed and destroyed. Or ignoring the lynching of a black man in the southern states. Whether or not the scale of harm was equivalent, the point was that these people were his neighbours, at least in the biblical and maybe even the literal sense and he had to do something. He took no convincing that evil triumphs when good people do nothing. His mind was made up.

"Elvira," he said finally, "I don't really know what to say. From what you've told us you have been through a living hell. But I will say this. You are safe now. You are never going back to that life. Never. And we'll do every single thing we can to help the other girls you were with. You can stay here for as long as you need to and when you decide what you want to do we'll help you. If you need further medical care I can arrange that. If you need legal help to remain in Scotland I have a good friend in an old Edinburgh law firm I can call on. I understand what you have said about your family in Belarus but, if you are willing, I would feel it a privilege if you would let us be your family in Scotland. I am ashamed of how you have been treated by my fellow countrymen. But that is now in the past. Sarah and I will do what we can to make things better for you from now on. That's all I can say."

And it was. Dalrymple got up, mumbling something, and left the room. There was a loud sound of nose blowing from the kitchen. Sarah sometimes found her husband's dogged, stubborn nature something of a trial but now she could see it was going to come into its own. After more than forty years of marriage, reading his mind wasn't hard. Pity help anyone trafficking in human misery in their city once he got his teeth into it.

When he had sufficiently recovered, Dalrymple came back into the room, a rather obvious question he had not yet asked in his mind.

"Elvira, can you tell me why you don't want the police involved in this?"

"Police are in the men who come," she said simply. "They do not say but we know. Sometimes he says a thing makes me think he is a policeman. Some men know each other or come in group and they speak. They say things make me sure. When Tati and I went in office we find a paper. It gives names. And letters. Some of the men I think is police have letters CID. I ask the woman cook for us what means CID. She say is kind of police. That is why Max think he is safe. If they come for him he say all the police who go with the girls. So police never any problem for Max. So I say no when you want phone police for me. David H: Pastor is the only one can help us. His name on another paper. The people Max is afraid of. David H: Pastor the only one to help us. You speak only him."

"But who is David H: Pastor?" Dalrymple pressed her. "Is that his name? Pastor? Or is his name David H and he is a pastor? How can I contact him?"

Elvira looked confused.

"I don't know. Only David H: Pastor. He will help us."

Dalrymple groaned in frustration.

"But how can I contact him if I don't even know his name?"

"Phone Gordon," Sarah said, as if it were obvious. "If he's a church pastor, Gordon will know who he is. Or if his name is 'Pastor' then we can search the phone book. You do the phone book. I'll contact Gordon."

More precious than rubies, James Dalrymple thought, not for the first time. The heart of her husband is glad in her. She does him good and not evil all the days of her life.

"Great," he said. "I'm on it."

Chapter 21

PLAZA DE ESPAÑA

The general opinion in Ribadeo regarding restaurants was that the Parador was good but expensive, the portions tended to be on the meagre rather than filling side, and the menu was more geared to international visitors who wanted something "*típico de aquí*" than meeting the tastes of genuine locals. Casa Pepe was good, though lacked the view of the Parador and tended to be something of a meatfest. So, partly by elimination and partly the genuine hard work of the owners and staff, San Miguel came out on top. It was perched on a little outcrop of rock at the far seaward end of the harbour and had uninterrupted views both inland over the Ria across to Castropol and out to sea. While red meats and chicken were available, it was fish and seafood – *pescados y mariscos* – that diners came for and were not disappointed. *Merluza*, *lubina*, *bacalao*, *percebes*, *navajas*, *gambas*, and *bogavante* were the order of the day and the reason David wanted to bring Gillian here for Sunday lunch. By October the tourist season was dying down and the families with holiday houses had gone back to Madrid or whichever other hotter-than-hell inland city they lived in the other ten months of the year, so a reservation wasn't in itself a problem. David particularly wanted a window seat and these were issued parsimoniously by the management; however, it turned out that the current *jefe* was actually a far-out cousin and remembered David from childhood holidays despite it being something like forty years previously.

"How did you manage to pull this off?" Gillian asked as they were seated.

"*Enchufe*," David answered.

"A plug?"

"Well, sort of. *Enchufe* does mean an electrical plug but more generally it means connections. A relative, friend, neighbour, someone you've done a favour for, a cousin or a colleague. Anything you like. When you've got *enchufe* there's almost nothing you can't get and almost nothing you can get without it."

"So bribery, corruption, and nepotism?"

"I suppose so, in the strictest sense, but it doesn't feel like that within the culture. It's just getting along and helping each other. If you have one window table left, who are you going to give it to – a perfect stranger or somebody you have a connection with? It's also like a reward for living here a long time and paying your way, like membership of the invisible society of the town. You have to earn it but once you've got it you're an insider."

"Not much room for equal opps there."

"Perhaps not. But we've got a window table, haven't we? Enjoy it."

They did – the table, the view, the meal, the service, and the sense of security, of being out of the firing line for a bit. Whether the police were just as corrupt as the racketeers had been was left sticking to the wall by mutual consent. David felt this must be what the Apollo astronauts felt like after finally landing on board the aircraft carrier, having been picked up out of the sea after re-entry: grounded and glad to be home but still a little bit giddy. Gillian, on the other hand, felt keyed up as she always did before presenting to a sophisticated academic audience who might spot some methodological error or missed connection in her research. But she was again enjoying the feeling of being back in Spain with a Spaniard. It was funny; David was just as Scottish as she was at home, but get him on Spanish soil and all of that seemed to burn off like morning mist. Naturally he dressed and spoke differently, but she would have sworn that he also walked differently, sat differently, and laughed a lot more. He relaxed like her dad did the minute you got him behind his drums.

That afternoon they had a siesta then drove to *Playa de las Catedrales*, a local wonder David insisted they visit. Gillian was impressed. It was as if someone had taken a rough saw and cut into the cliffs, gouging out a series of cuttings, arches, inlets, towers, and turrets, all in natural stone overlooking golden sand and rolling breakers. Gillian kicked off her shoes and paddled. They wandered as far as the tide would let them, hand in hand, then came back up to road level and found a table at one of the tourist bars. There was a sea breeze that wasn't exactly cold but tended towards the "bracing" so they kept outer layers on and sat quietly absorbing the atmosphere, looking at a few sails out to sea, and people watching. Eventually Gillian sighed and finished her drink.

"Sorry to break up the party," she said, "but I really need to check my presentation again. I'm on at 12.30 on Tuesday, just when the international delegates will be starting to get peckish, not yet working to Spanish meal times, so I want to make sure I keep them interested."

"Sure. We'll drive back, then I'll take a wander and let you get on with things."

David's laptop hadn't been returned yet by whatever CID boffin was crawling all over it or he might have spent the time doing a bit of work himself; instead, limited to email on his phone, he decided to find a quiet bar and just pick up his messages. He particularly wanted to see how Juan and Mrs MacInnes were coping, given that their pastor had yet again been plucked from their midst with very little notice. If they had been paying him they might have been looking at a clawback, but since they weren't they couldn't complain. However, complain Juan did. David sat in the dying evening sun on the *terraza* of the *cafetería* Linares sipping a chilled glass of Albariño and smiled at Juan's message. *David*, he started without embellishment. *I look forward to the day when you are no longer subject to criminal attacks and might want to think about pastoring a church.* Mrs MacInnes must have been helping him with the English. He could see her standing at his shoulder with a mischievous smile, tutoring him on Scottish sarcasm. *By the time this day arrives – if ever – I will myself have accumulated sufficient experience of the task, between short breaks running a restaurant, to offer some advice. My first suggestion would be to appoint a reliable second in command who can take over at a moment's notice without pay, guidance, oversight, training, or support. Failing this I would emigrate to Argentina and not come back.* Then he seemed to think the joke had gone far enough and flipped back to normal mode. *Seriously, David, hope all well in Galicia. No obvious progress here. The police seem to all be on holiday or have other urgent emergencies. Sam was ok at the funeral yesterday. PGC still seems to be closed and not coming back. Sandy and Sonia Benedetti came to church at Southside this morning. I'll let you know if there's any news. Besos a la señorita de mi parte.*

Well, if that was the worst thing in his inbox, then maybe he could keep on relaxing and leave Gillian to her prep. He ordered another Albariño and was about to start leafing through the weekend edition of *Voz de Galicia* when his phone pinged with something else coming in. There wasn't usually much spam on Sunday evenings so he flipped it open and read.

To: David Hidalgo

From: Andrei Navitski

Subject: PGC Church, Tatiana Garmash URGENT

That got his attention. The Linares waitress came with the Albariño and set it down with a *tapa* of sardines but he didn't notice.

Dear David Hidalgo Sir

My name is Andrei. I have not had the pleasure for contact you before. I live in Belarus. Please forgive my Inglish. It is a matter of urgency I contact you. I get your address from a hacker in Minsk, Rudi, who have it from a hacker in edinburgh name Spade. I think you know.

Rudi say me that you ask Spade help you find men who killed your friend. They put pictures on his computer to explain police. Spade tell you this was by a virus from PGC. This virus made by Rudi though he did not mean for killing. I hope you understand me. PGC pretend to be church by they are not church. They take girls of Belarus to the west for putting in business of sex. My friend Tati (Tatiana) one of these. She give much money to men for job in the west but no is job. Only they make to do sex. They bring them for sex house in edinburgh. No one can leave, no contact no one. Tati find your name in a list in the office. She worried they to kill you too. Police no help many police use girls as well. Tati say to trust only David H: Pastor. She does not know who is David H: Pastor but she is able send me a letter. I go to Rudi. He tell me he has message from Spade says me who you are. I want help Tati and others. She says me she is worried they kill all the girls when is finish. You live Edinburgh. Maybe you know police you can trust. Tati not allowed out of house only for shopping with a man, Mikhail. Tati is not know where is her house or other houses. She send me a plan to say you. This week Thursday she thinks they do shopping. Main street. Shop called Sally. Afternoon. Not sure what o'clock. If you can be shop Sally Thursday in afternoon look for her. If possible she be there. She look for you. Thank you David Pastor if you can help us. Tati is my best friend. I miss her. Please say me what you can.

Your friend

Andrei

David laid his phone down and looked about him. He couldn't believe what he'd just read. His name was being discussed in Minsk. It was on a hit list held by PGC. It was mentioned in a letter from a brothel in Edinburgh to a hacker in Belarus – or was it to a friend in Belarus who then took it to a hacker in Minsk? But whatever, this claimed that police in Edinburgh – surely not all of them – some police officers in Edinburgh were involved with organized crime, people trafficking, and prostitution. Tati, whoever she was, was trying to warn him through Andrei with extra information from Rudi, who got it from Spade. David felt his head beginning to spin and not from the drink. He left the second Albariño untouched, dropped a few Euros on the table and headed back to *O Retorno*.

Gillian looked up from her laptop and gave him a welcoming smile when she heard the door open, then she saw his expression.

"What's wrong? What's happened?"

He showed her the email without comment.

"I have to go back to Edinburgh," he said. "Right now. Sorry."

"How's it going?" Sarah Dalrymple asked her husband as she came through to the lounge with the phone in her hand. James Dalrymple had a copy of various Edinburgh telephone directories spread out on the coffee table and a notepad and pencil on the arm of the chair.

"Not too promising," he replied. "According to Google, Pastor is a surname, mainly in Latin America and the United States. There are three in Edinburgh and the Lothians though. 'B. Pastor' – B for Begonia, 'F. Pastor' – F for Frederick, and 'W. Pastor' – W for Wilfred. 'B' and 'W' had not the slightest clue what I was talking about. 'F' was out so I left a message. How about you?"

"Ask a woman," Sarah said, a little smugly, and held out a number. "Gordon says there are only two Davids he knows of who are pastors in Edinburgh with the second initial H. David Henderson is coming up for retirement and is on long-term sick leave with cancer so he couldn't help even if it was him. The other is a David Hidalgo. Only been around for about a year. Previously had a church in Spain but grew up in Edinburgh. Apparently he's made a bit of a splash already. Southside Fellowship in Newington. Gordon met him at a pastoral care conference. Southside seems to be doing well, which people Gordon has spoken to put down largely to Hidalgo's ministry. But the weird thing is that he's barely

213

back in Edinburgh after looking for a teenager who was abducted by a drug gang and taken off to Spain. So if it's crime-busting you're looking for, David Hidalgo may be your man."

James Dalrymple took the phone, thinking this must be what cross-channel swimmers would feel like just before the plunge. They'd prepared as well as they could, rubbed on all that goose fat, got the support team in place, but nothing could really prepare them for the cold grey waters, rough chop, crosswinds, squally showers, or numbing cold. He had a Belarusian girl in the spare bedroom who claimed she'd been part of a sex-trafficking ring tolerated and patronized by police. She had just recovered from attempted murder and maintained that the only person she trusted to help her was in Edinburgh. He had no reason not to take at face value everything she had said, but it still sounded so incredible that he wasn't sure how exactly he could start a conversation with a stranger on the subject. Still, Elvira was clearly worried that something was going on that made it imperative that David H. Pastor be contacted immediately. So here it was – final handshake with the swim support team and into the water we go. He dialled the number and heard it ring.

David Hidalgo stopped packing shirts and socks back into the case they had just come out of and picked up his mobile. A UK call but not a known number.

"Hello, David Hidalgo. Yes I am. What? Yes, I've had something to do with them. I see. Well, funny you should call right now…"

It took only a matter of seconds for both men to realize this was a missing-link conversation. To get any handle on PGC, David knew they needed someone who had got out, someone who could say what was going on from their own experience, particularly with respect to the police. Dalrymple knew he needed someone outside of their immediate situation to confirm what Elvira had said. David put the call on speakerphone for Gillian to hear and they spoke for almost an hour. If there was something she felt was missing she jotted it down on a Post-it and put it on the dresser where David was sitting. A picture began to emerge as James explained Elvira's story. Young, inexperienced girls from Eastern Europe hoping for a better future in the midst of economic meltdown were tricked into a life of servitude and slavery in a foreign capital far from home, with no friends or connections, no passport, no money, no liberty, little language, and soon little hope, dominated and controlled by men with a long criminal background who knew exactly what to do and say to control not only their bodies but also their minds. David found the story of Max's book of good and bad particularly chilling. The effect was to make the girls want to please their clients to get a good report and a promise of an earlier exit – so they became motivated to do what was required of them and didn't even need to be forced. It was diabolically perfect. James explained that Elvira was worried some kind of crisis or climax was coming, though she didn't know what. David confirmed Tati's existence from Andrei's message and described the plan he was proposing, though he confessed he didn't really get the details: a shop called Sally on Hanover Street some time in the afternoon of the forthcoming Thursday; Tati might or might not be there. He had no idea what shop it might be or how he was supposed to recognize a girl he had never met or seen. Of course she would not be unaccompanied – so a strong-arm minder or two, probably armed, given what they knew about PGC's methods. And they couldn't involve police since they were supposed to all be in cahoots. The whole thing sounded like a mountain of maybes.

"So what are we reasonably certain of?" James Dalrymple asked, slipping into research mode, his phone also on speaker with Sarah listening in.

"That PGC exists as a church," David replied. "That its main purpose is to front a network of brothels with girls trafficked from Eastern Europe. That the guys in charge have a long history of this kind of thing and don't hesitate to kill. That a police investigation is underway but seems to be stalling. That the church is now closed and the principals disappeared. So, at the very least, they know they're going to have to move on. That one girl has managed to get out – Elvira – and another has managed to smuggle out a message. That's Tati. That she seems to have access to a document with my name on it – probably not in complimentary terms. And that Tati has told her friend in Belarus that she thinks she'll be taken on a shopping trip this Thursday to a shop called Sally on the main street – I suppose that must be Hanover Street – but we don't know what Tati looks like and we don't know the shop."

"Winters," said a voice. "The shop is going to be Sally Winters."

"Sorry, who's that?" Dalrymple asked

"I'm Gillian Lockhart, a friend of David's. I'm sure the shop will be Sally Winters on Hanover Street."

"I'm sure you're right," another female voice put in. "This is Sarah Dalrymple."

"And what's Sally Winters when it's at home?" David asked.

"Lingerie and sex toys," Gillian explained.

"Oh, I see," he commented dryly. "Maybe that would make sense."

"Yes. Things of sex."

"Who's that?" David asked as yet another female voice joined what was becoming quite a confusing conversation.

"I am Elvira. I hear you talking so I come. Sex is right. When a girl go shopping they come with new underwear and toys. Some horrible things. You have to use with men who come. Tati will go shopping. Then you have a chance to get her."

"But how are we supposed to know who she is?" David persisted.

"Easy," Elvira said. "Tati is my best friend. I will show."

"So that's it?" Gillian asked. "So much for our romantic break."

"I'm sorry," David replied wearily. "What else can I do?"

They were back outside, sitting on the *terraza* of El Cantón on Plaza de España in the centre of the town, *cañas* in front of them along with a large platter of wafer thin *jamón*, a dish of olives, and some chunky local bread.

Gillian popped in an olive and took a sip of her beer.

"If you'd asked me a year ago if I fancied being a crime fighter's girlfriend the idea might have seemed quite appealing. It turns out to be not as much fun as you'd think."

"And nobody asked me if I wanted a part-time job fighting crime," David agreed. "It's ironic. People who think they've got boring lives want more excitement. We've had our fill of excitement and just want to be boring."

"Well, perhaps not exactly boring. I'd settle for normal."

"Define normal." David smiled and squeezed her hand. "All I'd say is that even this normal is better than normal was a year ago. We have our own plans. Apparently your dad approves of us. And you can't say we're not meeting interesting people."

"That's for sure. Speaking of interesting, what do you think of Sandy and Sonia turning up at Southside?"

"I actually find it encouraging. They've both been hurt and deceived but they don't seem to automatically want to throw the baby out with the bath water. Sandy told me about what they'd gained from PGC as well as the other side of things. He felt he'd connected with his faith in a new way and that it had probably saved their marriage."

"Wheat and tares."

"I knew you were going to say that."

"Personally, considering the amount of misery this whole thing has caused, if anything good comes out of it, that has to be a bonus."

Just then a tall man in a white linen jacket and smart jeans approached their table.

"Excuse me," he said. "I was overhearing you. Please forgive. You are English? Yes?"

"Well, Scottish actually. But English speakers."

"Well," the man continued hesitantly, "we were wondering. We have in Ribadeo a group to chat in English. But the couple who started us – they are teachers of English here and also from Scotland – they have had to leave us for a time. So we have no one.

I am Belgian but all the others are Spanish. If you wouldn't mind we would be very pleased if we could invite you to join us for a little time. We are there." He gestured towards a group of eight or nine gathered around two tables pulled together and now smiling and looking expectantly in their direction. David looked at Gillian, eyebrows raised. She shrugged, then smiled.

"Ok, I don't see why not."

They began gathering up their drinks and plates. David's phone buzzed again.

"Not another one," he groaned. "Can they not just leave me alone for a bit?" He tapped a few times to open the message then began to laugh in a release of tension.

"Listen to this," he said and held the phone up. The unmistakable hook from "La Bamba" started up and a voice began to sing *"Bamba, La bamba, Bamba, La bamba"*.

Gillian looked puzzled.

"Sorry," she said. "I don't get that."

"It's a message from Spade," David explained, looking down at the screen. "He says, 'Hope all going well and you are fighting the good fight. Andrei and Rudi send their best. Bank accounts as frozen as Siberia. Thought you might enjoy this.'"

"'La Bamba'?" Gillian asked, still in the dark.

"It's a joke," David explained. The lead guitarist of the band that had a hit with 'La Bamba', Los Lobos, is called David Hidalgo. I think he's telling us to cheer up – we're on the right track."

Chapter 22

CORSTORPHINE

David Hidalgo spent most of the flight back from Santiago to Edinburgh via Heathrow trying to remember what DI McIntosh looked like. He and Gillian had discussed the situation deep into the previous night. What a mess. It was one thing to be righteously indignant that a criminal gang was hiding behind a church with all the deception that involved; it was something else when you had a personal connection with a direct victim. Then there was the fact that those paid to protect us and enforce the law were hand in glove with the criminals and apparently lapping it up. It was beyond belief or comprehension. Clearly everything that could be done should be done, but David Hidalgo could not get his head around the fact that once again the matter had come to him. Why to him, for goodness' sake? Why not to some other concerned citizen with more aptitude and better connections? Wasn't he due a bit of a break and some peace and quiet? Was it just another "simple twist of fate" or was there some unseen hand behind it, moving, guiding, directing? Not so much a *deus ex machina* as *Dios en la machina*. Well, it had also come to James Dalrymple and that was something. Apparently he wasn't the only unwilling recipient of dastardly deeds.

As David and Gillian had argued back and forth about what to do now, two conclusions seemed to stand out. Firstly, David had to return to Edinburgh alone and, secondly, there didn't seem to be any way of helping without involving the police. Tati and Elvira had both been insistent that the police were actually the enemy but surely that couldn't be true – at least surely not every single policeman or CID officer in the entire city. Perhaps they should have stayed longer at the case conference to see what the specific plan of campaign was supposed to be. Gillian's point had been that the investigation was not secure, but what Tati and Elvira had said was that it wasn't secure because certain officers were playing for the other team. In this case it actually *was* conspiracy rather than cock-up. But surely not everybody. Neither of them had been impressed with DCI Stevenson's bullying, blustering, patronizing manner. Thompson they knew better and generally liked but he didn't exactly seem to be Mr Dynamic either. But McIntosh had come over a bit differently: calm, thoughtful, reasoned, and not intimidated by the atmosphere of the meeting. David wasn't sure if the obvious hostility to his presentation was simply the usual career cop's disdain for a jumped-up colleague with academic pretensions and accelerated promotion or something more sinister. Maybe those on the inside knew that McIntosh wasn't one of them and were also hostile for that reason. If they were users of illegal sexual services, maybe all his talk of the explosion in online pornography and how that fed into real-life prostitution and trafficking rubbed them up the wrong way. Maybe it was *both* conventional *and* personal. So, if there had to be some police involvement, then maybe McIntosh was the only way in. They decided to take a risk, trust their hunch, and see what happened – there didn't seem to be any alternative.

Both slept badly that night. Gillian couldn't help dwelling on the truly terrible fate of these naive, too-trusting girls who had spent all the money they could raise – or steal – just to buy into a life of misery and humiliation. She also kept going over her presentation for errors and assumptions. This was not the ideal way of preparing for a big event. In David's case, it was a question of how to take matters forward since it would depend on him as the one free to return. He had managed to get the last seat on Tuesday's flight, thanks to Skyscanner, but what if McIntosh wasn't interested, couldn't be contacted or, worse still, was himself on the wrong side of the law? Then all the risks that Tati must have taken smuggling out her cry for help and all the impact of Elvira's story would just be water down the drain. Blatov and Lubchenco would get off scot-free and the girls under their control would either simply be moved to another town or something worse that he didn't want to imagine.

First thing in the morning he sent McIntosh an email. Thank goodness Gillian had had the professional curiosity to ask about references and sources, which had prompted him to give her a card as they left the meeting. He let things lie while they had breakfast then he gave Gillian a kiss and sent her off to do battle with Regional Languages around the Celtic Fringe. Finally, unable to wait, he tried McIntosh's mobile. The poor man would hardly have had time to get his first coffee of the day and switch on the computer. Surprisingly he answered almost immediately.

"DI McIntosh."

"Hello. This is David Hidalgo. I don't know if you remember but we met briefly at a case conference last week. You were doing a presentation about prostitution and people trafficking."

"I remember very well. Your colleague Dr Lockhart was the only one in the room the slightest bit interested."

"Well, I think I could count myself in that group as well."

"So that makes three of us out of fifteen. What can I do for you?"

"Actually, I'm not entirely sure where to start. It's about the PGC investigation."

"Or non-investigation, you could say."

"What do you mean?"

"Oh, just a bit of a moan. Don't let me bother you with it. It's just that this is my area of professional interest and it looks like the largest scale operation of trafficking, false imprisonment, and forced prostitution we've ever come across in Scotland and one of the largest in the UK, and there seem to be absolutely no reliable leads as to how we can take things forward. In fact, everything we have had seems to have either ended up against a brick wall or been so thoroughly screwed up as to make it worthless. Forgive me. I shouldn't be bending your ear with my complaints."

"Not at all," David said, relieved at how the conversation was going. "That actually has a bearing on why I'm phoning. There have been a few developments you might be interested in."

"Go ahead. I am."

"Just before we do that, can I just ask if this line is entirely secure and if we can both speak freely? Some of what I'm going to say I would like to be for your ears only at this stage."

"Yes, I think so. I'm working from home all day today. I've got a meeting with my PhD supervisor next week and there's quite a lot of writing-up to do before then."

"After you've heard what I have to say, you may want to reschedule that appointment."

"I'm all ears."

Since McIntosh had already voiced some frustration, David thought that might be the place to start. He briefly explained where he was and why, then talked about how he and Gillian had felt about the official reluctance to see Mike Hunter's death as anything other than an easily explicable suicide. Then there was the failure to move sooner on Blatov and Lubchenco. Next the obvious insecurity of police computers, the shot through his bedroom window, and finally the disappearance of PGC's funds apparently due to an internal mix-up between specialist sections. And how did PGC know the money was about to be sequestered anyway? Perhaps he was speaking out of turn but it all just seemed like too many coincidences and muck-ups. Then he described the email from Andrei and phone call from James Dalrymple coming so close together and agreeing on so many details. McIntosh listened patiently with only the odd question for clarification or expression of agreement. Finally David got to the point.

"I'd really much rather not be saying this," he said. "But Gillian and I have spoken about it at length and we can't see any other conclusion. The investigation seems to have either been blocked or bungled in a variety of ways and the two girls, Tati and Elvira, are openly accusing CID and uniformed officers of being complicit in what's going on and actual users of the service – if I can put it that way. We were both impressed with your presentation in the meeting and couldn't think why you would be bothering to put so much effort into the subject if you didn't actually care about the issue. In the light of that, I'll be open with you: we've decided to come to you with our concerns and just hope you're not a bent bobby too!"

There was a moment's silence at the other end of the line and David wondered if he'd gone too far and blown it. When McIntosh spoke he was obviously choosing his words very carefully.

"First of all, David, if I can call you that, thank you for the trust you have put in me. I'll do my level best not to let that down. Secondly, I can assure you, if you're willing to believe me, that in no way am I personally implicated or complicit in what we're talking about. In fact, I feel like I've been banging my head off a brick wall for years trying to get this sort of stuff taken seriously. The matter of 'bent bobbies', as you put, is obviously extremely sensitive. Careers have been broken many times by allegations that turned out to be unfounded. The consequences of real corruption that never came to light are a little harder to evaluate! Next, I have to admit what you say makes a lot of sense from where I'm standing. I've been frustrated in terms of what's been happening but didn't actually have any tangible red light until now. What you've brought is a series of allegations from members of the public – victims if you will – and that can't be ignored, even by anyone attempting a cover-up. That sets wheels in motion much more effectively than if I'd simply been moaning about lack of action. So thanks for that."

David let himself breathe a sigh of relief. There'd be many fences still to clear but he'd at least got over the first hurdle without falling.

"What now?" he asked simply.

"What now is that I have to put my thesis to one side and get on the blower. Anyone doing academic research such as mine within the force is required to have an internal mentor. As it happens mine is Douglas Forsyth."

"Sorry, that doesn't mean anything. Should it?"

"Forgive me. Living in the bubble we expect everybody to know. Douglas Forsyth is Divisional Commander for Edinburgh. Big Boss. Head Honcho. He has a special interest in this and has always been very supportive. He's said to me that with him being so sucked up into policy and strategy, mentoring some academic work that has implications for direct policing keeps him connected with issues on the ground."

"So, yet another reason why you might not have been flavour of the month among the career cops around the table last week."

"Got it in one," McIntosh said, and David could hear the wry smile in his voice.

"My impression so far is that Douglas is a man of very strong convictions – and very happily married too, as far as I know. There is no way I could see him as being tied up with this sort of thing. Actually, I think you'd get on well with him."

"Are you going to approach Douglas Forsyth?"

"Today's Monday. According to what you've told me, Tati's shopping trip – if it happens – is going to be in three days' time. We haven't got long. You're coming back to Edinburgh, I suppose?"

"Early flight from Santiago tomorrow – first I could get. Change at Heathrow, then in Edinburgh about 11.30 or so."

"Right. I'll meet you at the airport; we'll take it from there. I'm glad you called. But I think I'm going to have a busy day and it won't be writing!"

The rest of Monday Gillian spent registering for the conference, finding the various venues, listening to the tedious, predictable welcoming speeches (with translation) from the Head of Department in Santiago, the Chair of the local Gallego Language Society, and the *Alcalde* on behalf of the Ribadeo Town Council. Then they were free from mid-afternoon. They ate in Casa Villaronta in Rua San Francisco, which they'd been told was the only place to get really authentic *pulpo a la gallega* – the real deal in local octopus. Wandering round the town arm in arm afterwards, they bumped into a couple of the English chatters from the night before and were happy to sit and natter, minds off PGC, Tati, Elvira, and whatever plan McIntosh was cooking up. Finally, they paseoed a bit more down by the Marina, then a few more drinks later and a light supper before early to bed. Big day for both of them tomorrow.

David didn't have any problem picking McIntosh out in the sea of faces waiting at International Arrivals. The two men acknowledged one another with a brief nod, paired up, and found a space just beyond the melee of family members and business connections. After a brief introduction and handshake, McIntosh turned to his right and introduced a figure David hadn't noticed up to now.

"David, this is Dr James Dalrymple. In between other things, yesterday I took a run out to South Queensferry and met Dr and Mrs Dalrymple and Elvira. I have to say I'm very impressed with the courage and resilience she's shown after all she's been through. You've done a fantastic job, Doctor, in getting her back to full health. She obviously feels very safe with you, which helps her talk more freely to us."

Dalrymple simply nodded.

"So, we have a meeting waiting for us. Gentlemen, shall we?" With that they headed out the main concourse sliding doors, across the complicated network of lanes, walkways, and crossings that fronts Edinburgh International Airport, then finally into the multi-storey car park. They collected McIntosh's unmarked police BMW, swung down three floors, then out onto the link roads and finally the trunk road into town.

"We're using a mothballed office in Corstophine," McIntosh informed them. "It's been pretty full-on since we spoke yesterday. I won't bore you with the details except to say we have a team drawn from a couple of different divisions – officers handpicked from the top. Some working in internal affairs – anti-corruption to you and me – and some people-trafficking specialists. They're good people. And maybe needless to say, this whole operation is off the radar. Officially I am relieved of everyday duties and now working as a staff officer to the Divisional Commander. Nobody is any the wiser than that. Everyone that was at the case conference thinks I'm off the PGC case altogether. We have a mix of DIs, DSs, and DCs. I'm in nominal command acting directly for the Divisional Commander but we'll be running this in a pretty flat way. Hope you can cope with that meantime."

David counted six around the table in a largely bare room on the ground floor of an anonymous set of offices just off the main street in Corstophine village. Four men and two women all in plain clothes each had a buff folder in front of them and were chatting quietly when McIntosh, David, and James Dalrymple came in. David and James each got a plastic beaker of coffee with UHT milk straight from the carton, then were introduced to the group. Rather pointedly, McIntosh did not mention the names of any of those gathered. If he had seemed at all diffident or defensive as he'd presented his findings in the case conference there was no sign of that now as he began the briefing.

"Hi everyone. We all know why we're here so I won't waste time repeating it. There are essentially two matters pertaining to the criminal conspiracy known as PGC. One is the internal issue of what connections there may be between serving officers and PGC, particularly in the light of allegations made by the two girls known as Tatiana and Elvira – and, I might add, in the light of certain features of how the case has been conducted. However, this is going forward in parallel and not for us to deal with in detail today. In relation to the primary investigation, since we have had great difficulty in making any progress on the number and whereabouts of any of the PGC houses and their occupants, it is imperative that we take full advantage of the only lead we have, which comes from Tatiana and her potential shopping trip. So that's what we're going to be talking about for the remainder of this meeting. Oh, and by the way, we have pretty up-to-date images of both men thanks to the activities of the church, which maintained a website." McIntosh tapped his laptop trackpad and took the lens cap off the projector.

Smiling photos of Max and Mikhail, whom David recognized, were projected up.

McIntosh continued.

"There are a lot of unknowns in this and it may end up being another dead end; however, we've got to give it our best shot. The gist of the matter is that Tatiana believes it likely that she will be taken on a shopping trip out of the house and into Edinburgh – she thinks on Thursday, in the afternoon. She only knows the shop as 'Sally'; however, looking at what shops there are on Hanover Street and, shall we say, the nature of what goes on in the PGC houses, we think it pretty likely we're talking about Sally Winters, a lingerie and erotica shop at 29b, Hanover Street."

McIntosh tapped his computer again and popped up an image of the shop taken from Google Street View.

"Twenty-nine B is on the right-hand side going up Hanover Street just next to a Santander Bank and before Rose Street," he explained. "Hanover Street, if you've forgotten, links Princes Street and George Street just opposite the Royal Scottish Academy. Copies of all the photos are in your packs."

"So, if Tatiana does go shopping on Thursday afternoon, on the face of things, it wouldn't be too difficult to identify her, intervene, pick her up, and detain anyone with her. Elvira has, courageously, agreed to be on site to identify her friend and make sure we know who the minders are."

"But that only gets her. What about the rest of the girls and the other houses?" David asked.

"You got there just before me," McIntosh replied. "What about the rest of the girls and the other houses, indeed. We can't just pick her up and throw anyone with her into the slammer. They might tell us their entire life stories but they may not; it may take time. According to Elvira there is a deep sense of unease among the strong-arm guys right now, as if there's some sort of showdown coming."

One of the unnamed team around the table spoke up.

"And do we know why Tati will be shopping? Seems a bit of a risk to take?"

"Good question," McIntosh replied. "According to Elvira, as well as individual clients, the houses stage what are called 'Specials' from time to time. A Special could be just for a single individual involving a number of girls and some other kind of additional services, but generally speaking it's a group event. Apparently student graduations, a significant birthday, a stag night, or even a retirement do can be the occasion for a Special."

David groaned and shook his head.

"That makes it sound like hiring a bouncy castle," he muttered. McIntosh pressed on.

"Friday nights are Special nights and clients often pay double what they'd be paying for what we might call 'normal' services. The girls are expected to look good and put on a good show. And for that, apparently they might need, shall we say, 'unusual' underwear, costumes, and other equipment. Sally Winters is a legitimate business. There isn't any suggestion I'm aware of that they are at all connected to what PGC does. But they are a stockist of exotic lingerie and what they call 'sex toys'. That includes bondage gear, electrical appliances, and lots of other things – stuff a Special night might involve. Elvira has also told us that Tatiana is considered something of a star attraction, so apparently Blatov likes to make sure she's looking her best. This seems to mean a trip to Sally Winters every now and then. Items of clothing have to be tried on to make sure they fit, etc. They can hardly order online with all the identification, payment, and delivery issues that would involve. You get the drift.

"So, to go back to the problem – what we need from this is not just to get one girl out and pick up one strong-arm minder. We want to know where each of the houses is, to get all the girls out, to apprehend all of the principals and their associates, and wrap up the entire operation. Serving officers implicated will be another matter and apparently the money has now walked so that may be hard to trace. But that's the brief. That clear to everyone? Anything to add?"

"Yes," David spoke up. "I'd just like to say how refreshing it is to be in an environment where the girls are the top priority for a change. So, from that point of view, I'm pleased to be involved. And of course I'll help with any information I have that might be useful. But beyond that, I'm not entirely sure what I'm doing here – or Dr Dalrymple, for that matter, if you don't mind me speaking on your behalf, Doctor?"

"James, for goodness' sake," the older man muttered. "But yes. I'm not a policeman and I'm not really planning on being part of a shoot-out at the OK Corral. Once this is all over I am certainly going to be taking some action on my own behalf to get this issue brought higher up the agenda, but for the time being, you know everything I know. So I'm really not sure what more I can add."

"Credibility and confidence," McIntosh said firmly. "Neither Tatiana nor Elvira has had a good experience with the Edinburgh police. They are going to need someone around they can trust whatever we do. Tatiana has said the only person she is willing to trust is 'David H: Pastor'. And we're asking Elvira to do a difficult thing. She trusts you, James. You will not be asked to do anything other than be there – if you're willing. It's what we'd call a 'confidence-boosting measure'. It may not be part of the main operation, but without your involvement, I don't think we could do what we're planning to do. I'd put it as strongly as that."

"So what *are* you planning to do?" David asked somewhat pointedly, giving up the fight on whether he was involved or not.

"I want Tatiana to come out shopping in Hanover Street on Thursday afternoon," McIntosh said crisply, "then go back into the house until Friday night. Then we'll bust the whole place, get all the girls, all the punters, all the staff, and all the cash. How exactly we manage that will form the second part of this briefing, but in the meantime I think it would be courteous at least to let Andrei in Belarus know we have heard, understood, and are acting on his information. David, you may still be at a degree of risk so you'll be staying with friends for a few days. And finally, if there are no more questions, I think we need to break for a bit and get some coffee."

"I think I need something a lot stronger than that," James Dalrymple whispered in David Hidalgo's ear as McIntosh closed the lid of his computer and one of his colleagues flipped the kettle on again.

"I just hope we're not needed on Friday night. It's my wedding anniversary. We were going to go to the Balmoral Hotel. If I miss that I'll need to move to Belarus!"

Mikhail Lubchenco turned the laptop round so that Maxim Blatov could see the screen and pointed to a line on a table of figures.

"Well, look for yourself. There's nothing there, I tell you."

"That's impossible. I moved it myself."

"Well, it's not there now." Mikhail was emphatic. "And I tried to look into the police network this morning. It's blocked. None of the passwords work."

Max paused for a second, then issued an order.

"Call Rudi. There must be some mistake."

"I tried. He's not taking our calls. I think we've been dumped."

"In that case I need to speak to Thompson."

Unusually, Maxim Blatov was not smiling as he tapped his mobile.

DI Thompson's personal phone rang. He flipped it open, saw the number, and immediately left his desk and headed out into the corridor. He only tapped it when there was no one within earshot.

"I told you never to call me at work," he hissed. "I don't care. You've brought all this on yourselves. You do that and you'll be locked up and they'll throw away the key. No. *You* don't know what *you're* dealing with. I might lose my job but you'll be going away for life. Think about that. I have no idea about the cash; we had nothing to do with it. No, I'm not willing to meet you. I'll see you on Friday evening. Then we can talk about this. And not before.

And don't ever call me at work again or I'll personally shop the pair of you!"

Chapter 23

HANOVER STREET

Tatiana had given up hope. Pat hadn't been in to see her for over two weeks, and she had come to the conclusion that he had probably thrown the letter away or handed it in and lost it or something else and didn't want to face her. But if he'd handed it in, why was she still able to walk and talk and feed herself? There was a lot of tension around the house but she didn't feel it was particularly aimed at her. Elvira had never reappeared, of course, and that was a loss. It had certainly seemed like she'd finally got out the only way she could. But maybe she'd somehow survived and was being kept apart from the others until she recovered and could work again. Or maybe Max had simply decided she was too much trouble and opted for "retirement" as it had said on the spreadsheet in the office. Either way, Tati was pretty sure she'd never see her friend again and that it was more than likely she was dead. That was desperately sad but it was what she was used to in this brutal life. She knew she was a commodity for Max, Mikhail, and the various men who used her. She would live as long as she could turn a trick and return a profit. When that day passed so would she. She couldn't stay in the house without working and making money and she couldn't be allowed to leave given everything she knew. These were men who lived at the expense of others and she was one of the others. How they'd got like that she tried not to speculate; she might end up feeling sorry for someone who had had a difficult childhood and had turned to crime as a way to survive on the mean streets of Minsk in the dying days of the Soviet empire. Well, plenty of other people had made it through without turning into monsters. There were always choices.

She mentally corrected herself: for most people at most times there were choices. What choices did she and the other girls have now?

She tried to maintain a positive attitude, to remember that she was a human being and that they could abuse her body but not steal her soul, but it was hard. She cut out fashion photos from copies of the *Evening News* that lay about the dining room and stuck them up on her walls to remind herself of what she once aspired to – a glamorous entrepreneur running a successful temping and office services business in London or Manchester or even in Edinburgh, looking good, feeling confident. She would have meetings with investors and clients, interview applicants, arrange transport and visas for girls from her home country and neighbourhood to come to the West, work hard, and make a life for themselves. Maybe they might get a British boyfriend, a nice flat in town, then a wedding and some kids. Or maybe some of them might start their own businesses too or else just get involved in the community and become naturalized. Maybe they would send some money home to the family or invite brothers and sisters over for a holiday. What about a Belarusian community right here in Edinburgh where they could speak their own language, eat their own food, listen to music, dance, tell stories and be glad that they were Belarusian but didn't have to actually live there? But all that was like smoke on the wind. She was destined to go the same way as Elvira; it was just a question of time. Somehow she had ended up a particular favourite of Max's and of some of his most valued customers, but that just pushed the inevitable a little bit further away – it didn't change anything. She was meat – eventually dead meat.

In the meantime she still had to play the game of pretending to live. That meant getting dressed up in kinky leather gear or some sort of sexy costume to please a bunch of drunken bums who sometimes could barely find their way to the bed by 12.30 on a Friday night. And for that there was another shopping trip tomorrow into town. She had grown to absolutely hate that shop. She wanted to contact Sally, if there was a Sally, and tell her what all the kinky gear and sex toys meant to her. If she had had any hope that Pat had posted her letter then she might have been keyed up in another sort of way. She might have hoped that David H: Pastor might have been there, that he would recognize her or she would somehow recognize him and that he would be able to rescue her from this living hell. She had almost even begun to wonder if such a man existed. When she could be sure no one would come in she had taken to peeling back that corner of wallpaper and reading the lists again, just to remind herself that the name had been written down somewhere and not by her. It was real; she hadn't imagined it. Whether he existed in the real world or not, someone had written down his name and seen him as a danger to PGC and its operators. Maybe they had imagined him as well, and he was just a figment of the collective imagination, like St Nicholas or the Easter Bunny. No doubt Jung might have some explanation for how they had all come to such an odd collective fantasy, but be that as it might, fantasy was what it was. David H: Pastor couldn't come to her aid because he didn't exist. The only things that existed were the men who inhabited both her waking and dreaming nightmares, who bit and licked and drooled and dribbled all over her. Who smacked and struck and pushed and panted, hour after dreary hour. And she had to somehow pretend it was fun or Max would "write it in the book". She wished she had taken that book out of the office, not the two lousy lists. Then she could at least have seen it for what it was – one gigantic lie to mess up their heads. Sometimes a girl would come to her with a smile and a twinkle in her eye and tell her that she had been with Roustabout or Soldier of Fortune last night and had done so well that Max had given her double points in the book. What a pathetic but clever lie. With no other source of hope or anything to believe in it was natural that sometimes the girls would cling to any passing branch or straw. *Max says that if I keep this up I could leave next year. Max says I'm the best in the house. Max says I always get top marks.* Tati didn't comfort herself by thinking about her top marks. When her mind had to be elsewhere, which was roughly five hours every day, she liked to fantasize about the marks she would give Max. What would be best – electrical cable or whiplash? A blunt instrument or something sharp and pointy? Maybe both – alternately. Or both together. She would ask him some meaningless paradoxical question, then whatever he said, she'd say, "Sorry, wrong answer, Maxy. What would you prefer – the whip or the chain?" Anyway, this was only a way of managing an unmanageable reality. It wouldn't change anything; nothing could. She had made an attempt with Andrei's birthday card. What had that achieved? It had probably been incinerated by the council or ended up in a landfill site by now – along with her dreams.

In the meantime, another evening of pathetic losers who didn't have a real girlfriend or who couldn't satisfy their wives or had such low social skills that the very idea of having a successful conversation with a real girl who had the choice of whether to listen to them or turn away was in itself a sexual fantasy. So they came to spend an expensive hour with her, a girl they could never hope to interact with in real life, far less get anywhere near a bed. And she had to giggle or pant and squeal as if they were amusing or exciting. Some of the girls in the house had had dreams of being actresses. Well, what perfect training. It was all acting, although the choice of parts was somewhat limited. None of them would be bold, impressive, dramatic actresses, just cheap little tarts turning it on for the punters. When it was finally over she went to bed with the start of some infection or other and tried to sleep. For all she hated the "Sally" shop, though, at least it was a change of scene. She got to look at normal people going about their normal business and could try to remember what it had been like to be able to decide what you would wear, what you would eat, where you would go, who you would talk to. Sometimes she would play a game with the girls in the house. "Anyone fancy going out tonight for pizza?" she would say in the middle of nothing. "Then we could take in a movie and maybe go dancing after. Anyone up for that?" It used to crack the place up. "Or a weekend in London – see a show or go to a concert? You might attract the attention of a nice-looking young man in the bar at the interval, give him the eye, sidle up to him, and sweetly whisper in his ear, 'Drop dead, buddy; I'm with my friends tonight and I'm sleeping on my own. Got that?'" They used to crease themselves and that made her feel good. She had poured some oil on their troubled waters and brought some humour and relief.

"Tati!" She heard a voice call her name. "Get yourself ready. I can't go today. Dimitri will take you. Leaving in five minutes. Ok? You hear me?"

Leaving in five. If she'd been leaving in five to see David H: Pastor that would have been one thing. But leaving in five just to try on underwear to tickle the fancy of some hopeless creeps with their brains in their balls? Well, it was a trip out at least. She put a pair of flat shoes on and grabbed a jacket. In some last pointless gesture she peeled back the wallpaper and pulled the lists out. What would it matter if she was caught? The papers that had excited them both so much that night had ultimately proved valueless, or whatever value they had couldn't be realized. There was no market for what she had to sell. She stuffed the two by now dog-eared and dilapidated sheets down her jeans, ran a brush through her hair – for what purpose she couldn't have said – and walked up the stairs to the locked and armoured front door.

Needless to say, Sally Winters hadn't existed in Scotland the last time David had lived here and he wasn't aware of any equivalent in Spain. The Great Universal Stores inch-thick catalogue had been the most exciting thing in that line in his childhood, although, to be fair, it was reasonably exciting for a twelve-year-old. Two days previously DI McIntosh had suggested that he and Dalrymple should at least familiarize themselves with the layout of the shop since this was going to be crucial. Having heard the outline in the briefing, they got the general idea and decided a bit of liquid lunch might be necessary first. Deacon Brodies on the Lawnmarket seemed as good as any.

"Do you mind if I ask you how on earth you got yourself

involved in this?" Dalrymple asked, as they navigated from the bar to an unoccupied table, pints in hand.

"I keep asking myself that same question," David replied gloomily. He did a brief resumé of Mike Hunter's role then mentioned Sandy Benedetti, the virus on a pen drive, the connection back to Belarus uncovered by Spade, the gunshot through his bedroom window, and, most recently, the email from Andrei and the list uncovered by Tatiana since confirmed by Elvira.

"Bloody hell," Dalrymple said and let out a low whistle. "And I thought our little incident over the past few days was dramatic. That does take the biscuit."

"Oh, and by the way, I also got engaged less than a week ago. My fiancée Gillian Lockhart is a Scots Language researcher. That's why we were in Galicia. She was speaking at a conference. So, one way or another, it's not been exactly what I was planning at this time of life."

"D'you know, I've been incredibly impressed with Elvira over the past few days. I've got to know her a bit. She's a little wobbly on her pins still but she's determined to show up for Thursday's event. She never stops speaking about Tatiana – 'Tati', she calls her. I just hope it all works – I mean, that she gets out for the day, that what McIntosh and his team are planning goes ahead, that they clean up every last one of them, and get the girls out safe and sound, of course. I'm still dumbstruck that this sort of thing goes on in our city. You read about it in *The Scotsman* and there might be some kind of drama on TV but it never really quite comes home to you that it's all going on right under our noses."

"Ah, well. That's the problem, isn't it?" David mused, taking another sup from his pint. "All human life is going on under our noses. There's a temptation to think that everything grizzly and nasty is banished to a housing estate somewhere else, but in my line of work you get every sort of person coming to you for advice and you find out that both the best and the worst exist everywhere."

"Yes, I've no doubt. The 'chiel amang us', as they say."

"I'm supposed to be in the spiritual care business, but the spiritual is impacted by the physical, the emotional, the psychological, even the economic. It's a Gordian knot and often there's no way of finding out what needs to get sorted first to have an impact on all the rest."

"I'm aware of that in my line too. The public tend to think the anaesthetist's job is just to send people to sleep while the surgeon comes in and does the clever bits. But we have a very particular kind of interaction with patients that the surgeons don't. In all but emergency cases the anaesthetist needs to meet the patient before the op and get to know them a bit – find out a bit about their general health and lifestyle and so on. Because we're not dealing with the cancer or the heart disease or the hysterectomy, people often open up a lot more to us than to the surgeons. They'll say things like, "Does it matter than I had an abortion last year? I've never told my boyfriend or my mum." So you might be the only person they've ever told, apart from the medical staff at the time. I've had patients in floods of tears about things they've never told anyone else that really had nothing to do with the anaesthetic or the operation – childhood abuse, rape, financial problems – or things they might have done years ago, like giving a child up for adoption, an affair, an assault. I had a man confess to bigamy once, as if he needed to get it off his chest before I knocked him out. So I know what you mean. Human life is endlessly surprising. But this has to be the most surprising thing I've ever been involved in. Bar none."

"Indeed – and the converse, what I call 'everyday heroism'. Take Elvira, for example – and Tati. We've heard about her from a couple of different sources. She seems to be a remarkable young woman. I'm taking a positive view on this – that we will get them out and she will get a second chance."

"Have you thought that if things go as we hope we're going to have maybe up to thirty young women with no means of support or place to go suddenly on our hands and no doubt all going to be suffering from post-traumatic stress disorder? It'll be like freeing thirty Al-Qaeda hostages or treating thirty victims of a motorway pile-up. Their physical health is going to be an issue but it's their mental health that worries me. Elvira only ended up in the Forth after she couldn't take any more and tried to hang herself. These girls are going to need a lot of care. I just hope the police have some plan in mind for that as well."

"McIntosh did mention something to me about it. They have specialist counsellors they can bring in, but he wondered whether the churches might be able to help in terms of accommodation maybe or some kind of semi-normal family home while things are being sorted out."

"Well, we certainly should," Dalrymple immediately agreed. "Isn't that what it's all about? Good news to the poor, freedom for the prisoners, recovery of sight for the blind, setting free the oppressed. Our guy Gordon quotes that so often I think everybody in the congregation should be able to recite it verbatim in our sleep."

"Anyway, I'm feeling a little oppressed myself right now," David announced. "The sooner we 'familiarize' ourselves with this place ,the sooner we can go home."

With that, two haddock and chips appeared from the kitchen, then rapidly disappeared, and half an hour later they were heading down Bank Street, past the Royal Bank building, then down the Mound, past the art galleries, then across Princes Street onto Hanover Street. Not much further on, David noticed the Sally Winters shop and felt his heart sink.

"Ever been in here before?" he asked nervously as they were closing on their quarry.

"Are you joking?" Dalrymple retorted. "My wife buys her underwear in Marks and Spencer. That's what made Britain great."

David wasn't quite sure how to take that but noticed a wry smile on Dalrymple's face.

"Ok, here we go," he said. "Deep breath and jump right in.

D'you think they'll reckon we're a gay couple checking out some bondage stuff or just sugar daddies shopping for our girlfriends?"

"Stop it!"

At precisely 10.30 a.m. the following day, Wednesday, Tracy Marshall, manager of Sally Winters, Hanover Street, got an urgent phone call from Head Office. She was in the middle of serving a good-looking, 35–40ish professional type shopping for something special for his honeymoon, which is always nice. He was a bit hazy on garment sizes and was trying to give her an idea just by holding out his hands in a vague sort of cupping motion. She was supposed to guess roughly what he had in mind. It could have been 34 DD or 38 F, for that matter. On the other hand, the beauty of most bondage gear is that one size fits all so that was easier. She took the call at the main pay station. It was the national head of HR. "Listen carefully, Tracy," she was told. They didn't need to say that; she was already listening very carefully. She would be approached within the next ten minutes by a plain-clothes police detective who would identify himself as DI Stuart McIntosh. DI McIntosh would explain to her a police operation that would be taking place in the shop the following afternoon. Senior staff were aware of the circumstances and had approved it. It would require all the regular staff to be given the afternoon off from 11.30 a.m. They would all be paid and told an unannounced stock take would be taking place. No one was under any suspicion – it was just a new procedure. Tracy would remain on site but would not interact with customers from that point on. From the point of staff leaving, two security staff who would in fact be police officers but in appropriate non-police uniforms would be stationed at the front door and would turn customers away on the pretext of a special training event. Those turned away would be given a £5 voucher for another occasion. From then until either closing time, or whatever time DI McIntosh decided, the entire interior shop space would be under Police Scotland jurisdiction. She did not need to know the precise nature of the operation. As an organization they were happy to be able to assist Police Scotland in a vital operation that would apprehend offenders, put an end to criminal activity, protect members of the public, and make Edinburgh a safer city. She would be paid time and a half for the entire day. There would be no danger to her whatsoever; however, DI McIntosh might at any time ask her to move into the staff room behind the main shop where she would stay until further notice. Two plain-clothes female police officers she would be introduced to today would be issued with uniforms and given some basic instructions as to how to operate the tills, etc. Further police officers and others connected with the operation would be posing as customers during that afternoon. No one else would be permitted into the shop other than those the door guards allowed. It was possible that nothing whatever would happen all afternoon, but in any case she would not discuss this phone call, the operation, or anything that did or did not happen the following afternoon. Disclosure would be considered as a disciplinary matter. The company gave the highest priority to assisting the police in their inquiries. Was that clear? Tracy agreed that it was, put the phone down, and looked around, eyes wide. Who might the detective be? The youngish professional type she had been serving came over and showed her his ID. DI Stuart McIntosh.

"Hi Tracy," he said. "Sorry about that pantomime a minute ago. Can we go through to your office for a few minutes?"

That Thursday afternoon Tati got into the car beside Dimitri. He was fat as usual, sweating as usual, and smelly as usual. But she knew the routine by now. She had the collar on and he had the remote. Why did they have to insist on testing it every time? Nowadays, knowing what was coming she was able to brace herself, but the message was plain: any mucking about and you'll be decked before you can say a word to anyone. It was hinted that at setting 5 the shock would do permanent damage. The instinct for self-preservation was still sufficiently strong that she knew it was pointless planning anything. Just go into town, park, walk to the shop, buy something, then back to the car and back to the house. Would it be so bad to stop at McDonald's and get a double cheeseburger with extra relish on the way? But she knew it was pointless to suggest it. Dimitri may have been lacking in intelligence but he knew how to follow orders. By this time she did too. Dimitri pulled the hood over her head and she didn't complain.

It was overcast and a bit hazy but dry once they had parked and started walking. There were shoppers everywhere and a fantastic diversity of fashion, hair styles, tattoos, piercings, even ways of walking. A group of schoolgirls charged along chattering like mad, every one of them with a mobile in their hand showing each other some funny video or a suggestive message from a boy that made them open their eyes wide in horror then fall about laughing. An elderly couple were making their painfully slow way along Hanover Street, careful to keep out of the way of other shoppers who might accidently bang into them or knock them over. They looked nervous and hesitant. Young urban professionals in expensive-looking sunglasses that were not in the least required strode purposefully along, talking on hands-free Bluetooth while swinging a leather briefcase. A young guy who couldn't be more than nineteen sat in a doorway with his dog. The very poorly written sign he had in front of him said *Spare some change. At least you've got a house.* She almost felt some envy. He might not have a house but as least he could sit on the pavement or get up and go when he wanted.

Tati was pretty familiar with Sally Winters after maybe three or four trips and knew which block it was in. But that was unusual; they didn't normally have security at the door.

"That's her! That's Tati!" Elvira said excitedly, standing in the bus shelter nearby wearing sunglasses and a high collar. James Dalrymple stood next to her holding a large shopping bag.

"Yes!" he said under his breath.

The plain clothes officer standing with them spoke into a concealed radio mike.

"ID positive. Subject with one male minder. Dark hair. Dark complexion. Very obese."

One of the guards at the door, who had just turned away a young couple, spotted them twenty-five yards away.

"Subject visual," he confirmed.

Elvira and James just had time to get into the shop and disappear towards the changing rooms.

Whatever was going on, they let Tati and Dimitri through. He usually enjoyed wandering through the shop imagining little Tati dressed up in whatever she was choosing. It was such a pity the girls were strictly off limits to staff. That was a cardinal rule and breaking it wouldn't just be a matter of a note in the file. So he had to use his imagination. His imagination was having to carry more and more of the difference between what he wanted and what was possible these days. He would seriously have to lose some weight and get himself together again. If they weren't even allowed to touch the girls, then where was the fun? So he normally just wandered around making sure he kept Tati in sight. She was free – in a manner of speaking – to choose what she wanted then go and make sure it fitted. She'd already been well warned about any attempt to communicate with the staff or trying anything cute.

It's a bit quieter in here than usual, Tati thought vaguely as she wandered around. Just two shop assistants and three or four customers browsing. She understood what was required and knew her sizes but trying something on at least drew the process out a bit. She picked up a couple of lacy bras, a body stocking, a thing they called the Addiction Dress, and some assorted ironmongery. What she really wanted was a pair of comfortable cotton pyjamas with a fleecy lining but they didn't stock that kind of thing. She took them towards the changing room. That was odd too. A male shop assistant was standing at the entrance to the little half corridor of four changing rooms and there was a new curtain installed that could block off the entire space.

Simultaneously as Tati entered the changing corridor a male store detective approached Dimitri.

"Excuse me, sir," he said. "I wonder if you would mind if I just had a look in that bag you're carrying. Over here, sir. That's the way. Just a routine check."

As soon as Tati entered the corridor the curtain behind her was drawn. But then the curtains of a couple of the changing rooms were pulled. It looked like they were all occupied. So why did they let her come in? And there were men in here. What? A woman with long dark hair and dark glasses stepped in front of her, grinning. What was going on? Suddenly the woman lifted the dark wig off to show short blonde hair underneath, then took of the glasses. It looked like... was it... Elvira! That was impossible; Elvira was dead. She gave an involuntary gasp and felt her legs giving way. An older man in a grey overcoat somehow materialized next to her and took her arm. Elvira – or whoever looked very like her – was holding her finger in front of her lips.

"Tati," she whispered. "It's me. I'm alive. Ssshhh! And this is David H: Pastor. He's real!"

Tati felt herself grow faint. The man in the overcoat put a chair under her and eased her down. She wasn't used to anyone helping her do anything. She let herself be gently lowered.

"Dimitri. Outside," was all she could manage to say.

"That's ok," a youngish man she didn't recognize said gently. "We've taken care of him. You're perfectly safe. Here. Drink this."

Meanwhile Dimitri was being ushered into a back room where two security guards made him turn out the entire contents of his bag and pockets. It transpired he had a pair of nipple clamps in one pocket and pink fluffy handcuffs in the other. That was impossible. He'd just come into the shop. What was going on?

"There must be some mistake," he stuttered. "This stuff isn't mine!"

"How right you are, sir," the detective smiled. "However, I'll just need to take a few details. Now. Your name, address, and nationality please..."

"Tati. Look at me. It's real. This is really happening." Elvira was kneeling on the floor in front of the chair. "It's almost over. Just keep strong."

Now the man in the overcoat was pulling up a chair next to hers. He took her hands in his. They were warm, strong, and comforting – not sweaty or filthy under the nails.

"Tati," he said. "My name is David Hidalgo. I am a pastor in Edinburgh. You found my name on a list. You wrote to Andrei in Belarus. He got your letter and got a message to me. The other men here are police officers but they are officers you can trust. Do you understand me?"

Tati nodded.

"I trust you," she managed to say. "Trust you. Elvira. How?"

"Dimitri tried to kill me," Elvira whispered, looking up, still grinning into Tati's face just in front of her. Tati's complexion was the colour of the white cubicle curtains behind them. "But he didn't. Maxi save me. Maxi belong to James. He help me." She looked half-round over her shoulder towards a tall older man standing just behind them and smiling warmly.

Tati gave a start but Elvira just grinned at her all the more.

"No worry," she said. "Maxi is a dog. Is beautiful. You see her soon."

"Ok, Tati, can I explain to you?" David H: Pastor was speaking, still holding her hands. "It's almost over but not quite. We'll get you out. You won't have to live that way any more. But there's one thing more we need you to do. We want to get all the girls out of all the houses. Will you help us?"

Tati nodded weakly, slowly recovering her senses.

"This man is a police officer who is going to get all the girls out of all the houses. He'll explain what we'd like you to do."

McIntosh got down on his hunkers next to Tati and held on to the chair back to keep his balance but didn't touch her.

"Tati," he said, "you have been incredibly brave. We're going to ask you to be brave one last time. Then it'll all be over. Max and Mikhail and all the rest will be going to prison for a long, long time.

They will never trouble you again. The girls will all get out. We'll do everything we can to let them stay in Britain. They'll get good medical care and a place to live in peace. But we need you to help us."

She nodded again, now in command of herself. She swallowed hard and sat up a bit. Then she felt something uncomfortable digging into her stomach and the tops of her legs. She straightened her back a little more, drew in her tummy and reached into the top of her jeans.

"This is for you," she said, handing the papers to David. "What do you want me to do?"

Dimitri was not a happy man when they let him out of the office. He didn't have any ID on him – no passport, no driving licence, no papers, no visa documents, no nothing. And how had that stuff got into his pockets? He guessed it must have been some kind of a training exercise. One guy would plant something on you then the others would fish it all out and treat you like a common criminal. Maybe they thought it was better training for handling shoplifters than just having somebody pretend, but he resented it. How dare they manhandle him like that! What right did they have to go through all his stuff? They had even found the remote for the collar. With all his stuff being dumped out of his pockets onto the tiny table it had fallen on the floor and split wide open, batteries going everywhere and the plastic cover pinging off. He'd a good mind to complain and get them to replace it but of course it was an illegal device anyway so he just shovelled it all up, swearing in Belarusian. It had taken an age. They had this huge form to fill in. When he complained they told him he could help them fill in the form or speak to the police – which did he prefer? So they worked through it in painful, tedious detail. His name – he gave a false one. His address – he tried to make something up but he knew nothing about Edinburgh and was stuttering and spluttering, which didn't look good, so he'd ended up giving the proper address rather than nothing. They were stupid store detectives; it wouldn't matter.

Then why was he in Edinburgh. Was he a resident or visitor? How long was he planning on staying? Did he have a preference for any of the tourist sites he might visit? What score would he give on a scale of 1–10 to the Castle, the National Museum, the Royal Yacht *Britannia*, the Royal Mile, Holyrood Palace? He didn't care about any of them; in fact, he hardly knew what they were and gave whichever number popped into his mind first. "Sorry, sir," one of them said. "You can't give a 6 to the Castle and the Royal Mile. They have to be different." "Then whichever number you want, please!" he shouted. "I don't care nothing for any of them. Will you let me go please. I don't do nothing. This not my stuff!" All the while he was wondering about Tati outside. She must be finished by now. She would come out and see he wasn't there. What would she do? And if she wasn't there what would he do? If she had done a runner he couldn't go back to Max and tell him he'd lost their star attraction. They would kill him dead for sure. *Sorry, Max, I just lost Tati. They caught me shoplifting some fluffy handcuffs. But I got off with it. Look – here they are. Sorry.* He knew it wouldn't go like that. Max would be smiling at him in that scary way. He wouldn't shout. He'd just say how disappointed he was and that he was sorry but something would have to be done. Then he would hand him over to Mikhail and Boris. They would finish it off. He'd be floating along next to Elvira in the Forth. But then one of the men pressed his finger to his earpiece, listening, and suddenly it was all over. "I'm terribly sorry, sir," he said. "There seems to have been some mistake. I do apologize for any inconvenience. Yes, you're perfectly free to go. There won't be any charges and the records will be destroyed." "Yes, sir," he said back. "You bet there is no charges. I keep telling you – none of that stuff is mine. Do I look like I need this things? I speak your boss. You get fired. How you bring me in here and say me a criminal? You the criminals. Yes, you. And you too. You the criminals. I get you all fired. I call your office tomorrow. Don't bother come to work. You finished. Now all my stuff please. Ok. I go."

When he got back out into the main shop he could hardly believe it. There was Tati, just waiting patiently at the main counter with a bag in her hand. He smiled but not at her. He had her well trained, for sure. Max better look out. One day soon he'd start his own house. Tati would work for him. Then Max could worry. These store detectives were idiots. Tati was just a stupid girl. Max was too confident. Mikhail was an uneducated fool. Dimitri was the smart one. They would all see soon. For sure.

Chapter 24

DUFF STREET

Tracy Marshall came out of the office after a boring hour spent reading *Heat* from cover to cover. She now knew everything about Charlotte and Gary's break up, had seen Peter Andre's secret night of passion pics, and taken the depression test. Turned out she was actually dangerously extrovert and needed to calm down a bit. Her mum would confirm that. She hadn't heard a dicky bird from in the shop for the full hour, and when DI McIntosh thanked her he seemed satisfied but didn't explain. So she decided to close early as there weren't any staff around anyway. If headquarters didn't like it, they could lump it. Since she'd dumped that loser Neville her evenings were free again. She pulled out her mobile and tapped on the Tinder app. After a boring day she needed some excitement. At least she was never lacking in accessories for a date night.

The police team gathered up all their papers and equipment. The changing corridor curtain was taken down. After Dimitri and Tati had disappeared, Elvira couldn't stop jumping up and down and hugging everyone. "Tati! Tati!" she kept saying. "We get you out, we get you out!" James found himself getting a huge hug with everyone else and didn't object. "Well done, Elvira," he whispered in her ear. "You did well." Nothing would have pleased him more than to meet Sarah in town and take them both to the best restaurant they could find. But maybe a shopping trip to Jenners, John Lewis, or M&S first: a complete new wardrobe, make-up, perfume, dresses, night things, *proper* underwear, sports stuff, casuals, the works. As her new adoptive family in Scotland and representative of her father in Belarus, he intended to take his responsibilities seriously, whatever it cost. He was not a poor man and nothing would give him more pleasure than hearing the plastic creaking under the weight of all the stuff Elvira had been denied for years. Every day would be her birthday now. And he also had a plan to repay whatever she had taken from her father with interest if it would restore relationships. But he knew that would be reckless right now. Until the girls were out and Max and Mikhail and whatever others he had heard mentioned but couldn't remember all the names of – until they were all locked up for good, Elvira still had to not exist. He made her put the wig, glasses, and high-collared coat on again, then shook hands with David and DI McIntosh and headed out. It would have to be Chinese takeaway tonight. Though he didn't know it, that was Elvira's favourite.

David looked round the shop one last time as the SWAT team got their stuff together, high fiving, all smiles. It had been a triumph – not the final triumph but a triumph nevertheless. He couldn't help feeling both a sense of elation and also a sense of anticlimax. Tati was real and he had shown that he was real too. He had met her, held her hand. Despite the temptation to run away and keep on running she had immediately understood what McIntosh was asking of her and agreed without hesitation. She was the real hero of what had just happened.

He felt a momentary pang and wasn't sure what it was, then recognized it for the familiar, dull, numbing realization that he would never have a daughter like her – or like anyone. Or a son either. Well, that was old news. He braced up and took a last look round the shop. Dalrymple had already disappeared with Elvira, their work over. McIntosh and his team would be having a debrief in the anonymous off-radar Corstorphine offices in about half an hour. Someone from the team would take him in an unmarked police car. For some reason they still seemed to want him involved, when all he wanted was to go back to his flat in Bruntsfield, put Chet Atkins on, open a bottle of Ribera del Duero, make a simple supper, and try to forget it all. No, there was one other thing he wanted. He wanted Gillian to be calling through from the kitchen. *I think this is sticking a bit, honey. D'you want me to give it a stir?* Then he'd put down whatever book he was reading, but keep his glass in hand and get up and go through. She'd be making a salad or something sweet to go with his *paella* or *rabo de toro* or *polla a la jerez*. He'd kiss her lightly or maybe put his glass down and devote a bit more attention to it. In about half an hour the supper would be ready and they'd eat together, then maybe snuggle up on the sofa and watch a romantic movie and leave the dishes till morning. But Gillian was in Ribadeo finishing off another day in her conference week, maybe planning to eat alone or maybe she'd met someone younger and more interesting and would allow herself to be taken out to *A Dorada* and wined and dined. No. He stopped himself. That way madness lay. The week was nearly over and she'd be home on Sunday. By that time he truly hoped the whole thing would be done and dusted – girls gathered up and these monsters in custody, every single one of them. A voice behind him jarred him back to reality.

"What do you think of this one? They've got it in my size."

He turned. There she was, right in front of him in her warm winter coat, holding up the most revealing undergarment he didn't even know the name of. He couldn't remember her looking more beautiful or more appealing. He dropped his bag and just wrapped his arms around her and squeezed. Neither of them said a word.

Tati sat in a daze all the way back to the house. She let Dimitri put the hood over her head and didn't even mind. Whatever they did, she wasn't in the dark any more. David H: Pastor *was* real. It was like a mythological hero from one of her childhood storybooks turning up in person to ask if she wouldn't mind helping out in a little enterprise they had on. The gods and heroes of old had overcome their petty jealousies and rivalries to once and for all overcome the powers of darkness. But they needed the help of a pure and virtuous human girl and had chosen her. Would she mind? Maybe that was a bit dramatic but no more unlikely. David H: Pastor had a plan. She needed to play her part, but mainly it just involved not giving the game away. She gripped the device in the form of a plain, cheap ballpoint pen they had given her tightly and wondered how exactly it would work. Would they see her location on a screen like a GPS, or was it something you could only view on a computer? But what if she were separated from the pen – if she was sent to another house at the last minute or somehow it ended up in the rubbish and was thrown out? She imagined going for a shower before the Special the following evening and coming out to find that all of her clothes had disappeared or been gone through. Stranger things had happened. Max was always smiling and relaxed, completely in control, but Mikhail was suspicious and would surprise everyone with a room check at ten o'clock in the morning. They'd all be turned out of bed and made to sit in their night things in the dining room while he organized his goons to tear their rooms apart. Contraband like a magazine that wasn't allowed or some pills in a quantity beyond what was permitted were all piled up on the dining room table and punishments were dished out. It might be a cold shower for ten minutes or not being allowed to leave your room for two days – except to work of course. If it was something bad then all the girls were punished. Once Mikhail got furious about something and made them all line up in the hall. He ripped the fire hose out of its holder and turned it on them at full force, totally deaf to the screams and tears. Then, soaking wet and frozen, they had to get down on their hands and knees for an hour and mop up the water while the minders stood round making obscene remarks.

She shook herself. It wasn't doing any good thinking about everything that might go wrong. Even if the pen was pulled out, snapped in two, and thrown in a waste paper bin, she was confident there would be another plan, another way. David H: Pastor *was* real. Andrei *had* got her letter. He had found the real man behind the name on the list. They had kept Dimitri busy while it was all explained to her. Best of all, Elvira was alive – and she was free! She was living with a Scottish family, and she, Tati, would be with her soon. They could go shopping together – but not in Sally Winters. If Dimitri only knew what was just about to happen he wouldn't be whistling like that as he drove. He wouldn't be driving back to the house at all. He would have stopped at the side of the road, taken her collar and hood off, and driven as fast as he could in another direction. But he didn't know – the fat, ugly slob. He seemed to have been sweating even more than normal, whatever had happened back in the shop. She would smell the disgusting reek right next to her, making her gag and choke. Well, not long now. Hold on, Tati. Just hold on.

David and Gillian sat as close as the seatbelts allowed in the back of DI McIntosh's police BMW and hardly spoke. Gillian just confirmed what she'd told David when he'd phoned on Tuesday night. Things had gone ok; nothing earth-shattering, but ok. Then she'd found she just couldn't cope with sitting in the audience listening to some hairy academic from Truro talking about compound constructions and tag questions in Cornish so she'd got up, gone back to *O Retorno*, switched on her laptop, and looked at flights. The earliest she could get was Thursday morning and she'd decided it might be best not to be a distraction in whatever was being planned. She'd emailed McIntosh, who had been happy for her to show up but only once the operation was over. That worked for her. Grabbing something called the Sheer Chemise with Crochet Trim was just a bit of devilment she couldn't resist. It seemed to have had an impact. She was worried she'd gone too far when she saw the look on his face. Anyway, all's well, etc. She put her head on his shoulder and gripped his arm. She wondered if she should worry about her husband-to-be taking so much interest in Eastern European sex workers between the ages of eighteen and twenty-eight but immediately dismissed the thought. And she hoped he knew that none of the tedious academics on the Celtic Fringe could hold a candle to him. *Hidden depths*, she thought. *That's what he's got. And I'm only beginning to find out what they are.*

"Ok, everyone. I think that went well. Any comments or feedback?"
The police team, plus David and Gillian, sat around the same

plain conference table in the same anonymous room where the last briefing had taken place only two days before. McIntosh was standing at the head of the table looking quietly satisfied and there was a relaxed atmosphere in the room, filled with the sound of general murmurs of approval. McIntosh went around the table and insisted on a comment of some sort from everyone. Gillian immediately noticed a marked difference in tone from Stevenson's at the previous week's case conference. McIntosh genuinely wanted to know what each member of his team thought or, if not, gave a convincing impression of it. David just gave a generally favourable assessment but didn't go into any detail.

"Dimitri was a pussycat," one of the guys remarked. "Complained a bit but didn't have a leg to stand on. No ID of any sort and couldn't even remember his address. I think the one he gave us eventually was actually genuine. What a numpty."

"I think that's a fair assessment," McIntosh concurred. "We've actually got surveillance on the property and Blatov has already been identified coming out. So one-nil to us at this stage, I think."

"Where is the property, if I'm allowed to ask?" David piped up.

McIntosh consulted his papers.

"Duff Street in Gorgie," he said.

"What?" David spat out. "You're joking."

"Why's that?" McIntosh asked, eyebrows raised.

"Spade, the hacker, lives in Duff Street," Gillian replied. "All the time we were meeting with him trying to find out where the virus had come from we must have been within a hundred yards of the main house."

"Looks like it. And Tati also provided the documents that Andrei made reference to – the White List and the Black List. I'm afraid your name is on the Black List, along with some other enemies PGC seem to have made along the way. But, perhaps more importantly, we've got the White List, with around fifty names – actual names, addresses, identifying initials like 'JP', 'QC', 'MP', and, believe it or not, 'CID'. PGC have clearly been both overconfident and careless. They must have thought they were impregnable given the number of powerful people who would not want their connections exposed, so there wasn't really any need for secrecy inside the house because they were never going to be busted. Too many vested interests. Well, we have a parallel team working on this stuff right now. Friday night is certainly going to be Music Night for a lot of important men who will not want to be facing the music. Anyway, it's not all going to happen by magic. We can be very satisfied in this afternoon's operation but we need to start planning Friday now. So I suggest you get yourself a coffee and we reconvene in ten minutes. Well done, everyone."

David and Gillian excused themselves, as there was no way they wanted anything to do with Friday night. David assumed McIntosh had included them in the debrief as a courtesy, which he appreciated, but that was it; their role was over. When the girls were out he certainly wanted to meet Tati and hear her story. She seemed a remarkable young woman who would have a bright future ahead of her. As regards the suggestion that the churches get involved in helping, he would certainly offer whatever resources Southside had to offer. He thought that Mrs MacInnes would be the ideal strong, steady, substitute granny to help some troubled young women get back on their feet again. But that was for another day. In the meantime they would leave the police team to the details.

"Just before you go, a big thank you for this afternoon, David," McIntosh said as they were getting their coats on.

"I won't say it was entirely a pleasure but I think we got a result."

"Indeed we did. Thanks to you both. I'll keep you informed. Assuming things go according to plan tomorrow night, there'll probably be a conference early next week. If we pick up servicing officers or we can get more intelligence then there will be suspensions and arrests. You'll probably see it on the news before you hear any more from me. So have a good weekend. Take it easy."

David slumped on the sofa as soon as they stepped into Gillian's place. She put a quick pasta dish together while he just lay and stared into space. They ate together on trays with a cheap pinot grigio. Brandenburg Concertos played softly in the background. They didn't speak much. She had a bit of cheesecake left over, which still seemed to be edible, so they finished off with that.

"What are you thinking?" she finally asked.

"Not much," he replied. "Small thoughts of a mollusc. I don't know who said that but that's about it."

"Well, my favourite mollusc anyway," she said and kissed his forehead. "It all went well. You should be happy."

He yawned and stretched.

"I am, but it takes its toll. I can't get over these girls, Tati and Elvira. Each of them is worth fifty of the hoods controlling them. After all they've been through they should be nervous wrecks but they're not. They are courageous, resilient, and at least in Tati's case, willing to live through another twenty-four hours or so till Friday night. I suppose she'll have to tolerate some other sleazy punter tonight. I can hardly stand to go to bed myself just imagining what she's having to put up with."

"Well, don't imagine it. You've done everything possible to change things for them. We both have. It'll be over soon. Then they can build something better."

"I just hope there isn't any lasting damage. I suppose there's bound to be after something like this. Maybe it's something you never get over. Either way, they'll need the best help anyone can offer. They've suffered in Scotland. It would be good if they could stay – if they want to – and get whatever help they might need here as well."

Dimitri was full of the story when they got back to Duff Street. Tati went straight to her room, but he grabbed a beer from the fridge and sat down with Yuri and Boris. He didn't dwell on why he'd spent fifteen minutes in the back office of Sally Winters, leaving Tati totally unsupervised outside, or how he'd been planted with unpaid-for items for a store detective training exercise. The point was that when he'd come out, there she was, patiently waiting at the desk. He had trained her well; she knew her place. She wouldn't dare cross Dimitri. He got them all laughing when he told them about the meek and obedient expression on her face. Then he started complaining about Max and Mikhail – how they were making such a fortune from the houses and not sharing with the staff. And not sharing the girls either. That brought grumbling agreement. Things had been good in the early days. Ok, so you weren't allowed to take a girl from the house you were working in, but as soon as the second, third, and fourth houses opened, you could work in one house and help yourself to the goods from another. And they were paid generously and regularly. So, good money and fringe benefits. Then it all started getting tighter and less fun. They were expected to work longer for the same money, then longer for less, then not touch any of the girls. That had all been Sasha's fault. He would work one shift in Duff Street then spend the rest of his time in Craigmillar helping himself to the goods, one after another, and leaving the girls not able to work the following day. He was a stupid Russian who had spoiled it for everyone else. Now things were more and more strict.

Max had had that same annoying smile on his face when he'd told them that things were changing. He patiently explained that his deal with the police was that they would turn a blind eye if certain conditions were met – no public nuisance, no admissions to casualty, no excessive use of drugs, no street prostitution, and no overpaid muscle throwing their weight around in city pubs and clubs. When any of these were breached – like that time he and Boris had been involved in a slight misunderstanding at Finnegan's Wake – then everyone took a beating. Max had tried to tell them it was because of the need to invest in future operations, build up the infrastructure, and get ready for expansion to some other locations. But Dimitri wasn't fooled. It was that creep Stevenson leaning on him. If you can't control your goons then we will, he'd probably said or something like it. So wages were cut and benefits restricted for everyone. *Who was running this show then*, Dimitri wanted to know, *Max and Mikhail or Stevenson and his buddies?* Dimitri had a theory. Max was blaming Stevenson but he was taking a bigger cut for himself and maybe sharing it with someone else. He snapped open another beer and belched loudly.

Recently things had been getting worse, he said. Sending him and Boris out to snuff out that little banker had been a big mistake. He'd tried to tell them but nobody was listening. When the perfect suicide scenario had turned into a murder inquiry Max had said that Stevenson and Thompson would make sure it didn't get anywhere, but supposing it did? It was their necks on the line, not Max's. Boris agreed, opened another beer, and passed one to Yuri. Then there was the pastor. He looked like he'd blow away in a strong breeze but he just kept on coming, whatever you did to him. If the shot had been on target that would have been one problem less, but Thompson had told them he'd had no choice but to put him in a safe house, so that was their one chance gone. Then he'd disappeared altogether. Phoning up the university and asking for his little girlfriend had been pretty stupid too. Still, at least he was out of the picture and not sticking his nose in like normal. It's no surprise that with all of that coming down around their ears the church had had to close, Max and Mikhail had had to drop out of sight, and he'd even heard that they'd lost access to the police computers. Sasha had told him he'd heard Max and Mikhail shouting in the office the other day about money in an account; maybe there were cash flow problems as well. What did it all add up to? That Max and Mikhail were past it and PGC needed new management. When Dimitri had seen little Tati standing at the counter waiting for him in Sally Winters this afternoon it had finally made up his mind. *Who was in?* Friday night at the Special would be the perfect opportunity. Max, Mikhail, Stevenson, Thompson, and all their other friends in one place at one time. It was perfect. But he had a few phone calls to make first to get all the little ducks lined up. Then roll on Friday.

Tati went straight to her room and lay on the bed. She could hardly contain herself. It was like drinking too much champagne or getting a new boyfriend; she wanted to giggle or laugh out loud. She certainly couldn't keep a smile off her face. But she had to compose herself in case someone came in. Only a little over twenty-four hours to go. She'd just have to make it through one more night of groping and fumbling, heaving and groaning, then it would be over. Of course she didn't know exactly what would happen or when but she was 100 per cent sure that something was going to happen, something decisive and final – something that would surprise them all. But especially Max. That would take the smile off his face. Permanently. It would all happen like clockwork, she knew. All she needed to do was keep this stupid grin off her face and behave exactly like normal. So she sat up, straightened her face, emptied the Sally Winters bag out on the bed, and started going through the stuff to get it all ready. She might be in the oldest profession in the world but she was going to act completely professionally. Roll on Friday.

From what Tati and Elvira had told them, McIntosh explained to his team – now they all had a fresh coffee in front of them – they knew there were seven houses, all run by PGC. The main house was in Duff Street, then further establishments were in Salamander Street, Craigmillar, Muirhouse, Wester Hailes, Granton, and Victoria Quay. They had tails on Blatov and Lubchenco already, along with anyone who came or went from Duff Street, so there was a good chance they'd be able to identify the houses even before Friday but, if not, it was almost certain they'd find their addresses in the records in the office in Duff Street. Blatov and Lubchenco seemed to feel so confident in their police protection that they were being negligent in their own internal security. "Criminally negligent," piped up one wag to general mirth before McIntosh called them to order again. So, assuming they could place teams in each location, they would go in at exactly the same time – 3 a.m. on Friday evening when the party was in full swing. If not, then SWAT teams would be stationed in each vicinity, ready to get an address as soon as they could access one, whether from office records or by persuading a participant in Friday's fun and games to cooperate in the hope of maybe some consideration in court. So that was it. Everyone knew their roles in the operation. They'd reconvene in the morning to go over it once again and update intelligence; in the meantime, go home, relax, unwind a bit, and roll on Friday.

Chapter 25

FRIDAY NIGHT IS MUSIC NIGHT

There was always a lot going on prior to a Special night. Mikhail would go around adjusting the decorations, making sure there was enough drink in the fridges and snacks on the tables and that broken lightbulbs were replaced. Each of the girls had to dress and was inspected from top to toe. Sometimes they were sent off to fix their make-up or even change into something more revealing. The end result was that everybody was totally keyed up. In the middle of this particular evening, Tati felt she was ready to explode, but she had to keep a straight face and behave totally normally. With about half an hour to go, Tanya came to her in floods of tears.

"I just can't do this any more," she sobbed. "I hate them. I hate them all. I can't go on."

It was so tempting to say, *Don't worry, Tanya. In a couple of hours it'll all be over and you'll never have to do it again.* But she couldn't. She just helped her dry her eyes and tidy up her mascara.

"You'll be fine," she said soothingly. "It won't go on for ever. Take it easy. I'll try and make sure you don't get one of the worse ones. I'll take Stevenson."

"Thanks, Tati," Tanya said. "Sorry, I know I have to. You're the best."

Tati let out a sigh of relief as she sent her back to her room to compose herself and went to change into her latest Sally Winters creation. *Great for your honeymoon with the man you want to spend the rest of your life with*, she thought, fiddling with the straps. Maybe even ok for a wild weekend in Grodno with a cool guy you met in a bar. Not so good just to be peeled off by a fat, sweaty man in his late fifties with bad breath who thinks you are his personal plaything.

Dimitri was keyed up too and also tanked up with a couple of shots to keep him steady. However much he boasted and blustered in front of Boris and Yuri, he knew that taking on Max was not in fact a piece of cake and carried significant risks. He thought he'd got the others on side and he'd made sure they had sufficient firepower if things got messy, but this wasn't going to be a Sunday afternoon picnic on the banks of the Svislach. As a result he was even more rude and aggressive to the girls than normal. Kristina ended up in tears on account of something he said and Mikhail tore a strip off him and told him to keep his fat butt out of the way and look after security like he was paid to. *Just a couple of hours, Mikhail*, he thought, *then you'll get yours. I've got a Special for you that you won't forget.* But he did as he was told.

Less than a hundred yards away McIntosh and his team were keyed up too but there was also something of a party atmosphere in the van. Sally Winters had felt like much the more speculative operation and that had gone better than could have been hoped. This was just sweeping up. It turned out they didn't even need the bug they'd given Tati once that idiot Dimitri had blurted out the actual street address of the main house. What an amateur. But it was still useful giving them local broadcast audio. And this was the first serious outing for the van, which was proving a huge asset. It had actually been the idea of Douglas Forsyth, the Divisional Commander, and he had fought hard for the resources to put it together and to keep its development confidential. McIntosh liked the joke in the livery on the side. A huge pantechnicon furniture van converted to two internal floors with a mixture of holding rooms with interview facilities, an incident room, hi-tech surveillance, and even a coffee machine was just exactly what this type of operation needed. That way they could transport up to twenty-four officers exactly to where they were needed in a single group, with all the facilities needed perfectly camouflaged, in built-up areas. Only a furniture van-sized vehicle would be big enough and, as it happened, nobody would bat an eyelid seeing it parked outside a block of flats. To complete the illusion, the van had "OUR MOVE" in huge letters on the side, with two fat blokes carrying a sofa as its logo. That was appropriate to the illusion but also very funny. McIntosh enjoyed the thought that Blatov, Lubchenco, and their lackeys had been calling the shots to date but now it was law enforcement's move. The audio feed from Tati's bug matched how she had described preparations for a Special night, though he would have loved to have heard a bit more of Dimitri's conversation just after they'd got back. Well, he'd find it all out in due course. In the meantime, Operation Top Hat – he had no control over the choice of designation – was sitting tight and ready to go. As well as his immediate team, they had a bunch of uniforms in body armour all wired for sound and video, night vision kit, two battering rams, stun guns and firearms, flash grenades, and a bucket load of other stuff you don't get in army surplus. He was ready.

David and Gillian were also keyed up on the other side of town. Having finally tracked down David H: Pastor, Elvira couldn't get enough of his visible, touchable reality and begged Dalrymple to let them get together on Friday evening. So James, Elvira, Sarah, and Paul had come over to Gillian's Marchmont flat, which had a considerably bigger living room space than David's. They drank tea or strong coffee and nibbled olives and savoury snacks but the conversation was desultory and vague. McIntosh had provided them with a receiver on the operational frequency, and it murmured away in the background with a load of coded comms abbreviations that meant nothing to anyone. David was surprised how calm and routine it all sounded. Elvira was high as a kite and chattered incessantly but he only managed vague monosyllabic responses or didn't even notice he was being addressed. Gillian looked after the guests with food and drink and kept a slightly nervous eye on David. She knew him well enough to know he didn't handle high-anxiety situations very well.

By 10.30 Mikhail was satisfied with preparations and allowed the girls to sit down and have a drink or pop whatever pill they wanted in moderation. Guests were forbidden to arrive before 11.00 p.m. so there was a breather. He would rather be ready half an hour early than two minutes late. This would be a big one. It was the first time Stevenson and all the insiders had come in a single group. That was somewhat risky but Stevenson had insisted. He had just hit forty years in the force and had a huge pension to look forward to. After all the rough he'd had to put up with it was time for some smooth. The silky smooth skin of a nineteen-year-old would do just nicely. When the door entry buzzer finally went Mikhail himself answered it. He took his role of master of ceremonies seriously. Max looked after what they called policy and strategy, but Mikhail's job was to keep the customers satisfied, and deal with what they laughingly called HR – a suitably dehumanized term for the resource they were managing.

"Mr Stevenson, nice to see you. We have a fantastic evening planned for you and your companions."

"Evening, Mikhail. Happy days are here again. Things have been getting a wee bit bumpy of late. You boys better get your act together again or you'll be wishing you were selling ciggies on the street corner. Oh, hello, darlin'!"

Six further burly men trooped in after him, laughing, joking, pushing, and jostling in high spirits. Their boss was leading the line. He'd have it all sewn up. And the girls were on him tonight. Mikhail ushered them into the main lounge.

"You've been redecorating, Mikhail," Stevenson boomed. "Very tasteful." Charlie Thompson just behind him wondered what his wife would have made of it. "Lurid", "disgusting", "an accident in a paint factory" might all be expressions she could have used. Anyway, she wasn't going to be asked to comment on the decor or any other aspect of the evening. As far as she knew, George Stevenson was hosting a wee celebration for his closest fellow officers in a converted bingo hall in Leith – a couple of drinks, maybe a band, then fillet steak all round, 'nuff said. After twenty years a polis wife she'd learned when to keep her doubts and suspicions to herself. Anyway, she'd be spending the evening with a friend called Barry that Charlie knew nothing about. So that was fine too.

The decor on the walls wasn't the main attraction, of course, and as each of the men came into the lounge they were met by a smiling escort who took their coats and hats, supplied them with a drink of their choice, then sat down draped around them as they had been trained to do. Tati made for Stevenson, leaving Tanya to go with Thompson, a slightly less disgusting choice. So drink was taken and Tati's pen – which she'd popped behind a pot plant, having been told to keep it as near to her as possible – relayed crisp, clear audio of light giggly voices, raucous laughter, obscene jokes, calls for more drink, and general congratulations to George, who was, without a doubt, a true survivor. One or two of the boys had even got him something, so there was also the sound of the unwrapping of crinkly paper and happy surprise. To remind him of their night of pleasure, Thompson and Carmichael had clubbed together and got him an expensive *Playboy* coffee table collection.

"Very nice – but not needed tonight, boys," was Stevenson's laconic response.

Around 11.30 the lights dimmed in the lounge, all but at the far end where a small performance area had been cleared. An eerie Eastern beat began, and Natasha, who normally worked in the Victoria Quay house, came on dressed as a harem girl. There was uproarious applause, whistling, and catcalling. It was a good job Natasha's English and for that matter her urban Scots wasn't too good, though the gist of it was plain enough. Gillian might have done a paper on twenty-first-century Scots euphemisms for sex. Natasha was a very beautiful girl, and once she started moving the noise died down right away as the guys sat round with their mouths open, transfixed by what they were seeing but also half-dying of anticipation for what was to come. Even Mikhail came in to watch. It was spellbinding. As a professional he could appreciate her style.

In fact, so engrossed did he and all the guests become that nobody noticed Dimitri, Boris, and Yuri edging into the room instead of being on door duty as they should have been. Yuri, as the slimmest, edged forward towards where Natasha was but nobody took any notice. The beat was building, Natasha glancing round enticingly from one gawping face to another as she spun, weaved, and swayed in time to the music. Boris stationed himself opposite Yuri and Dimitri was near the door. Everyone in the house was accounted for. They were all together in one place, just as Dimitri had planned. Everything was going perfectly.

At a nod from Dimitri, Boris yanked the audio cable out of the wall and the music instantly stopped. Stevenson and his crew hardly had time to protest before two sharp gun shots deafened them all. Dimitri was shouting. "On the floor. Everybodys! On the floor!"

Tati was confused. This wasn't part of the police operation, was it? Was Dimitri on the side of the police all the time? Mikhail had no doubts. He was swearing in Belarusian. He tried to stand up and Boris battered him on the back of the head with the barrel of his pistol. Mikhail went down, holding his scalp. Everyone else was frozen.

"Are you deaf, everybodys? I said on the floor!" Dimitri shouted again and let off another round just to show he wasn't joking. The girls immediately hit the deck or tried to hide behind the sofas, hands over their ears. Stevenson, Thompson, and the others weren't so easily phased.

"Come on now, fellas. What's this all about? You're spoiling a great party," he began, but Dimitri took a step forward and levelled the gun directly at his head.

"You want argue about it?" he asked. "What part you not understand, please?"

Reluctantly they followed instructions.

"Now, Mr Lubchenco. You. Get up. Come with me. We go office. If anybody's moving they gets a bullet, ok?" He walked over and half-lifted, half-dragged Mikhail off the floor.

"Change of management," he said sweetly. "A few things we need discuss, no?"

"Max will kill you for this," Mikhail spat out.

"Max is history," Dimitri said, trying to smile just the way he had seen Max do so often. "Right now, Max is my guest in Salamander Street house." He glanced at his watch. "And all other houses under new management too. Now come. We friends, no?"

Tati lay on the carpet quivering. She was sure this wasn't supposed to happen. *Where was David H: Pastor and his police I'm supposed to trust?*

"The computer," Dimitri ordered Mikhail, holding the barrel of his pistol to the back of his head. "The money. You show me where is the money I maybe let you live."

Mikhail gave a bitter laugh.

"That's funny," he said. "There is no money. Not any more. Max moved it to a safe account but when we looked two days ago it wasn't there. Nobody knows where it is."

"You think I'm a idiot?" Dimitri shouted. "You treat Dimitri like a crazy kid? You go to the banking. You show me the money or you never leave this room!"

"I can show you the account," Mikhail said wearily, as Dimitri pushed him into the office with a gun in his back. "I'd be happy to share the money with you if you could find it."

He tapped the keyboard to wake up the computer and started tapping and clicking. Dimitri, standing behind him, was aware of how much he was sweating. His mouth felt like the only dry part of him.

Back in the main room the police and the girls were all flat on the floor. Boris and Yuri were smiling at each other as they kept guns trained.

"Hey, Tati," Boris said, breaking the silence. "Get me a beer. Out the fridge. Now."

Slowly she began to get up and head for the door.

"No that one, you idiot. You're not going anywhere. I've got plans for you."

267

She opened the mini bar, took out a can, and handed it to him. The thought of trying to hit him with it occurred to her, but then she thought, *Who does that help? It's not like I'm on the same side as Mikhail. And where is David H: Pastor?*

In the OUR MOVE van, McIntosh had been listening to the unfolding situation with growing concern. What they needed was control, predictability, complete dominance of the situation; unpredictable, out-of-control events were the enemy. What was happening now was not in the plan. He decided it had gone far enough. There was no telling what was going to happen next. He moved the timeline forward. The original plan had been to let the party unfold, let the evening take its course. Once the drinking was over Tati had told them the men normally took their chosen girl off about half past twelve. Then what happened next varied depending on how much they'd had to drink. But they were usually finished by three and in a woozy, mellow mood. That was the moment to go in: when guards – and trousers – were down. The guards would be sleepy and relaxed. The action was over. But it needed to be coordinated with the other sites. He got a status update from each of them. There were no other Specials on so no particular activity. Normal comings and goings. Blatov had entered the Salamander Street house an hour ago and not come out. They were all ready to go on his mark; it was his call. He pondered for a second then made up his mind.

"Green for Go," he said calmly into his headset. "All units, all teams. Green for Go. Thirty second countdown."

The Duff Street team – designated the Alpha team – assembled in what served for a hallway in the van. Kit was given a last once-over check but there was no eye contact and no small talk. McIntosh gave them a countdown. Ten, nine… at three, the lead officer depressed the door handle and at "Go", they piled out and ran.

When Boris heard "Police, open up" coming from the door entry speaker, at first he thought there must have been some kind of joke. Maybe one of the evening's guests had arrived late.

Well, that was ok. They were all going to be lined up shortly, once Dimitri had finished with Mikhail. They would all have to drop their trousers and boxers and be photographed with a line of naked girls. That would be good insurance for the future, during what Dimitri was calling "the transition". So he didn't bother checking with Dimitri or Yuri. Another stooge in the line-up was a good thing. Maybe it would be somebody senior who could make their position even more secure. He opened the door just as the battering ram was being swung, took it right in the guts, and went down like a cardboard cutout. Dimitri in the office heard the commotion and turned round just long enough for Mikhail to grab his gun hand and try to twist it away from him. The gun went off into the ceiling just as two SWAT officers kicked back the office door and held weapons at them both. Four more piled into the lounge, the building layout exactly as Tati had described it in the changing corridor of Sally Winters. Yuri was on his own and immediately dropped his weapon. Stevenson looked up from the prone position and groaned.

In Marchmont, David reached across and turned the receiver off.

"It's finished," he said.

Chapter 26

BRUNTSFIELD

The final haul was one DCI, two DIs, four DSs and one lowly DC. Final reports could wait till the following week but there was a Saturday morning briefing, with a representative from each of the SWAT teams dealing with each of the different locations, plus McIntosh's core team. David was invited but declined; he had a sermon to prepare for the following morning. Gillian wanted to get her notes from the conference into some sort of order. Skiving off before the full event was over was not entirely kosher in academic circles but she had been in touch with Gary and explained. "Well, in the circumstances," he had said. "Just give me an overview of what you were at and we'll fudge the rest. It's just that any foreign trips have to be written up these days or the Faculty gets twitchy." By late afternoon she had it pretty much under control and thought she'd take a light pasta salad round to David's as a surprise. She knew he hated preparing to preach so close to the starting gun and would probably appreciate not having to cook. *Have to get that bedroom window fixed*, she thought, pushing open the heavy stair door.

As she expected, he was bent over his laptop – finally returned by the boffins – with a pile of books and three empty coffee mugs beside him.

"I thought I might give a final reprise on the wheat and the tares tomorrow – again," he said with an air of innocence. "But I'm fed up with that Scripture – if you're allowed to say that. So little wheat, so many tares."

"You should be elated, from what I hear, not depressed," Gillian said, trying to be bright. "Mission accomplished: twenty-nine girls in safe police care, eight police officers who will not be obstructing justice in future, and around 15,000 pounds in cash recovered, plus a quantity of drugs and other stolen goods."

"You make it sound like the Twelve Days of Christmas." He managed to crack a smile. "Eight cops in custody, seven brothels busted," he crooned.

Gillian laughed.

"And one sermon stalled," he added. "Can't seem to get my head around it. The parable has it all straightened out at the end of the age – but why not now? Why do girls like these have to go through stuff like that?"

"If you could answer that you'd get the Mastermind trophy home to keep."

He dropped his pen on the desk.

"Come on," he said. "Get your coat back on. Let's walk over the Links. It'll clear my head."

He climbed into his usual grey overcoat, screwed his fedora on, and pulled the door shut behind them. Outside it was bright with winter sun. They walked arm in arm down through the putting greens towards the Meadows, avoiding cyclists, joggers, mums with buggies, skateboarders, scooters, and one Segway rider.

"How long is it since we had that meeting at Mike and Sam's?" David asked abruptly.

"Four weeks today – exactly," replied Gillian, much better than David at dates and times, a fact they both acknowledged.

"Incredible," he replied. "Simply incredible. Three weeks of doubts, questions, one step forward, and two back. Now we've got a result I should be pleased. I can't quite understand why I'm not. Maybe just exhaustion from too much tension."

"I think it's understandable," Gillian remarked. "I've had my work to take my mind off things and you've had the brunt of the action, specially with that thing in Sally Winters on Thursday. Give yourself a break."

"I think I'll see the funny side in a few weeks. A stake-out in a sex shop – bizarre."

"No, Sally Winters," Gillian poked him in the ribs. "'Bizarre' is a competing brand."

That made them both smile.

They did a circuit almost as far as Buccleuch Street, then looped around behind the tennis courts and the back of George Square, continuing on along North Meadow Walk towards Tollcross, and ended up at El Quijote for a drink and a few tapas.

"*Miguel! ¿Qué tal?*" David shouted into the back shop and got some incomprehensible greeting back. In honour of the aborted trip to Ribadeo, David ordered *Estrella Galicia* beers and they sat for a bit watching passers-by on the pavement outside and listening to Omara Portuondo singing about how happy Cubans are over a not very good PA.

"Feeling better?" Gillian asked after the second beer.

"I think so," David admitted. "I don't always do my sermon prep over a couple of beers but it seems to be working. I have something in mind."

"Ok, now take me back to your flat, Romeo."

Walking up Bruntsfield Place, to where the common entrance to David's flat was clearly visible, he noticed two familiar figures going in. They got to the front door only a few seconds behind them.

"David H: Pastor," Elvira squealed, almost levitating with excitement.

"David," he replied. "Just David. How are you? And Tati. You look well. Both of you." He kissed both girls on both cheeks in the Spanish manner, not exactly sure what the norms were in Belarus, and it seemed to work. Gillian smiled encouragingly beside him.

"Good to see you both."

He unlocked the door and pushed it open.

"Coffee?" Gillian mouthed as he took the girls into the living room.

He nodded.

"How did you find out where I live?"

"We are detectives!" Elvira almost shouted excitedly. "Crime-fighting detectives!"

"James brought us," Tati said more quietly. "I was at his house with Elvira last night. The police, they have arranged rooms in a sort of hotel but we wanted to be together. He said they had a little extra bed he could put out. Mr McIntosh, he phoned and they said we could come. It was 2 a.m. before we got there but they stayed up for us."

"James, he cook us a real Scottish breakfast this morning," Elvira enthused. "It have everything. It was lunchtime before we finish it."

"David," Tati said shyly, "I want to say something to you. You have saved our lives. You have…"

"There's really no need," David interrupted. "I'm just glad…"

"No," Tati insisted. "I want to say. Many days I was in the house, I thought my life was over. Max. He had everything. We had nothing. No way to say anything to anyone. When Elvira and I were in the office and I saw your name on the list, it was the first time I thought there was anyone on our side. You play cards?"

"Sometimes."

"Well, it was like Max had all the cards and we had none. And there was no other player. Then, when I saw David H: Pastor on the list I thought, maybe there is another player after all. Someone else has a few cards. I didn't know if it would be enough to win the game but anyone with other cards was something. That was the first time. Then when Elvira almost died on her birthday I was so sad but it made me think about sending a birthday card to a friend. I wanted to send something to you but I couldn't. I didn't know who you were or how to contact you and I had to send something people would believe. Something not dangerous."

She looked down and smiled.

"I wanted to send you a secret message, like 'Help me, Obi-Wan Kenobi, you're my only hope.'"

That made them laugh. Gillian had just come back in with a tray and looked at them quizzically.

"First he's David H: Pastor, now he's Obi-Wan Kenobi," she said. "What does that make me?"

"No, you help us so much too," Tati protested. "I'm sorry. David was the only name I knew. You work together. James told us the story today. I am so sorry for your friend. Killing is normal for Max."

"By the way, I haven't had the full report from DI McIntosh," David suddenly said. "I've just heard bits and pieces. And nobody's mentioned Max. The last I heard they thought he was at one of the other houses. Have you heard?"

Elvira looked down.

"They did not find him," Tati said quietly. "They thought he was in a house but when the team went in he is not there. Or he got away. I don't know. Mikhail they have but no Max."

That put a dampener on proceedings and paused the conversation. Max was still on the loose, probably halfway back to Belarus or wherever his bolthole was by now. Obviously his operation was in tatters: all of the houses identified and taken; PGC church revealed for the sham it was; all his "merchandise" liberated. Spade had said something in a message about the bank accounts being frozen so maybe he didn't even have access to his profits any more. But he knew that was putting a brave face on it. Getting hands on Maxim Blatov had been a major objective of the operation, both to hold him to account for the damage done and take him out of circulation for a long time in terms of future operations. He had without a doubt been the brains behind it all. And, ultimately, what a brilliant idea. There was a certain degree of respectability in a church where small amounts of money could easily be laundered through the weekly offerings. Then it had become the front for grander schemes. In his desire for greater "respectability", to make his position even more secure, he signed up to the Council of Churches, but this had led to a few pebbles rolling down the hill, which had eventually turned into the avalanche that brought it all crashing down. Still, it wasn't a crazy idea. The more established he could become, the safer he would be from outside suspicion – and the harder it would be for church members to resist pressure from the pastor. As pastor or "prophet" of PGC, he could exert enormous mind control over his followers, and controlling other people seemed to be what made him tick, whether through the church, in the houses, or running networks all the way back to Belarus to entice the girls to get on that bus and travel all that way, willingly, eagerly, desperate to start their new life. Well, start a new life they undoubtedly did – just not the one they were expecting. So he could play his mind games not just in the criminal but also in the respectable world. And how much more control could you have than speaking on behalf of God? So the girls obeyed because they had no choices left, the strong-arm guys because they were paid to and got a share of the pickings, and Sandy and Sonia because they actually thought they were doing God's will. Max had it covered from every angle.

David thought he could just imagine the cynical cops clearing up afterwards, shrugging their shoulders and saying, *Well isn't that what church is anyway? Manipulation of the simple minded?* He wanted to come right back at them. *No, it's not. You've got it wrong. It's so much more than that.* It's teaching people to think for themselves in a complicated world where there are no easy answers but there is some guidance we can follow. We can let an ancient wisdom inform our minds, our judgment, and our relationships. Even if Jesus never existed and never said, "He who is without sin, let him cast the first stone", somebody did. And it has remained an incredibly powerful saying for the last two millennia. So let's start with that. There is something there that's still valid and authentic. As Gillian had said to him once, "Max is not 'us'. We are not him." But he doubted whether anyone who heard or read about the scandal would see it that way. The church was an easy target – yet another of Max's manipulations. And that's how the papers would play it.

Gillian hooked him back to reality by asking if anyone wanted another coffee. When she had made it he tried to recover a more positive frame of mind.

"I never heard how you managed to get your message out to Andrei," he said to Tati.

"A man called Pat," Tati said. "He is not a bad man, not like many of the others. Just lonely. I think I reminded him of his wife from forty years ago. Often he just wanted to talk. First of all I got him to make copies of Dimitri's keys so we could get into the office. Then, when I thought of sending a birthday card I asked him if he could post it for me, though I didn't have any money for the stamp." She smiled. "He was quite sweet."

David could see Gillian frowning and he knew what she was thinking. That sweet old man was exploiting people-trafficked sex slaves in Edinburgh. Not so sweet after all. He completely agreed with where she was coming from but he thought he could see the other side of it too. The wheat and the tares weren't just different people – one a stalk of wheat, one a weed. The good and the bad were totally mixed up in all our motives. Among Jesus' hearers then and in an old man looking for company in a brothel now. The church members who sat listening to his sermons. The police who had risked their lives last night rushing in not knowing what to expect. Even the regular punters who made use of the girls. They weren't monsters 24/7. They must have some good impulses too, even if they tried to gag the voice of conscience. Even himself. It was nice to be hailed as someone's saviour. He just hoped that underneath it all he wasn't in it for the praise, respect, and admiration. He had a harder time seeing the good side of Max though. Was there a stalk of wheat in there somewhere or just solid tares wall-to-wall? Or maybe there had been once and it had been crowded out and choked by the weeds, to mix up his parables a bit.

Anyway, this was getting a bit over-philosophical. Tati sat in front of David, happy and perfect, almost as if the last year had never happened. Free to come and visit, drink a cup of tea, and eat a Kit Kat without threats of violence, and that was something. Elvira's neck might carry that livid red band for weeks, months, or maybe even years but she was free to go into Accessorize and buy a beautiful Indian silk scarf to hide it if she wanted.

"So Pat posted the card and Andrei got the message after all." David tried to get back onto the subject.

"Yes. I haven't seen him since I gave him it so I thought he must have thrown it away and didn't want to admit it to me. But Andrei got it and he got in touch with you."

"I couldn't believe it when I read his message," David admitted.

"We were in Spain," Gillian explained. "Edinburgh to Belarus to Spain and back to Edinburgh again."

"Pretty good postman, eh?" Elvira chipped in, lightening the tone.

"We have to go now," Tati said reluctantly. "James said to meet him downstairs soon. Thank you again. For me you are always David H: Pastor."

David shut the door behind them, turned, and gave Gillian a hug.

"Now I'm even more exhausted," he said.

"Well, come and lie down," she said. "I think just lying on your spare bed's allowed."

Probably only two or three of the Southside congregation knew anything about what had been going on over the past three weeks. They knew that David had taken some time off to accompany Gillian to a conference in Spain. Maybe it had been some kind of post-engagement trip. Well, nothing wrong with that. They went so well together. A man that age needed a woman to look after him, after everything he had been through. And she hadn't had an easy time either, by all accounts. David Hidalgo was not Brad Pitt but he was a kind man who would love her and care for her. She, on the other hand, was a bit of a prize for a man over fifty. Maybe they might heal each other's wounds as the years went by. The only other thing widely known was that a good friend of David's had committed suicide. What on earth would drive a man to do such a thing? Only Mrs MacInnes and Juan knew more.

"Nice to have to have you back, Señor David," Irene MacInnes greeted him as he came in early. "Has all been safely gathered in?"

"Almost all. The biggest fish managed to get through the net but I understand they have all the small fry – and the girls, which is the most important thing."

She nodded. "That's good. It's the fate of these poor things that makes my blood boil. In Scotland too. I'm glad they'll be able to start again." Then a thought struck her.

"They will let them stay, won't they? I mean, in Scotland?"

"I sincerely hope so. But I suppose it'll all be tied up in red tape. I imagine they'll have to apply for visas then residency. After what they've been through, going back to Belarus seems like punishing them for being victims. A man called James Dalrymple is on the case though. Apparently he has a load of connections and thinks it might be possible to work something out. I imagine some of the girls might want to go home at least to see their families, whether they choose to come back or not. Tati and Elvira – the only ones I've met – I know they want to stay. They want to set up a business together to help girls from Belarus find proper work here and try to stop the need for traffickers."

"Very sensible." Mrs MacInnes approved of young women going into business for themselves. Made them independent. If it had only been more possible in her young day.

"Though they'll need some money for that," she said. "I just hope they get some help to get back on their feet – specially if it helps prevent others falling into the same trap."

David was just about to step up onto the platform to get his computer plugged in and his notes organized when he sensed someone else at his elbow wanting a word. It was Sonia Benedetti.

"Good morning," she said hesitantly. "Do you remember me?"

"I do indeed. Your welcome was the best thing about PGC. I remember you perfectly, Sonia."

She looked down and cleared her throat as if about to start a prepared speech.

"We didn't know," she began. "We had no idea what was going on. We thought it was a church. A bit unusual, but just a church. There were good things too. We liked Max before we found out. I know Sandy was very stupid. He broke the law. But we had no idea where the money had come from. If we had known…"

She tailed away, realizing she was beginning to repeat herself.

"I know that," David said calmly. "Sandy is in trouble for what he did but I don't think anyone thinks he knew what sort of enterprise he was shielding. And of course we know you had no idea about the money at all. Nobody thinks the worse of you, Sonia. Honestly."

She pursed her lips – the nearest she could get to a smile.

"So you don't mind that we might come to church here… with you?" she asked, clearly not quite believing it possible.

"Not at all. From what Sandy told me you had a genuine spiritual experience in PGC. It's obvious that there was something good about it and we know where all good things come from. You'd be welcome."

Sonia beamed.

"Thank you," she said. "For myself, Sandy, and the children. I'll call him. He didn't want to come up in case there was a problem. He'll be relieved."

So Sandy and Sonia were sitting in the middle of the congregation when David began to speak later on. He didn't choose to speak on the wheat and the tares, to Gillian's relief, as she sat listening. Instead he chose Psalm 40, verse 2: "He lifted me out of the slimy pit, out of the mud and mire; he set my feet on a rock and gave me a firm place to stand."

Juan and Alicia found themselves next to David at the coffee hatch after the service.

"You still keeping ok, *guapa*?" he asked Alicia as they waited in line.

"*Seguro que sí*," she replied. "Of course – and you? *¿Qué tal?*"

"*Adecuado*," he replied. "*Adecuado*."

"Ok."

"I hear you got a result," Juan prompted him.

"I think so," David confirmed. "It's been an exhausting few weeks but it's worked out. At least for the girls. Now they have to do the mopping up. All the police who've turned a blind eye..."

"Blind eye?" Juan asked with a frown.

"*La vista gorda*," David explained.

"Oh."

"So the police who let it all happen – and those that were actively involved. Plus, any number of charges to do with Sexual Offences Acts. It turns out one of the girls wasn't even sixteen."

Juan gave an intake of breath.

"Oh," he said. "That's bad."

"And it wasn't just police. Apparently there are lawyers, judges, politicians, you name it."

Jen MacInnes, on coffee rota that day, filled cups for each of them and handed them out. David backed off before saying any more given her recent history.

"So a bit of a mess. Shocking what lies just below the surface, isn't it?"

"Jeremiah 17, verse 9," Juan said, looking glum.

"You've got me there," David confessed.

"*Engañoso es el corazón, más que todas las cosas, y perverso; ¿quién lo conocerá?*"

"Of course. 'The heart is deceitful above all things, and desperately wicked; who can know it?' Who indeed."

Diana Krall was still singing "'S Wonderful" that afternoon and it still was – maybe even more than just a few weeks previously. Gillian now had an engagement ring on as she pottered about in the kitchen, chopping apples for sauce while David had a quick look in the oven to see how the roast pork joint was getting on. Crispy crackling – that was the thing. With a bit of luck he was free from being shot at for a bit and he had once again been amazed by the resilience of the human spirit. As well as Tati, Elvira, and all the other girls – survivors every one – David was also beginning to be very impressed by James Dalrymple, a dogged specimen. He went through to the living room with the wine. His dining room table could barely accommodate six, and while they were waiting James, Sarah, Tati, and Elvira sat on the sofa or in armchairs, each with a glass in need of topping up. James had already been sharing some of his plans with him. The legislation was all in place in terms of the offences. What was needed now was a robust system of ensuring that girls taken advantage of in this way were not subject to what felt like double jeopardy – trafficked into the country, subjected to appalling abuse, then chucked out for lack of the right paperwork. Sadly, immigration was not a devolved matter so he wouldn't be able to use his contacts in the Scottish Parliament, but he knew a few regular MPs as well and was going to try to get a private member's bill worked up that would guarantee specially favourable conditions for cases of trafficked individuals applying for UK residence. It seemed to be only a matter of natural justice, though he was aware that somebody would immediately start splitting hairs over bogus claimants and abuse of the system. Well, that was the game and he had to play it; at least he already had a few legal, medical, and public figures lined up to start a campaign. He had considered Joanna Lumley as a possible figurehead but Sarah had put her foot down. "You are not having tea with Joanna Lumley and pretending it's for a good cause," she had declared. Anyway, James was turning into quite a formidable bloke and David was pleased to have made his acquaintance. They would work together on it and pull in Gordon, James's minister, as well. Maybe they might bring something good for more than just the PGC girls out of it all.

Tati and Elvira were chatting quietly – though Elvira didn't do much quietly – in Belarusian but immediately switched to English when David came in.

"I'm sorry; I've not got any vodka," he said, circulating with the Rioja.

"Ugh! Vodka! Horrible!" Elvira said with a shudder. "It takes ordinary men – not wonderful but you know, ok – and turns them into pigs. I hate. This much nicer."

"You are from Spain?" Tati asked shyly.

"I was born here," David explained, "in Edinburgh. But I've lived most of my adult life in Spain. My father was Spanish and my mother was Scottish."

"I want to travel to Spain," Tati announced as if she had just made up her mind. "The country of David H: Pastor."

David had to refrain from groaning. Tati would have to get over that. He was just plain David Hidalgo, feet of clay just like anyone else. Gillian, however, seemed not to be perturbed as she came in with the starters – avocados with prawns in seafood sauce.

"Of course; it's a wonderful country. Come with us sometime. You'll love it."

"I want to travel everywhere," Elvira declared. "Everywhere – USA, Japan, Australia, Sri Lanka. Only place I don't want go is Belarus. And Russia. And Bulgaria. And Romania. But everywhere else. I go."

"That looks fantastic," Sarah Dalrymple said as they took their places.

"Very simple," Gillian whispered, "but we like it."

"James, would you care to give thanks?" David asked.

"Be delighted," Dalrymple replied and took almost five minutes to list all the things they as a group around the table had now to give thanks for.

"Just as well it's cold already," Sarah said under her breath but with a smirk when he'd finished.

Finally, after a relaxing afternoon of beautiful food – the crackling was superlative – and just as good conversation, James, Sarah, Tati, and Elvira left. Tati stretched up and gave David a peck on the cheek on the way out the door.

"We'll have to keep an eye on that," David remarked rather heavily as he closed the door.

"Don't worry, honey," Gillian said, putting her arms around his neck. "It's just a bit of hero worship. She'll get over it once she finds out what you're really like."

"Oh, thanks. That makes me feel a whole lot better."

He sauntered back into the living room and took another sip before sitting down, opening his laptop, and starting up his email client. It had been a busy day and he wondered if McIntosh might have been trying to get him. But it was an email from Spade he noticed.

To: David Hidalgo

From: SPADE

Subject: La Bamba

Hey Pastor – how's it going? My source – the virus maker of Minsk – tells me that the PGC are officially history. Better off the planet. I have an enormous pit in Minecraft I could drop them in. Who do I send my bill to for services rendered that put you on the right track? I was watching the whole thing out the window last night. Sooooo coooooool. I was expecting to see you in full body armour toting a bazooka. Well, maybe next time.

Anyway, just a little loose end to tie up. You may remember a certain matter of some missing cash. PGC's ill-gotten-gains. Well, a certain birdie – the hacker of Minsk again – seems to have amazing influence over money and conjures it from nowhere. And he has shared his secret with me. So I too am now richer than Croesus. And guess what. I have decided to share my good fortune with those in need. I believe there are 29 ladies in need. Click this link to see what lies in store for each of them. I can do this because "no soy marinero, soy capitán".

Cheers amigo

SPADE

Just keep digging, just keep digging

http://www.nestegg.com/default.
aspx?refererident=ET758D993KA35364MN20NDH4758837

David had a phobia about clicking on links he didn't trust but he accepted that Spade had proved his bona fides many times over. He clicked. It looked like a bank statement. The account held a credit balance of £689,655.17. He did the maths – £689,655.17 is almost exactly £20 million divided by 29.

Chapter 27

EDINBURGH EVENING

The following day and the week after that were the first David had felt to be anything like "normal" for a long time. It was a process, and he had good days and not so good. But whenever he was feeling a bit low and vulnerable he just had to think about Tati and Elvira. It seemed nothing short of miraculous. James and Sarah Dalrymple seemed to have more or less adopted Elvira, and since Tati was to all intents and purposes as good as her sister, she became a part of the family too. His son Paul found it all a bit bemusing but Sarah loved it. These were the daughters she had always wanted but never had. Of course they were not unscathed and Tati in particular had nightmares, but at least during the hours of daylight they seemed happy, well-adjusted girls. The police had provided a counselling service for all the girls, though it did tax the resources of the victims of crime support team. At least for Tati and Elvira, though, it was the love and domesticity of a normal family that had the most healing power. Sarah had rearranged the spare room to make it into a proper double and bought extra wardrobes, mirrors, bedside tables, and so on and fully involved the girls in the processes. Elvira could hardly contain herself when they went to Ikea and she was told to pick what she wanted.

David hadn't quite known what to make of Spade's final communication and thought even if it were to be taken at face value there were going to be difficulties in getting such bank accounts set up. He wasn't at all comfortable going behind McIntosh's back, but Gillian said to him, "For goodness' sake, just for once bend the rules a bit." So he thought he'd try it out with the two girls as a test case and spoke to Sandy Benedetti. Although he was still suspended by Salamanca Bank, Sandy had contacts and was able to make it happen. And lo and behold the cash did mysteriously appear. The Dalrymples understood and wholeheartedly approved, but after the initial conversation it was never mentioned again. However, when McIntosh suggested lunch one day David wondered if he had been rumbled and was for the high jump. He opted not for curry after the last time and they simply met in Henderson's on Hanover Street, loaded up their trays with veggie lasagna, moussaka, or something equally tempting and healthy, side dishes of salads, and some fruit juice, and found a vacant alcove deep at the back of the restaurant.

"All the paperwork done then?" David asked as they unloaded everything.

"Not entirely, but we're getting there. The evidence isn't hard to put together but the bulk of the burden falls on the Fiscal's office now. As I'm sure you know they prosecute in Scotland, not the police. For your ears only we've got seven currently serving police officers and a few retirees, a dose of other public and professional figures, plus the gang members themselves and various hangers on. It's a pretty big deal – unfortunately beyond the scope of my PhD or I could have had a field day."

"But…"

"Yes, the big but. We're still missing the major player."

"No leads?"

"A few, but nothing productive as yet. We've been on to European colleagues, however, and I think we're well on the way to rolling up the whole train of connections back to Minsk. Tati and Elvira and many of the others have been incredibly helpful in trying to nail it all down. They only ever heard first names, of course, but it's all served to confirm some previous suspicions and we are gradually sweeping them up."

"That must be very satisfying."

"It is. But I'm frustrated that a man obviously as clever and devious as Maxim Blatov is still on the loose."

"I'm sure. Well, at least we might hope that his particular guise of pastor and prophet won't be tried again. He's done it at least twice now and I would hope we're wise to it. At least in Britain."

"You'd like to think so, but unfortunately people can be naive and far too trusting. And sometime weak and vulnerable people are looking for someone strong to trust."

"I'm aware of that. Actually, I see a major part of what I do as encouraging people to think for themselves and work it all out in their own lives, not just depend on someone else's spiritual insights. We honestly do try to help people make progress for themselves, not depend on the pastor."

"Speaking of which – progress I mean – are you still in touch with Sam Hunter?"

"Not daily but yes, from time to time."

"Well, I hope you don't mind, but that was one of the things I wanted to see you about. Douglas Forsyth – you remember, the big boss – wants to meet her and personally apologize for how she was treated. Particularly as it turns out the detectives on the case were all tied up with those responsible and had a vested interest in not taking the murder idea seriously. How do you think that would go down?"

"Ok, I think. I can't speak for Sam but I can ask."

"He wants something low key, of course. He'll come out to her house – morning coffee or something, I suppose. But he'd like to make it personal. There might be a matter of criminal injuries compensation as well."

When David broached the idea Sam seemed caught off guard. "I don't know," she said. "I'm just getting over things." But on reflection she let it happen and it turned out to be ok. Forsyth was very personable. McIntosh and David showed up just to get over the introductions, then left the two of them alone.

"How did it go, if I can ask?" David ventured hesitantly when it was just the two of them left.

"Surprisingly well, I think," Sam said slowly. "He seemed genuine in what he said. He accepts that it wasn't dealt with correctly and of course there's no debate about the fate of the officers involved. He seems like a decent guy who really regrets what happened and is mortified over corruption like that in his own force. I'll not be joining his online Scrabble group, but it was ok."

David was relieved. One more loose end tied up, not just in a perfunctory way but leaving Sam feeling just a little less bad and that was worth something. As he was getting up to go he couldn't help but look around the living room and imagine the little group that had met there not that long ago. It had been a worthwhile venture to share good practice; however, he didn't have the heart for it any more. The group hadn't met since and he guessed it would now just quietly fade away.

It was as he was walking from Sam's to the bus stop that he got the first text message. His phone beeped just as he saw a number 16 coming round the bend and wondered if he could make it in time. He ignored the beep and dropped a gear for the last fifty yards. Phew. On board, settling down, taking in his fellow travellers, he remembered the text and fished out his phone. It was only a reference. Odd. He didn't remember subscribing to a Bible reading text alert programme. Mark 13:36–37. He had recently installed Bible Gateway so he looked it up: "Therefore keep watch because you do not know when the owner of the house will come back – whether in the evening, or at midnight, or when the cock crows, or at dawn. If he comes suddenly, do not let him find you sleeping. What I say to you, I say to everyone: 'Watch!'" It didn't take long for the penny to drop. Maxim Blatov: he was still at large, not in Belarus but here. Coming.

David immediately called McIntosh and they met at St Leonard's police station.

"They say it's not over till the fat lady sings," David remarked grimly, placing his phone on the table between them. "Not fat, not a lady, and not singing, but you get my drift."

McIntosh didn't even manage a smile.

"Thanks for letting me know right away," he said. "We have a team still on it and I'll pass them this information. In the meantime, what can I say? I don't suppose you want to go into purdah in a safe house all over again for goodness knows how long?"

"No, I've got a life, remember?"

"Absolutely. And you don't want to be walking around in body armour."

"Likewise."

"So what then? Ignore it?"

"Can't do that. It's happened. I think I have to just go on as normal – or as normal as possible. We all know we might be hit by a bus…"

"Or a tram more likely nowadays…"

"Whatever. The point is we all live just a few heartbeats from 'eternity', whatever you take that to mean. I don't intend to worry Gillian, James, or the girls with this. It may mean that it's only me he wants to upset. And it might be nothing more than that – just basic harassment and intimidation. We know he loves mind games – remember that disgusting book he used with the girls? He likes to mess with your head. So if I allow that to happen, I've lost the battle already. I just have to take things one day at a time and let what happens happen."

"Sounds like a theme for a country song. Are you a country fan, David?"

"Hate it with a perfect hatred."

"Well, there's another thing we have in common. So we can't give you a twenty-four-hour armed guard. You don't want to be in a witness protection programme; you're not going to try to move to Tahiti like that guy in *The Truman Show*. What will you accept?"

"My mum used to say, 'Take everything but blows.' What have you got?"

"Having run out of other options, I've one idea left. Hang on a minute."

McIntosh disappeared and came back clutching something small. He placed it gently on the table.

"Remember the live broadcast from Duff Street? We gave Tati one of these. Obviously, you can't broadcast live audio the whole time but when you push the clicker down that turns it on. It'll give a reasonable audio feed over about a hundred yards. Beyond that all we get is a blip to say it's been activated. If I give you this it would have to be on the understanding that you take it with you wherever you go – at least in the UK – that you don't fire it off accidentally, if possible, and that you don't try writing with it."

"Ok, I'm up for that. Did they not have something like this in *The Man from UNCLE* on the telly?"

"Bit before my time I'm afraid," McIntosh said with a grin.

So, after some training and testing, David took the pen and did his level best to remember to take it with him and not use it to poke debris out of the plug hole in the kitchen sink. The next text came a week later. Deuteronomy 32:35 – "It is mine to avenge; I will repay. In due time their foot will slip; their day of disaster is near and their doom rushes upon them." That was a little more specific and more worrying so he decided to share the situation with Juan.

"*¡Hombre!*" Juan exploded. "I still have some friends in Madrid who could sort this guy out!"

"Yes, no doubt," David concurred. "Me too. But not if we can't lay hands on him. I'm not telling you for the sake of doing anything; it's just to let you know. Please don't tell Gillian. You can tell Alicia if you want – we're more or less family anyway – but I don't want to worry anyone else. And certainly not Mrs MacInnes or it'll be on *Reporting Scotland*."

"*Vale. De acuerdo*," Juan confirmed. "Just don't take risks. Keep your eyes open."

Three days later Revelations 22:12 arrived: "Look, I am coming soon! My reward is with me, and I will give to each person according to what they have done." By this time David had the pen on his bedside table and routinely put it into the breast pocket of his shirt every morning and took it out at night. It was one Saturday evening when he'd just nipped downstairs to Ali's and Ayeesha's fantastic late-opening mini market, mainly for a box of their delicious marzipan sweets, that it happened. He got back in, pulled the door behind him, and somehow instinctively felt another human presence in the flat. Without even exploring, he took the pen out and clicked it. The tiny blue light on the clicker flashed once, twice, three times in the dark, confirming it was working. He put it back in his pocket and quietly laid his groceries down. What now? He'd always thought a baseball bat or a poker was traditional for intruders but how many households have a poker now? And he didn't play baseball. He could have just quietly opened the door again and slipped back out but that would have meant sentencing himself to a never-ending cycle of uncertainty. Who was that man who just went through the entrance door ahead of him? Who was following him a little too closely as he crossed the Meadows on a dark, winter night? Who was sitting, back on, as they ate in a nice Italian restaurant? At least this would finish it one way or the other.

The clinching factor was that he was alone. Gillian was out at music so whatever happened, at least she'd be safe. That was as it should be. He was the one who had connected with Spade, which had started the trail of connections that eventually brought Blatov down. Let the show begin. He quietly took his hat and coat off, went through to the living room, and switched on the light. Maxim Blatov was sitting at the table smiling serenely. He was fingering a heavy hand gun in front of him.

"Pastor David," he said warmly, "or should I say, David H: Pastor. From the first day we met I was sure our paths would cross again, that our destinies were somehow intertwined, and so it has transpired. How are you?"

David sat.

"I've been better," he admitted. "I suppose I don't need to ask what brings you here."

"Well, looking up old friends is always a pleasure. And since many of my old friends seem to be otherwise engaged, I'm here to catch up with you."

David was wishing he'd kept his coat on. A shiver ran through him. The curtains were still open and the orange sodium glow of the street lights outside cast an unnatural, unhealthy light into the room.

"From the first time I heard you speak I've wanted to compliment you on your English," David offered, stalling for time. "Hardly a trace of an accent and very natural expressions."

Blatov inclined his head.

"Coming from a linguist and a teacher I appreciate that. I've worked very hard on my accent over the years. It was important to achieve my goals."

"Of deceiving your congregations?"

Blatov made a mock scowl.

"Now, now! You put it so crudely. Of starting and running a successful enterprise in Britain. Has it never occurred to you that a church is just another sort of enterprise? It has a mission and goals, it has a product – of sorts – it has a market of course, and customers. It has an infrastructure and staff. And sometimes it may have, how can I put it, 'extension ministries'. You had that yourself in Madrid, I believe. All these houses for the addicts. You could say we had addicts' houses as well, I suppose."

"With a difference."

"And how would you characterize the difference?"

"Our addicts were trying to get clean. You were feeding an addiction."

"Nonsense." Blatov sounded offended. "We were providing entertainment. And the churches do that too. All these racks and racks of 'worship' music, garage musicians not good enough to cut it commercially selling to the Christian market. And the books, the bookmarks, the notepads, the inspirational artwork. It's all commerce – and you know it. We just don't try to pretend. That's the difference."

"And ruined lives? A by-product, or was that the main product?"

"Not so ruined from what I hear. Apparently all the little girls have been substantially enriched by their experience. I mean, in tangible terms, not just by broadening their minds. That's my money and I'm in the process of getting it back."

David found himself losing patience with the pretence, despite the need to spin things out. If the pen had sent a signal, if anyone was listening on a Saturday night, if they understood what the red light meant on the control panel, if they were able to raise a patrol, and if the patrol had a clue what they were supposed to do. So, in all likelihood, there wouldn't be any cavalry coming over the hill and he was only spinning out his last few minutes. He had been hoping for more. There was still a wedding to organize and a life to lead. A bullet from Maxim Blatov hadn't so far been in the plan.

"Excuse me – am I boring you, Pastor David?" Blatov said, still sitting across from him, still smiling but now also holding the gun. "I wouldn't want that. And there's no point waiting for help. DI McIntosh is on his holidays. I checked."

Yet again Blatov was showing that alarming gift for almost reading minds.

"Just one thing, before you pull the trigger," David said, racking his brains for what that one thing might be. He grasped a passing straw. "Have you never thought how things might have been if you'd been a genuine prophet, not just a sham?"

"But I was a prophet, Pastor David," Blatov protested with mock outrage. "I was. Have you not spoken to Alexander and Sonia? I changed their lives. And many others besides. Sandy only did what I asked because he owed me a debt of gratitude. I saved his marriage. I helped him get his job – and his house of course. Their family life improved immeasurably because of me. He says it himself."

"I know. But Sandy and Sonia have had to recover from discovering they'd been deceived, as have many others. Now they're trying to find out what's true. You could have told them that yourself."

"You mean to sincerely believe all that claptrap? I don't, you don't, not one in a thousand in pulpits around the land genuinely believe what they say on a Sunday morning. I think you're asking too much there."

"There are things we struggle with – I grant you – but I do believe what I say. And if I have doubts I'm honest. I tell them where the problems lie. What I'm saying is that you are a man with incredible gifts. What good you could have done with them instead of what you have done – maybe what you're still doing now, for all I know." David wasn't sure how long he could keep this up but he was giving it his best shot. Strangely, he seemed to have tapped into something that connected for Blatov, who still hadn't pulled the trigger and, even while he was still smiling, was thinking it through. The sodium street light outside the window had started flickering and somehow added to the garish, ghostly fairground effect. David dimly recognized the revving of a diesel engine of whatever device they'd sent to repair it.

"Are you seriously suggesting that I should believe all that Middle Eastern folklore?" Blatov demanded. "Adam and Eve, the walls of Jericho, the virgin birth, water into wine, and all the rest of it?"

"Lots of intelligent people do," David persisted. "Nobel prizewinners, MPs, judges, actors, businesspeople, scientists. It's not automatically nonsense just because it's outside your own experience."

Outside the window, over Blatov's shoulder, David could see the platform of the cherry picker slowly rising, the two men in it unusually not wearing hi-vis vests. They had got that together pretty quickly. He only needed to keep Max talking for a few minutes more. Just a few minutes more. Blatov just laughed.

"Well, we all know about MPs and judges," he said mockingly. "I've fitted them out with some splendid evenings' entertainment. So don't talk to me about the moral intelligence of MPs and judges, or actors or businessmen, for that matter. Some of the worst. At least a bent copper is an honest man in a sort of way. They never pretended that what they were doing was for any other reason than personal gain or pleasure. Have I ever told you about the Christian minsters we accommodated? I could write a book! But anyway. None of this is to the point. I am not going to write a book about my experiences. And neither are you, David H: Pastor."

Finally, Maxim Blatov lost his smile as he raised the gun and pointed it without a hint of a tremor at David's head. Without that mask of amiability he seemed to finally reveal the self-obsession and arrogance that lay beneath it all.

Suddenly the room exploded. David threw himself to the floor. Once again fragments of glass covered the carpet and pricked his palms and face. The front door came crashing in and uniformed officers filled the room. Blatov lay slumped across the table, blood pouring from his head. A friendly hand was on David's shoulder, a figure kneeling on the carpet beside him.

"You ok?"

He managed to raise and turn his head.

"I thought you were on holiday."

"Had to make it as authentic as possible. I just had an idea that if I slipped out of the picture for a bit it might precipitate something. Here. I'll help you up."

David sat up gingerly, brushing sharp needles of glass from his pullover and hands.

"I think we can say it did. Well done in reacting so quickly."

"I'd introduce you to the marksmen but they like to keep out of the public eye."

As they were talking, a stretcher team came into the room and strapped Blatov onto it. A medic was applying pressure to the head wound while another opened a dressing pack. Then he was gone. David was just getting up when a vision of loveliness in a black strappy frock burst into the room, ignored everyone else, and almost squeezed the life out of him.

"Thank God. Thank God you're safe," she said.

When the dust had settled, McIntosh insisted on a debrief as soon as David had had a check-up. They offered him a sedative in A&E and he put it in the breast pocket of his shirt just in case. The pen was still there. *I suppose I should turn this thing off,* he thought. *Don't want another SWAT team shooting the place up.* McIntosh explained that it seemed every time they were hopeful of tracking Blatov down it turned into another damp squib and he wasn't where they thought he should be. The thought occurred that maybe he had regained access to police computers and was anticipating every move. So, they put a big thing into all the databases that the inquiry was being scaled down, that Blatov had been identified and detained by Belarusian law enforcement, and that McIntosh was taking three weeks' leave while colleagues went to Minsk to do the interviews. The cherry picker had been a DC's idea – *if they could do it, why couldn't we?* David was about to start recounting his conversation with Blatov when McIntosh held a hand up and pressed a button on the unit in front of him. David heard himself remonstrating about how the mastermind's gifts could have been put to better use.

"Did you seriously mean that?" Gillian asked. "That, in another life he could have been a better man and used all of that for good?"

"Are you joking?" David asked. "He was a maniac. All tares and no wheat, as far as I can see. But I could have been surprised."

"Right now, I just want us both to live and not be so surprised," said Gillian. McIntosh offered them a lift home but they turned it down.

"I think we'll walk," David said. "I'd like to just walk through my city. Not to have to look over my shoulder. Be a normal bloke again."

"Whatever you are, you are not a normal bloke, David Hidalgo. That's what I love about you," Gillian whispered.

She kissed him lightly, then they gathered up their things and walked out of the police station into the Edinburgh evening. The air was sweet and smelled slightly of hops.

EPILOGUE

Several days later, on the other side of town, Sir Patrick Stenhouse sat at his desk – not the desk he had used in the Scottish Office up until just six months ago but the smaller, more personal one at home. A formal portrait of himself and Lady Mhorag on the day he got his gong stood at an angle on one corner. An old school photo of the twins matched it on the other side, and a copy of the *Evening Times* was open in front of him. A Macmillan Cancer Support letterhead peeped out from underneath. He let out a long sigh and looked first at one photo then the other.

As far as any of his well-connected and well-off friends and neighbours knew, he was a thoroughly decent sort. Not perhaps the ultimate high flier but a safe pair of hands in uncertain times. For more than a decade he had successfully steered a series of simultaneously dull and overconfident ministers – a dangerous combination – through the rapidly changing landscape of Scottish politics. Not something achieved simply on the basis of an expensive education and good RP vowels – though both of these he certainly had. Then the end to a long and distinguished career had finally brought the customary tap on the shoulder and change to his letterhead on retirement. Mhorag had only made it to Buckingham Palace with a bucketload of morphine so she could stand the pain, but the downside was only being partly aware of where she was and why. The twins saved the day and were wonderful throughout, allowing him to do the necessary with a fixed smile and the expected bonhomie. By the time they got back to Edinburgh he just drove straight back to the hospice and saw her into bed. He was called later that night and by 4 a.m. it was all over. Her last words were "I'm glad I went – you deserved it" and "You've made me very happy."

Some men would have kept a stiff upper lip, spent more time at the allotment, or turned to the Famous Grouse for company. Sir Patrick, as he now had to think of himself, was in reality very different from his calm and collected public persona and found it impossible to dissemble. He also hated gardening and drank only spring water. But he needed company. Not chummy golf club company and certainly none of Mhorag's friends, all pearls and bridge or else walking shoes and spaniels. He needed anonymity. Someone who knew nothing of his past life and did not judge. Someone with whom he could have some simple pleasure to dull the pain. Someone who could remind him of Mhorag when they still had time on their side.

How does a man in his sixties find such a thing? Obviously he pays for it. He found out about the House from multiple sources: rumours in the press, banter online, whispered, abruptly halted conversations by the water cooler. When he did finally make contact, at once terrified but also desperate for distraction, he knew full well how it might end. And so it now was proving.

He was never under any illusions about Tati's circumstances but always tried to make it as easy for her as he could, or at least not as brutal as he supposed some of her clients would be, though how sex for money under duress could ever be anything but brutal he couldn't imagine. Still, inflicting gratuitous pain revolted him so he tried to be gentle. She was exactly what he needed. Young, delicate, utterly lovely in a sweet elfin way but also intelligent, articulate, and sensitive. She asked nothing about who he was or why he was there but he rapidly found he had grown to trust her and he wanted to talk. In fact, the talking turned out to be much more therapeutic than the sex. He made up a career and a jovial, simple persona as an excuse for his healthy finances but about Mhorag he told the truth – more than he intended and certainly more than was safe. About Tati he asked nothing because he could guess. The couple of occasions she asked something of him he was grateful to comply. Getting a couple of keys cut. Posting a letter. It was the least he could do.

He knew it couldn't go on forever and now, glancing down at the paper again, he accepted that the party was thoroughly over. "Police Bust Celebrity Sex Ring" was the headline, with most of the detail on pages 2 and 3. Apparently Craig Morton (Chief Crime Correspondent) had had inside access to the operation and could reveal not only that fifty or so trafficked girls had been freed but that the hunt was now on for dozens of high-profile clients from the law, the church, big business, politics, and even the police themselves. Arrests had taken place, with more expected soon. Sir Patrick leaned across and lit his desk lamp as the evening light faded, though he didn't need to read the story again. He had been through it three times already in the way he would tackle an important briefing paper looking for some nuance or hint he hadn't noticed before. Some of the "big names" he knew already and others he could guess. It had been extremely decent of Douglas Forsyth to call him personally. They knew each other from a bunch of official committees and the Rotary. So instead of a squad car pulling into the drive and a bunch of goons crawling all over the house before dragging him off for cautioning and charging, he was at least allowed the dignity of showing up at the designated station for a prearranged appointment. The final outcome would be the same but the process a shade more civilized. Maybe.

Finally, after another half-hour in silence, glancing between the report and the photographs or out of the window into the beautiful garden Mhorag had slowly built up over twenty years, he closed the newspaper, dropped it in the bin, took out a sheet of cream conqueror writing paper and wrote: "To all my friends, colleagues and above all my beloved family…" He knew what he wanted to say and the text was completed quickly. He signed it simply, "Pat".

There were still hundreds of Mhorag's strong painkiller upstairs. From his research he reckoned fifty or so would suffice.

Want to read more David Hidalgo?
Book 3, *Sins of the Fathers*,
is coming in June 2019...

Prologue

MORÓN DE LA FRONTERA – LATE SUMMER

Nothing about the outermost security door had changed in the last seven years. Maybe a dribble of oil or a lick of paint, but nothing you'd notice. The mechanism was as robust and secure as it had ever been. Yet as it slammed shut the metallic clang was totally different. The sound of a door locking you in is different from one opening to let you through.

The preliminaries had been completed right after breakfast. His few personal possessions were returned and signed for, then a shower, a change of clothing, and on to the governor's office.

Governor Daniel Lopez was not a brutal man. He tried to make encouraging remarks to all the men about rejoining a world they might have left five, ten, or even twenty years before. And he forced himself to be scrupulously fair. Whoever the criminal, whatever the crime – murder, rape, fraud, armed robbery, or even ETA terror attacks – they all got their full ten minutes in a comfortable chair with a reasonable cup of coffee. But this morning he just couldn't bring himself to do it. The file of reports in front of him seemed to describe a model prisoner who had paid his debt and was ready to rejoin society. Excellent conduct. Polite to officers and professionals. No big fuss about guilt, innocence, or wrongful conviction. Fully engaged in the prison's eduction programme, particularly given that he wouldn't be going back to his former profession. In fact, he had shown a remarkable aptitude for the computer skills course and had not only passed all the modules but had repaired the education department's computers several times, and improved internet access and record-keeping.

It all looked perfect, but Lopez simply couldn't get past the uppermost conviction sheet in the file. He was used to shocking details but had never been able to get his head around this one. How was it possible? How could a man betray a trust so grievously and show not even the slightest sign of remorse? The prisoner was left standing as Lopez scanned the salient points yet again for some sign of progress; some acknowledgment of the wrong and harm done; some sign of a change of heart that would bode well for the future. After all, that was the key. New skills, improved self-confidence, and supportive outside contacts were important, but without the desire to be different they had little impact. Did the man in front of him convey any desire to be different? Lopez accepted there was no shred of evidence of it. So the prisoner was left standing. There was no friendly chat, no *café con leche* and no avuncular advice. Lopez abandoned the normal pep talk and said exactly what was on his mind. Then he regretting being so unprofessional. In any case, it seemed to make no more impression now than the many counsellors and psychologists before him had, according to the file. The prisoner simply kept looking ahead, showed no sign of emotion and refusing to respond in any way.

The man standing on the worn patch of parquet in front of the desk had more or less expected this reaction and let it wash over him. He had heard it all before. Let them think what they wanted. The only thing that mattered was that the metallic clang was behind him now instead of in front. It had been a long time coming. Of course, he'd used the time as much to his advantage as he could while studiously ignoring all the counsellors, psychologists, and social workers they had thrown at him. He had turned to the library first but was disappointed to get through all the worthwhile reading in less than a month. Then there had been a desperate time of nothingness when life had been reduced to eating, sleeping, staring at the walls, and counting days.

In desperation one Monday morning, Sandra, the cheerful, optimistic, well-intentioned education officer, had suggested an IT course after finally accepting that woodwork and pottery were achieving nothing. He'd started with little expectation just to fill a few more daylight hours but had been surprised to find that it fitted his type of brain exactly. It was cold, precise, and logical. Emotions were irrelevant and there was no need for psychobabble about how it made you feel. But that didn't make it mechanical. It was a science but also an art. The science was getting the right answer; the art was doing it in the most elegant, economical, and graceful way. He found it natural and raced through the modules before branching off into much more interesting investigations of his own.

Standing patient and silent in the face of Lopez's tirade he wondered what the governor would say if extracts from his last steamy email to Rosa from the admin office were to be quoted back to him. Or better still if it was shared with Señora Lopez. She was enjoying a comfortable life in the suburbs while her husband pretended to be heading off to yet another conference. In reality he was between the sheets with a girl half his age in a cosy little *piso* – paid for with the half of his salary she didn't even know existed. He smiled slightly at the thought and got another rollicking for it. It was a nest egg he was keeping for a rainy day but maybe he'd cash it in a bit earlier after this. When Lopez finally ran out of energy he told the prisoner to pick up his case and get out of his sight. That suited both parties just fine.

Five minutes later the now ex-prisoner was standing in front of an open door. He walked forward a few paces and stood silently under the deep blue dome of Andalusian sky. A dry scrubby hillside rose to his left and endless lines of olive trees stretched away for miles in front. The southern sun was relentlessness. Just like the so-called justice of the country. Politicians with fat bundles of Euro notes in plain brown packets went free, while the judge thought justice demanded fourteen years – seven with good behaviour – in his case. Relentless and unforgiving.

The time had passed painfully slowly without a shred of the normal camaraderie among prisoners when everyone feels they have suffered an injustice. The *Centro Penitenciario Sevilla II*, better known as *Morón de la Frontera* after the nearest small town, even had its own semi-formal system of prisoner support after a spate of suicides. The *Internos de Apoyo* – the "Support Inmates" – watched out for those about to slip over the edge and tried to respond with encouragement and care. No one cared about a man like him. Being in closed conditions – the *régimen cerrado* – meant he very rarely had anything to do with the so-called "normal" prisoners, but there were times when he did. Like when the trusted ones serving meals would spit in his soup as it was passed through the hatch. Or when the hospital orderly had fed him a massive laxative instead of the cough medicine he had gone in for. He had seen the grins and sniggers when he was brought straight back in doubled up in pain. Still, it was over at last. This time the slamming door behind him was neither a fantasy nor a daydream.

It took almost a full minute to calm his thoughts under the still ferocious late summer sun. He gradually gathered his senses, then finally noticed the tiny, peeling, red Seat Ibiza parked as far from the main entrance as possible. So she'd come. He hadn't thought she would, but she couldn't deny her own flesh and blood. He picked up his cheap cardboard case and walked over to the car. She didn't get out, or open the door, but continued staring straight ahead as he got in.

"You're here," she finally said.

"I am here, Mama."

"I've dusted your room and put clean sheets on. There's empanada and cheese."

The car's interior probably could have cooked the pie or melted the cheese. He wound his window down but it made no difference. The air outside was heavy and dead, like the atmosphere inside it.

"You can't stay," she said. "You know that, don't you?"

He wasn't surprised.

"It's ok, Mama, I'm not going to. I'm leaving."

"Where will you go?"

"It's best you don't know. I've got plans."

She grunted an acknowledgement, turned the key, and the engine coughed and started.

Plans. What a beautiful word. Big, beautiful plans. Plans he'd spent seven long years building, refining, honing, perfecting, dreaming. Beautiful, perfect plans. They would see what relentless and unforgiving really meant.

She pulled her black shawl tighter and kept staring rigidly ahead.

"Don't worry about me, Mama," he said. "I'll be ok."

"I'm not," she said, revving the engine. "I'm just glad your father's already dead. Please God I soon will be too."